Joy Dettman was born in Echuca in Victoria and now lives in Melbourne.

Joy, a mother of four, is a full-time writer and a published author of several award-winning stories and the highly acclaimed novels *Mallawindy*, *Jacaranda Blue*, *Goose Girl*, *Yesterday's Dust*, *The Seventh Day* and *Henry's Daughter*.

Also by Joy Dettman

MALLAWINDY
JACARANDA BLUE
GOOSE GIRL
YESTERDAY'S DUST
THE SEVENTH DAY
HENRY'S DAUGHTER

jacaranda
blue

JOY DETTMAN

PAN
Pan Macmillan Australia

First published 1999 in Macmillan by Pan Macmillan Australia Pty Limited
This edition published 2000 in Pan by Pan Macmillan Australia Pty Limited
1 Market Street, Sydney

Reprinted 2000, 2003, 2006

National Library of Australia
cataloguing-in-publication data:

Dettman, Joy.
Jacaranda blue.

ISBN 0 330 36196 1.

I. Title

A823.3

Printed by IVE

For Dad, and my trusted trio of plot testers,
Donna, Shani and Cheryl

the funeral

It happened on a Friday, on a day like any other. Stella
Templeton spent the morning starching and ironing the minister's vestments before preparing an early lunch. Her father had
another funeral at three, and this one was fifty-five kilometres
away, in Dorby. Stella was concerned. Her father was well past
the age of driving long distances. Still, he wouldn't be going
alone.

By one o'clock that Friday, four cars were lined up on Templeton's drive, and a crowd of Maidenville's elderly citizens had
gathered there. Stella watched Mrs Morris and Mrs Murphy
make a beeline for the minister's airconditioned vehicle. Four
more headed for a new Ford, also airconditioned. Five took their
places in Percy White's middle-aged sedan, and the rest piled
into Willy Macy's kombi van. The mood was not sombre as the
convoy headed east for a day out in Dorby.

Stella waved them away then returned to the house where
she washed the lunch dishes and polished the kitchen floor. By
two-fifteen she was dressed for town in a beige linen skirt, a
cream blouse and sensible brown walking shoes. Her hair still

1

damp from the shower, she pinned it back in the usual severe bun, applied sunscreen to her face and arms, then, donning her wide-brimmed hat and sunglasses, she walked downstairs.

Back in the kitchen, she glanced with disdain at the linoleum. It was worn, brown and rippled beneath the table, ripped before the sink, and almost through to the floorboards in front of the refrigerator. She wanted a new floor covering, but her father refused to spend money on the house.

Having taken her beige shopping buggy from the utility room beside the kitchen, she left the house via the back door and set off to walk the block and a half to town.

February was nearing its end. She would be pleased to see the last of it. The promised cool change had arrived last night, weakening as it blew north; there had been little cool and less rain in it. Now the early clouds had cleared and the sun was again beating down. Maidenville needed rain. Today the town looked brown, dusty, the street trees grey with dust, as weary as Stella for winter. She crossed over the road at the school's pedestrian crossing, stopping two cars on their way to somewhere better, then she walked on to the town centre, her hand brushing the sticky flies away.

Subjected to frequent facelifts, Main Street looked prosperous enough, but any character it may have had in Stella's youth was now well lost behind the facade of each modern fad; still, the business community was undeniably proud of their town – as the new sign near the park suggested.

WELCOME TO FAIR MAIDENVILLE, POPULATION 2,800. STAY A WHILE, it pleaded in small embarrassed letters.

Many of the surrounding farmers educated their children at the boarding school, and a few still used Maidenville's banks; enough did their weekly shopping at Spencer's supermarket, and on the nights of the school plays and concerts, the boarders' parents filled the two motels, but few passing travellers accepted the invitation to stay a while. Dorby was larger. Dorby had eight motels and the pokies, and the RSL Club; it had a K Mart that never closed its doors. The road between the two towns was well used at night, with early local traffic all heading east.

'What's your hurry?' Bonny Davis called as Stella entered the greengrocers. Bonny was a vibrant redhead, and dressed today in orange shorts and a multicoloured shirt. She too was in her mid forties, but few would have questioned her word had she claimed to be thirty-five. She fairly flared with colour and vitality. Beside her, Stella in her cream and beige faded clean away.

'I was hoping I'd run into you today, Stell. Have you got any spare pots in your shed? Just little ones.'

'Piles of them, Bonny. How many do you want?'

'A couple of dozen. I've been potting out those junipers I was telling you about and I didn't know I had so many. I've used up every pot I own.'

'I'll get Father to drop some around tomorrow. I think they breed in our shed.'

Templeton's shed was a town joke. A huge barn of a thing, it had been standing for over a hundred years, and in those years had accumulated two hundred years of junk.

'Have you thought any more about the raffle?' Bonny asked.

'I'm making a large clown. He's almost done, and a fine fellow he is too. I've been calling him Willy.' Stella smiled, and walked to the swedes, selecting two. 'It was accidental, I promise you, but he looks very much like Mr Macy.'

'That will go down well. The winner can stick pins in him.' The women laughed and began filling plastic bags.

'I used most of the filling on him, but there is more on order. I hope it arrives before the meeting on Thursday.'

Bonny's shopping was as colourful as her clothing. She purchased orange pumpkin, red strawberries and yellow bananas. Stella chose potatoes, brown swedes and greying brussel sprouts. They were the minister's favourites. Together still, the friends walked down to the butcher where Bonny bought orange frankfurts, pink chump chops and red minced steak. She paid cash. Stella chose lamb's fry for the minister's breakfast, and tripe for his dinner. Her purchases were jotted down on the minister's monthly account. At the supermarket, Bonny stocked up on specials for her tribe of growing boys. Stella chose tea, plain flour and floor polish.

The shopping bagged, the friends stood on, discussing the purchase of a new organ with Ron Spencer, owner of the supermarket, also the church organist. They were speaking of the two new bales of polyester filling, now overdue, when Marilyn, Ron's wife, finished with her customer, and leaned across the checkout counter.

'The third pin has fallen. Old Mrs Martin died,' Marilyn said.

The friends moved closer to the register.

'Died in her sleep this morning. They say that Joe got out at around nine, and he left her sleeping while he fed his chooks and had a shave. He went in with her breakfast at eleven, and thought she was still asleep. It was close to one when Liz got there with their dinners. She took one look at her and called Parsons around. Anyway, she was long dead.'

'It's this weather,' Bonny said. 'God, I wish it would rain.'

'That poor old fellow. How is he taking it, Marilyn?' Stella asked.

'They've got him up at the hospital. Liz was saying that the family don't think he'll ever come out either. He doesn't know where he is. Doesn't know she's dead. He keeps saying that he's got to get home and get Molly's breakfast.'

'Age is cruel. They've kept each other alive these past ten years,' Bonny said.

'Yeah, it's cruel all right. They've tried to talk to him about the funeral, but it's just going over his head. Liz said they want to do it Monday.'

That was the way of things in Maidenville, where everyone knew everyone else; no need for a death notice in the newspaper, word of mouth was swift. Before Stella and Bonny left the supermarket, the funeral plans were passed on by Lyn Parker, the Flag motel owner, and wife of John, the local solicitor. She was also president of the church guild. The conversation then turned to who would cook what, and who would make the sandwiches. The guild ladies always put on a light afternoon tea for the mourners.

At four o'clock, Bonny and Stella parted at the minister's tall cypress hedge, Bonny continuing on two blocks to her modern home, her supermarket bags swinging.

'See you Monday, Stell, if not before.'

'Bye, Bonny.' Already Stella's hand was reaching through the slot in the tall green gates. Now the bolt slid back, the gate squealed open, and she entered, bolting it behind her.

Her garden was a riotous blaze of disorganised blooming, a veritable jungle of flowers she kept locked away from Maidenville. This was her place, her escape from drab, and from community. She smiled now at her flowers and her birds flitting there, and her face lost its contrived years. She removed her sunglasses, the better to see the colours as her footsteps slowed on the long gravelled drive.

'Oh, you dear things,' she said, halting her shopping buggy and standing motionless there. She could see the small blue finch and his mate. They were the first pair she'd sighted in many years. She'd have to keep an eye out for cats. She didn't like cats, didn't like their eyes, and she delighted in turning the hose on any trespassing feline.

A single salmon-pink rose drew her glance, and drew her nose to breathe in its perfume. She nipped a few spent heads, eased an audacious weed from the earth. She filled the three bird baths, sprayed the ferns, then continued on down to the house, a staid, two-storey red brick construction built before the turn of the century. It had belonged to her maternal grandfather. Stella had never known him, but in her mind's eye, she always saw him as large, staid, red.

The old timber shed stood at the rear of the house, its high peaked roof overlooked by Stella's bedroom window and shaded by three giant jacaranda trees. Built to house both horse and

5

buggy in some past era, the shed still gave shelter to a horse collar, and harness, along with a 1936 Packard, a modern wheelbarrow an ancient wooden trailer, a cluttered workbench, and, when in residence, the minister's modern, church-supplied sedan. The walls were hung with cobwebs and the residue of years. Cycle wheels and car fenders hung from high rafters, ladders leaned, and boxes of the unnamed supported other boxes of the unknown.

A former horse stall, separated from the main shed by a partial door, was storeroom for the church guild. The polyester filling was usually kept here, its white snow bursting out of a hessian bale, but today the bale was sagging, near empty. There was a large plastic bag, overflowing with multicoloured wool. There were boxes of lace on a shelf, well off the floor, and two dozen completed clowns, packed in cartons, awaited their delivery to craft shops hundreds of kilometres away.

For twelve years Stella had been making her clown dolls, but they, unlike their creator, had escaped the boundaries of Maidenville. With the many hands of the guild ladies now knitting and stitching, the clowns brought in hard cash.

It was a busy shed, tool-filled, earthen-floored, its doors flung open to the garden. Stella spent much time there. In spring both front and side door looked out on a bower of blue but today the jacaranda trees were tired, their fern-like fronds drooping.

The town clock struck its long and painful five as she entered the shed that Friday. Her watch was one minute slow. She adjusted it, then took her rubber gloves from the workbench, carefully checking them for spiders before pulling them over her fingers. A new spray pack of weedkiller in hand, she stood reading the directions for use. There was a patch of couch grass growing against the paling fence her garden shared with Bill Wilson's neglected forest. Each summer she eradicated it, but each spring, devious roots burrowed beneath the fence to re-infest her garden beds.

'There are more ways of killing a cat than choking him with

cream, Mr Wilson,' she promised, marching purposely towards the side door.

Movement of shadow caught her eye. She turned, smiled. 'Good afternoon,' she said.

The shed's front doors, warped by a hundred years of rain storms and hot summer winds, sagged on aged hinges. Each closing dug two quarter-circles deeper into the earth, creating hollows where water lay all winter. They were rarely closed. Her visitor stood in the doorway, a tall silhouette against the white light of hard afternoon sun. He was tracing a muddy half-circle with his sneaker, pressing his footprint into the ooze.

'Father left the hose running while he was washing his Packard,' she offered, taking two steps to the left, attempting to see the face of her visitor. 'He's gone to Dorby for the funeral.' Then she smiled. 'Oh, it's you, Thomas. I didn't recognise you. You grow taller every time I see you.'

'G'day, Stell,' the youth replied. 'How's it going?'

'I'm well. And you, Thomas?' He was Ron and Marilyn Spencer's handsome son, and a long-term member of the youth group, a tall and well-built lad, barely sixteen. Although he had, up to twelve months ago, called her Aunt, she actually liked this youthful familiarity of the nineties, and thought of her own youth when young males would never have dared call an unmarried middle-aged woman by her Christian name.

'What time will he be back, Stell?' he asked.

'Who knows once they get to talking? The funeral was at three, and quite a crowd drove over. Father took Mrs Morris and Mrs Murphy, so I can't see them letting him get away much before six. Can I give him a message for you?'

'Na. I just thought I'd have a look at his old car.' As he walked towards her, he slapped the vehicle on its wheel-arch then kicked a tyre.

Stella flinched. It was her father's prized possession and he didn't encourage hand marks on the shiny black paintwork. She placed the weedkiller on the bench and walked to the car, offering the Packard her slim protection. 'You'd be welcome to come back tomorrow, Thomas. Perhaps the minister might start it up for you. He loves an excuse to show off his mechanical skill.'

'Does it still go?'

'Oh, my word it does. It's started up religiously every week. I tell Father he is like a little boy, playing with his matchbox car.' She smiled again.

'Do you still go?' the youth said. 'Anyone ever try to start you up, Aunty Stell?'

'Pardon?' Her smile now tempered with a frown, she stepped back from the youth.

'Do you still go?' he repeated.

It happened too fast for her conscious mind to accept, to assess. Her secure little world tipped, it tilted, it slipped into reverse. Too slight, and he too strong, she was flung to the floor, and all she had known became the unknown, and the unknown now became the known.

Boy. Child. Son of her friends. Ron's precious boy. Marilyn's baby.

The doors were wide open. The birds still chirped in the trees. Trucks rattled down the road, and Murphy's dogs barked.

This wasn't happening.

'No, Thomas ... No.' Her reaction time too slow; she was pinioned by his weight and his strong young arms. She tried to rise up, but her forehead slammed against the base of the Packard's running board. She tried to roll, and he pushed her face into the Packard's wheel. Her legs immobilised by his weight, her hands flailed uselessly as her cream blouse was ripped wide.

He was –

'No! No! Thomas. Don't do this. Have you lost your senses? Thomas!'

His jeans were down, and he was lifting –

'No! No! Thomas. Please, God, Thomas. Please.'

He was lifting her beige pleated skirt –

8

'No!'

He was ... He was ... He was ...

Then the world Stella Templeton had known for forty-four years was gone.

Time, sanity was gone. Consciousness left with it.

Sunlight had been replaced by twilight, muffled traffic noise replaced by a single motor. Stella saw the twin beams of light, highlighting a bird bath where no birds bathed, highlighting her garden. She was unaware of why she could see it.

Cold earth. Hard. Her back. Hurting.

'Father.' The word was raised in some distant place outside of conscious thought. The gates. The gates. She always opened the gates for the minister when he returned after a long day. She always had a hot meal ready for him when he returned.

But tonight the world was spinning on its edge, and no longer her world.

Where was she? Had she fallen?

The shed.

Her hand reached out, touched the car. She'd fallen. She'd hit her head on the car.

But answers came too fast on questions' heels.

'No,' she moaned, denying answers. 'No. No. No. No. No. No.'

Her head lifted. It slammed against the running board, bruising a place already bruised.

'Keep your mouth shut, Stell.'

And she remembered. And she remembered. And she remembered.

'Keep your mouth shut, Stell.'

She lay on the earthen floor, looking at the light in her garden. She heard the ancient complaint of the gates as they swung to. She heard the squeal of the bolt sliding home, locking him and his car in the yard. She heard the roar of an impatient foot on the accelerator. She saw car lights move to the house, light the house, then with no thought of whether she could, she rolled, coiled to her feet, and scuttled like an injured rabbit through the side door of the shed, across the vegetable garden, around to the back door, then upstairs to the bathroom, where she locked the door and stood in the bath, the shower raining down.

'Daughter! Daughter!' A door slammed open. His footsteps were slow, heavy down the dark passage.

She saw her face in the mirror opposite the shower. It was the face of a stranger, ghost white, a dark bruise beneath the hair line of her brow. Still looking at the face in the mirror, she let the water wash her blouse from her back, wash her bra straps from her shoulders.

'Daughter! Daughter?'

She heard his footsteps on the stairs, heard them still as he reached the small landing. Heard them climb again.

Slowly the water peeled away her clothing. Her slip was blood-stained, her cream blouse ripped, her beige skirt muddy. She stamped on the skirt, stamping, stamping it into the white bath, watching the pink water coil and trickle away down the plug hole.

'Daughter!' He was at the bathroom door. 'Daughter!' Now he hammered at the door.

Her nails were chipped, her legs bruised. Her neck stung, and her back pained. She raised a hand to her neck, fingered the broken skin, then rubbed soap into it. She scrubbed the external flesh, trying to force the soap to clean beneath her skin, and deep inside, to the part of her that would never again be clean.

'Daughter?'

Place of raw, aching pain ... and shame. And the shame. She needed a knife to rid herself of shame, to gouge memory of him from her, to wash him from her with her own blood.

'Stella!' Martin's voice now held concern.

'I ... I ... I ...' She tried to find the words but they were not there. Words were a rasp on emery. She looked at the door, shook her head.

'Stella, are you in there?'

'I'm ... I'm vomiting,' she said. And she did. And he heard her. He went away.

Stella stood beneath the shower, vomiting and soaping in turn; soaping and vomiting until the hot water became cold, and her father went to bed.

Martin was not particularly hungry. He had eaten well at the wake.

keep your mouth shut

Her limbs were lead on the mattress, weighing it down. Sleep was out there. Sleep and forgetfulness were hovering out there somewhere, but each time she released her grasp on consciousness, she heard the roar of hell's breath beneath her mattress. Old roar. Wind tunnel roar. Black roar. It was down there, an open maw of darkness waiting to suck her in. To suck her from sanity and into –

Her arms flailing, she refused sleep. For hours she fought her way free of sleep to rise to the surface of consciousness gasping for air while her heart threatened to explode.

'God. God, help me. Help me.'

At 2 a.m., she switched on her bedside light, but the light was too bright. She closed her eyes against it, and sleep came at her with grappling hands.

Evil, corrupt hands. Hurtful, prying fingers.

'God, help me. Don't let me think of it.'

Eyes wide then, she stared at the ceiling, stared at the whorls and roses of the patterned plaster cornice, her eyes burning, screaming out for their own rest. She attempted to pray, to seek comfort in the old chanted words, but she couldn't remember the words.

'We close our eyes when we pray. We know that God will hear everything we say.' Childish words, they were all that remained with her. A child's prayer. All others fled her mind like small grey mice, scattering in all directions when their hiding place in the shed was exposed.

'Foolish little words. Foolish little mice,' she whispered.

As the night wore away she grew colder, until in the hour before dawn she turned off the light and crawled from her bed to stand before the open window. It looked out on the jacaranda trees. She watched them turn from black, to grey, to green as she swayed before the window.

'*Keep your mouth shut, Stell,*' he'd said.

'Don't think. Don't think. Don't let me think,' she murmured. 'Our Father which . . . who . . . Our Father . . . who . . .'

Who are you? What form of God are you, that you would dare to allow this . . . this thing to happen to me? I have done all that has been asked of me – and more. I have asked for nothing. I have put my parents and their needs, the church's needs, the community's needs, before my own. Now this. Now this. How dare you? How dare you?

'*Keep your mouth shut, Stell.*'

Her mouth was dry, her lips sealed by dried saliva. Her eyes were sandpaper against her lids as she stared at the dew green haze, and at two early birds perched on a jacaranda bough.

Everything in nature has a pair. Except me, she thought. Bonny has Len. Marilyn has Ron. Even Father had –

'The animals went in two by two, hurrah, hurrah, the animals went in two by two, the ants and the lions, the kangaroos. Oh, we'll all be saved but we've got to get out of this rain,' she whispered. Then her hand went to her mouth, cupped her mouth, the second hand rising to cup the first, to hold insanity inside her.

God help me. I have lost my mind.

But what am I supposed to do but lose my mind? I can't live with this. How do I live with this?

Pretend it didn't happen. Push it away as a nightmare – away with the other bad dreams. You tripped over the pots in the shed, and ... and ...

Her eyes, blurred with their staring, began to follow a fluttering of blue. Unaware of what she was seeing, she tracked its odd flight down to the corrugated iron of the shed roof, then swept up by the breeze it circled, landed in front of the shed. She continued staring until the world slipped into negative and the blue became red. Blood red. Blood in the shed. And she cried out, but quickly gagged her mouth with her hand.

Where were her briefs?

Still in the shed.

'I can't let Father – oh, God. Dear God, let me be dead now. Take me,' she whispered. Please God, don't make me see myself in the morning. Don't make me face Father. I can't. I can't ever face him or this town again.'

Her nightgown, a calf-length floral thing, left her arms exposed. She shivered. For hours she'd been shivering, her core deathly cold. If I could weep, raise tears, they would warm me and wash my eyes, but there are no tears left in me.

'Mother,' she whispered. 'Mother.'

She waited for the voice she had forgotten. There was no reply, no remembered words of comfort.

'What can I do, Mother?'

'Stop that. Stop it,' she whispered. 'God, stop my mind from this thinking or I will begin to scream and it will never end.'

It was the one well used prayer that still had power. She made it have power.

Picture the ocean, waves breaking free over sand. Picture it, now grasp and hold it. Hold it steady. Make it grow.

And it came on cue.

A too blue postcard ocean wavered before her mind's eye. She willed it closer, until slowly the waves began to move in, break over white sand. Holding the vision, she rocked now to the rhythm of the waves, her eyes turned to the east, where a new day was creeping into the night sky.

New day. Already it was out there, way over the ocean. A clean new day to the east.

East. Sydney. Ocean.

I should have gone to Sydney, she thought. I planned to, but I have seen nothing. I have been here, doing what was asked of me. I have been a servant of this house, a servant of his church, trapped in this vicious, ugly little town with its vicious tongues and minds – and its vicious little boys.

She was aware of pain now. Her back, her neck, one arm was aching, and she hurt in that other place. His forced entrance had caused much pain, and he had taken pleasure in her pain. She had never known a lover.

Don't think. Don't think of it anymore. Think of the new day breaking over the ocean. Wild ocean, washing the world clean.

The image grew stronger. The waves grew wilder. She rocked with the waves, heel to toe, toe to heel.

Postcard ocean. Postcard from Bondi.

I miss you so much, Stell. We'll come here together on our honeymoon. Love from Ron.

Love from Ron. Love from Ron. Love from Ron.

Once she had dared to dream of love, dared to crave Ron Spencer's mouth on her own, dared to believe in love.

Love from Ron.

Ron's son. Handsome rapist. Only weeks ago she had baked and decorated his sixteenth birthday cake. Evil, vicious little boy.

I loved you, Thomas Spencer. I loved you. I hate you. Hate you. It is a new thing, hate, and it's hurting me. It's ripping out my heart.

But is it so new?

She shook her head, shook it until she stumbled and fell hard against the chest of drawers, catching the point of her elbow.

15

New pain washed over her. Clean pain. She grasped at clean pain, focusing on her elbow, allowing new pain to wash through her.

It could have been so much worse, she thought.

How?

He could have killed me to hide his guilt. It could have been worse.

Would that have been worse?

Again she shook her head. Better that he had killed me. Or better still that it had been a stranger who would be gone now.

He was here, in this town. A boy. Just a boy.

'*Keep your mouth shut, Stell.*'

He is here, and will be here, so I cannot stay here. I will have to leave.

'*Keep your mouth shut, Stell.*'

Who might I open my mouth to? Father?

'What you must ask yourself, Daughter, is, have you in some small way, perhaps in your manner, or your attire, have you perhaps led him to believe that his attention may have been acceptable to you?' she whispered. Martin Templeton. Our father, at any given time, could be relied on to take Angel's side, and though she was long dead Martin's conditioned response could not alter. Mankind is guilty until proven innocent. Precious Angel said so, so it was so.

What you must ask yourself, Daughter –

'Ask yourself. Ask yourself. What you must ask yourself,' she whispered. She had spent her life asking her father's questions, examining her mind until she could no longer be sure which was her mind, and which her father's mind. Every move she made was governed by the minister's voice, controlling her from within her own head.

She lifted her hands, looking at them in the early light, looking at her smallest finger, curled permanently into a C. She looked at the scars. Hard. Hard hands.

'*You've got hard hands, Aunty Stell.*'

Hard hands that once had held his tiny hands. Little Thomas. Baby Thomas.

She had celebrated his birth with his parents, had carried him, kissed his sweet baby face. How often through the years had she held that handsome child, and wished him her own son? And it could have been so. It should have been so. Ron said they would be married. At sixteen, she'd dreamed of a white wedding dress and a honeymoon at Bondi. Stella Spencer. It had sounded well on her tongue.

Stupid hard hands, trembling now – as they had trembled back then when Ron had placed the friendship ring on her finger.

'No. No. Not as then. Never again as then,' she whispered and quickly placed her hands safe beneath her armpits, as she allowed her mind to escape to that other time, that better time.

Ron had gone through school two years ahead of her, but near neighbours, they had formed a part of the group who walked to and from high school together each day. Then in the senior years, when they had walked too close on the footpath, their arms kept brushing, sparks igniting each time they touched.

One afternoon, as if by accident, his hand brushed her own. Eager fingers linked, and though her own hand grasped as firmly as his, she did not look at him, but continued walking at his side, eyes straight ahead.

That one hand had become a small miracle, living a life of its own. It throbbed, sending its heat up her arm and to her heart, and to her head, and her lungs so she could barely breathe, and barely walk, for there had been a throbbing in that secret place.

He had chosen her from the group. Not Bonny, not Marilyn. It was Stella's scarred hand he had chosen to hold.

Then, on the night of the end of year social when he'd walked her home, he drew her into the shadow of the cypress hedge and he placed his cool, chaste lips against her own. Just for a second. With her arms held firmly at her sides, she had given him no encouragement at all, but stood swaying there, on the footpath, drowning in the first wave of love.

School. A sanctuary. The community of teachers and students had allowed Stella to glimpse a world beyond the cypress hedge, outside of church restrictions. At school, she'd been free to live, to dance, to sing – not in praise of God, but in praise of life. Then Miss Moreland, the headmistress, chose her and Ron to play the leads in the school production of *West Side Story*.

How she had lived for the days when she and Ron rehearsed the musical. There were afternoon and evening rehearsals. She was blissfully, delightfully, never at home.

'The girl is never here,' the beige shadow that cast its gloom over Stella's childhood complained. 'I gave my health to give her life, but she is never here when I need her. Gallivanting around all night while I suffer alone.'

Ron and Stella had to embrace, kiss on stage. It was only a stage kiss, a brushing of cheeks, but the weekly rehearsals were becoming rehearsals for life. His arms grew more bold, his lips more demanding, and when the two met each lunchtime behind the school sports ground, his hands began their exploration of that first sweet love. His fingers unbuttoned her school blouse, and he touched her breasts, and he –

Drowning. Drowning. So much in love. They would marry when Stella turned eighteen, Ron said, then he gave her the ring with its small blue stones, and he said that it wasn't wrong. He said if you were in love, nothing was wrong. But she'd wanted to wait and be a bride in white, and it was only sixteen months. Only sixteen months.

She had waited too long.

Angel was sick again. Doctor Parsons came to the house twice a day, and Sister Brooks came twice a week, but Angel needed a full-time nurse, so Stella left school to care for her mother and the lead in *West Side Story* went to Marilyn Jones – as did Ron Spencer. They married three months after opening night, and Marilyn was already three months pregnant.

But she lost that baby while they were on their honeymoon. For twelve years, she hadn't been able to bear a live child. Then Thomas came, a fine healthy son for whom Stella had publicly celebrated, while imagining in the privacy of her own room that he was her son. Her own. How she loved the tiny boy, because she still loved his father.

'Keep your mouth shut, Stell'.

Oh, she would keep her mouth shut. What else could she do?

boiled eggs

At 7 a.m., Stella heard her father in the bathroom, which shared a wall with her room. Quickly she climbed into bed, pulling her quilt high. There was no lock on her door, and when Martin discovered the kitchen empty, his breakfast not waiting, he would come to her room, knock three times, cough, then slowly swing the door wide, filling the doorway as he had all the years of her life.

She heard him walk downstairs. Minutes later, his ponderous footsteps were again climbing. Now came the long silence as he stood, his ear close to the door. The three knocks. She waited for his cough.

It came.

'Daughter? Daughter?'

She feigned sleep, but from beneath her lashes she saw his heavy shoulder, his shaggy white head almost brushing the top of the doorframe. Her hands rose to cover her face as she rolled to her back.

'Are you ailing?' The question held an accusation.

'Just some virus, Father.'

He took his white handkerchief from his pocket and held it before his nose. He was afraid of illness, yet when the whole town succumbed to colds and flu, Martin Templeton went about his business untouched by disease, thanking God and his strong constitution for his robust health. It was neither God nor constitution protecting Martin. It was his distance from people, the space he kept between himself and the world.

His white handkerchiefs liberally doused with eucalyptus were used to good advantage when he preached in a church filled with a sneezing congregation. He hid behind these handkerchiefs. If someone sneezed, he chose not to breathe for the regulation thirty seconds he had decided it would take for the expelled germs to settle on someone else.

Martin also kept space between himself and his daughter. He stepped back to the passage now. 'Bed may be the best place for you then, Daughter,' he said, and he closed the door, locking the virus in.

In her mind, Stella pictured his progress downstairs. She saw him fling wide the back door, suck on the cool morning air. Only after considerable blowing of germs from his nasal passages would he return to the kitchen.

She lay listening to his bumbling movements as he searched unknown terrain for a meal. She heard the rattle of dropped pans below her, the splashing of water into the sink, the tugging at cupboard doors held shut by ancient snib, and his complaint when they refused to open to his will alone.

At eight-fifteen, he knocked three times, coughed, then entered her room, bearing a breakfast tray which he deposited on her bedside table. Quickly he returned to the door, his face pink with a breath held long.

Stella looked at his burned offering. Black toast. Weak black tea, a scum of leaves floating on top. She liked milk in her tea. He didn't know to add milk; but then he knew so little about her. She stared at the cup, and at the tray. Three times a day he sat with her at the table, ate with her, but he didn't know she took milk in her tea. Stella, a beige-coloured shadow, was only there to see to his comfort.

From the passage he said, 'Try to eat something, Daughter. We cannot afford to succumb to illness when we have God's business to see to.'

'Thank you, Father,' she said. 'Thank you.'

She heard the telephone at nine-fifteen, and she heard his commanding 'Hello. Hello. Hello.' A wrong number ... or perhaps a right number.

'Keep your mouth shut, Stell.'

Again her mind began its questions. Would her silence encourage the youth to repeat his action? It would break Ron's heart if she were to report it. She couldn't be responsible for that. And Marilyn. How does a mother, who had lost five babies before giving birth to a living son, survive the shame of that son turned rapist?

In this town she wouldn't survive it. And how could I survive the shame, survive the staring eyes, the questions, the silent accusations, and those not so silent? The town gossips, who used Doctor Parsons' waiting room as an airconditioned meeting place, would apportion guilt to her, deserved or not.

Better that I find a way to leave. I'll go to Sydney. Get work. I can type ... badly. I can sew ... a little. Perhaps I could set up my own business with the clowns? But how can I leave Father? I'll have to report it. If I let him get away with it once, he'll do it again.

She heard the telephone at ten.

'Hello. Hello. Who is it? Hello. Is there anyone there?' She heard her father slam the phone down.

Three knocks, a cough, and the bedroom door slowly swung open. Martin's head, white handkerchief held before it, peered around the doorjamb.

'Did you eat your breakfast, Daughter?'

'I've been resting. I'll eat something later.'

'Someone on the telephone. They keep ringing, then hang up.

Some parishioner with a faulty connection, do you think?'

'Perhaps a child, Father, who may grow bored with his game.'

But would he?

'Yes. Yes. No doubt you're right, Daughter. I'll ignore it. Let the confounded thing ring out. As you say, they'll grow bored.' And the head was gone, and the door closed, but the scent of eucalyptus lingered.

He was past his eighty-fifth birthday, at the age where the father becomes the child of his child. But she'd played the role of parent before. Always a mother, never the wife.

I'll have to go. He'll survive without me. He has the church. I must go. Now. Today. I'll pack a few things and go.

How? On the morning bus.

Too late. It's gone.

Tomorrow's bus then.

Money? What do I use for money? Ask Bonny?

She has no money to spare.

Miss Moreland?

No. No. I can never ask her. She'd know. She sees too much. Oh, God. God. God, what am I going to do?

The sun was out again, and its light too bright in her room. Her eyes closed against it and the dream began. She tried to will her eyes to open but she was already inside the dream, and when the black maw beneath her bed opened to take her, she gave up her fight and let it claim her, carry her away from the room, and from the house, and into the deep place. Be it hell or not, she only knew it was a place where there was no more thinking, a place where nothing could reach her.

Stella's new dress was white. Mummy liked white, and she got Mrs Thomson to sew it for her on her machine, and Mummy gave her some money, and said thank you, and Stella said thank you.

Mrs Thomson put pintucks in the top and around the bottom.

And Stella said, when Mrs Thomson went away, 'But, dearest Mummy, but I truly did want a red dress, like Bonny.' But Mummy only liked white.

It was Bonny's party when the clock said two Bongs, and she would be four. Daddy was taking Stella to Bonny's party, and they would have lots of cakes and some drinks and balloons, but she mustn't get her new dress dirty.

Mummy got her all dressed up and all ready to go before she had her rest.

She said, 'Sit there and be a good girl.'

Mummy was sleeping now, and making her snoring. It happened because of all the stitches Mummy had to get in her tummy. That was why she got tired and did the snoring. One day she showed Stella the place where she got sewed up with all the stitches, and it was all white and wrinkly. Mummy said the doctor took out all the bad, and one day Stella would get all the bad took away too, but Stella didn't want to have a big white line on her tummy, and she didn't want to sit still till Daddy came home either.

When the clock said Bong, Bong, one, two, then Daddy would come home. He said so. That was a long time yet.

She leaned back on the leather chair and lifted her knees so her bottom felt cool. The leather chair made her underpants and tights get all wet, so when your knees lifted up, then the air could get to your bottom and make the wet cool. A bit. She pulled at the knees of her white tights and wished she could have just sandals like Bonny.

Her shoes were hard and shiny white. They had a strap and a buckle. She mustn't put the buckle on the chair because it might cut Mummy's chair. She had to sit up straight like a good girl, then everyone would be happy with her.

Her bottom was getting all sweaty again, so she moved to the other side of the chair, where it was cool, and that made her bottom feel very cool.

She liked cool, but there wasn't any inside the house because

Daddy said now it was summertime. In the refrigerator it made cool. When you opened the refrigerator door, winter came out for a little bit, but Stella mustn't open the refrigerator because Mummy said.

It had cold water in it, in a big jug, and up the top it made ice-blocks for Mummy's special tea. Ice made Stella think of thirsty, and her mouth wanted an ice-block or a drink. She wriggled her feet, and thought of thirsty, and of the tap and lots of water outside in the tap.

She couldn't reach the tap in the kitchen, except if she got a chair, but Mummy might hear her get the chair, and she might hear the tap too. But she wouldn't hear the outside tap. Stella could reach that one easily.

Dearest Mummy was still making her snoring. Sometimes she slept for a long time, and sometimes she slept for a short time. Sometimes she slept for all the hot day and then she woke up and it was night-time. She didn't want to go to sleep any more, and that was the bad time.

Stella looked at the window-doors and at the little glass in them. There was one, two, three, four, five, six, seven, eight little glasses in the door, and the other door was the same. Daddy said they made sixteen little glass windows. The sun came through when the curtains got opened, when it was early, and the sun made like hopscotch shadows on the floor. But she wasn't allowed to play hopscotch, only outside. She liked outside.

Her mouth was very thirsty. She licked her mouth and, quiet as a mouse, she slid her shoes to the carpet, and on tippy-toe walked to the couch. Mummy had her mouth open and you could see her bottom teeth when the big snore went in, then her mouth pushed out a giant puff. Stella watched her for twenty-six puffs, and the clock didn't say Bong, Bong. One finger to her lips, she tippy-toed out the door to the passage then into the kitchen, but she didn't open the fridge. She looked at the chair, but she didn't push it to the sink. If she was very careful, and not got dirt on *her dress, and not got dust on her shoes, she could go outside. She was a big girl now. She was three now. One, two, three. And she knew how to be very careful.*

There were some trees outside, and some lawn, and a long black hose. She turned the tap, just a tiny bit, and she let all the hot water get out of the hose till it would get cold, and she was very careful. She didn't get any on her shoes, and when it got cold, she had a big drink and she didn't get any on her dress either.

Water was better than the refrigerator for making people cool. Bonny had a little swimming pool, and Daddy let Stella get wet all over in Bonny's swimming pool one day. She couldn't have a swimming pool, but she could make a rainbow with water. She just had to put her finger on the end of the hose, and point it up in the air, and when the sun shined on it, it made a rainbow, and some of the water fell on her, and it was like a tiny little rain on her hair. She only made a little rainbow, because her dress got wet and spotty, so she ran and turned the tap off with two hands, then walked up to the gate because the clock must be ready to say Bong, Bong, and then she could go to the party and get a red balloon – or even a yellow one.

She couldn't see through the gate, but she could reach the letterbox, and if she lifted the lid, she could see a little bit through. Just light through. She was looking at the light when the clock said its Bongs, but it was a silly old clock, because it wouldn't stop, and she wanted it to stop. It made six and eight and even sixteen.

Her mouth got sad. She knew that when the clock got to lots and lots of Bongs, then it had to go back and start at the one Bong, then you had to wait a long, long time before it made two.

She stood watching two cheeky birds while her face made its sad look that Mummy said was bad. She tried to make sad go away, but it didn't want to. She rubbed at her face with her hands, and tried to think of laughing things. Like when Daddy showed her a nest in the oak tree, and it had one, two, three baby birds in it, and they opened their mouths and said Cark, Cark, Cark when they saw her. They made her laugh. But she didn't laugh now, just made her eyes get wet.

Maybe there were some new baby birds in the tree. Maybe if she could climb up she could find a nest and when Daddy came home, she could show him, and there would be some laughing time with Daddy. And if she climbed up very, very high then she might see over the hedge and she might see Daddy's car coming.

But she'd get dirty, then Mummy would be sad and she couldn't go to the party. But if she didn't get dirty –

She walked to the front porch and very carefully, lifted her white skirt and sat on the top step, thinking big thoughts, and she said, 'Pressures Lord, make Mummy not wake up till Daddy comes home.' And she said, 'Pressures Lord, if Mummy wakes up before Daddy comes home, tell her that she must do some singing.' That made Mummy very happy when she was singing.

Stella undid her buckles, and she took her shoes off. She pulled her tights down and took them off too – pulled them until they slipped off her toes. Toes felt good when they got bare. She put her shoes on the porch chair, then she undid all the buttons that were in the middle of the pintucks and she took her white dress off, and her petticoat. Very, very carefully, she folded them and placed them on her shoes. Her underpants were white too, so she took them off, and all bare was very, very good. Now she could make a rainbow, and she wouldn't get wet, and she could be a bird in the tree and –

It was after one when she awoke to Martin's bellow from halfway up the stairs.

'Are you awake, Daughter?'

'I . . . yes,' she said.

'Pardon?'

'I was sleeping.' Her voice rose to penetrate the closed door and the distance between the speakers.

'Sleep is a great healer. Do you feel like a little lunch ...
perhaps a boiled egg?'

'No thank you, Father.'

'Pardon?'

'No. No thank you.'

'I ... I thought I might manage an egg. How might I ... how
might I go about it?'

'Bring the water to the boil. Allow the egg to – ' She sighed.
He would stand halfway up the stairs, calling his questions, and
she would call down her replies. It was too hard. Easier as always,
to rise from the bed and care for her aging child. Wipe away self,
extinguish self, bury self. 'I will cook your egg, Father.'

'Pardon?'

'Go downstairs. I'll be with you shortly.'

'Thank you, Daughter.'

Her back hurt as she moved from the bed, and there was more
blood. She showered, then dressed carefully, painfully. She slid
pantihose over her bruised legs, remembering the constant white
tights of her childhood. Hot. Too hot for pantihose today too,
but legs must be covered.

She was standing before her dressing-table mirror when she
saw the dark stain on her forehead. She touched it with a finger
tip. It was tender, bruised.

'Can't cover that one, dearest Mummy,' she whispered, and
she looked at her bed wanting to crawl back into it and pull the
quilt over her head, forget his eggs. 'Give up,' she said, but her
hand was reaching for her embroidery scissors. She looked again
at the bruise, then carelessly she combed her hair forward, drew
a careful part, and began cutting a fringe.

For too long she had drawn her fading hair back from her
brow; the new fringe refused to lie flat. Curls, given their
freedom, curled up, out. She dipped two fingers in the cold tea,
dampening the shorter clump of the hair, then combing it,
smoothing the fringe flat. Perhaps the sugar helped. Angel had
always liked too much sugar in her tea.

A plain cream blouse with its high collar did not hide the still raw scratch beneath her ear. She sought and found a near forgotten scarf, knotting it loosely at her throat. Hot. Too hot for scarves. Too hot for the airless blouse also.

Her window was wide open. Heat blasted through, drying her fringe into spiky clumps, sugar sweet. She combed it again, then, with a well-practised twist, coiled the long hair into a knot. It looked odd in the dressing-table mirror. The heavy clump of fringe, the green scarf. Odd. Un-Stella. She couldn't go downstairs like that. He'd know.

Give it up.

Her back ached; the bed called to her. She sat on its edge, wanting to lie down, to sleep, to hide, to die.

'Daughter?'

'Yes.' He wouldn't let her give up.

'What on earth are you doing up there? It's almost two.'

'I will be down shortly.' Her hair spilling free to her shoulders, she walked from the room and downstairs.

The kitchen was hard, stale with unchange. She had placed no stamp of ownership here. It was as it had been in her childhood, as it had been in her mother's childhood. Its small windows, now in shade, cast little light into this room that had for too many years soaked up the odours of boiled swedes and sprouts and roasts on Sundays. It couldn't change, and like the minister, wouldn't change. He saw no need for change.

The floor, the walls, the cupboards, were a worn brown. Perhaps in a time before, the linoleum had boasted a touch of colour, a dash of shine. Now it was flat, dull, always clean, but never clean. Each week, Stella wiped its surface with a liquid polish poured from a bottle, and for a time the kitchen smelt of the polish, but the floor refused to shine.

She walked to the refrigerator and to the cool blast of air, savouring it, wasting it. Large, new, twin-door, her father had bought it last year when the old Kelvinator finally died. This one jutted out from the wall, aware that it was out of place, out of time in this room; thus it did not associate with the brown canisters on the mantelpiece, nor the walnut antique dresser at its side.

Two eggs in her hand, she let the door swing shut, close off the cool, and she walked to the electric stove. Old too, but not as old as she. It stood on the hearth, directly before its long disused, wood-burning antecedent. She hated that wood stove with an irrational hatred, and chose not to look at it, not to clean it. She wanted it gone, had pleaded with her father for twenty years to have it gone; still it remained, bricked into the chimney, where the black soot of yesterday still fell in showers onto unused hotplates, scattering black beads to today's floor.

A small stainless-steel saucepan taken from the bottom shelf of a walk-in pantry; she stood immobile, studying its copper base, aware that it was the best money could buy in Maidenville. Martin had purchased the complete set when he learned from the television that aluminium was unsafe. She sighed, and carried the saucepan to the green enamel sink, an aged, chipped beast of a thing.

The entire house had this same inconsistency. The dark and light, the old and the new living incongruously, side by side. The lounge room was panelled in dark wood, its glass doors, that had once opened to the morning sun, were shielded day and night by heavy brown drapes, kept drawn against the dark side of the house, kept drawn against the forest of trees in the neighbouring yard, and against the eyes of the neighbour who owned the untamed forest. The minister and Mr Wilson had not spoken for fifteen years. Long ago, Stella had given up opening the drapes for Martin to close. Given up. Given up. Given up everything. Every dream. Every desire.

Within the lounge room, a modern, wide-screened television dominated. An electric heater covered the open fireplace, and a huge tan recliner chair awaited the minister's pleasure before it.

But against the walls, Angel's heavy, brown leather, lounge suite waited for Stella, as it had for all the days of her life. A dark room. Dark memories lived in that room. Sitting on a leather chair. Waiting on that leather chair. Always waiting.

The water was boiling. She gathered her thoughts and, with a spoon, eased the eggs into the boiling water. She turned the heat down to halfway, set the stove timer to four point five minutes, then stood watching the water boil while listening to the uneven rattling of eggshell on steel.

'Eggs,' she said. 'My God!'

'Daughter?' His head lifted in question.

'The water, Father. It ... it splashed ...'

A calendar hung behind the passage door. She stared at it, her shaking hand covering her mouth, while the eggs on the hotplate taunted her with their water dance.

From his position at the table, where he'd been writing on a notepad, Martin frowned. 'Perhaps you should return to bed. You are not yourself today.' She made no reply. He shrugged and returned to his writing.

Bread in the toaster. Butter from the refrigerator. Plates from the top cupboard. Knife, spoon, eggcups. She was forcing her shaking hands to function, but her mind was still on the calendar when the timer buzzed and the eggs were done.

He pushed the pad aside for her to place two eggcups and their eggs before him, the two slices of thick buttered toast on his right. 'Do you still feel nauseous?'

She shook her head, and returned to the sink. Perhaps it was his question, perhaps the smell of hot butter, perhaps habit, but she placed more bread in the toaster, and when it popped she buttered and ate it at the sink, while staring down at her ugly brown shoes on the brown linoleum.

I won't think of it. I will survive this thing. I will eat and sleep and the days will pass and I will survive this thing. What is done, cannot be undone. He didn't cut me, he didn't tie me, bind me, leave me to die on the side of a road. It is unlikely that – she looked at the table and at the two eggshells, empty already, and she turned again to the calendar. It is unlikely. And he is only a youth. There is little chance that he is carrying a disease. So much worse could have happened. So much worse.

'Do we take our meals at the sink now, Daughter?'

'I'm sorry.' An aged wooden chair pulled to the table, she sat opposite the minister, stirring her tea, and playing with her second piece of toast.

The table was as old as the house, as solid as the house, but she had covered it with a white lace tablecloth, then covered the lace with a clear sheet of heavy-duty plastic – safe from her father's frequent spillages. They had a dining room down the hall. It faced west, but its window was shaded by the front porch, and by two overgrown pencil pines. It was a good room, papered tastefully in some past era. The best of the old ornaments lived in the dining room. The antique lamp with its ruby glass bowl was on a fine old cabinet – both lamp and cabinet older than Stella's grandparents, but when Angel was no longer able to take her meals in the dining room, Stella and Martin began eating in the kitchen. Now the best room was used as the church guild's meeting room. Each week the women came to sit at the long oak table, to knit, to stuff and stitch the clowns, to pack them in their plastic bags, and to pass on town gossip.

The house was far too large for two people. Many rooms were rarely entered – except for dusting, and vacuuming. There were two small bedrooms downstairs; no doubt they had been the maids' rooms. Stella had claimed one for her ironing board and sewing machine. The second was still furnished with a small wardrobe and an old iron bed.

Allowing her mind to stray a while to the empty rooms, Stella's finger played with her father's fresh spill of sugar. Sugar grains were picked up from the plastic tablecloth, transferred to her saucer, one by one ... two by two ... three by three.

When he was small, Thomas had loved visiting the empty rooms, with their smell of age trapped there in old furnishings.

She'd allowed him to jump on the aged beds.

'Can we play trampolines, Aunty Stell?'

Until he was age seven, she'd been a second mother to him.

But memory of the good times only made what he had done that much worse. She shook her head, shook memory away.

'How could he?' she said.

The minister glanced up. 'I beg your pardon?'

'I . . . I . . .' She coughed. 'How will he go on? Old Mr Martin. They say he does not realise his wife is dead. They lived for each other.'

'Yes. I doubt he will survive long without her. It is hard to lose a partner.' He silenced, and again her mind was free to roam.

Another funeral. Flowers. She would have to go to the funeral, do the flowers. She would have to. Who would do the flowers if she didn't?

When?

Monday, no doubt. The family wanted it on Monday. Thomas will be back in the classroom on Monday, she thought. He will be sitting in the classroom with other children while we bury Mrs Martin. Age making way for youth.

God. He is only a child. Why?

In the past year, she had rarely seen him except at youth group, but even there his appearances were rare. Bonny's boy had been his best friend through primary school, but they had formed other friendships now.

Aunty Stell. She was honorary aunt to many children in town, but to Thomas, she had been more. She had walked him to school for years, waited for him at the school gate, listened to his spelling.

He had been her son. In those early years he had been as much her son as Marilyn's. Always too busy at the supermarket, Marilyn had seemed pleased to escape a mother's responsibility.

I will have to leave. Somehow. I will have to get away from here.

The minister cleared the table while she sat staring at an uneaten crust of toast. He dumped the saucepan, the dishes, the cups and glasses in the sink, then turned on the old brass tap, to splash its stream in a wide arc across the floor.

She heard him about his task and, as she sprang to her feet to save further chaos, the telephone began ringing in the hall.

'I'll get it,' the minister said.

Cloth in hand, Stella stooped, mopped the floor. She looked at the cloth, smudged brown, stained by dirt, or by the brown of the floor.

The ringing silenced. Studying the cloth, she listened to the commanding, 'Hello. Hello. Who is this? What do you want?'

Another wrong number?

A round-faced, battery-powered clock had lived for twenty years on the wall beside the sink. Now Stella stared at it, aware that the placement of the hands should mean something to her. 'Two-fifteen,' she said.

'Pardon?'

'It's two-fifteen, Father,' she repeated, her hands repacking the sink. She picked out a chipped glass, placed it in the plastic kitchen tidy beside the stove, before turning to the minister. 'Who was it?'

'That young pest again,' he said, and he leaned at the door watching her at work. 'You have an efficiency of movement, Daughter. Chaos bows readily to your hands,' he said. She made no reply. He coughed, gained her attention. 'Do you think I should report these confounded calls?'

'It's two-fifteen,' she replied.

'Yes. The day has flown. I have had nothing but interruptions this morning. Shall it continue all afternoon, I wonder?'

'It's Saturday. It's ... It's Miss Moreland's day. I've got to go.' She turned the water off.

On Saturdays, she sat with Miss Moreland in her bright little unit discussing world affairs and cricket scores and watching the tennis. She never missed a Saturday. Miss Moreland's birth certificate might state that she was ninety-six, but she was younger in mind than many forty years her junior.

'I'm late. I have to go, Father.'

'Should I report the calls, Daughter? Get Johnson onto the young hooligan?'

'What will be gained by reporting him? What good will it ultimately do?' she said, unaware she was answering her own unspoken question. 'Please leave the dishes. Please don't touch the dishes. I'll do them when I return. And don't use that cloth.' She pointed, then took the cloth in her hand. 'Look at it, Father. That came off the floor with one wipe. It's past time that we considered a new floor-covering.'

'It's functional enough, Daughter.' He dismissed her words.

She tossed the cloth into the kitchen tidy, then walked towards the stairs.

'I don't believe you are well enough to go out today, and certainly not well enough to walk the distance. You should perhaps consider returning to bed.'

'Perhaps I could take the car?'

'I may need – '

'It will only be five minutes away, Father.'

'I dare say I can leave my work and drive you there – if you are determined to go. I need to fill the tank.'

'If you'd register the Packard – '

'It would be seen as wasteful extravagance,' he said, quickly ending that conversation.

'I'll have to go. I'm already late.'

His head bowed, his frown grown deeper, he looked at her feet, at the floor-covering. He followed a new ripple to the fridge where the linoleum had worn through to show its hessian backing. 'Yes,' he said. 'Yes. We need milk. I'll pick some up while we're out.'

'I'll get the milk.'

In the bathroom, she looked at the basin, rust-stained. It

looked like blood. She shivered and turned her eyes away from it. This was a dark room, old. Everything was old. She looked at her face in the mirror. She too was old. Stained.

Behind her, she could see her father's face reflected in the same mirror. He leaned against the door, watching her run the comb through her hair, watching her again wet down her fringe. His mirror image frowned.

The mirror was large, and not so old. She had installed it, hoping it may lend a little light to the room. 'A wasteful extravagance. I manage well enough with the shaving mirror,' her father had said, but she'd bought it anyway. Bonny helped fix it to the wall with the aid of Len Davis's electric drill and some small green wall plugs. They'd done it six or eight years ago when Stella had been strong enough to argue.

'You don't look at all well, Daughter. I'll feel happier if I deliver you safely to Miss Moreland's door.'

'Look at me, Father. Look at me for just one moment. Please see me. I am old. I'm almost as old as my own mother was when I was born,' her reflection replied.

'And you are in no fit state to drive today.'

'I was driving at seventeen. I have had my licence for twenty-seven years. Twenty-seven years,' she stressed.

'But you have not driven the new car, and perhaps what I am attempting to say, Daughter, is today is not the best day for you to begin driving it.'

She turned from the mirror and stood facing him, waiting for him to clear the doorway, and when he did, she walked downstairs. His shaggy head shaking, he followed behind her, through the back door and out to the shed.

'You won't drive through the centre of town, Daughter. You'll go around via the pool. Don't attempt to cross the highway at the railway line. The traffic is fierce there.'

'As always, I will do as you say.'

At the shed door, she remembered her missing briefs. Heat rushed to her head as her eyes scanned the floor, her leaden feet walking her towards the Packard. Then she smelt him. The stink of his youth was still inside the shed. His sweat. His sex. His footprint was in the drying mud. Heartbeat. Hammer. She turned, ran by her father to the side door where she grasped wood, cowered, unable to run further.

He glanced at her as he walked to his car. 'Will you get the gates, Daughter?'

Blood was flooding her head, beating in her brain; his command had no power to move her. Her hands covering her face, she trembled in the shade of the jacaranda. She would not open the gates again, allow the outside world in. She didn't want the world. Didn't want to live in such a world. She would stay here. Just stay here. Die here.

The plaintive beep of a horn. And his voice. It would not be denied. She turned to the house, to the gate, then her eyes caught the flutter of blue. They followed the odd spiralling flight as, caught by a breeze, a jacaranda blossom fell to the earth beside her shoe.

'It's too late,' she said.

'And while you stand there dreaming, it grows later still.'

She stooped and picked up the flower, cupping it in her palm as she looked beyond it to the tree. 'It does not bloom in February. Has the world gone mad?' she whispered.

'Daughter?'

'It's February. It's blooming, Father. The jacaranda.' He returned to the door, frowning down from his great height. She turned to him. 'It's too late for it.'

'I agree. And you are not at your best.' He sighed. 'I have considerable work – '

'No.' She shook her head. 'Do you see it, Father? Look. Do you see it too?'

He followed her pointing finger to a cluster of violet-blue blossom. 'The trees have a habit of blooming, Daughter.'

'But never a second blooming. Never in February.'

'God's hand at work in our garden, no doubt. Now, if you

are still determined to go about your visiting, then I suggest you get the gate.'

'Yes. Yes.' She walked to the gate, opening it then stepping back, her eyes turned to the shed and to the jacaranda foliage, visible above its roof. Two more clusters of blue. It was there. It was.

The beep of a horn moved her from the drive to the footpath.

'Hop in, Daughter. Easier for me to drive you than worrying about the car all afternoon. It's no effort to me at all. Perhaps you'll feel like walking home.'

A shake of her head and she was at the driver's side door, waiting there, waiting, until reluctantly, Martin vacated the seat. His face pink, his jowls trembling, he watched her take his seat, select drive, release the handbrake and slowly ease the car away.

'The power steering is rabid. Watch the kerbs when you're cornering. And the brake is dynamite. Take care, Daughter,' he called after her. 'Remember, the car belongs to the church.'

Miss Moreland's house was three long country blocks east and one west. Martin watched the car out of sight. He did not see his vehicle make the turn across the highway. It appeared to be continuing east, travelling towards Dorby.

the black packard

The minister made his grudging way back to the shed, his mind with his new car. Unmarked yet, it still smelt of the showroom – and he liked it that way. The church supplied his vehicles, and so they should, he thought. Much of his work was out of town. He had given his life to the church, but, had he not chosen to follow his father's vocation, Martin Templeton would have made an admirable motor mechanic. He had a shelf in his study specifically for mechanical books. Each year at the church fete he sorted through the second-hand books for old magazines he could not justify purchasing at the local newsagents. Wallowing in the intricacies of motors was his secret vice.

The Packard, like the house, came to him with his wife, and he had grown to know the old car more intimately than he'd ever known dear Angel. 'A strange woman,' he muttered, dusting her father's car, loving it, wiping finger marks from its wheel-arch with one of his own outgrown singlets. He kept a bag of rags beneath his workbench, discarded garments he used as polishing cloths and to wipe the grease and oil from his fingers when he delved beneath the bonnet.

On his knees, he was peering beneath the old vehicle when the telephone again paged him.

'Confound that thing,' he said. 'Confound its ill-mannered interruptions.' Head up, he counted the rings. Most callers gave up if the phone wasn't answered after twelve rings. He always followed this rule. With effort he stood, listening, counting. The phone continued to ring. Sixteen. Seventeen. Eighteen –

His oily rag in hand, he crossed the garden to the back door, flinging the flywire wide, picking up the phone and bellowing his frustration into the mouthpiece. 'Hello. Who is this?'

'Old age pinching this afternoon, Martin Templeton?' an equally peevish voice replied.

'Miss Moreland. Do forgive my ire. I have been the recipient of innumerable nuisance calls today. Any work I have attempted this morning has been interrupted by some young hooligan with a penchant for telephones. Is Stella there? She has taken the new car. Not familiar with it, I'm afraid.'

'She's a better driver than you ever were, Martin Templeton.'

'Has she arrived, madam?'

'Not yet. Where is she?'

Martin's mind began charting the car's course to Miss More-land's unit, seeing his small white vehicle smashed on each corner. 'She left a few minutes before two-thirty. She was . . . is not . . . not herself.'

'Speak English. Is she sick?'

'No. No. Luckily she inherited my constitution rather than her poor mother's. She may have stopped off at the centre. I noticed that we were out of milk,' he added, attempting to convince himself, more than the caller. He looked at his clock. Almost fifteen minutes had passed since his daughter had driven away. It didn't take that long to buy milk in Maidenville. He should have put his foot down, refused her the keys. It was six months since the army reunion in Sydney. That was the last time she had driven, and that had been in the six-year-old Ford. Why he had allowed her to drive away today he didn't know. 'Remind her about the milk. Better still, tell her to give me a call when she arrives.'

'If she's not here by three, I'll call back.'

'Thank you. Don't forget to remind her we need milk.' Martin placed the phone down then, his rag tossed to the table, he made his slow way upstairs to his study where he sat scanning through his bible, looking for inspiration. He had barely taken up his pen when the phone jangled again from the hall. 'That will be Stella,' he said, 'or the police.' He sprang to his feet and hurried downstairs. 'Good afternoon,' he said.

There was no reply.

'Who is this? What do you want? Have you got the right number?'

The caller replied with heavy breathing, and Martin slammed the phone into the receiver.

Thomas Spencer was stifling his laughter as he returned to the storeroom of his parents' supermarket. He was supposed to be filling shelves. He did it every Saturday, and he hated it.

For minutes he stood on the cool cement floor, imagining the face of old Templeton. It was almost as good as Stell answering, he thought, visualising the old bull-moose slobbering into the phone. He'd do more than slobber if old Stell ever told him what'd happened. But he knew she'd kept her mouth shut like he told her to because he'd seen the cop car driving down Main Street only half an hour ago. It went straight by.

He reached for a carton of tomato-sauce bottles, and hefted it onto his shoulder as his father walked through.

'Nice to see a smiling face for a change, Tommy.'

'You've got a better view than me.'

'Why don't you use a trolley? You'll drop the lot one day.'

'She's cool man. She's cool.'

Ronald Spencer continued on through the storeroom, his brow permanently creased in a frown.

'Nagging old shit,' Thomas muttered. His father was always nagging him to use a trolley. Thomas ignored him. He liked the look of his shoulders beneath the carton, and he stopped now in front of a mirror over the main freezer, shifting the carton to his other shoulder. He stood there, viewing his still new manly physique. Twelve months ago, he'd been one of the smallest in the junior football team. This year he'd be one of the biggest. He looked good too. Girls liked him now. They more than liked him! He hoped Kelly Murphy would walk in and see him flexing his muscles, see what she was missing out on. He was giving her a rest for a while, letting her learn that she wasn't making the rules any more. He was making the rules these days.

Nobody came in.

He walked to the sauce shelves, placed the carton on the floor, then with his Stanley knife, slashed the cardboard carton, waiting for the wound to gape open like a slit throat, to expose the glass veins of clotted red blood. 'Die,' he hissed, slashing again. 'Die.'

The whole town must have lived on tomato sauce. Every Saturday of his life he had to fill the tomato sauce shelf. He even dreamed of filling it some nights – of spilling a pool of red to the tiled floor. If a Saturday ever came when he walked past the shelf and found it full, he'd know the world had come to an end and the whole town was dead, pulped, pulverised, blood running in pools down the street and into the drains and on into the river.

'Blood,' he said, then checked quickly over his shoulder. No-one heard him. His mother was serving a customer.

He didn't know there would be blood with old Stell. From what his mother always said, he was sure she would have been like Kelly Murphy. Hot. Easy. When he'd done it to Kelly the first time there hadn't been any blood, which wouldn't be likely because she'd already had an abortion. Everyone in town knew about it. She and Sean Logan, who used to work after school in Smith's Garden Supplies, had been at it since Kelly turned thirteen. Sean was seventeen. He'd wanted to marry her too and keep the kid, but Kelly's old man was one of the mean Murphys. He wouldn't let Sean get near her, warned him to get out of town or he'd end up under it.

Sean got out, and Kelly started doing it with anybody, just to nark her old man.

She was the first one Thomas had done it to, his second was one of the boarders from Dorby, Leonie someone-or-other. They did it on the night of the school social. Leonie lived in at the school all week, then went back to the farm at weekends.

'Boring,' the youth said as he carved two deep slits into the shelf. 'How can they stand being locked in all week?' It was bad enough going to school every day, without staying there at night.

All the out-of-town kids got a late pass on the night of the school social, and Leonie what's-er-name made hay while the sun shone. She made a lot of hay that night; he hadn't been the only one who got onto her. Half the football team had already done it before him, and the other half were lining up for their turn after him. It hadn't been much good, like sharing your condom.

Old Stell was something else. 'Radical, man,' he said. 'Animal.'

Animal. The way it was meant to be. None of this sensitive new-age guy bullshit the whole world was pushing down your throat these days. Just hit 'em over the head with a club and drag 'em home to your cave by their hair and give it to them in the dirt.

'She liked it,' he said to a sauce bottle. 'She really liked it.' He turned the bottle upside down and rammed its top into the now empty carton. It dented the cardboard, but didn't go through. He looked over his shoulder again before slashing the carton with his knife – a horizontal, and a vertical – then with the bottle gripped before him, he hit the cross dead centre. The bottle penetrated. He ground it in, deeper and deeper, thrusting with his pelvis, grinding it in like he'd ground it into old Stell.

Then the carton collapsed and he almost went down on top of it.

'Tommy?'

'What do you want?'

'What are you doing there?'

'Nothing.'

'Can you get some small packets of self-raising flour please? Mrs Wilson is waiting.'

'Yeah,' he replied, then muttered low. 'Let the old bitch wait.'

I didn't know there'd be blood though, he thought. He had thrown his under-daks out this morning, but his old man wouldn't miss 'em in the wash. Plenty more where they come from – they got them wholesale from the supermarket.

He'd gone for a ride around town before he came to work this morning, and he'd dumped his daks in old lady Murphy's garbage can, then ridden his bike on past the minister's house. Nothing was moving there, no cop cars, no nothing. He rode by the cop station too. It was just as dead.

Bloody hick town. Nothing moved before eight. He hated it. Hated it like he hated this lousy supermarket. Hated hearing how lucky he was that his parents were putting money away for him to go to university in Sydney, money they saved by paying him a pittance to do the job they'd have to pay someone else ten dollars an hour to do.

As if they couldn't afford to send him to university without him working, and who but they ever said he was going to go to university anyway? You needed good marks to go to university, and his marks weren't worth shit – not since he'd discovered sex. It was a drug. The more you had, the more you wanted. If they hadn't made him work, then he might have found time for sex and school work.

'Their fault. Hardly any of the other kids at school are expected to work and study too, and they get a lot more than me for doing nothing.'

His old man and lady expected him to go down on his bended

knee and thank them for letting him lug boxes around all Saturday morning and half his holidays, while they doled him out ten lousy bucks a week. Ten bucks? It was nothing. He could get the dole if he left home. He'd be rich. Have a fortune coming in every week.

Never mind, he thought. I take what I'm due.

He unscrewed the top from the small bottle of sauce and slid his finger inside, slid it up and down, up and down, then he withdrew it, smelt it. Squatting there, he looked long at the bloody finger before licking it clean.

His mother was working the checkout and, between customers, she sat around knitting the legs of Stell's stupid clown dolls. Thirty stitches, sixty rows of garter stitch. She could do it blindfolded. He could do it blindfolded! Stell had taught him to knit when he was six or seven, before he knew any better.

He used to watch her stuffing all the bits before she stitched them into clowns. She made him one when he was a kid. For years it had sat on his window ledge and laughed at him – until one day he'd cut its head off.

'That stopped its laughing,' he said.

She used to let him play in the stuffing, pass her handfuls of it. He could remember the feel of his hands, deep in the white fluffy fake wool stuff that she stored in bales in her shed.

That's why he went there yesterday. Stuffing.

It was his father's fault. He'd sent him around to tell Stell that the new bales of stuffing had arrived, and that he'd drop them around when they closed the shop on Saturday. But he didn't tell her his father was coming for a visit. He did his own stuffing instead. More fun than stuffing clowns.

He chuckled, and again slipped his finger into the mouth of the bottle, feeling the smooth silk of glass, the sucking, the pressure of fluid. Again he licked his finger.

'Tommy?'

'Yeah.'

'What are you doing down there?'

'Nothing.'

'I asked you ages ago to get some self-raising flour for Mrs Wilson. She's still waiting.'

'And getting a free read of your magazines while she's waiting,' he said, replacing the bottle top, sliding the sauce to the front of the shelf. A bead of red oozed from beneath the lid. He wiped it away with a finger, licked the finger clean.

'Who were you trying to call earlier?'

'No-one,' he said.

'I heard that Thomas has got himself a little girlfriend,' Mrs Wilson said.

'Have you, Tommy?'

'That's for me to know and you to find out,' he replied, adding quietly, 'Stupid old cow.'

'Who is she?'

'No-one. Leave me alone, why can't you?'

'Get me some self-raising flour for Mrs Wilson, then I will.'

Nagging old bitch, he thought but he stood and walked again to the storeroom, returning with a box of self-raising flour packets. He ripped it open, walked to the checkout, tossed one to the bench, then returned to study the packets. They had pictures of scones on the back.

'Scones in the oven,' he whispered, 'Maybe I gave the old Stell some self-raising power – got my scones baking in her old oven. I wonder if she's too old.'

His mother was too old, old and fat as a pig. She'd had her bits cut out by old Parsons. Now she had to swallow hormone pills to stop her shrivelling up. He sometimes thought of doing it to her, like his old man used to. He used to watch them doing it when he was a little kid. His old man was so scared he was going to die, like his other five kids had died, that he couldn't sleep unless the cot was in their room. Thomas had slept beside their bed until he was nearly five. And he'd watched them when they thought he was asleep.

He didn't know what they were doing, it looked like they

were playing rudy trampolines on the bed, but one night he'd wanted to play and his mother had kicked him out to a bed down the other end of the passage.

She was the boss at the shop, and at home, but it was his father who made him work at filling shelves. 'Teach him responsibility,' he said. 'I worked with Dad from when I was fourteen, and it didn't do me any harm.'

Didn't do him much good either, Thomas thought. Weak bastard.

His parents couldn't stand the sight of each other, but they spent every day together. They went to church together, crapped on at parties together, saving up all their hate until they got home. Then they screamed all night.

He didn't listen any more. The same shit got said, year after year. It got boring after a while.

His old man slept in the sleep-out now, and his old lady tossed down pills and whinged about him sleeping in the sleep-out. She looked about sixty. If he'd been his old man, he would have been sleeping out in the sleep-out too, or sleeping some place else. His old man was only forty-seven, but he looked fifty.

Saint Stell wasn't too fat, or too grey. 'Wow!' he said. 'Radical.' She hadn't screamed, or put up much of a fight. She'd sort of flaked, accepted his visit as she might have the coming of the holy ghost.

He giggled.

With her head under the Packard, he'd been able to watch himself in the paintwork. It was something else, like doing it in front of a mirror. He hadn't wanted it to end, and he'd lasted longer than he ever had with Kelly.

'What are you laughing about, Tommy?'

'Just thinking of scones,' he said. 'How long it takes them to cook.'

'You can cook something for dinner tonight, if you like. Go home early and get it started.'

'Hire yourself a maid.'

'You used to like cooking. You used to make biscuits with Aunty Stell.'

'I used to like a lot of shit,' he muttered, then added, 'I might just knock you up a big batch of scones and surprise you.' Again he laughed, and Marilyn laughed with him.

Mrs Wilson put the magazine down, paid for her purchases and left as two more customers came in. With the supermarket and the liquor store, his parents had the town wrapped up. If you looked at the average hick in Maidenville, most of their money went on food, drink and smokes, he thought, as he filled two more shelves, waiting, waiting, until his mother got busy checking out an old dame with a trolley full of pet food, and his father was tied up selling grog, then he walked to the telephone and dialled Templeton's number without even looking at the numbers he'd written on his wrist.

'Hello,' Martin Templeton said.

Thomas stood blowing into the phone until the image of the fat old fool, standing there, going red in the face, got to him. He had to cover the mouthpiece while he giggled.

'Hello. Who is this? Who is there?'

Thomas knew old Templeton wouldn't recognise his voice, he was past recognising much of anything. He wanted to heckle him. Say something. No fun in it, unless you did something. He blew a raspberry.

'Templeton here. Who is this?'

'Templeton?' Thomas said, keeping his voice low and using his American accent. 'Ah yes. Are you the Templeton on the main road, sir?'

'Yes – '

'Then you'd better get off because there's a road train coming through fast,' Thomas said.

The old bastard slammed the phone down.

'Got you, fat stuff. Got you a beauty – and I'll get you sooner or later, Aunty Stell.'

an ill-planned escape

Stella had been aware of the red light on the dashboard for minutes, but had not realised its significance. The windows were down, allowing the wind to whip her long hair, knot it, cleanse it. And she had felt cleansed because she had found a focus. Escape.

The car was different to the Ford. Things were in different places. 'Fuel gauge?' she said, and her foot sought the brake. As her father said, it was dynamite. A touch and the tyres grabbed, but they were on the narrow bitumen – if not, she may have lost control, rolled the car, ended it all on the Dorby Highway. Carefully now, she pulled off to the side and turned off the motor.

The hum, the noise of the wind, the grey blur of passing land had lulled her, allowing her mind to move away to a future somewhere, far, far away from Maidenville. Perhaps she would have flown as far as Sydney, driven east until stopped by the ocean, but flight had been stopped by a red light.

Her father had mentioned filling the tank. She'd forgotten. Jennison's service station must have been closed last night when he returned from the funeral, otherwise the tank would have been filled then.

The problem of fuel forced her mind back to grapple with the moment. There was probably enough in the tank to get her to Dorby. Her father said the car went on the smell of an oily rag – but she had no money to buy more if she made it that far. She never carried money, hadn't for years. Her father carried the money. He paid the bills. She had accounts at the department store, and at the butchers, and at the supermarket. If she went to a fete, her father handed her money to spend, as he had since she was five years old.

Long ago she had suggested to him that she might have a credit card. Everyone used them. Marilyn had bought an expensive red racing bike for Thomas before Christmas, ordering it from Sydney; she'd paid for it with her credit card, just gave the number over the telephone. Bonny always bought the boys' clothing on hers, but the minister didn't believe in credit cards.

'It encourages living beyond one's means, Daughter. In my situation, I see the harm this can create. Too often young lives have been ruined by their greed for more. I have seen families split asunder by credit cards. If you require money, you may come to me. When have I denied you your heart's desire, Daughter?'

Not since the day she asked for money for a pair of jeans.

Denim jeans. Everyone was wearing them. The new jean shop had just opened in Main Street and –

She was twenty-eight. They had buried precious Angel on the Monday, and it was Bonny's birthday barbecue on the Saturday. Martin had said it was too soon to go out, but she was going anyway, and Bonny said that everyone would be wearing jeans.

Her mother had never allowed Stella to wear trousers, but she was dead, and her rigid reign was over. Stella wanted a pair of blue denim jeans.

Her father had shaken his head, so she'd bought two metres of denim and a pattern from the department store and she put it on his account. The jeans were baggy, and they looked home-made. She had wanted them to be tight, like Bonny's, but she wore them to the barbecue and she drank two fast glasses of wine.

Steve Smith and his band had been playing there that night, and somehow, blame the wine, blame the blue jeans, or the freedom, Stella began singing with Steve. Everyone said she sounded terrific, that she had lifted the band. 'You ought to cut a record,' they'd said.

'How about it? I mean, joining us. We could use a female lead,' Steve said when the night was over, but she'd shaken her head. He was so much younger, and his guitarist and his drummer were only boys – barely twenty. Then she'd accepted another glass of wine and Bonny had said, 'Do it,' so Stella said 'Yes. Okay then, Steve. I mean, why not?' And she had another glass of wine to seal the agreement.

A dark door had closed behind her, and now a very fine portal was swinging wide open; Stella, feeling wildly wonderful, ran through it, just to find out what was on the other side.

'It is not fitting, Daughter, this caterwauling all night with that long-haired lout. This driving all over the country with three males, and unchaperoned. It's not fitting at all for one in your particular situation, and so soon after your dear mother's death.'

'But, Father, I am paid to sing. It's wonderful to be paid for doing what I enjoy, and to be able to buy what I want. I have few enough talents, and I want to sing. I want to live my own life, earn my own money.'

'Do I not pay for your needs? You smite me to the heart with this late desire for independence – and will you take those damnable trousers off and turn that damnable recording off?

Must it play night and day? Since your dear mother died, I have grown accustomed to a silent house.'

'I have to learn the song before Saturday,' she'd said to him, but the borrowed tape-recorder moved into her room and she kept the volume low. It was her first rebellion, and too long placed on hold.

Three months passed before she stopped gallivanting around with the band to concentrate her energy on the church choir – a small enough sacrifice if it might buy her the rest of the week.

Through the long years of precious Angel's illness, Stella had, in the privacy of her own room, penned tales of love, spilling the self that sheltered within to paper, freeing that self from Angel, God and Martin Templeton. She'd begun typing her tales on the minister's ancient Royal, and posting her compositions away to the women's magazines. For several years, her writing had kept her both busy and happy, until one magazine had posted a cheque instead of the usual rejection.

Ron Spencer cashed that cheque at his supermarket, and with her ill-gotten gains, Stella had gone shopping. She bought six copies of the magazine and two pairs of fashionably tight jeans from the jean shop.

But keeping a secret in Maidenville was like trying to hide a pumpkin in a bowl of undergrown apricots. Martin Templeton, the omniscient, bore down on Stella, a copy of the magazine in his hand. 'Daughter! Daughter! What is this I see?' Stella cringed from his disapproval. She bowed her head and clenched her hands and she waited. 'What you must ask yourself, Daughter, is what would God think of time wasted on this ... this ... this puerile trash ... this ...'

She had not been expecting praise. Praise had always been a stranger in the minister's house, but she had seen no wrong in her writing, and if she'd captured rotund little Doctor Parsons in his summer-winter uniform of baggy check shorts and wide-brimmed gardening hat, wouldn't he have been amused by her description ... even delighted? Wouldn't he have shaken her hand and said, 'Keep that chin high, Mousy Two'?

'I ... I didn't use your name, Father. I didn't for a moment consider using your name. See.'

'Does that not, in itself, tell you, Daughter, that inside your heart of hearts, you were ashamed of what you had written? You cannot hide shame from God. Destroy it. Shred it, and swear that you will pen no more of this ... this ...' Words deserted him.

Stella took the magazine he had crushed in his huge hand; she smoothed it, looked at the illustration. It was just an innocent love story, the tale of a boy and a girl and an odd little detective. Of 'Silver Sand', by Lea S. Temple.

Lea S. Temple. Weeks had been spent in choosing the name. She'd practised it, over, and over, had finally printed it on the cover of a short novel packed ready to post away to Mills and Boon. They paid well for romance. Perhaps enough – this magazine had symbolised her true beginning. It was the promise that there could be a future for her. Publication. Fame. Fortune. Eventual flight from Maidenville.

'Destroy it, Daughter. No good will come of it.'

Her hands were no longer driven by her will, but by his. She felt them grow hot, burn as they had that day ... that other day. As from a great distance, she watched the scorched things slowly tear two pages from the magazine. Twin craven cowards, they shredded the pages, handed him the pieces.

'Do you have more of this?'

Head down, she nodded. 'Then let us be rid of it now, Daughter,' he said, tossing her dreams into the open fire.

The cheap paper burned to ash before she walked upstairs to her room.

Her manuscript was in the top drawer of her desk. She picked it up knowing her hands would give it to him, let him place it on the coals. Palms would join and she'd mouth the words of a prayer while her future burned. Then she thought of Doctor

Parsons and her chin lifted. High. Higher. The heavy bottom drawer of her dressing-table was eased silently to the floor and into the cavity she dropped the novel, safe with the six magazines and many exercise books, safe with the postcard Ron had sent her from Bondi, and his friendship ring with the blue stones. The drawer slid back on its runners, she closed it with her foot and stood dusting guilty hands. Cool hands. Even cold. From her desk she took a writing pad and, after scanning it briefly, she walked downstairs and handed it to the minister.

Several years passed before she discovered Angel's fine metal knitting needles and a bag of knitting wool.

While others of her age lost their waists and energy in breeding the new generation of bored Maidenville youth, Stella remained slim and active. Perhaps there was something to be said for virginity after all.

Her garden had become her child, and a wilful ward too. It began when a teacher sent her home one day with a handful of bean seeds to grow in a jar. She had placed hers in the garden, and daily watched the miracle of birth, and later of death. Thereafter she carried seeds home from other gardens, and she learned early to nip cuttings from overhanging shrubs. Each birthday, Doctor Parsons had bought her a bulb to plant, and in later years he had become adventurous, ordering exotic bulbs for her from Sydney. The little doctor loved her garden.

Then Steve Smith, who now owned Gardening Supplies down the bottom of Crane Street, started bringing her his sickly discards, and Stella's friends offered their dying plants when, after a meagre blooming, they curled up their leaves in suicidal pact. Stella nursed them all back to health, and found space for them in her garden. Forty years of undisciplined planting had created a wilderness, where narrow gravelled paths wended their way through the masses of blooms to tiny hidden lawns, and to bird baths. Large and hardy shrubs protected their tender relatives.

Rare bulbs sent up their stalks to bloom, and the common geraniums, massed behind them, raised their own expectations higher.

Martin, who had a penchant for order in all things, could find no reason to disapprove of the disorderly garden, for each Sunday – summer, winter, autumn or spring – Stella filled his church with blooms. She picked bouquets for each new mother, and she knitted her colourful clown dolls for their offspring.

Every babe her father baptised received such a toy. Soft cuddly things, with contoured faces, each one was unique; they were coveted by those outside the Anglican congregation, and the few Stella knitted for the church fete sold as soon as they hit the stall.

It was the January of her thirty-sixth birthday and she'd been seated in the garden, watching the birds while adding the finishing touches to a large clown – a gift for Bonny's fifth son. Because of their friendship, this doll was receiving special attention – the eyes were wide and innocent, the smile wry, the hair a carrot red. It was almost done when the minister had come to stand before her. 'For the Davis child,' he'd said.

'Yes, Father – and I believe it looks a little like him.' She'd held the clown up for inspection, smiling at its cheeky face.

This morning her father was not in a smiling mood.

'Your thirty-sixth birthday today, Daughter,' he said.

'Don't remind me.'

His 'Yes' was long and thoughtful. He stood on, studying her attire until she looked up from her sewing.

'Is there something you wish to discuss with me?'

'Your dear mother has been dead eight years. It seems less.'

'The years are flying,' she replied. A long silence grew, an uncomfortable silence she had to fill. 'My jacarandas have grown so tall. It seems like only yesterday I planted them and worried that the frost would kill them.'

'Yes. Yes. I have been meaning to speak to you about your mother.' He coughed, looked over his shoulder to the house and to his bedroom window, then he took two paces back. 'Your mother's wardrobe.'

'Perhaps I should pack her things up for the opportunity shop. I've been wanting to for some time.'

'No!' His head was shaking adamantly. 'Indeed, you should not!' He stepped from foot to foot, seeking the correct approach. A bumbling great ox of a man, Martin had measured six foot five before age bowed his shoulders. Thankfully, Stella had not inherited his excessive height, nor his heavy bones, but his hair was as thick as her own, it curled as her own hair curled. Perhaps his too had once been the same shade of gold. She couldn't remember him other than grey.

'What you must begin to ask yourself, Daughter, is – ' He coughed again, uncomfortable with personal issues, and he looked towards heaven for inspiration to continue. 'Having now reached middle age, perhaps the time has come to ask yourself, would God deem that ... that outfit suitable for a woman of your years, and your position in the community?'

She'd been wearing jeans that day, and a light T-shirt, through which she could see the shape of her small breasts – and worse. Her nipples were large. A bra did little to camouflage them. When she went out, she used two tissues, placed strategically, but at home, in her garden, she had seen no need for tissues. She blushed, folded her arms across her breasts. 'I'm comfortable in jeans, Father.'

'Around the yard. Convenient for some of the more strenuous tasks you take upon yourself around the garden perhaps; however, I know your dear mother felt that trousers on a female encouraged unladylike posture. She could never have been accused of unladylike posture – in her early years.'

'Wearing a skirt while trimming the top of the hedge might be seen as extremely unladylike by some, Father.'

Again he'd looked heavenward, his face growing pink at the mere thought of his daughter's bare legs. He'd swallowed, his jowls appeared to swell as he lifted a finger high. 'I am speaking of the way you go about town, Daughter, and well you know it. I am speaking of this new habit of wearing those damnable working trousers to church! As you are aware, your dear mother left a full wardrobe, unworn in the last ten years of her life. She was never one to stint on her costumes. Thousands of dollars are invested in those wardrobes. I suggest you might look them over, choose some of the more suitable items for your own use.'

'Father! How could you suggest such a thing?' She had picked up her sewing and walked ahead of him to the house.

Two years passed before she'd asked him for money for a new pair of jeans. He shook his head.

Time had a habit of laying waste to most rebellions, as it did to stretch denim jeans. When the vibrant patches she'd stitched to knee and seat did not shame him into parting with his dollars, she thought to play a more devious joke. Her mother had not been as slim as Stella, and her garments, though purchased from expensive stores in Melbourne, were drab, hung long. But the joke backfired, her new garments gained her a rare smile of approval from the minister.

She'd again headed for her sewing machine, but having had the best, had spoiled her for the rest – and his approval was taking on an importance. He was all she had, all she would ever have, and she needed his approval. Eventually, the wearing of Angel's colourless pleated skirts and twin-sets had become a habit. Certainly the old wardrobes were overflowing, and the fabric in these garments, though drab, was of a quality rarely seen in Maidenville. In time, Stella adjusted the suits, the pleated skirts, the tweed jackets. The many virtuous blouses were washed, pressed carefully, and again put to use. The beige woollens kept out Maidenville's brief winter chill, and Angel's many petticoats were soft against the skin. What did it matter? At forty, Stella had become a part of the background in Maidenville. Who was there to notice how the church soloist was clothed? Who was there to care? It was her voice that was sought after, her reliability, her eagerness to serve.

'Who's doing the roster for Meals on Wheels?'
'Stella Templeton.'
'Who's supervising the youth group this week?'
'Stella said she will.'
'Who's bringing the afternoon tea today?'
'Stell.'
'Who is doing the flowers for the funeral?'

Who else but capable old maid Stella? Always there, but never seen.

Ron Spencer sometimes saw her, smiled at her. But he was long married to Marilyn, and his friendship ring hidden away. Although first love may never truly die, Stella stopped dreaming her foolish dreams, her frustrated love had been given in full to Ron's small son. Little Thomas. How she loved him. Of all the children in Maidenville, she had loved him best.

Her thick golden curls were the last to conform to middle age. Slowly her shoulder length hair evolved into a loose French twist, which developed quite naturally into a severe bun where grey began its slow erosion until the gold gave up the fight. It too turned beige. No overnight reversal of the caterpillar and the butterfly, but more a gradual decay, a giving up, until at forty-four, little Stella Templeton, sweet golden canary, trapped inside the minister's cage, had become a small beige sparrow, its wings finally clipped – fair game to a youth, eager to try out his new-found weapon.

Tears were blurring her vision now as she stared at the road ahead. Tears were pooling against the lenses of her sunglasses. She rarely wept, and she shook her head at her tears; freed from the lens, they trickled down to her lips.

'God,' she said. 'God. I have to stop this.' She breathed deeply, held the breath, trying to regain control while she

58

removed and wiped her glasses on her skirt. She wiped at her face, blotted her eyes, then glanced at her reflection in the rear-view mirror.

'God. If anyone should see me. I can't sit here.' And the key turned in the ignition. She was certain the car would not start. But it did.

'I have to keep going. I cannot face Maidenville, or that boy. I can't, so I have to keep going. Just drive until the car stops, then get out and walk. I have to. I'll find a way to get to Sydney.' But she sat on, wasting precious petrol and allowing the tears to drip away. She couldn't stop them. She didn't try.

As a girl she'd dreamed wild technicolour dreams of Sydney. It had spelt freedom, and she'd been disappointed to wake from her dreams. Now she dreamed in black and white, and the Sydney she visited was a desolate place, where she walked dark streets alone, seeking, always seeking an address, or a building. She woke from these dreams, relieved to be safe in her own bed, in her own room. Safe in Maidenville. In the last few years, she had become afraid of life. But what was it she had feared? Rape in some strange city?

'God help me,' she whispered as she looked out across the blurred landscape. 'Still, this flight was ill conceived. I'll wait until tomorrow, until Father buys some petrol. I'll pack a case tonight, and ask Father for twenty dollars – for a haircut. Thirty dollars. I'll take some of the finished clowns with me. I'll take the ring. It must be worth something. Perhaps a couple of the old ornaments. The ruby lamp would have some value if I can get it to Sydney. I'll get a job. Something. Housekeeper. Nanny. And if I can't then I'll ... I'll apply for the dole. I'll survive.'

Fool. You should have gone ten years, twenty years ago.

'Yes. Yes. I have been a fool, but I will go tomorrow.' She dried her eyes on the cuff of her blouse, and replaced her glasses.

The sun was high, and too bright for weeping eyes. A hard, glaring land, and so dry. Crops had been harvested, now pad-docks rested, brown beneath the cover of grey stubble. Summer was nearly over, but in this part of the country it was sometimes hard to recognise where summer ended and autumn began.

Five crows were squabbling over some dead thing on the road ahead. Two hawks were circling. Waiting. Birds of the heat. How did they survive in this dry, dry land? Where did they drink at night? The river was miles away.

The little car was like an oven. She turned the airconditioner on, and she wound her windows high. She had been born to heat, had lived with long dusty summers and short winters of sometime mud. Here, farmers spoke in the thousand hectare, and of how many tonnes to the acre. Houses were sparse, neighbours miles apart. Maidenville serviced this land, and the high school educated the children of this land. Some rode the school bus daily, but many were weekly boarders at the old school.

She had boarded for three months back when she was twelve. She'd started her periods when she was twelve and in her memory the two were ever joined. She'd loved the safety of boarding, the shared bedroom, the friendships and unchanging routine. She'd loved the every morning of waking up and knowing exactly how the day would be. A wonderful time. Her best time.

A white van was coming towards her. It looked like Len Davis's, Bonny's husband, the roof-rack loaded high with ladders and trestles. Quickly Stella selected drive and the car moved forward. Len tooted his horn as he drove by. She waved a hand and continued on to the intersection where the road ended on a well surfaced highway. Many signposts pointed to distant towns.

Dorby 23 K. Sydney 544 K. Maidenville 32 K.

Her father still spoke in miles, refused to acknowledge the existence of kilometres; thus she spoke in miles, had for half of a lifetime been converting kilometres to miles for him, doing the arithmetic in her head.

'How many miles is 544 kilometres, Daughter?' he'd ask, and she'd reply, '325, or near enough, Father.'

At what age did I learn the trick that appeased his desire to ignore change? she thought, but she shook her head. She couldn't remember. At what age did I learn the trick of putting each day behind me? She couldn't remember that either. 'Poor Father,' she said. 'How did it happen? How did I allow myself to get to this day? Why didn't I run for the axe that day? Why didn't I scream?'

Still looking at the signposts, she selected reverse, then she turned the car around. 'Twenty miles to Maidenville. Twenty miles on empty. We are both running on empty, little white car. Will we both make it back?' she asked, and she looked at the clock on the dashboard. 'Miss Moreland will be thinking I've forgotten about her.'

the grand old dame

There was never a time when she had not known Miss Moreland, former headmistress at the high school, former Sunday-school teacher. A frequent visitor to the house when Stella was a child, she had been supportive, coming when she was called; she could always put things right. Once she'd taken up her scissors to level a child's hair, to put things right, and her school-teacher hands had been gentle.

Like Stella, Miss Moreland had been tied for years to an invalid parent. They had that in common, and perhaps it helped to forge this strange friendship. But Miss Moreland celebrated her mother's death by retiring from her position at the high school, then setting off to see the world on her mother's hoarded money. Only when she began to run short of cash did she curtail her travels, sell the old house, and buy a modern unit at the retirement village behind the hospital.

Her stance upright and proud, her thick hair rinsed a champagne blond, a touch of make-up, carefully applied, Miss Moreland refused to be considered as one of the elderly. Few in town had known the grand old dame's age until she broke her arm, when her date of birth was exposed to hospital staff. Within days the news had filtered across the town to become the main talking point at tea parties.

Calculations were made by the town busybodies. 'She must have been in her sixties when she'd taught me in form four. I was sixteen in form four. She must have been over seventy when she retired from the school, and well into her eighties when she went on the cruise to New Zealand. She couldn't have been far from ninety when she went to India. My word, she could have died there amongst the heathens.'

Miss Moreland had no fear of gossip, age, or gods, be they Anglican or heathen. Having travelled to the far end of her life, she looked to her ultimate death with great interest, as many might look towards a grand tour of Europe. Death was one of the few places she hadn't been; still, if her plane was running a little late, she had no complaints. Her bags were packed and in order, and when her flight from Maidenville came in, she would freshen up her lipstick and fly away with a wave of her hand.

The old rocking chair on her front porch was her one concession to age. She was seated there now, rocking, watching for her late visitor.

'You're late, my girl. I thought you'd absconded with the guild's funds,' she called as the car drew to a halt in her drive.

As with Bonny, being around Miss Moreland always made Stella aware of her own lack of colour. Today her old friend looked a young and vigorous seventy-five in her grey slacks, and shirt of red and grey.

'I went for a long drive, my dear. It has been so long since I've managed to wheedle the keys away from Father, I took the opportunity to ... to just drive. I forgot the time.'

'Forgot to put your hair up too.' Miss Moreland stood and pulled at a corkscrew curl that the wind had found free to tangle. 'You look like an underfed mouse with dreadlocks. If Arnold Parsons got a look at you today, he'd have good reason to call you Miss Mousy.'

Stella ran her fingers through her hair, gathering it. Habit twisted it into the familiar knot, then she remembered the scratch on her neck. She let the hair fall back. Her hand straying to the scratch, she drew a curl forward.

'It's Mousy Two. He began it way back when I was three or four. I tell him frequently that he is giving me a complex, but he tells me it's a compliment.'

'Some compliment.'

'It's from a tale of two mice swimming in circles in a vat of cream. He told it to me long, long ago, and I often wish I could remember it. I used to buy old nursery rhyme books as a child, hoping to come across it, but I never did.' She removed her sunglasses. 'You look well as usual. I do like your shirt.'

'I got it at the department store yesterday. It cost enough – and don't you go trying to turn the subject on me. Your father said you weren't yourself this morning, and for the first time in his life he may be right. Have you looked in a mirror lately?' She led her guest indoors where she propped her before a mirror that took up most of her small hall.

Stella peered at the face of the stranger. Her eyes were deeply set and bloodshot. The half-circles beneath them stood out like bruises. 'I didn't sleep well.'

'More than a sleepless night caused that, girl. A good howl caused that. And what's with that fringe? Your hair never took well to a fringe.'

'It's – it was overdue for a change, Miss Moreland.'

The old lady's eyes didn't believe her. 'Anything you want to tell me, girl? I'm a good listener.'

Stella shook her head. She stepped back, took a brush from her handbag, flattening her fringe, tidying the wayward curls. She managed a lame smile as she dropped the brush back in her bag and began delving for the knitting she always kept by her side. Unable to look the old woman in the eye, she drew the knitting from the bag and began winding the wool.

Miss Moreland stood, hands on hips, feet planted wide,

studying her. 'Your father said you've been getting obscene phone calls. Is that what's troubling you?'

'No. Truly, I'm fine.' Or I will be soon, she thought. So my virginity has been sacrificed upon the altar of youthful greed, but I have grown accustomed to sacrifice. Tomorrow will be easier, and the day after tomorrow easier than the one before. I have to go on.

The old lady was speaking. Stella hadn't heard her. ' – haven't had a decent one for twenty years. My own fault. I always took the wind out of their sails. You know, I used to get a real kick out of those phone calls. Might have even shocked a few perverts into giving it up for life.' Stella smiled, her mind back on track as she was ushered into the open-plan lounge/dining/kitchenette.

'Never let them know that they're shocking you. That's the trick. Give them back as good as they give you,' Miss Moreland added.

'I haven't ... Father had a few calls this morning. A bit of heavy breathing, I believe. I'm sure it's nothing,' she said.

Her Saturday afternoons in this modern little unit were never a duty. Her mind never wandered, not in this place. Conversation never lagged. Miss Moreland was a friend, a dear friend, and one with whom she could relax, be herself, speak her mind and shame the devil – or God. As she watched the older woman preparing tea, buttering scones, for one fragment of an instant she thought of telling her the truth, of opening her mouth and sharing the shame. Freeing it to words may make it less, she thought.

Shame stifled her beginning. She felt her heart begin its mad race and her face begin to burn at the thought of exposing herself to this town. And exposed she would be. She looked at the telephone hanging beside the sink. Miss Moreland would be on the phone to Sergeant Johnson in the time it took her visitor to form three words. What was the use? It is over. In a week ... in less than a week, I will know if there are to be any further complications. But by then I will be in Sydney. I will put it behind me today. What is done cannot be undone. Time will heal.

Doesn't time always heal? When Ron and Marilyn announced their surprise wedding, I got over it, even though I thought Ron still loved me, that he was filling in time with Marilyn, waiting for me. And when I gave up singing with Steve's band, didn't the disappointment fade after time? Of course it did. I will be fine once I am away from here, but until I go I have to keep behaving in the same way, keep my chin up, and smile. Give no-one reason to question me, and learn to deal with the problems as they arise – as I have always done.

Silences were rare between these two, but today a silence kept growing, and though Stella tried to do what her mind bid her do, her thoughts continued their wandering.

Miss Moreland was no fool. Questions rarely brought the answers desired, but if she waited, watched and listened, answers often had a way of coming unbidden. When they didn't come this day, she tried her second ploy. She asked an innocent question. 'Did you get to watch the golf yesterday?'

'No.' Stella's heart thumped in her throat, and her mind returned to the shed and to the smell of the earth, and her blood on the earth, and the stink of his sex. She could still smell it in her hair. The wind had not blown it clean. She had washed it and washed it last night, had used the last of the shampoo on it; still it smelt of him. Her hand rose to her hair. She drew a strand forward, smelt it. Have to cut it off, she thought. Go to the hairdressers and get it all cut off.

'What's wrong with your hair today?'

'I ... I washed it last night and rather foolishly went to bed with it wet. It dried wild. I'm ... I'm thinking of getting it cut like Bonny's.'

'What did you get up to yesterday?'

'Nothing.' Her voice was defensive, her heartbeat erratic as guilt rose like a wave in her brain. Guilt planted by God, and her mother, to cower the innocent. Blood rushed her cheeks, her brow. Her hands began their burning.

'Did you go to the funeral?'

'No. Father went to the funeral.'

'Wouldn't be much of a show without Punch, would it? I hear he's got another one on Monday.'

'Monday. Yes. Yes. A lot of relatives are from out of town. The two boys.'

Again the silence.

'Did you see Bonny yesterday?'

'Yes.' Stella's chin lifted. 'We were speaking about ... she said she'd potted out a lot of junipers, and we thought we might have a separate gardening stall this year. There is so much in my own garden. I'll have to get into the shed and – '

Her mind went away to the shed, and the rape and the silence grew long again as she sat, shoulders hunched, counting stitches with her fingers, recounting stitches while the old woman stared at her bowed head.

'Stella Templeton. What in God's name is the matter with you today?'

'I ... I didn't sleep well.'

'We've been through all that. Spit it out. I know there's something troubling you and don't deny it. I've known you too long, girl.'

'I'm fine. Really.'

Miss Moreland rose, walked to her cupboard, selected a bottle then poured a portion into a glass. She added water from the tap. 'Here then, get this into you.'

'What – ?' Stella took the glass.

'Down the hatch with it and don't you give me any arguments. You're as white as a sheet and if you're not going to tell me why, then drink this down then go home to bed. I don't know what your father was thinking of, allowing you to come out today.'

'I'm quite well, really.'

'Pseudo martyrs are two-a-penny in this town. And I can assure you that the town and I will survive without you for a few days. You go home to bed, and if you don't feel any better in the morning, then give Parsons a call, and have a check-up.'

Stella sat handling the glass, peering at its contents, thinking of Doctor Parsons and if perhaps he would be the one to tell. He would understand, and he could keep a secret – but would he keep this secret? And what could be gained – unless she pressed charges against the youth? And what would Marilyn do if she did? And Ron? What would he think of her?

'Drink it. Get it into you, girl.'

'What is it?'

'It's brandy and water, and it's gotten me through every emergency that's arisen in my life in the past seventy-odd years, and God willing it will keep me going long enough to get my telegram from Queen Lizzie. Now down the hatch with it and go home. I will brook no argument today, girl.'

Stella emptied the glass, then she left.

The minister was waiting for his car at the front gate. She stopped the vehicle, climbed out, and handed him the keys.

'Did you buy milk, Daughter?'

'Milk?'

'I asked Miss Moreland to remind you.'

'No. No. She didn't remind me. The petrol is ... is very low.'

He watched her back as she walked down the drive to the house, then with a shake of his shaggy head, he climbed into the car, roared the motor and drove away.

The phone began ringing as Stella entered the kitchen. She heard it, but her mind refused to make the connection. It continued its high-pitched ring, jarring against her eardrums until habit saw her walk to it, reach out and silence it, place the phone to her ear. 'Stella Templeton speaking,' she said.

'Did you like it?' he said. 'I did.'

Her tongue still burned with the taste of brandy, and in her stomach, the brandy tried to rise. She gagged, dropped the phone.

'Glad you're keeping your mouth shut, Aunty Stell.' He waited for her reply and when there was none, added. 'I might come and visit you again one day.'

He didn't know he was speaking to the panelled wall.

the tour

Martin wandered in later, a carton of milk in his hand. Minutes passed before he tracked the muffled beeping to the hall, and to the dangling telephone. He shrugged, placed it on the cradle. So there had been another call. Juvenile delinquents, with nothing better to do than to play pranks on busy people.

'Daughter?' he called at the stairs.

There was no answer. He walked to her door, stood a moment, knocked three times then coughed. The door wouldn't open. She had obviously placed a chair behind it. He knocked again. 'Daughter. Are you all right?'

'Go away, Father. Just leave me alone, please.'

It was a reply that had plagued the years of his wedded life, and one he hadn't missed. Always more confident preaching to the masses than communicating with individuals, he stood shaking his head, his mind forming questions he might ask.

It appears that something has seriously upset you, Daughter, he might say, or perhaps, What is it that has caused this upset, Daughter? Let us talk it out, and see if we can find a solution. No, he decided. Least said, sooner mended. She had asked to be left alone, so he would respect her wishes. He stepped back.

Her mother had been a highly strung woman, who had not enjoyed the duties of a wife, nor had she accepted the responsibilities of motherhood as he might have hoped. Was his daughter now going down the same path of melancholia? Anger for breakfast, silence for lunch, recriminations for tea. Martin shuddered. Having been through it once, he had no desire for a repeat performance.

Storms pass, he thought. Stella has always been a sensible girl. She will weather this storm far better alone. She's had one of those damnable phone calls. Never a worldly girl, it has upset her, and rightly so. That and the virus. Yes. He nodded, and took three more steps towards the stairs.

There was much on his mind today. The telephone had not stopped its ringing while Stella was out. Barely had he placed it down when the damnable thing would call him from his work again. But he'd been pleased to take the final call. It was from one of the few men he had, in his life, named friend.

Martin and Patrick O'Sullivan, a Catholic priest, had weathered the war together in Africa and France. They had travelled home on the same boat when the war was won, and they still kept in touch. Patrick had telephoned this afternoon from Sydney. He'd spoken for twenty minutes, attempting to persuade Martin to fill a gap on a planned tour of their former battlegrounds. Patrick had the persuasive tongue of the Irish.

It was a fully guided tour, he'd said. No luggage to handle, no stress. Quality hotels all the way. They would be picked up each morning at the hotel door, and dropped off there each night. Comfortable airconditioned buses all the way.

And France. To see Paris again. Martin loved the French – loved anything French. Hadn't he intended returning to France after the war, and to the young French lass who had initiated him into a more giving love than he had known with Angel?

And London. Wonderful London. The tour would take in Churchill's bunker, left as it was on the day the war ended.

Untouched. A small segment of trapped time – and trapped from a time Martin had understood. He was out of touch with the nineties.

Africa? Well, he could take that or leave it, but it certainly would be an experience. The tour was also taking in Germany – only the edge, but quite enough.

'And a weekend of sightseeing in Switzerland, beautiful Switzerland. It is certainly tempting,' he said to the stair rail, neither up nor down. His thoughts silenced, he listened again. At least there was no uncontrolled weeping coming from his daughter's room. His wife had frequently shaken the very foundations of the house with the intensity of her weeping.

What age is Stella now? Forty – . He did some mental additions. Angel had been forty-seven when Stella was born. 'Forty-four last January,' he said.

Middle age could be a difficult time for a childless woman. I could not leave her alone in this state, of course. Still, it may be a temporary upset, and probably is. She may be fine in the morning. It would do no harm to call the tour organiser, sound him out. No harm at all.

The tour, then only an idea, had been suggested to Martin in October. He'd given the embryonic plan careful consideration, but when it came time to pay his deposit, he'd decided against it. After all, at his age, anything could happen in six months.

'As indeed it has. As indeed it has,' he muttered.

According to Patrick, things had altered considerably in six months, and for the better. Harold Smithton, a pernicious little pustule, had passed on, and a second member, Matthews, a know-all ferret of a man, with whom Martin had no patience at all, had been struck down by a stroke. The possibility of ending up in a twin room with either one of these in the other bed had caused the hackles to rise on the back of Martin's neck.

'However,' he said, 'it is sad of course for their families, but death comes to us all.'

Patrick had mentioned that the organisers were eager to fill these two vacancies, and at a possible discount to the latecomers. If the vacancies could not be filled, the cost to other members would be increased, which was possibly – probably – one of the reasons Patrick called him, pressured him to go. Martin was aware of that.

'However . . .' he said, one finger raised.

It was a trip he had fought against taking, convincing himself he was beyond the age of travel, that he could not take the chance of striking bad weather, could not leave his church – and Stella – for three weeks. The other considerations, the ferret, the pustule – 'No longer considerations,' he said, smiling broadly.

The cost of the trip was of no real concern. Although he was not personally a rich man, he was comfortable. The house willed by Randall De Vere to Angel now belonged to Stella. Martin had supervised the drawing up of his wife's will, signed only months before she died. Doctor Parsons and Miss Moreland had witnessed it. This left Martin, to all intents and purposes, dependent on his daughter for shelter.

Over a period of time, as his own investments came due, he transferred them to his daughter's name, until by his seventy-seventh birthday, he had been able to collect a full pension, and had been living well on it for the past eight years, supplemented, of course, by a small allowance and other extras from the church.

Martin still managed his daughter's money, still looked after her investments. During the years of high interest, he had doubled her holdings, and when the bottom fell out of interest, he'd considered himself lucky to have seen it coming. All available cash had been locked in to long-term bonds which were still paying well, the only annoyance being Stella's tax bill that crept higher each year.

She knew nothing about her money. She had no experience in handling money. Finances were, after all, a male domain, and all letters with windows were placed on the hall table for Martin to open. Like her mother before her, Stella signed where he placed his small pencilled cross.

The money for the tour would come from her accounts.

'Perhaps a little out of each,' he said.

The discomfort of the twenty-odd hour plane trip could be his greatest concern now. Seats were not built for one of his stature. Also, Martin had a fear of enclosed spaces, specifically if those enclosed spaces enclosed others; he disliked the idea of breathing the recycled air of unknown parties. After all, too little was known yet about the transmitting of these new diseases, he thought, and the physical discomfort of remaining a virtual prisoner of one small seat for those twenty-odd hours would play havoc with his bones.

Never a small man, he had spread in the latter years of his life, until seats in public places, bus seats, even toilets seats, had become minor embarrassments. The world was fitted out for the average, and Martin was anything bar average. However, he argued silently with the stair rail, what is a little discomfort compared to the delights of meeting with old friends, of three weeks of freedom from clerical duties? And France. Wonderful France.

He silenced his thoughts and listened, one hand to his ear.

Stella was a strong girl, and capable. He respected these traits in his daughter. Even during the worst years of his dear Angel's . . . illness, Stella had not succumbed to tears. Always a courageous infant. A pity she did not marry. A great pity, he thought. Women need children – most women need children, he corrected mentally. He had once had dreams of a grandson; but if it was not meant to be, then it was not meant to be.

The silence of the house, without the movement of Stella, unnerved him. In truth, the trip was looking better by the minute, the discomforts shrinking in importance. Perhaps I should consider going. Perhaps I owe it to myself, and to Stella. It would give the girl some time alone. Perhaps that is all she needs. Time alone to come to terms with whatever is troubling her.

During his wife's frequent bouts of melancholia, he had found it safer to walk away. At times, in the early years of their marriage, she had seemed the better for the time alone.

As he stood, motionless, halfway up the stairs, he heard Stella cough. Heard movement in her room. He waited for her door to open. It remained closed.

'Yes,' he said. 'Yes. Far better for her to work it out herself.' And he tiptoed ponderously down to the telephone.

He'd scribbled the number of the tour organisers on a pad beside the phone. It was a Sydney number. He dialled it and waited for the voice to reply.

'Good afternoon. Martin Templeton speaking ... Yes. I have spoken to you before I believe ... Yes. The Reverend Martin Templeton. From Maidenville. I am calling STD, so we will keep this as brief as possible.' He took up his pen, opened a new page on the notepad. 'Yes,' he said. 'That is so. Now, it has been brought to my attention that you have had two recent cancellations on the tour ... Yes ... Yes, of course. The tour. Europe ... battle-grounds. Yes.' He drew small boxes on the pad, interlinking them. Boxes, within boxes, within larger boxes. He turned the boxes into cubes.

'It does appear that I am now able to get away ... Yes. Very interested. No. No. Not a problem ... Health? Not a problem. I am as healthy as the proverbial horse. A widower ... Sadly, yes.' He found a W amid the boxes, darkened it.

'Passport? No. I have not had the need in recent years. Can you perhaps look after that small detail ... ? Yes ... Yes. Having served my country, I should think so.' The small page of the notepad was filling with his doodling. He wrote *photograph* at the bottom of the page, and *Chemist* beside it. Then a question mark. He darkened the question mark. Turned it into a face, drew stick arms on the question mark's line, lengthened it, drew feet with large box boots.

'Of course. Now, just one or two questions, if I may. The tour is fully catered? All meals. Wonderful. Except for one free day in Paris ... Ah yes.' And he wrote *Paris!* 'Just the one free day ... I had hoped ... Yes. I had hoped for more time in France.' He underlined *Paris!*, circled it.

'Right. We will of course have breakfast and the evening meal on that day – . Excellent. Now this business of shared rooms. No. No. No. Allow me to put this to you, if I may. I assume, as I am to be, more or less, filling a vacancy, that there will be a reduction in the overall cost. Yes?' The pen returned to a box. He drew small dots within it, continued the dots.

'No? I was led to believe ... Yes. By Patrick O'Sullivan ... Yes. That there may be as much as a six hundred dollar discount. Yes. The deposit paid by the deceased was not refunded, according to Patrick – . To be sure. To be sure. I am of course a pensioner, and on a limited income you understand, and as a widower, I have grown accustomed to my privacy ... Yes. My own room. Yes. Having lost two of your party, I would assume that you now have one room freed. Yes. I certainly would.' His eyes on the pad, he frowned at it, then removed the page. The pressure of his pen had driven deep into the page beneath it, so he removed it too, then a third page.

'That sounds fair. Of course I would expect to pay extra for my privacy ... which will no doubt be covered by the six hundred dollar discount. Yes?

'Then I look forward to meeting with you also ... The cheque will be in the mail this evening ... Passport forms at the post office. A photograph. Yes. And you will send me the itinerary ... Thank you. And you, sir. Goodbye.'

He looked at his watch. It had taken almost fifteen minutes on normal daily rates. Still, the church paid his phone bill. He placed the telephone down, and with a weighty skip, walked to the kitchen and tossed his doodling in the waste bin. He picked up his keys from the dresser, flung the flywire door back to slam against the brickwork, and he made his way through the garden to the true love of his life. The flywire door jammed open.

* * *

The Packard had thirty-seven thousand miles on the clock. It had never spent a night out of doors, and it could, with near honesty, claim it had only been driven to church on Sundays – although, not in the past twenty years. It was Martin's pride and joy. He kept it in immaculate mechanical condition.

The key in the ignition, he pressed the starter and the motor sprang into life. He backed it out of the shed, then like a large child playing motor cars, he drove it backwards and forwards, backwards and forwards, up and down the long drive until his stomach suggested it was six o'clock.

Martin normally ate at six, but when he crept to the kitchen window and peered in, he could see no movement in the dark room. He returned to the shed, where, beneath light, he examined the vehicle again. There was some substance on the running board.

'What is this? Who has been in here?' He looked closely at the spill, his hands held behind his back, then he shuddered. 'A quick wash perhaps, just to be on the safe side,' he said.

By the time he was done, the sun was low in the sky, and his stomach told him it had definitely missed its dinner. Still no call from the back door, and no light in the kitchen. He entered wearily, flicking light switches as he went, placing his keys on the dresser.

'No dinner tonight, Martin,' he commented, listening at the foot of the stairs. Silence. No light. No movement. 'Things are coming to a pretty pass,' he stated to the stair rail and to no-one in particular.

Back in the kitchen, he turned in a complete circle. Dare he approach an egg or two, attempt to boil them? He took one from the refrigerator, and stood studying its fragile shell. A Packard piston fitted his ham hand better. With a shake of his head, he returned the egg to its container. Never interested in acquiring kitchen skills, he had left the preparation of food to his women; still, he could manage bread, and Stella kept a well stocked refrigerator.

He selected cheese and lettuce. He mutilated a tomato, squashing it near flat onto the lettuce. He shook on salt and pepper, sighted a glass container half filled with pineapple slices, adding one to the mound. A dollop of mayonnaise in its central hole, he topped it with another lettuce leaf, then a second slice of bread. Standing at the bench he halved his sandwich in two bites.

'Not bad. Not too bad at all,' he commented, splashing water into the electric jug, plugging it in, and setting out tea making requisites. After two more such worthy bites had demolished his sandwich, he repeated its construction, twice.

Stomach satisfied, Martin walked, with his over-full cup of tea, away from the chaos of the kitchen table. Spilled tea left a trail up the staircase and down the passage carpet to his study.

Tomorrow was Sunday. His sermon needed honing. This he did on his tape-recorder. He had yet to read his words aloud, to seek out missed commas, and to find the most effective spaces in which to draw breath. This could only be done with a practice reading, or two.

'But first things first,' Martin said, taking up his cheque book and an envelope. 'Strike while the iron is hot, Martin. Allow no second thoughts to raise false doubts.'

Minutes later the letter was stamped and waiting on the hall table to be dropped in the postbox on his way to church, and he was back at his desk, reading his sermon into the microphone of a small tape-recorder. After rewinding it, he pressed 'play', turned up the volume, then sat back. Hands linked across his round stomach, he listened, enthralled by his own words, his own voice.

'Rousing, Martin. It has a certain exuberance about it that has for some time been missing. Perhaps God has noticed you have grown a little stale. Perhaps it is his hand that is guiding you to Europe. Wonderful. Wonderful. Let us hope that the girl is over her little drama by morning, and well enough to type it up for me.'

frilly knickers

Stella was up and about the business of his Sunday morning breakfast of tomatoes on toast when Martin came downstairs at eight. Apart from her new hairstyle and her missing smile, all appeared to be as usual.

'Feeling better this morning, Daughter?' he said, seating himself, and tucking into a breakfast unlikely to repeat on him during the sermon. He had learned his lesson with sausages, as with eggs and bacon, yet his constitution required a substantial meal with which to break his fast.

'Yes, thank you, Father.'

'Tomatoes. One of God's gifts to man. I used two last evening ... made myself some dinner,' he said proudly, and with only the barest hint of accusation in his tone.

'The tomatoes have done well this year. I'm sorry, about last evening. I feel much better this morning.'

'Well enough to type up my sermon?'

She looked at the clock on the wall. 'Yes, Father.' She would wait until he was at church, then she'd pack her things, and after lunch –

'And to accompany me to church, no doubt.'

'Pardon?'

'You are well enough to accompany me to church?'

'No, I believe I will stay home today.'

'I thought you would have shaken off the virus – after your excellent sleep.'

'I am, as I said quite well. It's just – .'

'Just?'

What was the use? Sooner or later she would give in. Easier to do it now than later. She could leave tonight. Wait until he was settled in front of the television. His wallet would be on the kitchen bench. Better not to ask, but to take – .

Monday. The funeral. I will have to go to the funeral on Monday. How can I not go to the funeral? So I will leave on Monday night – and ask him for money for a haircut.

'Your mind is wandering, Daughter.'

'I . . . I have a slight headache, Father, but if you wish me to go with you to church, then I will take an Aspro, and go with you.'

'I certainly wish it, and God demands your splendid voice to override our Mrs Morris's baritone.'

God demands your voice? God demands. God is too demanding.

Her hands were burning, and she wished that God didn't demand her voice today. Her face wanted to cry, not sing, and she didn't want to go to church and she didn't want to think about her hands and she had to, because she had gloves on, and they made her hands hurt worse.

And when they had driven up, Marilyn and Bonny were already there, and she'd said, 'Hello, Marilyn. Hello, Bonny,' and she made her face smile.

And Marilyn waited until Mummy and Daddy walked away and then she'd said, 'What have you got gloves on for in the summer? You only wear gloves in the winter.' And she'd said, 'Just because you mother is called Angel, you don't have to always try to look like an angel in stupid white all the time.'

Marilyn's father was dead, and he didn't just die from old age. He made his own self die, so everybody had to be kind to Marilyn and her brothers, the teachers said, so Stella thought of that instead of saying what she wanted to say.

'It's just ... Mummy said I have to wear them, just because I have to sing a stupid solo.' That wasn't the truth, and Stella's face felt all red like it always did when she didn't say the truth.

Then Marilyn said. 'You only get to sing the solo because your father is the minister, and my mother said he thinks he's God himself and if I had a minister father, then I would be allowed to sing too. I can sing as good as you can.'

Bonny, who couldn't sing at all and didn't care about being kind, who just said the truth, even if it was kind or not, said, 'Shut up and leave her alone, Marilyn. You're just jealous and you know you are. Green eyes. Cat's eyes. Green eyes. Cat's eyes.'

Marilyn cried, and Stella didn't want her to cry, or to be jealous. Sometimes she wished she couldn't sing, not even a little bit – but she could, and that was because Mummy was nearly a famous singer who went to London with Grandfather when she was eighteen, and she'd had special singing lessons to turn her into a soprano. Now everyone said Stella would be able to sing like Angel when she grew up, and one day she would be a famous singer. Angel couldn't be a famous singer because she got nerves and got a breakdown, so she just got married instead of being famous, then she blamed everybody because she wasn't famous.

It was a bit funny having a mother who was called Angel. Marilyn always liked to make fun of that too, but it was Mummy's proper name, not just a made-up name. It was on her certificates from the special school in London. Angel Joy De

Vere. Grandfather's name was Randall De Vere – but he had been dead a long time.

Stella couldn't sit with her friends. Since she turned eight, she had to sit in the front of the choir, and she had to smile, even if she didn't feel a bit like smiling. And she had to put her hands together while everyone prayed too, and today that made them burn more, but she didn't pray, she just stared at the beautiful stained-glass window over the door. When the sun caught the glass colours, the tortured body of poor Jesus looked like it was moving on the cross, trying to get away. She felt very sorry for him, because she wanted to get away too, but she couldn't. She told him that she knew how he felt – like she had holes in her hands too, but her cross was the hard wooden pew, and the nails that were holding her to the cross were all the people's eyes.

Doctor Parsons was sitting near the front. He winked at her, but he shouldn't wink in church. Then his mouth said without any voice, 'Keep that chin up, Mousy Two,' and he touched his own chin.

He always said that. She liked him to call her Mousy Two. Sometimes it made her giggle. He was a funny little man. He was sort of like Peter Pan, like he couldn't grow up, but he sort of looked like Grumpy, from the Seven Dwarfs.

He always went to church too, and she always went to church – always and forever and he was always and forever in that same seat. His wink made her feel better – even if he shouldn't have done it – and then it was time to sing the solo, she sang it very well, because it was about Jesus's pain, and she looked at the glass window while she sang and she pretended she was singing it to him. She knew all the words – she knew all the words of all the hymns, because the singing was the best part about going to church, except Doctor Parsons. He was the extra best part.

She had to sit beside precious Angel. She didn't like sitting there, because sometimes, if her smile just got a bit tired, or if *it slipped into a yawn, precious Angel squeezed her hand, or pinched her leg, and her father without even stopping his sermon said things like, 'We give our smiles to God and our yawns to the pillow, Daughter.'*

This morning she didn't let her smile slip, because she didn't want Angel to squeeze her hand.

After church was the very extra best time, because sometimes Doctor Parsons came for dinner after church, and he stayed all afternoon and played chess with Daddy, and he talked to Stella, and sometimes he let her show him her garden, and sometimes he sat on the lawn with her and let her tell him all the stories about how she got the flowers, and he let her show him the birds' nests that were in Mr Wilson's forest of trees on the other side of the fence.

One day Stella planned to fly away with the birds ... to climb the very tallest tree in Mr Wilson's yard, and flap her arms and fly away – to somewhere.

'The sermon, Daughter. Time is wasting.'

'I'm sorry. I ... I was miles away, Father.'

She took time with her dress that morning, and though her hair still hung long, she turned it under, subduing it with pins. It looked different but almost modern. She needed colour. Her complexion was naturally fair, but today it looked like marbled clay. She needed a touch of lipstick, or a blusher like Bonny used, but it had been years since she'd bothered with make-up. She searched her dressing-table, found some flesh-tone zinc cream, and applied some to the scratch beneath her ear. It stained her collar, drawing attention to the scratch. She changed her blouse, turned the collar up at the back, then searched her wardrobe until she found a small hat. It was the colour she had called burnt orange at eighteen. Just a scrap of a thing, it looked well enough with her tan and grey check skirt, but ridiculous with the green scarf. She found a pink thing, then a scrap of blue.

'Daughter. We are going to be late.'

'Coming.' She snatched up a string of large amber beads. The telephone rang as she walked downstairs, fastening the necklace.

'Get that damnable thing, while I get the car out,' the minister called. 'Don't become involved. We are late enough already.'

Stella approached the phone as if it were capable of biting her. She snatched it, held it far from her ear.

'That you, Stella? I need more stuffing for my peanut pillows. Can you bring some to the church?' It was Mrs Carter, the church guild, peanut-pillow queen. The shed was already storing garbage bags full of these little travellers pillows that hadn't sold at the last fete. And still that woman made more. Stella did not reply.

'Did you hear me Stella? I need more stuffing. Ronald Spencer said he delivered two bales to you yesterday afternoon.'

'I . . .'

'You are on your way to church and so am I, so if you can bring me up a couple of supermarket bags full then you'll save me coming around there this afternoon. I've got my granddaughters up for the weekend. They're going to stuff peanuts for me.'

A long silence followed. Stella was picturing the shed and the contents of the shed. She didn't want to go inside it. Bonny's pots too. She promised Bonny some pots.

'Well, can you or can't you bring it with you to church?'

'The shed is locked.' She was unaccustomed to lying – and what a stupid lie. The shed was never locked. Keys hung undisturbed on rusting hooks. This was Maidenville, where country habits had not changed in decades, where violence and robberies were still city problems. But Maidenville was changing. Maidenville had spawned its own rapist, and Stella Templeton had told her first lie.

'Well, can't you unlock it? I don't have a church-supplied, airconditioned car, like some.'

Stella took a deep breath, she held it, held her words.

'Are you there? Are you there, Stella? Stella?'

'I'm sorry. It's a bad line. Call me back.' She placed the phone down and ran.

'Who was it, Daughter?' her father called as she flung the front gates wide.

'A bad connection.' Lies are like rabbits, they multiply, Stella thought.

Martin drove as he had at twenty, but in that era, his had been one of the few cars on the road. He diverted, without signalling his intent, and he pulled into a no-standing zone to reach out and post his letter. Then he made a screaming U-turn, barely missing a lad on a cycle as he roared away to Hospital Street.

Miss Moreland was waiting at the kerb, dressed this morning in a skirt of black and white hounds-tooth, a short red jacket, and white silk blouse. Stella vacated her front seat, admiring her old friend's new outfit that made her own more drab.

'What a beautiful blouse. You look stunning as usual, Miss Moreland,' she said.

'I'd like to return the compliment, girl, but in truth you don't look much better than you did yesterday. What is ailing you? What's ailing her, Martin?'

'I'm fine. Perfectly well, Miss Moreland. Perhaps the humid weather has an effect on my complexion.'

'You can fool some of the people some of the time, girl, but you never could fool me. You look like you've been to hell and only come halfway back.'

Martin left them to it as he drove the near straight line down to where Main Street intersected with Church Street, aptly named. The two main churches had been erected on opposite sides of the street. The Catholic's steeple was two metres taller than the Anglican. Their stained-glass windows were larger too, and more ornate, and the Catholic pews of English oak were polished by more behinds than the Anglicans. But too long banned from breeding, priests were a dying race. Maidenville's Catholics had no priest in residence, tall steeple or no tall steeple.

They made do with spiritual leaders, married men, who could perform neither marriages, baptisms nor burials. They imported their priests from Dorby. Not so the Anglicans. For over sixty years, Martin Templeton had been marrying, baptising and burying his congregation.

He parked the car in front of the new church hall, in the shade of a tall gum. He pulled on the handbrake, then noticed his passenger staring at the previously dull mission-brown door. His eyes followed her gaze.

STELLA WEARS FRILLY NICKERS had been painted there by someone adept with a yellow spray pack.

'My God,' he said. 'What young scoundrel is responsible for that?'

Stella leaned forward, peering between the two heads in the front seat. A cold hand grasped her throat as her heart turned to ice in her chest. Would it never end? Would he not let it end?

They turned to her, spoke together.

'I'll take you home, Daughter. No-one has seen you. I'll explain that you are unwell.'

'Ignore it,' Miss Moreland commanded. 'Ignore it I say, girl.' Swinging the car door wide, Miss Moreland placed her shoes purposely on the ground, effectively breaking Martin's escape.

'Stella is the one we must think of in this instance. We will deliver her home.'

'Run from some young scallywag? It's probably the same one who's been making those nuisance calls. He's looking for a cheap thrill, and if he sees you scuttling for home, then he'll get his cheap thrill and he'll do it again. Come along, girl.'

Cold. Stomach. Limbs. Scalp. Cold. Stone cold. Stella made no reply. Let them decide between them. I no longer care. Let someone else argue the matter for me, decide the matter for me, she thought, her eyes focused on the mission-brown door with its message. He would never let it end. He would paint his signs and hound her, drive her from the church, and from the street, and from the town. Or make her a prisoner in her house, locked away ... locked away from ... from what?

From a life I have never had. Haven't I always been locked away by decisions made for me by others? By mother ... and then by him.

She looked at the minister's heavy face, now turned to her. His mouth was moving, creating words that could not penetrate the ice of mind. The motor still running, his foot tap-tapping, the accelerator was growing heavy with his own desire to escape. He needed escape.

But what about me? What about me, she thought? What do I need?

I have no needs. I am a cardboard character, placed in fiction to fill any given function. I remain faceless, only given name so I may be quickly identified, then dismissed.

Stella wears her mother's clothes.

Stella satisfies a youthful greed.

Stella moves to her father's will.

Stella is forty-four, or sixty-four.

It is unimportant. Stella serves.

Nurse needed to care for the invalid. Male lead wishes to escape from the responsibilities of his wife. Give the part to the Stella character. Female lead not cut out for motherhood. Let Stella look after the boy. She'll handle it. Dress her in background beige. Free them to play their more important roles, to continue the plot without complication.

And if the Stella character becomes a complication, then write her out. No-one will miss her. Let her smash the car up on the highway, or just lock her up at home, safe behind the cypress hedge – as precious Angel was locked safe behind the hedge when she became a complication.

Stop this. Stop it now.

Why should you stop? Don't stop. Look at her. Look at precious Angel, recognise his lie.

Ugly Angel. Too sick to sing the solo any more. But never

sick enough. Not until the day she died. Until the day Doctor Parsons came with his bag, and his smile, and his baggy shorts, and pronounced her dead.

That wonderful day. Think of that day of rejoicing. That day, when the Stella character wrote her own brief lines. Stella character dancing a crazy dance, barefoot in the garden, wearing a garland of salmon rosebuds in her hair, and when the minister came searching for her, and found her barefoot, bare legged in the garden, she hid her smiling face from him and she handed him the garland, and he had named it a fine wreath.

Martin's voice rose above the hum of the motor. Had a minute passed or an hour? How long? Stella looked at the back of his head, then at Miss Moreland's moving mouth, and she strove to force the faces into focus.

'Will you be cowered by some vicious child? I think not. On your feet before anyone sees you trembling in there like a mouse in its hole. Move your feet, my girl.'

Stella's hands still gripped the front seat. Her feet refused to respond to the order.

Miss Moreland opened the back door and took Stella's arm. 'Out of there. I gave you credit for a bit of guts.'

'One of the young hooligans from your youth group, perhaps, Daughter. Have you given any ... cause to ... ?'

The abused fictional character found her voice and it was high in its own defence. 'Father?' Tears rose with it – tears still too close to the surface; she would break down soon, and then it would all end.

Fictional character screams rape in churchyard, and is carried off to a psychiatric ward.

'Be off with you and your damn fool questions, Martin Templeton. Take yourself into your church. We won't be far behind you.' Miss Moreland slammed the front passenger door with a vicious swing – enough to make the car and Martin shudder.

Another vehicle pulled into the shade beside them. Martin

nodded to the driver, then turned to take one last look at the sign. He flinched, turned off the motor and climbed from the car, closing his own door with a gentle click. His back to the church hall door, he said, 'Perhaps if we march in together, show a united front, Daughter.'

'United front? Against some little scoundrel who needs his bum paddled?' The old lady nodded towards the church. 'Off you go. Stella and I will speak a moment, as we usually do, then we will mingle a while. Buzz off Martin Templeton.'

He locked his door, checked the rear passenger side door. 'Don't forget to lock up, Daughter,' he said.

'No, Father.' The character had learned her few lines well.

As the minister walked across the yard towards his church, Stella climbed from the car. Two more cars had pulled in. The Scotts, Steve Smith and his mother. Steve with his still long blond hair tied back with a rubber band. All eyes were on the sign.

'You've been chosen this week, girl. If you can ignore his game, let the cheeky little beggar see you laughing about it, then he may move on to someone else.'

It was the obvious explanation. No-one knew of the rape. This was just the work of any one of a dozen youths with a spray can. Why was she cowering here from a popular game? Hadn't the supermarket windows been sprayed over on New Year's Eve? Stupid woman.

She stood, her legs barely capable of supporting her. She breathed deeply, making much ado about collecting her handbag. No-one knew. No-one would ever know – unless she told them. And she would never tell them, except by her behaviour. Her life had been one of control. Angel's control. Her father's control. She had learned mind control, she could and did choose a face to fit the situation. Her back to the sign on the church hall door, she sucked in a deep breath.

'Good morning, Miss Moreland, morning Stella,' familiar voices greeted the duo.

Stella turned to a speaker, and with lifted chin, forced her facial muscles into a smile. 'Good morning, Mr Scott. It appears that we have a new sign-writer in our midst. We've just been admiring his handiwork,' she said, then at Miss Moreland's side she walked to the church door, nodding to family groups, stopping to chat a while with the elderly, taking the arm of near blind Mr Bryant, and guiding him to his seat. She nodded to Ron Spencer, already seated at the organ, but she didn't meet his eye, then she took her place with the choir, between Mrs Morris and Miss Moreland.

'Did you see it?' Mrs Morris's beetle eyes were seeking prey.

'We certainly did, Mildred Morris. As did the entire congregation. Someone with a penchant for clotheslines. It wasn't you, was it? As I recall, your spelling was always creative. *Knickers* with a K, Mildred.'

Mrs Morris peered closely at her neighbour. Her eyes, darting, fleet things, searching for a weak spot, an entrance to the new victim's juices. 'Do you?' she said.

Stella turned to her in amazement. 'Do I what, Mrs Morris?'

'Gord love me. That came out all wrong, didn't it, dear? What I meant to say was, would they have seen . . . you know? I mean, your smalls. Lace?'

'I don't hang my underwear on the cypress hedge, Mrs Morris, nor do I hide it in my wardrobe. Perhaps you should join our new sign-writer at the clothesline one Monday. Some time after ten-thirty. I usually have the underwear out by then. Shall I expect you for morning tea?'

Miss Moreland let loose one of her frequent belly-laughs. It brought the wrath of Willy Macy down on her.

'Knickers to you, you old wowser,' Miss Moreland hissed over her shoulder.

Safe laughter was just one small step away from tears, and Stella gave in to it gladly. She became caught up in the blissful relief of safe laughter, and received a near forgotten nod of disapproval from the minister.

'And knickers to him, too.' Miss Moreland whispered. 'Frilly ones.'

Separated by fifty years, the friends hid behind hymn books, valiantly attempting to compose their features as the organist began to play the first hymn.

It has been too long since I felt his disapproval, Stella thought. I have been too good at my fictional role, too pliant, bending too easily to the director's will. Why?

Habit, her inner voice replied. But habits can be broken.

She sang her solo. It was not her best rendition of 'Amazing Grace'. She caught Miss Moreland's eye during the third verse, and it was enough. Anything would have been enough. Though she strived to continue, laughter was infectious, others began smiling, giggling behind hymn books. She had to cut the solo short with a coughing fit, excuse herself, and go in search of a glass of water.

'Brazen,' Mrs Morris muttered. 'Her poor mother would roll over in her grave.'

Willy Macy nodded his mute agreement.

yellow fingernails

Steve Smith and his aging band were still popular with the older generation. They played at the hotel on Friday nights, and they supplied much of the music for weddings and twenty-first parties, but there was little money in it. Steve's living came from the nursery and gardening supplies. He never went to church, but he drove his widowed mother there each Sunday then filled in an hour at his business until it was time to pick her up again.

This morning he was using his hour well. Having sandpapered the vandal's handiwork on the church hall door, he was slopping a rough coat of paint over the faded sign when Stella and Miss Moreland returned to the car.

They stood talking with him, and were joined there by the minister and the entire Spencer family.

'G'day Aunty Stell,' the rapist smiled his most winning boyish smile.

Stella ignored him and turned towards the car. The laughter had helped, and the Aspro, swallowed with church water, had taken away the ache in her back. 'Do you have the keys, Father? I need a tissue,' she said, searching her handbag.

'One moment, if you please, Daughter.' He stood with the youth, smiling benevolently. 'As I said to your father, nice of you to grace us with your presence this morning, young Thomas – and some time, if I recall correctly, since we last sighted you in church.'

'Yes. It's been quite a while, sir,' the youth agreed. 'I was half expecting the roof to cave in on me.'

Marilyn laughed. 'Quite some time, Mr Templeton. I was as surprised as you when he said he was coming with us this morning.' She reached for her son, brushing his long hair back from his brow, but looking by him at the door, the yellow near hidden now beneath a fast coat of brown.

Thomas was looking at it too, a wide smile on his lips. 'You've been stirring up emotions in the old town, Aunty Stell.'

'That's not nice, Tommy. Small things amuse small minds, and smaller minds take notice, I always say, Stell,' Marilyn replied. 'We were all that proud of the way you just chose to ignore the whole stupid thing, weren't we, Ron?'

Stella looked at Marilyn, at the prematurely grey hair – hair she had dyed at twenty-eight, and gave up dyeing at forty. She was eighteen months older than Stella, had started school late. Stella had commenced at four. Doctor Parsons saw to that.

She turned to the church where the little doctor was trying to get away from Willy Macy. He caught her eye, nodded, and touched his chin, and she heard his unspoken words. 'Keep that chin up, Mousy Two.'

Good little man, she thought. Her chin lifted.

'Tommy was saying in church that he's never heard you sing better.' Marilyn was still speaking.

Still she didn't reply. Ron was standing back, his eyes on her. He smiled. She looked away, felt her scalp crawl. Don't blush. Please, God, don't let me blush. Please, please, God. I've got to get away. I can't –

Thomas was speaking again. She turned to him, and his eyes held her own.

'Except for that day I caught you singing in the old shed. That was really something else, but you were singing a different song that day, weren't you, Aunty Stell? A more modern song. I'm into modern songs.'

Her face began its burning. She looked at her shoes, rubbed at her brow, her cheeks.

'You look as if you're feeling the heat, Aunty Stell? Does she look well to you, Mum?'

'And you look exceptionally pleased with yourself this morning, Thomas Spencer. Has anyone checked your fingernails for yellow paint?' Miss Moreland said.

Steve Smith stopped his painting. He turned and stared at the youth.

But to youth go the nerves of steel. Thomas extended steady hands before him. 'Look, no fingernails,' he said. His hands were long, slim, his fingers tapered, his nails pared down to the quick.

Miss Moreland took his hand in her own, stared at it, looked at the palm, then up to his face, to his eyes.

'Well. Well, I never did – ' she started, then she dropped the hand as if it burned her and quickly turned to Stella, taking her arm. 'Help me to that car, girl. Laughter might be the best medicine, but it didn't make it down to my old legs today. Not as spry as they used to be. Maybe I'm getting old.' Again she laughed, allowing the others to laugh at her great age as she and Stella walked away from the group.

Stella clung to the older woman's arm, carefully placing one foot before the other, afraid she may fall before she reached the sanctuary of the car. Youth and its certainty, she thought. He is so sure of himself. So obviously guilty, yet so innocent. 'Feeling the heat, Aunty Stell.' Just a youth showing concern for an honorary aunt, but his words had been chosen with care.

Clever, handsome Thomas. His jeans were the best money could buy, his casual sweatshirt complimented his dark good looks. He was, if possible, more attractive than his father had been at the same age. Taller too, or has Ron grown shorter, Stella thought. Dear Ron, with his greying beard. Dear Ron, so clever at school, so bright, and able.

Able to transfer his love with his stage kiss to the new leading lady, her inner voice whispered.

She shook the thought away.

Thomas had not inherited his father's gentle smile. His smile was his mother's, as were his teeth. He had Marilyn's green eyes, her smaller, more classic nose, her high cheekbones – and her hair, dark, thick, as Marilyn's had once been.

This is not a youth who turns to rape. This is the boy who has every girl in town following him with her eyes. How did it happen? Why did it happen? Did it happen? Have I gone mad, and cannot tell where reality ends and mania begins? Is madness genetic?

She turned away, glanced at Steve Smith, still working with his paintbrush, his back again to the group, and she turned her back and looked down at her sensible shoes.

'What a fine young fellow he's turning out to be. A son to be proud of,' the minister said, walking up behind the two women, his car keys jiggling. He opened the car door and allowed Stella to escape inside.

'Humph. That is a matter of opinion,' Miss Moreland scoffed.

Stella wound the window wide, and Steve Smith turned, waved his paintbrush. She lifted her hand and waved back.

'Now, there is a son any mother could be proud of,' Miss Moreland said.

'That long-haired lout?' the minister replied.

doctor parsons

From the shady side of the church, where he always parked his bike, Doctor Parsons watched Stella's escape. What's ailing Mousy Two? he thought, and his eyes squinted into the late morning sun, striving to see more as the minister's car drove by.

Parsons didn't like the heat, and it didn't like him. Donning his old straw hat, he dragged it on hard, low, fixed it lower by sliding its loop of elastic beneath his beard. He hitched his socks up to meet with his knee-length shorts, then straddled his bike, all the while watching the minister's car. It backed out slowly, turned crazily, and crept away.

'Safe to hit the road, James. To the surgery, and spare the ponies,' he said to his aging bicycle, and he pedalled off behind the car, his bright blue eyes near closed against the glare.

A small room beside his waiting room was where he tossed his hat. He never called it home. Maidenville would never be home. He was just filling in time, just swimming around and around in circles, still looking for a way out – as he had been now for the past forty-odd years.

He had arrived on the Monday afternoon train with his old bicycle, a Gladstone bag, and a brand new medical degree. Great expectations had carried him the long hot miles from Sydney. His prospective employer ran a one-man practice in a thriving farming community – or so it had said in the advertisement. He'd applied for the job in writing, and twice in the following month, had spoken to Cutter-Nash on the telephone. The job sounded good – the money offered, more than good. His grandmother had bought him a new suit for the interview and paid extra to have six inches taken off the trouser cuffs. She had packed his spare shirts and underwear. With complete confidence that her grandson would quickly prove there was more to him than his four foot nine inches, she'd bought him a one-way train ticket to Maidenville.

It was mid afternoon when he'd stepped down at the station and the 114-degree heat rose up from the bitumen platform to suck his fair skin dry. He saw no sign of the thriving town, just one half-dead dog, and two crows waiting for it to fall over.

Maidenville had sounded green, neat country-village green, and Parsons had spent his hours on the train seeing himself as the revered village doctor in his new pinstriped suit, with its fashionably wide lapels, but Maidenville, the reality, now sprawled out before him, white on blistering red. No green. No neat. Just another outpost, a few miles east of the black stump. The afternoon sun glared off the corrugated-iron roofs and windows, hitting him between the eyes whichever way he turned.

'When's the next train out?' he had called to the stationmaster, busy swatting flies.

'On Saturday, lad.'

'Saturday?'

'Saturday.'

'That's five bloody days.'

The stationmaster placed his fly swat down and counted the days off on his fingers, slowly. Only after the second count did he agree. 'Five right enough,' he said, reaching for the scabby growth on his forehead, picking at it.

It was probably cancerous, Parsons thought, hunting flies from his eyes. 'Get your doctor to have a look at that thing,' he said. 'It ought to be seen to.'

'Got a bigger one on me neck. What are ya, boy? You wouldn't be that new quack we're all sweating on today?'

'No. I'm just a little lad, sweating on the Saturday train and his granny.' He paid for his return ticket, tucked it safe into the rear compartment of his wallet, picked up his bike, and wheeled it across the road to a department store. Out front, they were selling cheap straw hats. He bought one, and a pair of too large khaki shorts, which he put on in the fitting room, stuffing his new interview suit into his Gladstone bag. He no longer needed it for the interview because he wouldn't be taking the job, but he had only thirty shillings left on which to survive until Saturday. Maybe Cutter-Nash wouldn't see a colleague starve.

'Where might I find the doctor's surgery?' he asked the aging shopkeeper.

'Old Cut-n-Slash. What do you want with him?'

'Not a lot,' Parsons replied.

'He's got Mick Murphy's eldest boy up at the hospital. Past the Post Office, then two blocks east. You can't miss it. It's brick. Got a Moreton Bay in front.'

Parsons found riding east was preferable to riding into the sun. Three blocks east he saw clinker brick and Moreton Bay. He was drinking hot water from the garden tap when he sighted his prospective employer exiting the building.

Cutter-Nash was an Errol Flynn of a man, sixty-plus, tall, his features fine, his thick hair dyed a dead flat black. At that moment it was sticky with blood. Parsons frowned and ran his head under the tap while watching the older doctor frog-marched down the verandah and tossed overboard to the flowerbed.

'Matron brained him with a bedpan. He was trying to cut young Mick's bloody leg off,' Mick Murphy explained, dusting his hands. 'You're not the new one, are you?' he asked, and when Parsons nodded, he added. 'Christ. You're a bit short on. Ah, well, beggars can't be choosey, can they lad? Get yourself inside then. Young Mick is bleeding like a stuck pig.'

The bike propped against a post, Parsons took off his hat and allowed Mick to shepherd him to the operating theatre. At least it was cool in there, and the two staff members, both sixty-plus, looked pleased to see him. He took his time washing the dust off, and more time in checking out a broken but otherwise healthy leg, then he stitched up Cutter-Nash's slash and set the break while Mick looked over his shoulder.

Matron Firth was a one-woman army. She made two of Parsons. They were in the hospital kitchen drinking a well deserved cup of tea, when a third giant, wearing a dog collar and toting a middle-aged female in his arms, came bullocking down the corridor.

'Knitting needle. She used a knitting needle,' the giant said, and he fainted. The female escaped, leaving a trail of blood and snarled invectives behind her.

Parsons decided to forgo the cup of tea and make a run for it. Three hundred miles on a bike and a residency at the Sydney asylum was starting to look like a preferable future. He stepped high over the fallen giant, donned his straw hat and walked out to Cutter-Nash, still sleeping peacefully where he had fallen. This was his mad bloody thriving community, so let him deal with it, Parsons thought, kicking the older doctor's imported shoe. Cutter-Nash snored on. Mick Murphy wandered over, preparing to aim a kick at the opposite end of the sleeping man.

Parsons shook his head. 'Tut-tut,' he said.

Mick was built like a truck, all chassis and cab. His shoulders were three foot across, and his massive head had somehow been attached to a barrel chest, with no need of neck. He'd probably make a better friend than enemy.

'Dirty, murdering, mongrel bastard of a dog,' Mick said, but he stepped back from the sleeping doctor and offered his new mate a smoke.

Terrible noise was issuing from the building, Matron Firth adding to it with her bellow for help, so Parsons placed the smoke in his breast pocket for later, then beckoning Mick to follow, he re-entered the shade. Together they brought the bleeder down and Mick sat on her until Matron Firth and Sister Balwyn tamed her with chloroform.

Parsons washed his hands again. He picked up Cutter-Nash's favourite tool and did the old cut-n-slash trick. The male was stillborn, but he found a second baby cowering high in the womb. Unlike her deliverer, she had been forewarned about Maidenville; she didn't want to come out, and when he got her out, she chose not to gasp on Maidenville air.

'Breathe, damn you,' he ranted. 'Give me a wail, baby, or this town will be wearing my guts for garters before sundown.' He should have known better than to ask. Didn't he have his return ticket to Sydney safe in his wallet? But the infant had sniffed at the scent of responsibility; she wailed. Two hours, two pints of good old Murphy versatile blood and a rough hysterectomy, done with Matron reading the instructions over his shoulder, and it looked like the crazy mother might even live to tell the tale.

Bedded down that night in a disused verandah ward, Parsons had not heard the Maidenville buzz as news of the semi-dwarf doctor, who'd come in on the Monday train then spent the day performing miracles, was passed from mouth to mouth until it reached the town's upstanding citizens.

They'd arrived in force at the hospital in the early morning, before the sun spilled too much heat to the air, and they recognised a good thing when they saw it, even if it did come in the shape of an undernourished jockey in his Bonds jockey shorts. Matron made them tea and toast while Parsons' elastic gut wrapped itself around the outside of a huge country breakfast.

They offered the young doctor good money to stay on in his

verandah ward, all meals thrown in. They offered to get the cook back and to import two more nurses, and a part-time woman for the office. The chemist swore he wouldn't dispense any more of Cutter-Nash's scripts, and all the while Matron Firth's big brown eyes pleaded with Parsons to accept the offer, bribing him with more toast.

'You're the fifth quack we've had in the past twelve months. The hospital is bloody dying, and so are we,' Mick Murphy said, and a bloke from the menswear store upped the ante. He offered a three-piece suit, tailored to fit, plus three new business shirts. Then the old bloke from the cycle shop said he'd be willing to donate a new Malvern Star bike with gears.

'I've got a suit. Don't need a new bike.'

'We'll fix up one of the rooms here as a surgery. I'll give you full board free at the hotel,' the publican offered.

Parsons dipped his knife into homemade fig jam, just like his grandmother made. Then he scraped it off. He didn't want their jam or their offers. He wanted Sydney, and Granny's jam. He wanted to go home.

Cutter-Nash had regained consciousness halfway through the hysterectomy and tried to reclaim his operating theatre. If not for Mick Murphy, who had refused to leave Parsons' side, then there may have been more blood spilled in there that day. Mick had flattened Cutter-Nash, tossed him on the tray of his truck and dumped him fifteen miles from town. But the old doctor would be back this morning, and Parsons now knew why. Cutter-Nash had a vested interest in the hospital's medicine cabinet. Mick and Matron Firth liked a good gossip. The man they called Cut-n-Slash was a womanising drunk, a butcher and a morphine addict, Matron Firth said. Mick's description hadn't been so kind.

At nine o'clock, the businessmen began leaving. Shops had to open their doors, but Martin Templeton arrived to take their place in the hospital kitchen. He was big enough to make four of Parsons. 'You were sent here by God,' Martin said. 'He has work for you to perform here, lad. It is your duty to remain and do his work.'

'Yeah. Well you be sure to give him my apologies on Sunday, Rev. I'll be hanging around here till the Saturday train, and that's it. That'll give you time to move the patients to Dorby hospital,' Parsons replied.

As it turned out, there wasn't a lot of hanging around to do. A landowner got himself gored by a rampaging bull on the Wednesday, three women decided to pop their infants on the Thursday, and old Jennison from the garage set himself and a car on fire on the Friday.

It was a conspiracy, and Parsons knew it, a Maidenville conspiracy to keep him there. The nursery and the four functioning hospital wards now full, the committee had to call on volunteer staff, and borrow two nurses from Dorby. They hired a couple of Murphies to help the local cop with his day and night patrol of hospital verandahs because the chemist was keeping his promise. Cutter-Nash was in withdrawal.

Saturday had eventually dawned. Parsons and his bike were waiting at the station when the owner of the hardware store, also mayor of Maidenville, came puffing up one side of the station, just as the train puffed into the other.

'You got it, boy. It's yours,' he bellowed. 'I'll throw in an airconditioner.'

'What?'

'He's cut his own bloody throat. Old Cut-n-Slash. Slit his throat from ear to ear last night with his own bloody scalpel. The practice is yours, boy.'

'Life happens,' Parsons said. He wheeled his bike from meagre shade back into full sun, knowing he didn't want the bloody practice, didn't want Maidenville, but also knowing he didn't want to leave his patients and his now semi-functioning hospital.

At the hospital mortuary he got to examine his deceased colleague with his mate, Mick, and the local cop leaning over his shoulder. It was bloody suicide, Mick decided, but not a soul in town cared if it was or wasn't.

'He could a done it himself. Maybe. Shit happens sometimes, lad, and when it does, the best you can do is bury it deep and keep your mouth shut,' the old constable said.

Over the years, Parsons became a master at keeping his mouth shut.

Although he hadn't planned to remain forever, he never seemed to catch his train out. The stationmaster kept getting skin cancers, the locals kept breeding, limbs kept breaking, bulls gored, and people got singed. He'd been looking at houses, planning to move Granny, but she had enough sense to drop dead before he had the chance. So he was alone now, with no place to go. He had a real feel for doctoring, and he swore he could sniff out need at fifty paces. Maidenville had been needing bad. His bills eventually got paid too – if he bothered to send them out for long enough, and he had a good body of pensioners to service.

Old Cut-n-Slash, to the last, had managed to read blood pressures without more than a bruise or two, and to prescribe high blood-pressure pills and aspirin for arthritis. His waiting room provided a meeting place for aged busybodies. When Parsons took over the practice, the oldies looked down at him with a jaundiced eye, but they didn't vacate their chairs.

Parsons had never found an assistant prepared to remain for more than twelve months, so he'd never found time to look for a wife – no-one over the age of ten was short enough anyhow. He'd never found a car which enabled him to both reach the brake and look over the steering wheel at the same time, but a five-minute peddle took him from one end of town to the other, so he told himself he didn't need a car.

Back at the surgery that Sunday, he wheeled his bike into the hall, and walked into his waiting room. Cool. He'd left the airconditioner on. He flung his straw hat to its peg, and looked around. He'd never updated the furnishings in his consulting rooms, nor had he altered his summer-winter uniform, but there was a pastry shop next door to his surgery, and he liked his food. His waistline had thickened, and the size of his baggy shorts grew with the passing seasons, but not so his legs. They remained cordy, twin pegs, carved from local mallee roots.

He wore a full beard now. It protected his face from sun and wind burn, and his beard helped to hold his hat on. It also saved him shaving time. His hair, trimmed when necessary with scalpel or surgery scissors, was sparse on top, and the silver blond of his youth had slowly turned to white. He wore it long enough to tuck it into his collars. His shirt sleeves were always buttoned at the wrist, and his long socks always sagged around the ankles of his brown leather sandals. In the winter, he added a plastic bag to his hat, and a plastic raincoat to his uniform.

When Medicare was introduced, with a solo practice such as his, it had turned an old timer's clubroom into a goldmine. Given licence to bulk-bill the old and the young, the rich and poor alike, charity was out the window and billing the government was in. No-one sued him for over-servicing. Maidenville was an old town, full of arthritis and high blood pressure. As more of Maidenville's population reached pensionable age, and came to fill the waiting room, profits increased which enabled Parsons to install bigger and better airconditioners.

His refrigerated, dimly lit retreat was a fine place for unshielded eyes to scrutinise their neighbours for signs of decay. Catholic and Anglicans sat side by side, shivering, while placing silent bets on who would be the next pin to fall. And if there appeared to be no death imminent, perhaps there was a life, or even an emergency, to brighten up an otherwise long and dreary country day.

Parsons' receptionist, a local widow who answered to the name of Sister, came with the practice. She refused to make appointments, but used the old 'first in best dressed' appointment system. Seventy-five if she was a day, near crippled by arthritis, she rode to work each morning on a motorised three-wheeler, then hobbled into her office with the aid of a walking frame; but once seated behind glass, only the brave dared question Sister's authority.

'Life happens,' Parsons said, if people complained about the long wait on hard chairs. 'So catch the bus to Dorby and pay for the privilege.'

Many did. There were umpteen doctors in Dorby, and the hospital was modern.

Martin Templeton telephoned Parsons the following morning.

'I have the Martin funeral this afternoon, so I'd like to make an appointment at ten for an influenza shot.'

'See Sister,' Parsons replied. He was younger than Martin by a decade or two, but they were drawn together by a love of chess and by the church. Parsons, raised Anglican, was now one of the church elders. He liked going to church on Sundays, and even if he didn't get a lot out of Templeton's sermons, he got a kick out of heckling him, also the Sunday services supplied the doctor with most of his invitations for home-cooked meals.

'I am a busy man, and I have neither the time nor the desire to freeze in your waiting room all morning. If you refuse to make an appointment, is it within your capabilities to make a house call?'

'I could. Are you sick?'

'Of course I'm not sick. I merely require an influenza injection.'

'House calls to the healthy are termed over-servicing. Is Mousy Two sick?'

'You obviously consider yourself a humorist. My daughter is well enough, and when did you last service myself or my daughter?'

'Are you accusing me of rape or buggery, Templeton?'

'I have told you before, Parsons, I do not like your particular brand of humour. And it does not suit one of your position in the community.'

'You don't say? Did I ever tell you I'm not too fond of your bloody sermons either? Speaking of sermons, I saw our Mousy Two at church yesterday. She didn't look well enough to me. Invite me around to dinner and I'll give her the once over, and you, your injection. I won't even bill Medicare for it.'

'I do not mix social and business intercourse. My daughter and I are not seeking charity, nor do I respond well to blackmail.'

'Then come down to the surgery like everyone else, you cantankerous old coot.'

The phone was slammed down. Parsons chuckled, placing his own phone gently in its cradle while he probed his ear with an index finger.

'Poor little Mousy Two,' he said.

Parsons would have been the first to admit that Stella Templeton didn't fit the description of mousy. A sweet-natured, vivacious kid, she was sliding too fast into colourless middle age – fading into the crowd. By mixing often with the elderly, she had become one of them, old before her time.

'Pity,' he said. He'd liked the look of her the day she was born, and he'd watched her grow. Her little pointed chin held high, her eyes constantly scanning – like him, she appeared to be looking for a way out.

He'd set her broken arm when she was three years old. That was the day he'd named her Mousy Two.

Blame it on his adored grandmother. She used to tell him a rhyme about two little mice who fell into a vat of cream.

Mousy One and Mousy Two, in search of cream once strolled
into the farmer's dairy, where Tom the cat patrolled.
Poor Mousy One and Mousy Two, in fear jumped in a vat,
full up with cream. 'Far better we were eaten by a cat.

'We're going to drown. We're going to drown,' cried timid
  Mousy One.
'Oh goodness gracious dearie me, our little lives are done.'

But Mousy Two, her chin held high, was circling round and
  round.
'Please don't despair, keep swimming, a way out may be
  found.'
With cream upon her whiskers and cream upon her chin,
  she swam around in circles, allowing no cream in.
And come the morrow, Mousy One lay dead there in the
  vat,
But Mousy Two upon a raft of golden butter sat.

Poor little mite. She'd been looking for birds' nests in the oak
tree. Martin had found her on the lawn. He'd wrapped her in a
towel and driven her to the hospital. It was when the doctor tried
to remove the towel that he began to ask his silent questions.

He had never seen a three-year-old child so afraid of her little
naked body, nor had he met a father who dared not look on the
beauty of his own naked child. Something was smelling bad. He
asked no questions, but pinned the tiny mite into a toga while
her huge tears dripped, and her tiny jaw remained clenched.

His size usually helped him with kids. He could get around
most, but it wasn't until he told her his grandmother's rhyme
that her wide blue eyes had looked at him. She allowed him to
wash her cuts then and check out the break in her arm. He'd
said the rhyme again as he and Matron Firth set the small arm
in plaster, and when it was dry, he'd drawn a picture of two
long-nosed mice on it, one with its chin held high.

Little Stella had raised a giggle. 'That one is Mousy Two,'
she'd whispered. 'I like that Mousy Two, cause her has put her
chin up high so she can get out.'

Until last Sunday it had been a long dry time between sweet
Mousy Two's giggles.

He'd watched her and the grand old lady attempting to control their mutual hysteria in church, and he'd understood it. He and his grandmother had known that same lack of control. Just a glance, the twitch of a lip and they'd be off. That morning, Parsons felt that old twitching call to join the giggling duo, then he recognised the desperation in Mousy Two's laughter. It was a frantic straw-clutching giggle. She looked bad, pale, nervous as a mouse. She wasn't well enough. She wasn't well at all.

Surgery hours were from nine to twelve Monday and Wednesday, and from two to four on Fridays. The queue was always orderly. Those who came by car, first took their place in line, seemingly marking it with their spore before returning to the comfort of their cars. There was no argument. And when Sister unlocked the door at a quarter to nine, the queue filed in, to queue again in front of her window while she wrote their names on her written queue.

'Old Mrs Thomson is waiting in her car. She was after me, Sister, at number five, and young Barbara Bennet is vomiting. She had to run over the road to the public loo. She's after Mrs Murphy, at number seven.'

It worked well. Only an emergency could throw the list into chaos.

On the final Wednesday in February, Doctor Parsons had such an emergency. Bert Holden was brought in, a bloody towel wound around his hand. The waiting room buzzed as a patient was evicted and Bert hurried into the doctor's room.

'How did he do it, dear?' Mrs Morris asked, her small brown eyes, dug in between low eyebrows and high cheeks, like hungry cockroaches in a pudding bowl of stale rice custard.

'Well, he took the day off for the funeral, of course, and he was helping me cut up the pumpkin for the Meals on Wheels. He's bloody useless with a sharp knife. I'm always telling him to be careful. I've left it roasting in the oven. Hope old Parsons isn't too long, or it's going to burn.' Liz Holden was loud. Heads lifted, turned to the new arrival.

'Sit down, dear. Here, have this seat by me. You look all of a bother. So long as your oven isn't turned up too high, pumpkin will be all right for an hour.'

'Cut his hand cutting up the pumpkin for Meals on Wheels.' The news was passed in the half-circle that made up the left of the room. Slowly it was gathered in by those who waited in the hall with Parsons' bike.

'Hope you washed that pumpkin well, Liz,' Mr Bryant, the ancient and half-blind wit, said from his corner.

'Didn't think you took Meals on Wheels, Mr Bryant,' she yelled back.

'Only when our Stella's cooking,' he replied. 'She drops me off a freebie on Wednesdays.'

'As you were telling me, about the way she came into church yesterday. You were saying, Mrs Morris – ' Mrs Murphy prompted her friend of the bosom.

'I was saying I don't know if I would have been game to show my face in town again. That's what I was saying. But she was almost brazen about it. Behaving like a giggling teenager. Laughing about it, my dear, and in front of the whole congregation,' Mrs Morris said.

'I wonder if there's any truth in it.'

'I always say that where there's smoke, there's usually a fire. And at her age too. Lace always gives me a rash. I prefer comfort, myself.'

'I used to make all mine, but I don't seem to find the time since Dave and I tied the knot.'

'I buy those Cotton-tails myself. A hundred per cent cotton they are. You can buy a packet of three for eleven dollars at the department store at the moment. They're made in China but they seem quite good quality,' Mrs Morris admitted.

'Have they got a good wide crutch in them? I like a good wide crutch.'

'Crutch? Whose crutch? Who's got a rash? Did I miss something?' Liz bellowed.

Soon those who were not in the know learned what had been written on the church hall door. For minutes the room hummed, melding the ones waiting there.

Slowly, lace led back to Cotton-tails, which led to corsets, and corsets led to stomach ailments, until the clusters segmented again, and Bert exited, his hand stitched and held high in a sling.

'Be seeing you,' Liz yelled, jingling the car keys as she followed her husband from the room, unaware that all eyes were following the line of her knickers beneath her skirt.

Everyone now knew that she made all her own knickers since she did that stretch-sewing course at the high school. She found they stayed up better than the bought ones, and the crutches, that she reinforced with calico, lasted years longer. As the door closed behind her heavy buttocks, other patients came under scrutiny.

'Young Barbara Bennet. Look at her. She might have done well to keep her knickers on, my dear.' Mrs Morris's words were spoken behind a hand.

'Do you think she is?' Mrs Murphy leaned forward, staring blatantly at Barbara.

'Pregnant. Plain as mud on your face.'

'Could be.'

'Look at her eyes. If she's not pregnant, I'll eat old Parsons' straw hat and have his sandals for seconds.'

'She's only my second grandson's age.' Mrs Murphy's bottle-top glasses were lifted and held forward, gaining her a closer inspection.

'Can't be more than fifteen – sixteen. Terrible isn't it? The youth of today. My word, but I do not know what our old world is coming to, and that's a fact.'

'I wonder who's the father, Mrs Morris?'

'Probably that cousin of the Watsons who spent Christmas in

town. I saw them riding off to the river on their bikes,' Mrs Morris nodded knowingly.

'You don't say.'

The diagnosis made without need of Doctor Parsons, the likely father named without need for blood tests, they turned their faces to a young woman and her twelve-month-old baby.

'He always looks such a sickly little pet, doesn't he?'

'He certainly does, Mrs Morris.'

'I wonder – is that a bruise on his dear little arm?'

'I do believe it is,' Mrs Murphy whispered as again her glasses were used as dual magnifying lens. 'Yes. He's bruised from wrist to elbow.'

'As they say, like mother, like daughter. Her mother nearly killed her youngest one time. I saw her take to him with a broom handle, and if I hadn't wrestled it away from her, he mightn't have been alive today. Did I tell you about – ?'

And when their own names were called by Sister, and their own backs unshielded from neighbours' knives, vacated chairs were not vacant long. There were new fish to fry, new reputations to singe.

'Mrs Morris doesn't look at all well. Did she say what was ailing her?'

'Her hubby is going for the invalid pension. He's ten years younger than her. She's here to prime old Parsons before she sends her hubby to him.'

'What's wrong with him?'

'A bad back, or so she says. Not that you'd guess. He was helping his son fell that big gum tree over her fence. They cut it into foot blocks and stacked it up against my side fence. It's got a terrible lean on it, and I can't afford a new fence, not now that Dave has retired.'

'He could be going for the carer's pension, dear. She's been on the pension for years. I've often wondered why he isn't on the carer's.'

'She doesn't look at all well lately – that terrible complexion.'

'She's five years older than I am, you know.'

'She looks it too, dyed hair or no dyed hair. Not that I'd say that to her. Of course, her mother died young. A growth in the breast if you remember.'

'Yes. It's in her family. She's very pasty-faced lately. Oh, look. Here comes Reverend Templeton. I wonder what's up with him?'

At fifteen minutes to twelve, Martin Templeton bumbled his way through Parson's entrance hall to the waiting room, hoping it had cleared. The room was still full. His expression, not pleased, he hid it with his white handkerchief. He hadn't been inside Doctor Parsons' rooms since he sprained his ankle fourteen years ago. Looking around him now at the staring faces, he pondered their possible diseases. It would be just his luck to go down with some virus after posting off the cheque, but the tour organiser suggested he have a flu injection. He hated injections. Didn't want to be here.

'Good morning.' Many voices muttered, and many eyes measured him for a box. He was more than old enough, but God help his pallbearers.

He nodded, and spoke his communal, 'Good morning.'

'There's still seven before you. Do you want to wait?' Sister, safe behind the glass window that sealed her into her tower of power, asked.

'No. No. I certainly do not want to wait. Thank you. Thank you. If you could tell Parsons that not everyone has the time to sit and await his pleasure, and that if he is prepared to run his business in a businesslike manner, to make an appointment for me, then, and only then will I return.' He turned his back on the room and departed, relieved to be away. Shooting slightly disabled germs into one's arm had always sounded like an admirable way to catch disease, rather than a prevention. He'd do well enough without it.

delayed rebellion

Martin had learned long ago to wait for the last day of the month before making withdrawals from Stella's bank accounts. By doing this, he neither missed out on interest for the month past, nor for the following.

From the stove, where she was cooking his breakfast of lamb's fry and bacon, Stella watched him place two slips of paper on the table, tucking them beneath her bread and butter plate – as he always did – as he had with her mother. Without a word, he walked out the back door.

'Father. Don't go away now. It's almost ready.'

'Two minutes,' he called.

'You'll get sidetracked in the shed like you always do,' she warned, but Martin was back within less than a minute, a huge and dusty leather case in hand. She frowned as he took up the clean dishcloth and began wiping the dust to her newly polished floor.

One eye watching him, she served his meal, buttered his toast, poured two cups of tea, then served herself a small bowl of cereal.

'Father. Your breakfast is on the table getting cold.' She sat, moving the withdrawal forms to the side as she set her bowl down. He was usually seated first, his knife and fork raised in expectation and ready to pounce when she placed his meal before him. He has been behaving oddly for several days, she thought, or am I behaving oddly? Am I seeing him and the world through different eyes?

She had done the flowers for the funeral on Monday, but had not attended. Instead, she'd packed a small case, planning to leave on Monday night, to take the car and drive, but her father had sat watching television until eleven. Tuesday, he usually spent at his desk. She'd decided she would go before lunch, but Tuesday came and went, and by Wednesday, she wasn't certain that she wanted to leave.

Since Sunday, Stella had not been beyond the cypress hedge. She had not seen Bonny – or Marilyn; had spoken to no-one, other than her father. It was he who telephoned the church guild ladies on Wednesday afternoon, explaining, that as Stella was unwell, the Thursday meeting would be held at Bonny's house. He had taken the boxes of wool and clown parts to Bonny in the late afternoon and Miss Moreland had caught a lift back with him.

They'd found Stella on her knees before the sink, tacking down the edges of a new tear in the linoleum.

'So this is what Parsons prescribes for illness?' the old woman had said. 'You're flogging a dead horse there, girl.' Then she'd turned to Martin. 'Why don't you do something with this room? It's enough to depress a saint with a gold pass to the hereafter.'

The minister had cut the conversation short. 'Quite functional,' he'd replied, making a fast exit to his study. But he rarely gained the last word with Miss Moreland.

'You can't take it with you, you mean old coot.' She had laughed then, and she'd walked to the open window, reaching out to touch a jacaranda blossom that brushed at the window sill.

114

'It's late, isn't it? Should be thinking of dropping its leaves, not flowers.'

'Very late. I've never known it to bloom in February.' Stella had placed her hammer on the table before joining her friend at the window. 'I believe it is attempting to come inside, my dear – trying to brighten up this terrible, terrible room.'

'Great minds think alike.' She tossed a plastic department store bag to the table. 'I thought it might brighten you up a bit, girl,' she'd said.

The bag had contained a delightful blouse, all blues and greens and lilacs, and this morning, Stella was wearing it in celebration; she'd woken around midnight to the familiar stomach cramps, and never before had she welcomed them. Relief. So there was to be no testimonial to that day, a day she could now truly put cleanly away. Place it behind her with other days.

She looked down at the blouse, delighting in its colour. It was like wearing her garden on her back. Wrapped safe in her garden, neglected these last days, as had been her other duties since the rape.

The weather remained fine, and not too hot. Today she would spend outdoors with her flowers. It was a place of memories, where old blooms and the surprise of new blooms, from seeds long buried, or blown in from other gardens, never failed to please her. She would pot out the little jacarandas for the fete, and some of the smaller oaks. It was not the right time of year to disturb them, but she trusted her green thumbs.

And the tomatoes. They were rotting on the vine. She must get to them, pick them, give some away. She had seedlings to plant out too – and the couch grass beside Wilson's fence to spray. Perhaps she'd reach over and give her neighbour's forest a few bursts of weedkiller too, she thought.

Her eyes turned to the window now as memory of the child she had been, came from a place too long put aside. She had spent her childhood in that garden, or in the shed, or up a tree.

It was a good place to hide in, and large enough to deter the most determined seeker. Her hands went to her face, covered it, and she breathed deeply between her fingers.

Put it aside, she warned. Don't look at it.

Her maternal grandfather had died many years before Stella's birth. He'd had this house built in the centre of two large country blocks, which left an abundance of space for the garden – space that had not been put to good use until Stella began tilling the earth. She had told Bonny once that her garden, to some small degree, compensated for her lack of a child. Perhaps it did. It was certainly her creation. Seeds were sown, and watched over, small plants nurtured, and she gained so much pleasure in watching small sick plants grow strong and tall.

The three jacarandas were her adult children. Almost thirty years ago she had purchased them at a church fete.

She smiled, remembering that day – her father hurrying her from the house, handing her a brand new five-dollar note; it was so new, she hadn't wanted to spend it.

'Poor Father,' she whispered, and again her hands went to her face, covered it, but her mind was wandering back now, back to the day of the crisp five-dollar note.

'Off you run, Daughter. Quickly now. Have a day in the sun,' he had said. 'They'll have food there. Buy your lunch today.'

It had been a wonderful day of freedom. For hours she'd wandered the stalls, eating hot jam-filled donuts while trying to decide between a small figurine, five second-hand books by Agatha Christie, and some writing paper. Then she had come upon the three sickly little trees, their roots restricted in small clay-filled pots. They were marked at fifty cents each.

She planned to keep money enough aside to save one, to take it home and free its roots to the earth, but she had not been able to decide which one's need was the greatest, so when Mr Scott offered her the three for one dollar, she was jubilant. She had handed over her dollar note and, while he placed the sickly trees in plastic bags, she'd run back and bought the books.

116

Steve Smith was at the bookstall. He'd helped her carry the trees home, and he'd stayed on to dig the holes beside the shed.

'The shed and the house will give them a bit of protection from the frost,' he'd said. 'I'll build you a bit of a frame around them – that's if you like.'

Each winter for three years she had covered the trees with plastic bags stretched over taller and taller stakes, but soon the jacarandas had outstripped their planter. Now they no longer needed her care, but cared for her, supplying shade with their graceful foliage, adding their colour to her life, giving shelter to her birds.

There were birds out there this morning. One was only inches from the window. Head to the side, it looked directly at her, winked.

She smiled. I will find a way to survive, she told the bird. Haven't I always found a way? Soon I will return to my meetings and to my responsibilities. When I am ready, but until I am ready, my garden and my birds will support me, and as Miss Moreland says, Maidenville will do well enough without me.

'Father. Your breakfast. It's not nice, cold. What on earth are you doing with that old monstrosity?' she asked, eyeing the case again, frowning over the dishcloth, new yesterday, now only fit for the rubbish.

'It is a little antiquated. Its clips don't appear to hold. What happened to the small leather case?'

'It's ... perhaps the budget could be stretched to supply some new luggage,' she replied.

He walked away from the case, leaving it on the floor, tossing the soiled cloth to the sink before taking the seat at the opposite side of the table. He picked up his knife and fork and stabbed at a slice of liver, chewed on it. 'You cook well, Daughter. A mite more pepper perhaps.'

She passed the pepper, then pointed to the withdrawal forms

beside her plate. 'Do I have my own accounts, Father?'

'No need to concern yourself with it, Daughter. Just sign where I have placed the cross. I am using a little of it this month to top up the cheque account.' She continued to look at him, and he turned his attention to his plate. But she made no move towards the pen. Her head down, she stirred the cereal into the milk, waiting for him to continue. Frequently called on to sign his papers, she rarely looked further than his small pencilled cross, placed beside the space for signature. Today there were two forms. Why? Why two?

'Why the two, Father?'

He swallowed, coughed. 'I have been meaning to tell you – we are leaving in a little over three weeks. Catching the bus from Maidenville on the twenty-third of March. We fly out on Sunday the twenty-fourth.'

'We?' she asked with interest. Was he planning to take her away from Maidenville? A holiday, perhaps to a Queensland beach. Had he known what she was planning to do? She smiled. 'You mean . . . has this bought on your new interest in luggage?'

'I feel I am being guided by God's hand to return to the old battlefields of my youth. Yes. The tour I was considering back in October. You may remember, Daughter. I've decided to go.'

'Oh.' Disappointment was cold acid in her blood, but she hid it well – a master of the hiding, practised at the lie –

'I thought you had made up your mind not to go. You said . . . the weather . . .'

'Yes. Initially. I felt that the weather might restrict one's movements, and thus spoil the tour for me; however, it has recently been pointed out that we have received off-peak rates. Had we booked the trip to coincide with Europe's summer, the cost would have been considerably more. I also feel that it is God's will that I journey there at this time, Daughter. Perhaps he has a task for me to perform.'

She filled his teacup, passed the sugar. 'If it is what you want.

If you feel you are being led there,' she corrected, 'then of course you must go. You will certainly need to think of new luggage. Something with wheels on it, and some new winter woollies, and perhaps a new waterproof jacket. A warm cap.'

He nodded. She watched him add three heaped teaspoons of sugar to his cup and stir well. She knew the cost of the trip. In October he had spoken to her about it, discussed it at every meal. Did she have that much money in her accounts? She had always assumed her total worth to be somewhere around five hundred dollars.

'I know I can rely on you to see to my needs, as always. I'll require clothing for twenty-one days. Unless the hotels have a laundry service.'

'I'm sure they do ... at a price. Perhaps you could hand rinse – '

He laughed, interrupted. 'Laundry is a woman's domain, Daughter. I am, of course, not entirely happy leaving you here alone, but you are looking much improved.'

'I'm quite well now, Father, and capable of coping alone for three weeks.'

'If I leave the petrol tank full and a hundred dollars with you, that should see you over the three weeks.' He saw her expression and added, 'Of course, if you have need for more, then Miss Moreland – or any one of the congregation would not see you begging.'

'It appears that I have no need to beg.' She tapped the forms with the handle of her spoon. 'Or are you absconding with all of my worldly wealth? What was the final cost of the tour, Father?'

Her question silenced him long enough to empty his plate, to wipe it clean with a crust of toast, to drain his cup.

She knew he was not pleased. Head bowed over his toast and jam, he ate in silence. Stella pushed her plate to the side, then taking up the pen she signed the blank withdrawal forms. It was easier than arguing.

He had been watching her. Now he stood, took the forms,

placed them in his satchel, and without a word he left the room, returning later, dressed for the town.

Stella left her dishes and followed him to the back door. 'Father?'

'Yes?' He checked his watch, impatient to be gone. 'I posted, on Sunday, a cheque to cover the full tour. It is no small figure, Daughter, and at present, not covered by sufficient funds in the cheque account. The postal service to Sydney, being reasonably efficient, I fear the cheque will have been already presented for payment. There is a fee for – '

'I understand. I understand. Can you also understand my desire to know why you have access to my accounts, but I am denied this same access? Or am I? Can I walk into the bank and make a withdrawal?'

'Finances are a male domain, Daughter. You have never questioned my handling of these matters before.'

'No, oddly enough, I haven't.' Why? her inner voice asked. 'Surely, Father, it would be a simple enough matter to arrange a ... a small credit card on one of my accounts. I assure you I would not abuse the privilege.'

'I have no fear that you would. It is ... is one of these trends of the modern world that I have chosen not to follow. You can surely understand my abhorrence of a world without cash. It is alien to those of my generation.'

'But a world I have grown with, and not so alien to me. Am I, must I, remain trapped in the time warp of your generation? I am only forty-four. I have, no doubt, many years in which to survive an ever-changing world. I must move with it or ... or sink. Go down without a bubble, Father.'

'*We're going to drown. We're going to drown,*' cried timid *Mousy One.*

'*Oh goodness gracious dearie me, our little lives are done.*'

'We'll discuss it later, Daughter.'

'I would like to discuss it now. What is the actual balance of these accounts?'

'They vary – from month to month. Enough of this now. Do I deny you, Daughter?'

'I'm middle-aged, Father, and still dependent on you for my every need. I'm living in the past. This is the nineties. If I have no income of my own then I must be eligible for some social security payment. Everyone else in town appears to be.'

'Are you destitute? You are certainly not.'

'What qualifies as destitute? It may have been well enough in your youth for maiden daughters to remain dependent on their parents, but I would like a little independence now. Freedom.'

'Freedom?'

'Freedom to – ' She almost said it – almost said, to run from Maidenville, but she caught her tongue, and added, 'Freedom to walk into . . . into the hairdresser's, have my hair cut. We don't have an account there. What if I should like to have it washed and set each week like Mrs Morris?'

'God forbid it, Daughter!'

She had never before expressed interest in her bank accounts, so the minister had never been forced to lie. And he did not wish to lie to her. Always content to live the way he dictated, Stella had previously shown little regard for the papers he placed beneath her nose for signatures. Martin's problem now was how he might wriggle out of this one, and get things back the way they were. Her bank accounts were overly healthy at the moment. As investments came due, he'd been cashing them in, building a pool he intended investing in shares. Interest was too low for his liking. Hang the young home-buyers.

Halfway through the back door, he turned, returned to the room, allowing the door to slam shut behind him. 'A woman's hair is her crowning glory; however, this . . . this leaving of it loose – as you have been doing these last days. It is not for me to say, but you must ask yourself, isn't that sheepdog style more suitable for a teenager?'

'It's quite comfortable, but I've been thinking that perhaps I should have a little of it trimmed off.'

'Anything but Mrs Morris's starched wig. Shall I leave an extra twenty, fifty dollars?' A conciliatory smile, a grand offer.

She rejected his offer. 'I have no idea of what it might cost, and that perhaps is the point I am trying to make, Father.'

'Then let us get to the point, and quickly.' He checked his watch, looked at the kitchen clock, stepping from foot to foot, eager to go, but forced to remain.

'The point is, that I am out of touch with living. At the auxiliary meetings, women in their sixties and seventies consider me to be of their generation, but they know more about managing money than I. I don't know the price of things, Father. I've always bought what was required, no prices asked. I walk through the supermarket and never look at prices. I trust Marilyn to bill me – to bill you, for the correct figure. The accounts are sent to you. It is as if I don't exist. Mail comes addressed to me, from the banks, but you handle it. I don't dare to open my own mail! I am forty-four, and a reasonably intelligent woman ... or I was once. And this floor. I want to buy a new floor-covering for in here. It's disgusting. It's ... it's revolting. As you say, we are not destitute, so if I have the money in my accounts, then I'd like to spend some of it on a floor-covering that I have some chance of keeping clean. Why can't I?'

'Come, come, Daughter. This argument does not suit you – and if I might say – is perhaps a mote extreme.'

'Perhaps. Perhaps it is. But ... but you tell me you are flying off on a tour. Did you ask my opinion? No, you did not.'

'So the father must now ask the daughter's permission?'

'No. No. I don't know what I mean, Father, but can't you see that a little money of my own might help give back to me some self-worth?' She had gone too far now and endeavoured to step back. Her head bowed, she looked at her hands ... scarred, ringless, aging hands.

'A new floor may give you self-worth?'

'Yes.'

'Self-worth?' He stood shaking his head. 'Surely it is not self-worth we seek, but what we are worth in the eyes of God! Do you think he cares if we have floors or not?'

'I care. God doesn't have to clean it. I do – and, as always, you confuse me with your arguments.'

'Confusion this morning is a two-way street, Daughter.'

She sighed, turned away, accepting defeat. What was the use? But the worm of rebellion still lived within her. A deep breath, and she turned to him again. 'What I mean, Father, is that a little independence, might, at this particular stage of my life, be in order – a safety blanket against some emergency.'

'Emergency?' Martin could not perceive of any emergency in Maidenville that might require the outlay of hard cash.

'I'll be out of touch with you for three weeks. In that time anything could happen. A broken window – as when the bird flew against the lounge room doors last summer. A minor accident in the car. What if something should happen while you are overseas, if I had to go to you?'

'God forbid! And the glazier would send an account.'

'Yes. Of course he would. You have all the answers, and I have none left.' She turned on her heel, and her rubber soles squealed against the aging floor.

His face had turned red, his jowls were swelling. Her attention on the sink, she let the hot water run over plates.

'Planes are safer than the average family car, these days – they say.'

Safer than the average family home, she thought, as she turned the water off. 'Of course planes are safe, and of course there will be no emergency.' She knew him too well. He might profess total faith in his God, but he had no desire to walk through the pearly gates and shake his maker's hand. She spoke on quickly, pacifying, calming a frightened child. 'I use that only as an example, Father. It will be a wonderful trip, and I'm pleased that you decided to go. I suggested that you go originally, if you remember.'

'Yes. Yes you did. We are flying Qantas. They have the best safety record.'

'They certainly do.' She began clearing the table. 'What are you doing about a passport? You need a passport to travel.'

'I sent off the forms on Monday with a confounded photograph. George Jones, the tour organiser, is rushing it through. They lined me up in front of a screen at the chemist's and snapped before I was composed. I look like a criminal. All it requires is the number and the arrows on my jacket. Now I really must be on my way. We'll have to leave this discussion until later. Perhaps we'll talk about some new linoleum when I return.'

'Yes, Father.'

'I assume the department store will have suitable luggage.'

'I was looking at a rather attractive case there some time back.'

'And I must get some new spark plugs for the Packard. I'll get the car into A-one order before I leave.'

She nodded, tame again, the way he liked it.

'Not good for a fine old car to sit idle. Motors, as mankind, have a habit of dying when unused. Far better to wear away than to rot away.'

'I can run the Packard for you while you are gone.'

He laughed. 'You would remember how to drive it?'

'I was driving it at seventeen. For years I drove Mother around town in it.'

He shook his head, dismissing the idea.

'Have you really forgotten the past, Father? Have you been able to erase it totally from your mind – ?'

He cut her off mid-sentence. 'Indeed you did. Indeed you did. I have not forgotten, Daughter. Your dear mother liked the Packard. It came to me with her, you know. I only allowed the registration to lapse when she no longer had a use for the vehicle. Never learned to drive it herself, of course. Your mother was never one to demand her independence.' It was a good line on which to make his exit. He opened the door.

'About the credit card, Father.'

He looked heavenward. 'You are determined to have it, Daughter?' Frustration, and the desire to escape this house and be about his business was threatening capitulation.

'It would give me a feeling of security while you are away.'

'Then damn it all, I cannot deny you that security. We'll go into the bank before I leave. Get it underway.' Capitulation could be delayed. Decisions could be made tomorrow, next week, but after he had transferred some of her money into a small account. Perhaps a thousand, or two thousand. Yes. Two thousand. That would be the way to go, he thought. Present her with the book, rather than a confounded card. Give her some small independence, if her desire for independence was so great that she should stand here and argue for it. What in God's name has got into this girl? And the timing of her rebellion is not good, he thought. 'I should be back by eleven, Daughter. If young Cooper and his intended arrive before I return, give them tea.'

'I'll come with you. We can look at the cases together.'

'In that outfit? You look like a floral bouquet.' He eyed the shirt.

'Miss Moreland bought it for me at the department store. She said it looked like my garden. I thought perhaps they may have another, and we might see a nice light jacket for you there. I feel I would like to get out of the house today, and I have nothing more pressing to do.'

'The dishes, perhaps. And the young couple will be here – '

'Dishes have a habit of waiting for me, Father, and Mark Cooper and his bride will surely wait for you.'

the rapist rides

The night throbbed with silence, or perhaps it was his own heart-beat. Nothing moved. The town was stone cold dead. Keeping away from Main Street and the streetlights, Thomas Spencer had ridden his bike out to Boundary Road, then cut back via the river road, his only light, a slim pen-light torch he'd helped himself to from the shop.

They won't miss it, like they never missed the bottles that walk out of the liquor store, the youth thought. He had a good business going with black-market booze and cigarettes.

It was sort of eerie, riding through the trees along the river, sort of like a science fiction show, he thought. A sky of stars, but no moon. This slim channel of light slicing its way, like a laser knife, through the pitch blackness, leading him on, and into – 'The outer limits,' he said.

Rabbits scuttled from the road as he passed by. He swung his torch onto them, attempting to get their eyes, dazzle them. He nearly got one too.

He and Kelly had got a rabbit that way one night. Hypnotised it with the torch, then grabbed it and wrung its neck while its little chin trembled. They sprayed a yellow stripe down its back, and hung it from a noose on Kelly's old man's front porch – like a voodoo sign. Like saying 'Lay off us, man, or we'll send in the zombies to do you.'

The old bastard just cut it down and gave it to his dog – paint and all. Free tucker, he reckoned, or that's what Kelly said. Kelly wasn't a bad-looking babe, but how she got that way with her gorilla old man and his emu wife, Thomas never could work out.

He caught the eyes of a second rabbit, but it blinked, hopped. 'If I used me big light, I'd could get you, you jumpy little shit,' Thomas warned.

So far the calici rabbit virus hadn't reached Maidenville. Maybe it never would. Nothing else ever got this far away from civilisation, he thought. 'Flat, red, dusty, dead shit hole. Only thing it's any good for is for bike riding. Look, no hills,' he told the land around him.

The nearest hill was sixty kilometres away. Every year the state school took a bus load of first grade kids there for a picnic, just so they wouldn't start believing the bloody world was flat and that they were all going to fall over the edge of the earth if they ever left Maidenville. He'd gone there with the school, and he'd wanted to see what was on the other side. He still wanted to see what was on the other side, and one day he would too. Just take off, and ride. That's what he told his mother last night.

'Fat old cow,' he'd told her. 'One of these days I'll just take off and ride.'

Freedom. That's what he needed. Cut loose. No more supermarket shelves, no whingeing, no-one telling him what to do and when to do it.

'Freedom, man. Just gone, man.'

He shone his torch into the trees. 'Pow. Pow. Pow,' he said, picking up the twin green eyes of some night thing, probably a feral cat, also out after prey.

He had a big modern light on his bike. His parents only ever bought him the best, but he didn't use it when he went wandering in the night. It was a dead giveaway – lit him and his bike up like a moving Christmas tree. Anyway, he liked the dark. He couldn't see the flat, and the dust, and the pathetic bloody town that didn't even know how pathetic it was. Tight-arsed bloody hole of a place, seething with secrets hidden beneath its respectable skirts. He knew its secrets, heard most of them from his mother, and nosed the rest out like a bloodhound.

Kelly was supposed to call for him at midnight. He'd waited out front until one, but she hadn't turned up. Either she was trying to make him beg for it, or else her old man had locked her in again.

'He's jealous that she's putting it out for everyone and he wants some himself, but he hasn't got the guts to take what he wants. Gutless old shitter,' he said. 'I'd like to do him, cut him with my knife. Slit his fat old gut and let it all spill out. Here dog. Come and get some free food – choice gorilla belly.'

The river road brought him in at the top end of town. He circled Murphy's block, but there was no sign of Kelly. Maidenville was locked up, battened down for sleeping. It belonged to him tonight. He rode down the main street, wishing he had a brick to toss through the supermarket window, but he didn't have a brick. Then he was at Templeton's hedge, and he skidded to a halt, leaning his bike against it while he peered over the top of a gate as tall as he. Just like old Templeton to have a two-metre gate nobody could see through. He's got a privacy complex, old bull-moose guarding his virgin heifer ... virgin no more. Thomas chuckled.

He liked old Stell's garden. It was cool, green – like one of them oasis things that they have in the middle of deserts. You come on them when you're dying of thirst and you bury your head in cool. Slake your thirst, he thought. He had a thirst tonight that needed slaking real bad, but it wasn't for Kelly. He was glad she hadn't shown. She was too easy, boring after a while.

She'd do it any which way, and once you'd done it every which way, what else was there to do?

'Plenty.'

He couldn't get old Stell off his mind lately. The little breasts and the big hard nipples. 'Wow. Power, man. You've got the power. May the force be with you,' he said. With old Stell it had been like ... like the power, like something else ... like doing it to your mother, or to a little kid. 'Yeah.' Like watching a stupid little kid's mouth tremble, its big innocent eyes blinking at you, pleading for one more chance ... then you socked it to them, then crunched their necks. It would be like crunching a rabbit's neck.

'Snap. Crackle. Pop.'

Templeton's house stood out like a tall dark lump against the lighter dark of sky. It looked like it was staring down its nose at the Wilsons' and old Bryant's low-brow squats, like old Templeton stared down his nose at half the town. 'Superior fat old fart. You wouldn't be looking so superior if you knew where I've been,' he said.

The gate was easier to scale from the inside, but he wouldn't let that stop him. Grasping the top, he heaved himself up, the soles of his sneakers walking wood. He gained a toehold in the slot for the letterbox and in the hole where the bolt ran. Then he was straddling it, and jumping lightly to the ground on the other side. He laughed. That miserable old fart's gate couldn't keep him out. Not any more. No-one could keep him out – not if he wanted in, wanted to slake his thirst.

His sneakers on gravel made no sound; he crept down the drive until he could see Stella's bedroom window, sort of ghosting with the light from the street. It was open too. He knew which room she slept in, he'd been in there with her plenty of times when he was a stupid little kid. He stuck a toy mouse in her knickers drawer once, hid it under her frilly knickers. She always wore frilly knickers – black ones, pink ones, blue, and soft little bras that made his mother's look like they were made to hold up a cow's udder.

Only the night before last, he'd sat for hours in the big jacaranda, watching Stell brush her hair, watching her take off her little bra, and put on a nightie. The light played her shadow on the blind and it was like watching a giant television screen. It turned him on, just watching her. It was sort of like watching blue movies in black and white, but knowing it was all there behind the screen waiting for you, waiting for you in true and vibrant flesh tones, and when the show was over you could walk around to the back of the television and go for it. Stick it to her while her trusting old eyes blinked and begged. Give it to her until she went limp.

He started wanting it real bad, wanting it at the back of the television, wanting it in colour, wanting it so bad he had to take her once-white knickers from his pocket and create his own patch of colour with them.

He'd kept the knickers with him for two weeks now. Kept them in the pocket of whichever jeans he was wearing. Used them for –

'Remembering,' he said. They were getting past their use-by date.

Standing now beneath her window, he unzipped his jeans, and he remembered the Packard and the dirt floor again ... remembered it good.

The knickers were silky stuff. Real slow, he rubbed them up and down, up and down, building the vision in his head, building it until he was ready to explode with it, but he held on to it, never wanting it to end. Sometimes, lately, the visions in his head were better than the real thing with Kelly. He couldn't get rough with her, or she'd set her old man and uncles on him, but in his head, he could get as rough as he liked with old Stell.

Tonight he was changing the story. He'd tamed her with his knife, and now she was licking him, licking him good. He sucked in a long breath and let the pictures grow. She was up on her knees now, straddling him ... backwards, and he'd put his knife down, and his two hands were around her, pinching her little boobs with their big nipples sticking out like stalks out of green apples. He was driving her into a frenzy, and she was moaning and begging him and licking him, up and down, up and down, her tongue was silk ... warm silk. She was –

'Shit.'

He finished too soon, and held the knickers high. I ought to put them in the wash for the old man. Might bring back pleasant memories, he thought. Placing his foot in the fork of the jacaranda closest to Stell's window, he began his climb, high into the tree, his pen-light gripped between his teeth.

They were good climbing trees. He knew where the branches forked, and which branches leaned across to her room. He could easily get in her window from this one. It was wide open tonight. She always left her window open, except in the rain, but even then she left the top down. Still, it might be pushing his luck with her old man only three rooms along the passage.

He thought of the top floor layout as he moved further out on the limb. There was a long dark passage with rooms both sides. Old Templeton's room was over the front door, Stella's at the other end of the passage, down the back. Plenty of space in between, as long as he shut her up fast.

The limb swayed. His weight gain in the past twelve months had its downside. Too thin to hold him, the branch groaned and its leaves swished against her window.

Then it cracked.

'Shit!' he hissed, moving quickly back, her knickers in his hand.

'Maybe I'll hang them on the tree,' he thought. 'Or ... or nail them on the church door. Yeah. Yeah. Yeah. Nail them on the church door next Sunday.'

A light came on at the front of the house, in old Templeton's room.

'Shit man. Must have a hundred-watt globe in that bed lamp,'

Thomas muttered, freezing back against the trunk. He clung there, watching the window, half expecting to see the old bull-moose's head emerge, almost hearing the bellow. The town kids knew that bellow well. It used to be a dare in grade four, to climb in and pinch the minister's apricots.

The light in the bathroom was turned on. It bathed the foliage above Thomas, turning it from black to a bower of soft green, scattered with jewel-like blue.

A long intake of air and a slower release. 'Far out,' he whispered. 'I'm in the magic faraway tree, Aunty Stell, with old Saucepan Head and what's his name. Far out, man. Far out.'

In silence he waited until he heard the cistern's hiss, heard the water sluicing down the sewerage pipes only feet from him. He waited until the bathroom light was off, and the night, and the tree, black once more before he began the climb down.

But the soles of his expensive runners were thick, spongy; his left foot wedged in the fork of the jacaranda and Thomas, thrown off balance, fell heavily to the earth, his ankle twisting as his foot was dragged free of the shoe.

'Fucking tree. Fucking old maid bitch with her fucking tree,' he hissed through gritted teeth as he rubbed the ankle, soothed the raw skin. Minutes passed before the pain abated and he was able to stand, to climb, to retrieve his shoe then limp slowly down the drive.

It wasn't until he was on the footpath and mounting his bike that he thought of it. He pushed the frilly knickers into the letter-box. Still cursing, he peddled away, one shoe on, and one shoe off, the bike labouring now as it followed the slim pencil of light home.

pondering underwear

The only feminine underwear Martin Templeton had sighted at close range, had not been what you might call smalls. His wife had always worn full cotton bloomers in the summer and knee-length woollen bloomers in the winter. And his grandmother, who had raised him from the age of four, wore calico, split-crutch drawers. Martin recalled, with some embarrassment, studying that odd piece of apparel at length one day while it swung on the clothesline. With a six-year-old's logic, he pondered its construction – and its purpose. In time he reached the conclusion that it was indeed her drawers. These strange items always hung with his own and his father's drawers. It took more time for a six-year-old mind to deduce that the inconvenience of the long skirts Grandmother refused to discard in favour of more practical fashions, would have made normal bodily function, in the narrow confines of an outdoor lavatory, tedious; thus the split-crutch, which might only require the raising of her skirts and the spreading of her legs. Or did she bother to sit on the lavatory? Did she just spread her feet where she stood? Hadn't he seen her doing just this on their way home from church one morning . . . a telltale puddle left in her wake? Eventually he had to ask his small boy's question.

His father, also a clergyman, was a dominating and impatient man. Unable to keep his young wife, he certainly was not one to tolerate his son's questions on female apparel, and worse.

Martin blushed with the memory, and a hand went to the broad seat of his trousers, to brush at the ghostly sting of the razor strap.

He had no recollection of the woman who bore him, then made her escape before being trapped by a second child. No photographs of the absconding wife were allowed in the cold house where Martin had lived, but trace-memories told him she had been a tall woman. And certainly, he had not inherited his great height from his father's side, only his profession.

'Those we didn't know, we cannot miss,' he lied as he inserted his hand into the letterbox and withdrew his telephone account, a pair of white briefs, and the receipt for the cheque he had sent to the tour organiser.

Initially he thought the briefs a soiled handkerchief. Held between finger and thumb, and at the greatest possible distance from him, he then noted the elastic waist, and the lace-bordered legs.

Quickly he walked to the rubbish bin, dropping the offensive item in, relieved that it had been he and not his daughter who emptied the letterbox that day. He prodded the white cloth low with the rake handle. The letters held at a distance he hurried inside, where he ripped them open, shook the undefiled contents to the kitchen bench, tossed the envelopes into the kitchen tidy, then stood at the sink soaping and re-soaping his hands, scrubbing at them with a nail brush.

Stella had been watching his actions, now he caught her frown. 'Wretched youngsters. I don't know what this world is coming to,' he muttered.

'What youngsters?'

'God knows,' he said wiping his hands on a tea towel, which

he tossed into the kitchen tidy. 'They are placing their confounded rubbish in the letterbox now. If I catch the young scoun-
drels at it I'll have their hides.'

'Their empty drink cans again, Father?' Stella asked, retriev-
ing the towel, and taking it to the laundry.

'No. No. A soiled ... a soiled handkerchief, or the like.'
He was seated when she returned, and she watched a smile of
satisfaction spread across his features. 'My itinerary at last.
I thought there may have been a hitch.'

She stood behind him. 'As they say, it's all happening now,
Father.'

'Yes. Yes. Look here, Daughter. Two nights in Switzerland.
Lucerne. Oh my word, I do believe I'm beginning to look
forward to it. I dare say we should begin the packing – if just
to ascertain how much we can fit in the case.'

'You still have over a week. Everything will become crushed
enough without packing it too early.'

'Perhaps we should have a trial run.' He was on his feet again,
and heading for the stairs. 'Could you bring the bathroom scales.
I dare say that should give us an idea of weight. They only
allow ... I believe they said twenty kilograms. Check it for me,
Daughter, then tell me how much that is in pounds. Kilograms.
Who on earth understands their confounded kilograms – ?' His
voice faded as he disappeared upstairs.

Stella followed him, doing the conversion.

The case had been packed and repacked umpteen times by the
twenty-third. When Stella saw it loaded into the luggage compartment of the bus that would transport Martin to Sydney, she
was pleased to see the last of it, but she hoped that the plane
seats might be a little wider than those of the bus. The minister
looked like a stressed whale compressed into a sardine can.

'Take care, Father. Stay well.' She stood at the door, her hand
to her mouth, knowing she should say more, wanting to say

more. 'Try to keep moving your feet. It helps with circulation,' she called as the door unfolded, closed, locking her out and him in. She ran to the window, and he turned to her.

Not prone to displays of emotion, Martin raised a hand, and a tight apprehensive smile. Then the bus pulled away from the kerb, and he and his case were gone. A wave of something akin to fear for him, or perhaps love of him, washed over her, and some precognition of doom brushed at the hairs on the back of her neck. Was this to be the last time she would see him?

It is as if I am being pared down to my core, readied for ... for ... She knew not what. Her hand raised, waved to the exhaust fumes, waved until the vehicle turned the corner and was lost to her vision.

Things ought to have been said that were not said and she knew it. Perhaps she should have kissed him goodbye, held his hand and begged him to stay.

She never touched him. Not since she had been a tiny infant had she held his hand. She sat with him in the evenings, she sat beside him in the car, she washed his underwear, ironed his pyjamas, starched his vestments, the collars and the cuffs of his shirts, but she never touched him. Never.

Until this morning. He was standing before the bathroom mirror combing his hair, and she'd stepped forward, taken the comb, and flattened the thick hair standing up at his crown.

His old face had softened, and his smile was a strange thing. A boy's, coy. 'Thank you, my dear,' he said.

My dear? Strange words in reply to her own odd behaviour. As she had placed the comb down she'd remembered a time before, of combing his hair, remembered the feel of it back then. Thick hair ... not white. What colour had it been?

He would have been in his mid forties. Angel had been forty-seven when Stella was born, and Martin six years her junior. He would not have been grey by that age. What colour had his hair been? She couldn't remember. Why didn't memories come in

136

colour? But she could remember the colour of the comb. Blood red. And she could remember entangling it in the thick curling hair, and she could remember Angel had cut the comb free with scissors. Then she'd turned on the child, and –

Anger. Such anger.

Standing at the kerb, she stared unseeing into the distance, her hand rubbing at a scar on her calf. Her mind was away, traversing the years, taking her back to –

Doctor Parsons, the little boy man with Grumpy's face and his small hands. He wasn't grumpy though, just looked like him. She liked Doctor Parsons. That day he had put two funny white sticky-tape stitches over the cut, then bandaged it.

'*Mousy One and Mousy Two, in search of cream once strolled into the farmer's dairy, where Tom the cat patrolled.* Good heavens! I remember it,' she said. '*Mousy One and Mousy Two, in search of cream once strolled into the farmer's dairy, where Tom the cat patrolled.*'

She stood, repeating the words, attempting to force more to come. And they did.

'*We're going to drown. We're going to drown,*' cried timid Mousy One. '*Oh goodness gracious dearie me, our little lives are done.*'

'He'll be jake, love.'

The voice startled her. She turned, for a moment bewildered, unsure of her surroundings. It was one of the middle-aged Murphy males, seated in his equally middle-aged car. Her hand moved to her mouth, unsure if he had heard her words, but aware she had spoken the childish rhyme aloud. She blushed.

'Don't worry about him. Take more than bloody England to kill old Martin Templeton. He's as tough as old boots, love.'

She flashed her fine white teeth in what served as a smile for strangers. 'He's eighty-five, and far too fond of his creature comforts, Mr Murphy.'

'Do the old bugger good. Bring him down to earth with a bloody thud.'

Waving a hand to the middle-aged Murphy, she walked around the corner to the minister's car.

He had parked it there, and unwillingly handed her the keys. 'Drive it carefully, Daughter. The keys of the Packard are on top of the dresser. Take care backing it out of the shed. Its steering is like a truck's.'

Stella turned the key in the lock and as she swung the door wide, a blast of warmth rushed out. Heat still had a hold on the land, and though the sun was still low, it carried an early sting. She sat, placing her hand on the steering wheel.

Hot. Her hand sprang away. It was burning hot. She looked at the hand, expecting to see blisters there, but she only saw the scars.

'*You are not behaving rationally, Angel. I kissed the child goodnight. I tucked her in.*'

'*I know all about daddies tucking their little girls in . . .*'

'Stop this,' she said, 'Look forward, not behind. That is the way it has always been, and a far, far better way. I will look forward to my three weeks of freedom, and to sole use of this car.'

It fitted her well, and it was her own to drive for three long weeks. Perhaps she might take a trip to Dorby, ask Miss Moreland along for the ride. With her old friend at her side she might be brave enough to go to the RSL club for lunch, even look at a poker machine, maybe feed it with a few cents. The three weeks would fly by all too soon, and it would be wonderful not having Father underfoot as he had been for the past few days.

He had fussed, and she had fussed over him, trying to prepare him – as she might prepare a child heading off on his first school camp. She'd typed him a list.

```
Left pocket, handkerchiefs.
Ties in right side pocket.
Underwear front zip compartment.
Dark shirts, left side case. Casual for
travelling.
```

White shirts, left side case. For dinner at
night. Fold neatly.
Will do for several wears.
Keep case neat. It will make finding things so
much easier.

A European early spring ahead of him, she had purchased two
fine woollen sweaters and told him to wear them beneath his
shirts. Unable to buy a lightweight jacket in his size, she'd
settled for a shower-proof thing with a hood. It looked like a
tent but was small enough to roll into a neat package he could
keep with him in his flight bag.

So many instructions she'd given him, but how many would
he remember? How would he survive without her to anticipate
his needs, to organise his days?

'He'll be fine. He will be fine and so will I. I'll paint the
kitchen, and the cupboards. Perhaps I'll think about a new floor-
covering too. Surprise him when he gets home. It wouldn't take
long. They'd put Bonny's new tiled floor down in a day. Three
weeks. They will no doubt fly.'

She started the motor and followed the bus's path down Main
Street.

Four weeks had passed since the rape. She had stayed far away
from the shed – when she could, and when she couldn't, she'd
found ways of entering it when her father was pottering there
with his car. On the days of the church guild meetings, when
the other members came to her house, she always managed to
take someone with her to store the clown body parts, or to select
more wool.

As Doctor Parsons frequently said, life happens. With certain
reservations, in the past three weeks, life for Stella had settled
back into its familiar, its near comforting routine of meetings,
and church, of hospital visiting, and her Wednesdays of Meals

on Wheels. She had cooked biscuits for the street stall, and worked her small clown faces; she had served. Since the day of the painting on the church hall door, there had been no such repeats. In fact she had only sighted Thomas Spencer twice, and then from a distance. She ignored him. He had been erased from her heart, and from her head. To her he had become one of the many non-people who happened to share with her the town of Maidenville.

Being born in a small town, raised there, most faces were familiar; as was the Murphy male at the bus stop; yet she could not put a name to his face other than his family name. He could have been one of eight, most of them older than she. They all looked like old Mick, their father – all shoulders and no neck.

She knew Young Mick Murphy, the eldest of the eight, and she knew Spud. She now recognised Dave, who after his first wife died, married Mrs Morris's neighbour and crony. She also knew the second youngest, Pat Murphy, but only because they had once shared a classroom. Of the others, she had never bothered to fit names to their faces. They didn't move within her circle of acquaintances.

As in any community, there were the various levels and societies in Maidenville. That she might be known by the middle-aged Murphy meant nothing. She was the minister's spinster daughter, his only daughter. Everyone in town knew Stella. As they knew Polly Daws, a mother of seven, who had not allowed her single state to prevent her raising a family.

Stella had also known Polly since school. She always smiled at her, gave Polly a nod, even called her by name, but she never stopped to pass the time of day with her, as with many of the Catholic families. They passed on the street as strangers might. There were some people, who for various reasons Stella had been known to cross over the road in order to avoid, others she crossed the road eagerly to greet. That was the way of her small town. Hers was a church community, a hospital community. She knew the nurses and their families, and the hospital auxiliary

140

members. She named both Bonny Davis and Marilyn Spencer, friends. They had gone through school together, and though their lives may have forked at the intersection of puberty, both Bonny and Marilyn going into early marriages, they remained close friends. The church saw to that. The church brought them together each Sunday. They worked on the same auxiliaries. They manned adjoining stalls at church fetes – and they knitted clowns.

Bonny had five boys, all redheads like their mother. Her third son, Peter, was the same age as ... Stella saw Peter riding by as she closed the gate. For a second, her feet almost tripped over each other in their desire to run.

'Aunty Stell,' he called, and did a wide wheel around.

Could she turn the entire youthful population of Maidenville into non-people because of one bad apple in the barrel?

Of course she couldn't.

She waved a hand to the youth, and waited inside the gate. 'Good morning, Pete.' She smiled at his snub-nosed face, and wondered why so many red-headed children seemed to wear the same features, as if cloned from some ancient red-headed ancestor. He was a lovely boy, bright, helpful.

He skidded his bike to a halt beside her, sliding the earphones of his radio down to his neck. 'You haven't seen my pup around anywhere, have you?'

'No, Pete. I haven't.'

'Some useless idiot must have opened the gate. Now he's gone. I've been everywhere.' He readjusted his earphones and pushed off.

'I hope you find him,' she said, but he was away, locked into his music.

She climbed back into the car, drove it down to the shed, parking it beside its much larger relative.

Then she opened the door and stepped out.

And she could smell him. As soon as she opened the door, she could smell the heat of him, the sweat of him, and his sex,

a smell previously unknown to her, and one she would never forget.

He had been in here.

No. You're mad. It has affected your mind. He wouldn't come here again. Never. Stop it. What are you doing to yourself?

But it wasn't in her mind. It was in the shed.

No. You stupid woman. You are imagining it. You see Bonny's boy, and you want to run from him too. It's sick. You are sick. Your mind has become twisted by it, and I will not allow it to be so. I will not waste my life in fear. There have been no phone calls from him for two weeks. He has forgotten about it, and so must you. It's over.

But it wasn't over; Thomas Spencer had been in her shed while she was at the bus stop and she knew it. He had been lying low, waiting for her father to leave town. Now he had come back to keep his promise.

'No.' She stamped her foot. 'No. Get a grip on yourself, Stella Templeton,' she demanded. 'You've been good. You've been fine. Father is ten minutes out and already you are panicking, conjuring up imaginary demons in your head. I will not live in fear for three weeks. I will not. It is only the scent of ... of ... of a stray ... pup. Perhaps young Pete's little labrador, or a stray dog, a male dog.'

Who has left his stink behind him – all the better to find his way back to you, my dear.

She shivered. Standing in front of the shed, the sun warm on her back, she looked down at the place where her own foot had stamped. Beside the imprint of her sensible rubber sole was a second. A sneaker sole, clear in the soft red dust. Rings and stripes. Twin rings and stripes.

Stealthily, she stepped back, her eyes straining now as she looked into the interior, dim because of the brightness of the morning sun. Her heart was racing as cold tremors passed through her, from head to feet. She looked at her hands, trembling hands. For two weeks they had been steady.

142

He has left his scent and calling card, the voice from within whispered. If you dare to search inside the shed you will find more evidence. He has lifted his leg against the wheel of the Packard. You know it is true. Don't deny it. He found good pickings beside the wheel of the Packard, and like a dog he has returned to sniff his old scent and spread a little more. That is the way that it is with dogs.

'I am not afraid of dogs,' she whispered, but her lips trembled as they spoke the lie. I will not become a victim of my own imagination. I am not like my mother. I am not like my mother. It is an old footprint. Others had been here. Half the town wears sneakers.

She turned her back on the shed and walked to the house, but with her hand on the doorknob, she baulked. What if he is inside the house, waiting for you?

She backed off and returned to the shed. Arming herself with a heavy hammer, she walked purposefully to the storeroom and flung the half door wide. Only her toys, and her bales of polyester wool. She moved back, looked behind the Packard, and beneath the Packard, and in the Packard. She opened its boot and peered into the dark interior. She checked the old trailer, the bench, and beneath the bench and she saw the dampness there, and the hammer in her hand shook.

'The floor of the shed is always damp – so much lower than the garden. If he was here, then he is no longer here,' she told the hammer, and she walked to the back of the house and reached for the doorknob.

Her hand refused to turn it. 'Stupid woman. What are you doing to yourself? Control this panic. Get on top of it.'

You should have locked the door. Why didn't you lock it?

For minutes she stood there, her hand on the knob. She could hear Mr Wilson on the other side of the fence. Familiar. Four houses down, Murphy's dog barked. Loud music was coming from the north side.

Open that door. He will be working at the supermarket. He

always works at the supermarket on Saturday mornings.

But the supermarket doesn't open until nine, the inner voice replied, and her hand left the doorknob and moved to her mouth.

Then I'll go back to town and I'll walk into the supermarket and I'll see him for myself. I'll see him with my own eyes and stop this foolishness.

And next time you'll lock the door, Stella, her inner voice said.

'Yes. Yes. I will. I will find the keys and lock all the doors,' she whispered.

Thomas was on his knees, stacking the tomato sauce shelf. Relief and revulsion fought behind the cage of Stella's ribs. She wanted to run home, lock herself in, but she couldn't run. Marilyn was on the checkout, knitting a clown's legs by rote. They spoke a while about the shade, and of what colour might best set it off.

'White and gold, probably, and I'll give him green eyes,' Stella said.

'I thought we could use that green lace Bonny bought at the Dorby market.'

'Too yellow, I think.'

'You always know best, Stell.'

Ron came to lean on the dividing wall between supermarket and liquor shop, and Steve Smith, shopping for his weekend slab of stubbies, leaned on the checkout bench. They asked about her father's trip, and she spoke to them of his new case, and of how he ended up twelve kilograms overweight.

'He had packed five pairs of shoes. I talked him down to three, then at the last minute tossed out his brown brogues. The trouble is, all of his clothing is so large. His shoes make four of mine. One of his sweaters takes up the room of my three-piece suit.'

'We're not all slim like you, Stell,' Marilyn said, and Stella turned away to stare at Thomas's back, and at the soles of his shoes. Rings and stripes. Circles within circles.

They were the same tread.

The group laughed. Stella hadn't heard the joke, but she flashed a smile as fake as the smile she had flashed at the middle-aged Murphy.

They didn't notice. The world was too busy about itself. Each friend, only an ear in which to pour their week of words, but she had no more words to pour, except the words she couldn't speak.

Your son is a rapist. Your son is a rapist and I should have reported him. Why didn't I report him?

Because I know this town too well, as I know Marilyn too well – always a barb to her comments. 'You always know best, Stell.' 'We're not all slim like you, Stell.'

Stop this. What am I doing to myself? Marilyn is a good friend. She has been my friend since childhood.

But she doesn't look at me as she might look at a friend. She hasn't in years. Not when Ron is around. Her eyes never leave him. She smiles at me, but she stares by me at Ron, watching him for one false move, one misguided smile.

Look at him. His arms folded, protecting himself from accusations. Poor Ron, he appears to be shrinking year by year. She is devouring him. Swallowing him up like the praying mantis, eating her mate.

She has a bitter mouth. It loves to chew on gossip then spit out the pips. It thrives on another's shame. Listen to her mouth.

'Did you hear about young Leonie Matthews? She's nicked off to Melbourne with a bloke who's been working for her father. She's only sixteen, Tommy's age. They say she's a real little moll. Her mother ought to be shot the way she lets her run around.'

Leonie's shame today, and her mother's. It could have been my shame, Stella thought. Marilyn would have passed it on just as easily – with the change from her till – sidetracking her listener with her words while handing back a dollar less, multiplying her profits as she multiplied shame.

Stop this.

She would cut me dead in town, and many would walk at her side. This town thrives on drama, and on the shame of others.

Stop this.

Why?

Because the truth is too painful?

Because I know this town – as I know I made the right decision for me on the night it happened. But I will not fear the pain of truth any more. I will look at it, and I'll be very careful. Careful of Marilyn, and of her son. I know where the house keys are and I will lock myself away safe from them.

Her mind far away, Stella's mouth continued smiling. They were speaking now about Willy Macy, who had lost his wife to a passing carnival man fifty years ago.

Lucky lady, Stella thought. She got away from Maidenville, but she still adds spice to many meetings.

'Marry in haste, regret at leisure,' Marilyn said, casting a meaningful glance at Ron. He turned away.

Praying silently for a run of customers who might free her to run, Stella nodded, and smiled, seeing all, saying nothing, while her eyes sought escape. No-one came in. Eventually she lied. 'I must run, Marilyn. I've got so much to do today. With Father rampaging around the house like a giant two-year-old, I've let everything go this past week.' She had known Marilyn all her life, now she had to invent lies in order to get away, away from her friend and her friend's son, the rapist with the stripe and circle tread on his sneaker soles.

The refrigeration section was at the rear of the store. Stella stood before it, scanning the array of cheese. So many to choose from, and with no need of more, she could not justify buying what she might not use. The minister had trained her well.

Reaching across for a packet of tasty, she didn't hear the rapist creep up behind her on his ring and stripe-soled shoes, but she smelt the stink of him, and the smell of his hair near her face. A packet of cheese slices snatched, she attempted to squeeze by him.

'Good morning, Aunty Stell. Not playing speaks today? I thought I was your favourite nephew.'

She would not speak to him. She would not see his face. She would not acknowledge his existence. But Thomas was not one to be ignored. Like a wolf shepherding his fleeing prey into a corner, he cut off her escape.

She tried to go the other way.

'Maybe I should call you Miss Templeton, now,' he said, the toe of his shoe lifting the hem of her pleated skirt. 'Do you think I'm too big to call you Aunty Stell?'

The aisle was narrow. Protected from his parents' view by the shelves, Thomas Spencer's arms were placed on either side of his prey. He pressed against her, forcing her forward against the refrigerated cabinet.

'Can I do anything for you, Aunty Stell? Can't waste time though. I'm a busy man.'

His mother's laughter muffled the sound as the edge of Stella's palm was used with a cutting action. She hit him between wrist and elbow, and as she hit, she pushed by him, dropping the cheese to the floor. He stooped, picked it up, offered it to her. 'Don't tell me I haven't got what you want, what you came looking for. We Spencers always aim to please, Miss Templeton.'

Again she heard the laughter, then his father's words. 'Since when did you ever aim to please anyone but yourself, Tommy?'

Stella had snatched up a second packet of cheese. Now she hurried with it back to the checkout.

'You okay, Stell?' Steve Smith asked.

She knew her face was red, and her stupid hand shook as she offered the cheese to Marilyn. She busied her hands with her handbag as Thomas, who had followed her to the register, leaned on the bookshelves, watching with interest.

'Just rushed off my feet, Steve,' Stella replied.

Steve Smith caught the youth's eye and stared him down while wondering how close Miss Moreland might have been with her suggestion that his nails might be checked for yellow paint. Young Tom Spencer had turned into a wild little shit these past twelve months. Steve stared at Marilyn, wondering if she was aware of the kid's growing reputation. Probably not. Marilyn knew how to make money and that was about it.

She'd been his neighbour through primary school. As he leaned there, he allowed his mind to wander back to those earlier years when he'd spent his life reading by the window, listening to his parents discussing the neighbours' habits.

Marilyn's old man had hung himself when the youngest boy was three, and Steve's parents thought they knew why. Marilyn had two brothers. The oldest was a dead ringer for his old man, but everyone knew who had fathered the youngest. He had the Murphys' big head, no neck and short legs.

'Lucky she was a girl, that's all I can say. She's the dead spit of him. Those eyes, and her hands,' Steve's mother had once said of the younger Marilyn. Now he tried to see what his mother had seen, tried to pick the one who had fathered Marilyn. She wasn't a Murphy. Too tall, dark as a gipsy once – exotic, for a few years, with those amazing green eyes.

'Don't take any notice of what Tommy says, Stell. He thinks he's someone now. Just like his father, got every lovesick female in town making cow eyes at him,' Marilyn said, sliding the cheese into a plastic bag, writing cheese plus butter in her account book.

Steve saw it. Cheese: $2.76. Butter. $1.08. His mouth opened in mute protest as he looked at the plastic bag. Only one item. He looked at the account book. Closed.

'Yeah. He's getting to be a light-fingered little shit, too. I don't know who he gets it from,' Steve commented, picking up his slab and walking out behind Stella. His beer dumped in the back of his ute, he walked to Stella's driver-side window as her car began to move away.

'Hold it, Stell.' She braked, but didn't look at him. 'Just a hint. You can take it or leave it, but I always pay cash in there. I'd check your account next time it comes.'

'I – I trust them.' Stella wanted to go, but he leaned on.

'Yeah, I know you do.' He silenced, and she touched the accelerator. The motor roared. 'Has that kid been giving you a hard time?' She shook her head, but her hands, her mouth trembled. 'I've been hearing a few whispers about him, Stell. Mavis Larkin reckons her girls saw his face at their bedroom window a couple of weeks back. Has he been – ?'

Stella shook her head again and her car moved back.

Steve stepped away.

She was back in the drive and unsure of what route she'd taken to get there, or of how many cars she'd passed on the way. She didn't park the car in the shed, but left it in the shade of the oak tree, close to the front door. Let the leaves fall on it, let the birds decorate it at will, she would keep it close, keep the keys close. Habit saw her walk to the gates, swing them shut, but she stopped before sliding the bolt home. Better to leave them wide, ready for a quick getaway. Gates would not keep him out, only lock her in.

It required work with a shovel to release the right-hand shed door from the earth which the years had heaped against it, but ten minutes of digging saw it freed, and closed. It had a bottom bolt that had once slid into a buried galvanised pipe. Stella knew it was there, somewhere – unless it had rusted away. She'd kicked her toe on it many times as a child. For minutes she chipped at the earth with her spade until she struck metal, and had she unearthed a gold nugget, she would not have been more pleased. Clay had compacted in its central hole. She poked at it with a screwdriver, then searched for a better tool. A rusty wood auger, hanging on the shed wall for a hundred years served her well. It drew the clay out, and eventually the door bolt was forced down, driven deep, then the right-hand door was bolted to the left and a heavy padlock clipped into place.

The shed grew suddenly dark. She turned on the light, and spent the next half hour hunting for the key to the side door.

It was hanging on a hook, beneath ancient dog chains and an aged army hat. She had seen the hat and the dog chains there for all of her life but she couldn't remember the dog, nor had she ever known the man who had worn the hat. She wished she had known the dog, and perhaps the man who wore the hat, but they were from a time before her time. Rusty. Dusty. How could they have waited so long undisturbed? How could her father believe he might return to that time and find it undisturbed?

She looked up at the high ceiling, and down to the floor. Junk. The worthless accumulation of years had been packed into this shed. Old chairs, their tapestry seats now woven of cobweb. Old picture frames in a corner, bound together by ropes of dusty web. Her own small bicycle tied high from a rafter with cobweb.

When had she ridden a bicycle? Where had she ridden it, except around and around the garden in small circles? Never on the street. Why had he bought it? Why offer her a freedom she could never have?

She shook her head and took the old key in her hand. It was heavy, rusted; it refused to turn in the lock. But she found a can of oil on the bench and she squirted a liberal amount into the keyhole. For ten minutes she stood lifting the door, rattling the key amid the rust and cobwebs.

And it turned, and the lock slid into its slot. Some things sustain.

The two keys in hand, she walked inside, took a third key from the top of the kitchen dresser and locked herself in the house.

The time was nine fifty-five. Her father had been gone for an hour and a half. Already it seemed like days.

the twisted clowns

The keys held tight in her hand, Stella walked each old room, checking windows, locking them. She checked the glass doors in the lounge room, unopened for many years, then she retraced her steps to the bathroom. Its window was small, and always open at the top. Now it refused to close. She greased the old runner with soap, and hurt her hand attempting to hammer the jammed window, to no avail.

Downstairs again she required a key to get out, a key to unlock the shed where she selected a hammer and her father's small oil can. Shed door locked behind her, back door. It took an hour, but she persisted until the bathroom window closed, and the rusting old lock finally moved. Fear had exhausted her.

At eleven she escaped the house. Invited for lunch, she arrived at Miss Moreland's, armed with a carton and two large plastic bags filled with clowns. They were beside her now on the couch, and hands busy, she unpicked large stitches from the neck of one rather twisted clown while the older woman went about the business of lunch.

Stella had borrowed a little control from two Aspros. Her

heartbeat had steadied. She would be okay. Everything was locked, her three keys, now tied together with red wool, were in her bag. She would be okay.

'A salad day, girl. The weather is still holding.'

'Yes. It's a glorious day.'

Stella refused to treat her friend as elderly. It was one of the reasons their relationship sustained. She never offered help in the kitchen, but sat and allowed Miss Moreland to play the hostess. And she was a wonderful hostess. Perhaps it took her a little longer these days to achieve less perfect results, but Stella enjoyed being waited on, as she enjoyed the conversation. Only here in this modern little unit could she let down her guard. But not today. She'd watch her tongue, be careful.

'I thought you were in the business of making those things, not unmaking them?' the older woman commented, pointing with her too sharp knife at a now headless clown.

'They are Mrs Morris's batch. She uses her own form of galloping horse stitch, and has no idea that she should attempt to match the sewing thread to the fabric. I end up unpicking every one she does and consider myself lucky that she does so few.'

'Tell her. This is double handling, girl.' Miss Moreland was not one to mince words. She had attempted to pound some basic concepts into Mildred Morris's head fifty-odd years ago, and failed.

'I don't mind really. They look so lopsided and pathetic, I like giving them a second chance at life. To be quite truthful, I wish I had time to assemble them all myself. See this one.' She held up a doll wearing a strange twisted smile. 'See its neck. It is quite screwed, but when he is unpicked and restitched, he will have a sweet wry smile. I particularly like this fellow's face.' The small head freed, she took up a needle and began making her own small stitches. 'Since we started accepting orders, we have had to accept all offers of help, and also become more professional with our finish,' she said.

Stella's knack with wool and embroidery had snowballed. The

guild received regular orders from craft shops around the state, and from two in Victoria.

'Your hand is shaking like a leaf in the wind, girl.'

'The silly thing. It was fairly trembling when I told Mrs Carter that we were overstocked with peanut pillows, and could not continue to supply filling.'

'Mmmm.' Miss Moreland murmured, not interested in Mrs Carter or her peanuts. 'One thing I always noticed about you, girl, was your nerves of steel. No matter what happened, you handled it. You nursed your mother for years and never let it take the smile from your eyes. You baby that bombastic father of yours, who anyone else would have brained forty years ago, but you still managed to go about the town with a smile for everyone. It's gone, girl, and though you might still flash your teeth regularly, there is no smile in your eyes.'

'Must be old age. I sent Father off with three of Mrs Carter's peanut pillows. Let us hope that they give him some comfort on the plane.'

'Stop trying to change the subject. What happened to you?'

'Happened?'

'What has happened to your eyes?'

'Nothing.'

'I don't believe you, girl.'

'I'm fine. Really.'

'You're far from fine. Anyone bar a fool could see it. Are you worrying about your father?'

Stella grasped at that straw. She nodded. 'Yes. Possibly. A little.'

'No. It's more than that. You've discovered fear. It's written all over your face.'

Stella flinched. She looked up to the eyes of her inquisitor, then away, back to her sewing. She couldn't tell her. Not now. 'I admit I am a little afraid of sleeping alone in the house. It's so cut off from the neighbours. And that darn hedge, it gives me the spooks when I come home at night. I've been asking Father to get the White boys to trim half a metre off it. I'm actually considering getting it done while he is away.'

Miss Moreland took a tomato from the refrigerator and tossed it from hand to hand, her eyes still studying her visitor. 'Fear is a demon,' she said. 'If you can slay your demon with young Whitey's chainsaw, then slay it, I say. It wouldn't cost much.' She turned her attention and knife to the tomato, slicing with cavalier strokes, missing her fingers by narrow millimetres with each cut. 'We are all born without fear. You only need to watch a daredevil child to see that. I always believed that one of the reasons we spinster women outlive our married sisters is because we are saved the lesson of fear.'

'You had a sister?'

'Married a mean wowser then died in self-defence thirty-odd years ago. I've got two nieces somewhere, but they took after their father. Haven't seen their prune faces since Cara's funeral.'

'I always wished I had brothers and sisters.'

'You should have had a brother. You were one of twins, you know.'

'Me? A twin? No.'

'You were. One of a pigeon pair. The boy died at birth.'

Stella shook her head. 'Good Lord. Why didn't they tell me? They never ... never once mentioned it. Why wouldn't Father tell me?'

'Not something he wanted to remember. I shouldn't have told you either. Me and my big mouth.'

'A brother. How different life may have been.'

Miss Moreland washed and shredded lettuce then turned again to her visitor. 'I always say, girl, you can choose your friends, but family and neighbours you get stuck with. I never missed family, not after Cara went. I never regretted not marrying. Oh, I considered it a few times, had a few flings, but I always shook the coots off when they started talking marriage. Maybe I was attracted to the wrong ones, like you.'

'Like me? Who?'

'Look at young Steven Smith. He's been after you for years, never looked seriously at any other girl in town, but you won't give him the time of day. You could do a lot worse than Steven.'

'Steve? He's only a – he's so much younger than I. And he certainly did have other girlfriends. Many. You old match-maker!'

'Just time-fill while he waited for you to get over Ronald.' Miss Moreland laughed and began apportioning shredded lettuce to plates.

Stella kept her head down. Was her feeling for Ron so obvious?

'My only regret is that I never bore a child. I would have liked to have had one, if only to see what sort of a botch I might have made at child-raising. If a husband hadn't been a pre-requisite in my day, then I might have bailed up some likely lad and sent poor Maidenville into a spin. Still I didn't learn the pain of childbirth, nor did I spend my life fearing for some tiny life I brought into the world. The more we love, the more we have to lose, girl.'

'Then perhaps I'm lucky I only have Father to worry about. He has been like an obstreperous infant these past two days. This morning he looked quite pale. I believe he is actually pet-rified of flying. You know, my dear, what never ceases to amaze me, is how those who profess total belief in the hereafter are the ones who seem to fear death the most.'

'Fear grows like a poisonous fungus in this town. It feeds this town. Half of its population are of pensionable age. Maidenville is no longer growing.'

'Yes. I noticed that little art supplies shop in Crane Street has closed down. Half the shops are empty down there.'

'The town is dying, and its people know that it's dying and they know that they're dying with it, and one day soon they're not going to wake up. It will be their own name in the obituary column. *Loved mother of Harry, loved granny of Debbie Lee.* They know it's coming, and that there's not a damn thing they can do about it, bar hope that everyone else goes before them. Maidenville. Ha. They ought to change its name to Senilityville.' Stella laughed.

'That's more like you, girl.'

'Perhaps we should hit the old sign with a spray pack one night.'

'I'll be in it, if you will.'

Again they laughed, then the older woman said, 'Why don't you get out?'

'I did think seriously about it a few ... a while back. But where would I go? My life is here – the only life I have is here in Maidenville, and I'm afraid I'm far too old to start again.'

'Old. You're only a pup.' Miss Moreland carried two plates to her small dining table, then came to stand before her guest, her legs planted well apart, the knife in her hand pointing. 'I don't know what it is that you're fearing, girl, but it's something big and black and it's eating you alive. Your skin looks like mud, and I guarantee you've dropped half a stone in three weeks.'

Stella placed her sewing down. She stood shaking the hair back from her face. 'Well, I'll make up for it today. I fear I'll eat you out of house and home, my dear,' she said. 'I could eat a horse.'

'Hungry are you, or just not in the mood for a lecture? Okay, I'll save it for later. Come and eat before it gets hot.'

They washed the dishes together then sat before the television keeping half an eye on a golf tournament. Miss Moreland had taken up a clown doll. 'He looks like he's running from his pursuer, running full-tilt ahead while looking back over his shoulder. Poor little clown. Which demon is on his tail, I wonder?' Stella reclaimed the doll. She began snipping with her small embroidering scissors. In silence the old woman watched her guest's hands, capable hands, not trembling now. 'I can't keep my mouth shut when I see that something is not right with you, girl. Wish I could sometimes, but I like, I respect you too much to turn a blind eye to your trouble.'

'I hope we can always feel free to say what is on our minds.'

'I'm too fond of saying what is on my mind – or so they tell me. The last of the big-mouthed Morelands my old dad used to call me.

'A definite advantage in your particular profession,' Stella said.

'Perhaps. We were always teachers, a natural genetic selection occurred over the generations as we tried to pound knowledge into uninterested heads. You know, I'm not a one for gossip, but that boy's hands, those nails bitten – no, pared nails, pared by a knife down to the quick. I was looking at them again this morning.'

'What boy?'

'Young Tom Spencer. Up at the supermarket.'

Stella sprang to her feet. 'A drink of water, I think. Would you like a drink?'

'Not now. You know, I've seen hands like those before. How old is Marilyn?'

'She's older than I. I started school at four and a half. Marilyn was six.'

'I thought so.'

'What is your devious head working on now?'

'Just some old gossip better left buried. Speaking of heads, give me one of those twisted dolls. How many have you got there?'

'Only this lot. The others have to be packed in their bags and tagged. I'm posting another two dozen off on Monday. Sydney ordered a dozen, would you believe, and we've got orders for four from three other shops. I sent off ten last week. I don't think we're going to be able to keep up the supply.'

'Fashion is fickle. They may find something new in six months.'

'Perhaps they will. Did you see our new tickets? Lyn Parker did them on John's computer.' She took a sheet of stick-on tickets from her bag and passed it to the older woman. 'They look quite professional, don't they?'

'You're only a bit of a girl still. Why don't you take the business away from the church guild, set up your own co-op. You and Bonny and Lyn. You're the workers. You could let in a couple of the other girls; go for it while they're hot; get yourself some independence, then get out. Go and see the world.'

'I couldn't take them away from the church. They've always been ... always belonged to the church.'

'The church? The church is rolling in money, made by the likes of you. It doesn't need it, but you do. Stick it in your pocket and let it buy you a holiday. Fly to China, and walk the Great Wall. See something. There's a wonderful world out there, girl. And more is the pity that I started looking at it too damned late. I'm too old to go gallivanting on my own any more. That's where a husband might have come in handy. You're not too old to find one, you know.'

Stella laughed. 'Perhaps I should place an advertisement in the local paper. "*Wanted, seasoned traveller, must have strong back, and be able to lift heavy cases. View matrimony.*"'

'Preferably rich,' Miss Moreland added.

Again they laughed.

'Maybe one day I'll fly away to some place,' Stella said. 'I planned to, but there was always something to keep me here – some reason why I had to put it off for a week, or a month, or a year. Father is almost eighty-six. I could never leave him now.'

'He left you fast enough. How old are you?'

'Forty-four last January.'

'Menopause? Is that what's troubling you?'

Stella's chin lifted. 'No. No, it certainly is not. Not at all.'

'Haven't found a lump in your breast, have you, and you're too modest to go and see old Parsons about it?' Her eyes refused to leave her visitor's, seeking a truth in those eyes she could not glean from the smiling mouth.

Stella shook her head, but kept it low.

'No. You're no damn fool, and the look I see in your eye when you think I'm not watching isn't the common garden variety fear. It's terror, girl. When you're free to think, you let some personal demon back into your head.'

'There are no demons in this flat, just Mrs Morris's dear twisted clowns.'

'I didn't teach fifty years of students without learning something about life, something about people. Oh, you might shake your head at me, Miss, but it's in your eyes. Even when you laugh they're like lost marbles in lightless pits.'

Stella stood. Too close to breaking now, she turned her eyes to the window, clenching her teeth and each muscle in her jaw, as she had as a child, tightening her aching face against tears threatening to spill. It would be so easy to weep in this woman's arms and gain comfort there. But she had learned long ago that there was little value to be gained from tears.

'Can we please change the subject, Miss Moreland? I promise you that whatever may be troubling me will not be the better for an airing. This little flat, and you, have for years been my escape, my sanctuary. I love to come here. I love to be with you. Don't drive me back to that . . . that mausoleum today. At the moment I have no answers for you.'

'If you're afraid of staying by yourself, then come and camp out on my couch, girl. There are worse beds.'

'I mightn't like the house, but I'm not afraid of it. Nor do I . . . do I fear my own company.' She turned to face the old woman. 'I have never run from fear, Miss Moreland, never shown weakness, and I don't intend to start now. I will be fine. If I am left to work it out for myself, I will get on top of whatever is troubling me and I will be fine again, my dear.'

'Sometimes it's safer to run, girl.' Those old knowing eyes watched her guest, saw the tension on her face, and cursed the town anew. What was there in this town – who was there in this town capable of – ?

She had been acting strangely for weeks. There was some gossip about the Spencers. Was that it? Were she and Ron having an overdue affair? That might explain her coldness to him and the boy in public. The guilt of it would eat her alive.

'Are you having a fling with one of our fine upstanding citizens?' she asked.

'Miss Moreland! You do have a truly wicked mind.'

'I'll get to the bottom of it, girl, or my name isn't what it is.'

'Thank you for caring. And I do know you care, my dear, and I promise you that when I have an affair you will be the first to know. I also promise you that if I find I'm not sleeping well while Father is away, then I'll be pleased to use your couch.' Stella walked back to her clowns, picked one up. 'Look at this poor mite. I do wish Mrs Morris could content herself with stuffing the toys. She's spilled her coffee on its collar. I'll have to give it another one if I can find some lace to match.'

'Toss it over. You get on with your packaging.'

Miss Moreland sat unpicking the small collar while watching the hands of her younger friend, checking and tidying each doll, then the plastic bag held open with two palms, she slid the clown neatly in, using her thumbs. One twist, and a small sticky label sealed the plastic bag.

Made for you in Maidenville, Australia, from Australian wool.

She'd said enough on the subject. 'Quaint things. Where did you get the pattern?'

'It evolved. I play. I like to create. Always have. I used to write, as you may remember, and lately I have felt the desire to try it again. Finding the time to start is holding me back.'

'No money in it, unless you write a best-seller. More money in these. They're very professional. Why don't you start your co-op?'

'You have a money fixation today – and don't imagine for

one moment that I haven't considered packing up my clowns and running. But, would you believe, I badgered Father into allowing me to apply for a credit card a few weeks before he left. Always believing I had a small balance, from when mother died, I now find I don't need the money from the clowns, Miss Moreland. I am, by Maidenville standards, a reasonably wealthy woman.' She slid another clown into a plastic bag, sealed it and tucked it in the carton. 'It also appears, by the interest payments that are paid into my passbook, that I have considerable investments, even some shares. I asked Father – asked him why he had kept me ignorant of my money. He said – ' she smiled as she continued. 'He said it was his fear that I may be pursued by a gold digger. So it looks like we can delete the "preferably rich" from our newspaper advertisement.'

'Your mother inherited the lot when old Randall died. He owned half of Maidenville at one time.'

'I never knew my grandfather.'

'Didn't miss much. He and Cutter-Nash were thick as thieves. Devils both of them – and you can thank God it wasn't Cutter-Nash who brought you into the world, or you would have gone the way of your twin.'

'Not much loss,' she said, then forced a smile. 'Father always said he would have been a childless widower if not for Doctor Parsons. Was Cutter-Nash as bad as he is painted, or has his reputation been expanded upon – like poor Mrs Macy's?'

'Dora Macy married Willy on the Saturday, and left him the following Friday.' Miss Moreland laughed. 'I never could understand how she stuck it out for a week.' She stood and walked to a modern wall unit, where she picked up an aged photograph album. She opened it, stood turning pages until she found the one she was after. 'That's Cutter-Nash. He was twelve years older than I. There was a time I considered marrying him. Old memories that bless and burn, eh?'

'What a fine looking man, Miss Moreland.'

'He was that – apart from his eyes. Jaguar eyes. Always on

the hunt for prey, and those – ' She cut her sentence short.

'So?'

'So you can multiply all you have heard about him, by ten, then double it. Someone told him when he was a youth that he had surgeon's hands – but he had the heart of a butcher, and about as much skill. I'll tell you something that might shock the frilly knickers off you, and I've never told another living soul. He aborted our baby when I was just seventeen.'

'My dear!'

'Shocked your pure little heart now, haven't I?'

'I believe I have become immune to shock lately. No. No. I didn't think ... I mean, in those days. I didn't know they did abortions back then, and certainly not in Maidenville.'

'He did plenty, and there were plenty more of his own that he missed. I can walk the streets of Maidenville today and pick his grandchildren almost as easily as I can pick Mick Murphy's.'

'He does look a little familiar.'

'Yes.' Miss Moreland turned a page quickly. 'There you go. That's me at seventeen. Wasn't I a Miss Modern?'

'What a beautiful girl you were,' Stella looked at her old friend. 'And what a terrible waste that your own child, that a part of such a very special person, was lost.'

'And a part of him that the world is better off without.' Miss Moreland pointed to another photograph. 'That's your grandfather. They were an evil pair, old Randy De Vere and Cutter-Nash. I could tell you some stories about your grandfather that would make your hair stand up on end.'

Head to one side, Stella waited for more, but the album was closed with a snap, put away.

'Suffice to say, you can blame him for what your mother was, but what use raking up the past. Let the dead keep their secrets, I say. Spend old Randy's money, girl. That's the only worthwhile legacy he left you.'

'Money gives freedom, offers choices. It's a strange feeling though. It is there, but not much use to me unless I spend it.

Perhaps if I had a companion to travel with, I may catch a plane to some place.'

'Maybe we'll fly off together, girl. What does it matter if I die here or in some paddy field a few thousand kilometres away? As long as I die with my shoes on, and I get to wear my red dress at my funeral.'

'I believe I may badger you into putting your money where your mouth is – when Father returns. Oh, and speaking of Father. He has arranged for Mr White to lead the congregation tomorrow. We couldn't get a replacement minister on such short notice. I'll pick you up at the usual time.'

'Percy psalm-singing White? God help us all. You know his father would roll over in his grave if he knew Percy was standing up in the Anglican pulpit. Old Red White was a dyed-in-the-wool communist. He courted me for a while, you know. I was quite fond of Red, but my father didn't like his politics. Such is life, girl. Such is life.'

all tuckered out

'I told you to stay away from her!' Marilyn Spencer stood over her husband's bed, her fists clenched, her face red, her eyes flashing green fire.

'I hardly said two words to Stella. I was talking to Bonny.'

'You give each other looks, and I can hear her brain, hear her thinking. "Can he still be fond of Marilyn? Dear me, how has she allowed herself to go to fat. How terrible for poor dear Ronald." The skinny old maid bitch, with her bloody lovesick eyes.'

'I carried their shopping out to the car – '

'And opened the car door for her. And held it. You don't need to speak to her! I see the way you look at her when you think I'm not watching. Bloody hangdog cur of a man – you haven't got the guts of a louse, you haven't. The only reason you still play the organ in church is so you can hide behind it and look at her, smile at her behind my back.'

'Then join the choir and you can sit up there and watch me.'

'Oh, no. I can't sing as well as Stella. You'd just make comparisons. You always have. How was she in bed, anyway?' Ron rolled to his side, offering his back to her abuse. '"Stella was always clever with her hands. Stella was always creative." I bet she was!'

'I've had enough of your stupidity. I'm tired. I've been on my feet since seven this morning and I'll be on them again in six hours. Go to bed.'

'You can't even touch me any more. You won't even share my bloody room.'

He rose up on his elbow. 'And who decided they wanted me out here, eh? Who told me to get the hell out of my own room?' His voice rose now, matching hers. 'I'm sick of your jealousy, Marilyn. You get in one of your moods and you try to take it out on her.'

'Now you're defending her.'

'I'm not defending her. But what has she ever done to you?'

'What's she ever done to me? What's she ever done to me? She ruined my bloody life. I never had a chance with you. She was in our bed on our honeymoon. And your mother. "Stella is such a gentle, well raised girl. Stella is this. Stella is that. Stella's father is a minister, you know. Poor Marilyn's hung himself. Not a very stable background."'

'Take a pill. You get yourself wound up and you don't know what you're saying, and Mum never ran you down. She did a lot for you.'

'Bullshit she did. "Poor Ronald, she can't even give him a child." I heard her. I heard her with my own ears. "Stella would have made him a wonderful wife. She's so good with children." That bloody old maid bitch! And when I finally had a baby, she tried to take him away from me.'

'That's a lie, and you know it. You were always asking her to take him, and she never said no.'

'Never said no. Didn't say no to you either, did she, you liar?'

'Don't judge everyone by yourself, and she's been a second mother to Tommy, and a good friend to you. You couldn't have coped without her when Tommy was small.'

'I had to work.'

'You didn't have to work. I wanted to put a junior on when Dad died – '

'So you could feel her up in the storeroom.'

'You're sick, Marilyn. You need help.'

'And you're not a bloody man's bootlace. I never had a husband. I tied myself to a bloody lovesick worm. She had you. She's had you all our married life – '

'I've never touched her.'

'Don't you give me that shit. We all knew you were doing it.'

'Oh, Christ. I want a divorce.'

'Divorce? So you can go to her and cry on her shoulder. I'm not divorcing you, you bastard. You're stuck with me until the day you die.'

'That's your decision. I hope it makes you happy. Now get out of my room – '

Thomas's window was only a metre from the sleep-out louvres, and they were open tonight; he'd been getting an earful for hours. It got boring after a while. Anyway, he had his own problems.

Parsons had given Kelly a prescription for the pill, but her old man wouldn't let her take it – or so she said. Now she was in the pudding club again, and blaming him for it because he didn't use a condom. All the others had used a condom, so it had to be his, or so she'd said today after school.

'It's cool,' he'd said. 'So get another abortion.'

The trouble was, she didn't want an abortion. She wanted him to nick off to Sydney with her and play mummies and daddies in some hole with a kid that could have belonged to any one of two dozen. Maybe he might have taken up the offer a few months back. Got out of town, gone on the dole, but he had better options now. Bigger fish to fry. Maidenville by night was full of opportunities with old bull-moose Templeton gone.

It was after one when the noise in the sleep-out settled down, but he couldn't sleep. Around two he got out of bed and took a couple of the pills his old lady had left on the kitchen table, and he downed them with a half a glass of whisky. He was used to beer and her pills, but mixing them with his old man's whisky made his head buzz and his muscles feel like they were made of unravelling silk.

He needed space – empty space – so he got on his bike and rode around town, feeling his muscles sort of smooth out, knit up, slip into overdrive.

'She's cool man. She's cool.' Everything was cool now. Even the town clock doing it's Dong, Dong, Dong, sounded cool. 'The lonely death knoll on the hill that never was. Dong. Dong. Dong. Maidenville swallowed up by the earth, but still the clock dongs on. It's a great donger.'

He laughed as he pedalled on, swerving from side to side on the empty road. He was on a high now, hyped up, his bones trying to break out of his skin, jumping around like the Davis's pup that he and Kelly had drowned down at the river.

Stupid little mongrel, it had followed them up the street one night, let them pick it up. They tied it into a plastic garbage bag and threw it in the river, and watched it try to run free while the water crept up. It was still running when the bag disappeared around the bend. Tonight he knew how it felt. Like his bones were locked in some place, trying to run, cut loose, but there was a bag stopping their escape.

When he got to Stell's gates, he found them wide open. 'Maybe she's expecting me,' he said. 'Been on her own for nearly a week now. Never disappoint the ladies, Thomas.' He laughed, choking on it, trying to hold it in. Keeping close to the shadows, he dismounted and leaned the bike against the open gate before creeping through the tall shrubs to the shed.

The doors were shut. Her doors had never been shut against him. He liked that shed, liked poking around in it, finding stuff that you never saw anywhere else. 'Old bitch,' he said, trying the side door, wanting to kick it in, but knowing if he did, it would set every dog in the neighbourhood barking.

'Stupid old maid bitch. You think locked doors can keep me out if I want to get in. You stupid old bitch. You can't keep me out if I want in. No-one can.'

A part of the shadows, he crept around to the back of the house, feeling like a silky black Indian stalking his prey. The wire door wheezed open, and he reached for the doorknob, turned it.

Nothing.

He turned it again, pushed against the door. 'Locked up like Fort Knox. Who do you think you are?' he snarled.

His pen-light drawing a pale line on the gravel, he followed it up the side path to the twin glass lounge room doors. They were made up of small square panes. One door had a snib and bolt at the top, with the other one locked to it by a key. That key was always in the lock. He knew this house, knew it well. Old Stell used to watch the kids' shows on television with him in this room. The dark room, he'd called it when he was a kid.

'Can we go in the dark room, Aunty Stell?'

Wilson's trees next door stole all the light, even in the day time; at night it was a black hole. The trees, mainly gums, were creaking and moaning tonight, shedding their leaves in the wind. It was a good night to be out. No-one would expect anyone to be out. There was the smell of fire on the wind too. Some place was burning.

He stood in the space between fence and wall, and he sniffed at the air. Everything was cool tonight. Everything was new, cool – even the moaning of the trees. They sounded like the souls of all the people old Templeton had buried; an army of souls coming back to get him. But he wasn't here, was he? He was in Africa. Thomas gave a ghostly moan that ended in a giggle. He tried the door, knowing it would be locked, but also knowing that this would be the best side of the house for a break-in. With the end of his torch he tapped the glass, gently. Just one good tap would knock out a pane, and he could reach in and turn the key.

She'd be in bed, and she'd have her bra off, and maybe she'd have her knickers off, and he'd just peel back her nightie and –

'Coming ready or not, Aunty Stell,' he whispered, but he couldn't get up the nerve to tap that glass.

He rubbed at his groin with the pen-light. Rubbed slow. Nothing was happening. Maybe it was scared she might tell this time. But she didn't before, so why should she this time? He unzipped his fly and his hand worked hard on unresponsive flesh. He tried encouraging it with his fantasy of old Stell's silky tongue. It was all tuckered out and he wasn't in the mood anyway.

Maybe it was the pills and the booze, he thought, but he liked the pills and the booze, liked the way it made him see things from a different angle.

'You'll save, Aunty Stell. I got two more weeks,' he said, gliding back to the cypress hedge where he picked up his bike, wishing he'd nicked a spray pack from the supermarket. Paint her hedge. Paint it yellow. Paint her drive yellow.

'Just follow the yellow brick road.'

He was giggling, looking at the hedge and planning his artwork when the pedal of his bike caught on the leg of his jeans. His reflexes were slow tonight. He tripped, fell against the hedge, and the bike fell on top of him. The outside growth looked green and soft enough, but behind it, the branches were sharp. They scratched his face, gouged at his shoulder.

And the silky Indian was gone, and Maidenville looked like shit again. He scrambled to his feet. His bike weighed nothing, and he tossed it to the gutter, then he kicked the hedge, angry at that which had dared to reach out to him, hurt him, to rip his new shirt, make his shoulder bleed. He kicked the open gate, then he went after his bike and he kicked it too, threw it at the hedge.

'Fucking bastard. Fucking bloody hedge.' His arm was bleeding. He sucked on it, spitting blood as he hiked back to the dark side of the Templeton house, where he stood wanting to smash the door. Just get a brick and toss it through. Just get a knife and cut her, make her bleed too. But he didn't have a knife, only his bloody torch.

Angry, breathing fast now, he peered over the paling fence into Wilson's yard.

Wilson didn't used to have a dog, but he whistled softly just in case. Waited. No barking, no scuttling in the long grass. Easing himself up, he scrambled over the fence, prowling through the tangle of grass and overgrown creepers until he stumbled on an open garage.

It was a treasure trove. Thomas found exactly what he needed ... exactly what he was looking for.

the hedge fire

Dream and reality had intersected somewhere along the line. Stella heard the fire siren, but in her dream it came from an airfield, perhaps one she had seen in an old war film on television. The voices of men penetrated her dream; officers, shouting, giving orders. Then came the knocking. Persistent. And awareness of strange light. Flashing light. Still close to her dream she sat upright, her eyes scanning familiar walls.

In the week since her father had left, she had slept badly, and last evening, Friday evening, it had taken her hours to fall asleep. At midnight, she swallowed two Aspros – not for a headache, but in the hope of gaining some much needed rest. Deep sleep had taken her then, carried her away to that airfield and the burning plane she knew was her father's.

She slid from her bed and ran down the passage to her father's room. There was a wall of flame outside his window. The cypress hedge was burning; flames shooting metres into the sky dwarfed the men in her drive.

'Stell. Are you in there, Stell?'

She pushed the window high and called down to the one knocking at her front door.

It was Chris Scott, head of the voluntary fire brigade. He looked up, saw her there. 'We're letting her go. Not much use saving a blackened skeleton. Some young hooligan's been getting ideas from his city friends.'

'I'm coming down, Chris.'

'Better shut your windows or you'll end up with a house full of smoke.'

The window closed, snibbed, she dressed quickly, and hurried downstairs and out through the front door.

'Is the shed safe from sparks? It's old wood. Do you think I should move Father's Packard out?'

'It's safe as houses. We got onto it early.'

'Who reported it?'

'Old Wilson. Said he got up to go to the loo, and saw the flames. Rang the brigade. But it's no bloody accident. Someone's doused the length of it with petrol. You could smell it when we got here. We found the can too, and Jennison reckons it's the one old Wilson gets his motor-mower juice in. I wouldn't put it past the old coot to have done it himself. Taken the opportunity to get in a hit below the belt while the minister is away.'

'No. No. He wouldn't do that. He and Father mightn't be on the best of terms, but he is no firebug. Thank goodness he saw it.' She stood well back from the wall of fire, waving to a group of dressing-gown clad neighbours who were enjoying the pre-dawn drama from the opposite side of the paling fence.

The hedge was as old as the house. Stella had known for years that the dead wood in the interior would go up like a bonfire with the least provocation.

By dawn only the embers were left. The men went in with axes then, felling the last of the standing wood, knocking over charred gateposts, and what remained of the aged wooden gate. As the fire truck drove away, the sun came up to peer between

Mr Wilson's forest of trees, and for the first time in her forty-four years of life, Stella could watch a vehicle drive beyond the hedge.

She stood on when the fire men had gone, stood immobile, watching the weak light grow stronger. She could see the post office on the corner, and the town clock, and the two church steeples. The sun was catching them, lighting sun fires on steel. It lit the Catholic steeple first, then touched its Anglican neighbour.

'My God,' she breathed.

Light glowed like fire on the swimming pool across the way, and it painted the side wall of Jennison's service station. She could see the second floor of the new high school building. Then the cars began, cars full of people off to somewhere, but they slowed as they drove by, to peer in, to see what had been hidden behind the hedge, just as Stella was peering out.

To her, it was like looking at a scene through some formerly unknown window, some wide window that looked out from a secret room, to which she had only now found the key. She had been locked out of that room, its window hidden from her all the days of her life.

'I wanted that hedge gone. For years I have planned to cut it back. Now it is gone.'

She didn't return to bed, but continued the work of the firemen, raking up, encouraging the smouldering trunks to burn away by feeding the fire with smaller branches and garden refuse.

Many walkers stopped to stare, or speak. Miss Moreland walked over at ten. She found a different Stella, a girl with long wild hair and black hands; a smudge-faced, laughing Stella. They drank tea on the front porch, then together they toured the garden, propping up damaged plants, removing those too far gone to save, and just looking at the new vista while Stella spoke of a picket fence.

'Go and have a look at your garden from across the road, girl, then decide if you dare to lock it away again. There is little enough beauty in fair Maidenville.'

'I believe I am a little afraid of my new freedom – like a prisoner who has served her time and has now been tossed out on the street, unprepared. Perhaps I've become institutionalised, my dear.'

'Well, in my book, you've overpaid your debt to society. Both gate and hedge are ash, and you are free, girl, and I'm here to see you get used to it fast. Consider me your parole officer. Now if you've got a sharp pair of scissors, I'm going to cut a few inches off that hair. And if I ever see it pinned up in a bun again, you'll go back into solitary.'

Stella showered all the ash away before Miss Moreland took up the scissors.

So soothing, those old hands combing her hair, touching, cutting. Stella relaxed, left the fate of her curls to the cavalier scissors, and when it was done and the scissors placed down, she felt the loss of those gentle old hands, if not of her hair. There was so much she wanted to say, wished she could say, but like her father, she was uncomfortable with personal issues.

'Thank you, my dear. I believe you just saved Father thirty-odd dollars. I have been intending to have it cut these past weeks, but couldn't raise the necessary incentive.' It wasn't enough. It wasn't what she wanted to say. 'Thank you too for your care, and support, and for your friendship.' But it still wasn't enough, so she took the old hands in her own, and she kissed them.

'Kissing, now is it? You'd better cut that out or you'll have this town calling us a pair of raving lesbians, girl,' the old lady said, but she left her lipstick smudge on Stella's cheek.

At one they drove to the coffee shop for a light lunch. Later, with the money Martin had left on the dresser, they bought a new letterbox from Steve Smith, and a bag of pre-mixed cement so they might set it in the ground.

All that remained of the old gatepost was the rotted wood

beneath the earth. A small crowbar and a trowel removed it. The flashy red letterbox was put in its place and held upright by Miss Moreland while Stella tamped the earth around it, then poured in the mixed cement. By three it stood beside the drive, waiting open-mouthed for some long-banned junk mail.

The friends washed their hands and drove again to the centre for a well earned coffee, then for an hour they walked the long street, peering into shop windows and wandering into stores.

The shoe shop in Main Street was closing down. They had a bargain table out front and Stella picked up a pair of white sandals with five centimetre heels. 'Only twenty dollars, marked down from sixty-nine.'

'Try them on, girl.'

They felt right, made to order, made for narrow feet that had once looked fine in strappy sandals, for feet that had once loved to dance all night at church socials.

'I love them,' she said, and she paid for them with her credit card, just for fun.

They walked next door to the chemists. Miss Moreland wanted a new lipstick. She chose two, then chose a matching blusher and a brown eyebrow pencil, a light foundation, but when the assistant handed her the parcel, she removed the brighter lipstick and handed the parcel to Stella.

'That is not my style, Miss Moreland.'

'Then it ought to be. Take it, girl. It matches your new shoes.'

'It cost you a fortune!'

'Money is only as good as what it will buy. Take it! Your parole officer has spoken.'

Stella smiled. 'Oh, well – if it will save me from another forty years in solitary.'

In the middle of Main Street, they laughed. It was very un-Stella. People turned to stare at her, so she hid in the electrical goods store. Miss Moreland found a rose pink lightshade there that she thought might add a bit of life to the lamp in the minister's lounge room. Laughing still, they bought it.

Money was fun. Spending it was euphoric.

They wandered to the whitegoods department, glancing at microwaves, then at the stoves.

'That's the same as the one Bonny bought. It has a fan-forced oven, and it cooks so evenly.'

'That's what you need, girl. So buy it.'

'Heavens no. The old one is . . . is still functional.'

'You sound like your father.'

Stella ran her hand over the smooth white surface, allowing it to rest there. 'It would probably takes weeks to install it. I'd want to put it in the chimney. Get rid of the old wood stove – '

'Ask him.'

'No. Father would have a fit.'

'But he's not here. Be a devil. No harm in asking.'

Then the salesman was at their side and desperate for business. He kept dropping the price until it began to sound like a bargain, too good to miss out on, and somewhere along the line the decision to buy had been taken out of her hands. The only problem now appeared to be the installation.

'We'll do it Monday. Rip out the old stove. Stick an exhaust fan in the chimney.'

'Monday? You mean next Monday?'

'The one that comes after Sunday, girl. Sold,' Miss Moreland said, and in a smiling daze Stella followed her friend to the department store.

They looked at jackets, browsed amongst the hats. Miss Moreland bought a cheeky thing, as red as sin. 'It'll match my funeral dress,' she said.

They were laughing as they loaded their last purchases into the car boot, and when they were ready to leave, they didn't want to leave. This had been a day like none before. If this was freedom, Stella loved it and she wanted more.

'Are you tired, my dear?'

'Tired? Me? Why should I be tired?' Miss Moreland scoffed.

'Then let's try the coffee shop's special. They've got savoury pancake filled with avocado and prawns. My shout. Or my bankcard's. Save us cooking dinner.'

They parted at seven-fifty at Miss Moreland's front door.

'I won't be going to church tomorrow. That crazy old Willy Macy is leading the service. Percy's psalm-singing I'll tolerate, but I refuse point-blank to sit through Willy Macy's twaddle.'

'Do I have my parole officer's permission to stay away too?'

'You set one foot inside that door and I'll see you go down for life.'

'If you put it that way.'

'Have you heard from your father?'

'Nothing. Still it's only a week since he left Maidenville. Then the flight out of Sydney was not until Sunday afternoon, so I dare say they wouldn't have arrived in Africa until the Monday. He would have been exhausted. Lord, I hope he is up to this trip.'

'He's tough as old boots. They made us to last in the old days.'

'I thought he might give me a call, let me know he had arrived, but he's more likely to send a postcard. Bonny was saying at the meeting on Thursday that it takes over a week to send a card from America. When her mother flew over for John's wedding, Bonny said she was back before her postcards.'

'Don't you go worrying about him. Thanks for lunch and dinner, girl. We'll have to do it again. I'll come around and have a look at your stove on Monday.'

'He said it could take two days.'

'Then I'll see it on Tuesday. Enjoy your freedom, girl.'

the birds

Mr Wilson never went to church, and he'd found himself a tree cutter who didn't mind working Sunday. At seven-thirty, a chainsaw began its roar outside Stella's lounge room, and limbs began falling.

She took her breakfast upstairs to her father's study. Its window looked down on Wilson's property, and from her seat at her father's desk she could watch the worker, at home in the trees, his chainsaw, when not in use, dangling from his belt on a long rope.

He is in his natural element, she thought. A young Tarzan. He worked with a safety belt, snibbing it to a limb below, before beginning to cut the limb above. One hand above the cut, he sawed through, or almost through the branch, then pushed it from him to crash to the earth below.

She stared like a child, afraid for the worker, but enthralled by his lack of fear. There was no-one to comment, no-one around to ask if God might deem it a suitable occupation for a woman of her maturity, no-one to care if she sat at the window for one hour or three, staring at the agility of the worker, who looked more primate than man, swinging from limb to limb, from tree to tree.

He saw her there in the late morning and he waved to her, then mouth grimacing, he mimed the cutting off of old Wilson's head. The old man was standing well back, bellowing instructions that couldn't compete with the chainsaw.

Stella laughed, reading the worker's hand signals clearly, and laughing at the final mimed punt kick of an imaginary head. She couldn't recognise the worker beneath his cap and ear muffs, but he looked like one of Percy White's boys. Probably the youngest, she decided. Parsimonious Percy had been the town woodman for years. He had handed the business over to his sons.

She placed her two hands to her ears, miming earmuffs. The worker smiled, and held up a thumb. 'Good.'

She repeated the sign. 'Good.'

The two, high above the ground and Mr Wilson, shared a private joke, laughing at the self-important little man down below.

'Silly woman,' she castigated herself. 'You're acting like a child this morning,' she said. 'He must think you quite moronic.' But it was not her opinion, only the opinion of her conditioning, and her inner voice replied. What rubbish. He likes the fact that you are watching him. He is proud of his skill, his ability in the trees. And rightly so, he's an artist of sorts. By watching him work you are admiring his art no less than you might admire the skilled paintbrush of an artist.

'Yes,' Stella agreed, and she sat on. 'Perhaps I should consider the purchase of earmuffs. They may save me from unwanted advice when I am trying to weed along the fence.' Mr Wilson was over-generous with his doubtful wisdom; one of the few areas of garden Stella neglected was beside Wilson's fence.

'Or perhaps I'll get one of those radio things with earphones, like Bonny's boys always seem to have attached to their heads.

I'll buy myself one. Yes. On Monday I'll march into the electrical shop, pay for my stove and ask to see their range of radios ... and I might look at their cordless phones while I'm about it. Have one installed in here, in the study. It would save Father's poor old legs.'

She went off to collect her knitting. It appeared that the White boy intended felling her neighbour's entire forest. It could be a long and noisy day, if an interesting one. But she should keep her hands busy while she watched the timber fall.

The Wilsons had lived next door since before her birth. They had planted, or allowed nature to plant, a miniature forest in their backyard. The trees were old. Dead branches fell at will, and frequently over the minister's fence. Mr Wilson had long been a thorn in the side of her father. A loud little man, he called himself C of E, but he hadn't been inside a church since his wedding day fifty years ago, and he'd told Martin he didn't intend seeing the inside of a bloody church again until they carried him in, feet first.

Martin had sworn he wouldn't bury him.

'I've got ten years on you, you cantankerous old coot. You won't get the bloody chance.' Wilson always got the final word.

The war had been raging for most of Stella's life, and she could understand her father's attitude towards him and his trees. The forest had annoyed her. Their lounge room saw no sunlight at all, and falling leaves constantly blocked the spouting. Martin was too old and heavy to climb these days, so the ladder work fell to Stella; however, the forest annoyance had recently become danger. A huge branch had come crashing down while Mrs Wilson had been hanging out the washing. Her clothesline, an old but solid contrivance, saved her from certain injury.

But I doubt it was your near miss that did the trick, Mrs Wilson, Stella thought. More likely my hedge fire, and fear of the local firebug. Whatever it was that encouraged her neighbour into parting with his dying forest, it could only be looked on as a plus. He may even get around to mowing his grass.

I'll have so much more light in the backyard; although it is beginning to look quite bare. Won't Father be in for a dreadful shock when he returns? No forest beside him, and no hedge before him. While he is not here to hold it back, the outside world is encroaching on his own secret little realm.

'My goodness,' she said. 'Perhaps I should take up my pen again. *His Secret World*, by Lea S. Temple.' She could see it, just as she had in her youth. The idea always came with a cluster of words, then imagination began filling in the spaces.

Deranged wife stalking the dark rooms at night with a kitchen knife. Minister screaming into the telephone in the wee small hours of the morning. The child . . . the small child hiding in the dark garden . . .

'Stop this nonsense,' she said. 'This is a childish habit you have long put behind you. Stop this nonsense now.'

It was late afternoon when she saw the birds gathering outside her window. Their trees were gone, their nests, their perches now a pile of timber in Wilson's backyard.

'Poor birds,' she whispered. 'I had given no thought to my birds.' Each time she looked outside there appeared to be more gathering. The branches were thick with birds. Strange. Like heavy fruit weighing down the boughs of the apple tree. Feathered fruit.

A shiver travelled down her spine. She thought of a picture show she'd been to with Ron. The birds gathering, attacking.

His secret world.

Again the words played in her mind. The scene was coming, the words spilling, wanting to spill to paper, but this would be no love story, no Mills and Boon.

The house loomed like a dark entity behind the hedge. Birds gathered, their small beaks blood-flecked –

Again she shook her head.

How odd, she thought. There are hundreds of birds. I hadn't realised that Mr Wilson's trees would have given home to so many. But of course. Of course they must have. Where else have my birds lived? Oh, you poor dears. Where will you sleep tonight?

So many different varieties. She walked across to her own room and looked at her jacaranda trees. Birds by the score were perched there and more kept coming. As they flew in from their day of play and feeding, they circled and called, then came to jostle for position on the boughs, and to glare at her window with their wide accusing eyes.

'Some portent of doom ... the gathering of birds,' she said. 'Starlings? Sparrows? Didn't I read somewhere that they are the harbingers of death?'

Sparrows pecking at the window, trying to get in. The child, hammering at the window, trying to get out. Daddy. Daddy. Daddy.

Silly woman. Your imagination is running away with you. And why not? Why not indeed? Wasn't it always a better world?

Slowly she returned to the study, her fingers running through her hair. Freedom. She liked the bounce of her neck-length bob. Where Miss Moreland's scissors had not cut so straight, the curls had sprung up to conceal the mistakes.

'Samson in reverse,' she said. 'My imagination stolen by my hairpins.' Her hand reached out for paper. She shrugged, inserted it into the old typewriter and she began.

Time went away to that other place.

So carefully she removed the white stockings and the pintucked frock. Now her small hands folded them, then placed them carefully on the chair. She felt cool in her pretty white briefs, her legs delightfully bared to the breeze. But shouldn't she remove her white briefs too? Mustn't get them dirty. Dirty was bad.

The oak was a grand climbing tree, and she a small bare monkey, free in her natural element. Green leaves rustled around her like the pages in her favourite book, and the birds, initially afraid, lost their fear of this small intruder. Soon they went about their business of love and courtship. The child sighed too deeply for one of her tender years. How she envied the birds their wings to fly.

Daddy said they flew south for the summer, flew to where it was cool. She liked cool. She flapped her small arms. 'I'm a birdy. I'm a birdy.'

The voice from below startled her. From her perch high in the branches, she looked down now at the greying hair, and at the mouth screaming its words.

'Dirty, filthy naked little slut. I'll show you naked. I'll show – '

The town clock and the fading light halted her fingers, but beside the typewriter were seven double-spaced text-filled pages. Where had they come from?

'Good Lord,' she said. 'Good Lord. Where have I been?'

the first of three

The Templeton house was not a good place to be come Monday morning April Fools' Day, and Stella was feeling in a young and foolish mood. The workmen had arrived in force at eight-thirty. She left them to it. For an hour she typed, then she dressed for town and walked to the bank, walked into the bank.

It was rather frightening, filling in that first withdrawal form, and she felt like a bank robber as she passed it to the teller, but when the green notes were handed to her, it seemed so little. It was soon gone anyway. She paid cash for the stove, then stayed on at the electrical store listening to the pros and cons of radios and headsets while fearfully eyeing a computer.

Would it be possible for a person of her years to learn the intricacies of those things?

At the same time, Mrs Morris and Mrs Murphy were seated in the doctor's surgery. They had delivered Young Mick Murphy there. Now they waited to taxi him home. Young Mick was sixty if he was a day, but until Old Mick, his father, died, he would remain, in name, forever young.

This morning, he looked older than his father, and the two

friends discussed the possibility that he might not live long enough to ever become plain Mick. They had the two best seats, right next to Sister's glass window, where armed with camouflage magazines they had settled in to do a little overdue research. From these seats they could glimpse Doctor Parsons when he walked his patients back to the waiting room after the consultation. They watched five patients walk in and walk out, and they made their own diagnoses.

Mrs Morris and Mrs Murphy could glean a lot of information from the expression on both doctor and patient's face – if they caught a glimpse of them in the hall before features were composed for the outside world. From these seats, they could eavesdrop too on the latecomers who presented themselves at the window, and they always got a close look at any emergency before the injured party was whisked out of sight behind the passage door.

Phone conversations could be, and were, frequently interpreted from Sister's one-sided monosyllables and verbal shorthand, and if the friends were sometimes a little off dead centre, then they sometimes hit the bull right in the eye.

They agreed that Sergeant Johnson looked like stroke material when he entered the surgery around eleven that Monday. He was sweating profusely and his face was red. In his rush to get to the office window, he pushed past old Jim Bryant, almost knocking his white walkingstick from his hand.

'Sorry, Jim,' he said, steadying the older man. 'Sorry about that. I have to see the Doc in a hurry. 'Scuse me, everyone. Can you get him out here now?' he said to Sister.

'Take a seat. He's with a patient.'

'It can't wait. It's Miss – ' He saw the town gossips leaning towards him and he turned his back, dropping his voice to a whisper.

'Oh, no,' Sister said.

The old gossips moved closer, their ears straining now as Sister dialled through to the doctor's room, speaking quietly into the mouthpiece, her hand guarding her words.

'It's Johnson. Yes. It's Miss – you know. Yes. I'd say so, by the look of him. Yes.'

Johnson pushed in front of Mrs Morris and took charge of the telephone. His head through the glass window of the office, he said, 'G'day, Doc. Yeah. It's me. Hate disturbing you like this but – yeah. Yeah. As bad as it gets, Doc. Worse. I need you. Need a clear head before I go bringing in the young bloke. He's city – yeah. Yeah. Yeah. You know. That's right. You know. Yeah. That's right. That's what I'm trying to say. Yeah. Much appreciated.'

Mrs Morris, grasped her neighbour's hand, their eyes on their respective magazines, widening with disbelief. Near rigid on their chairs they waited for more. But there was no more. They'd have to fill in the gaps, which they would do admirably.

Johnson put the phone down and Doctor Parsons came out, ushering Mrs Cooper before him.

'But what about me blood pressure, Doctor?' she said. 'You didn't take me blood pressure today.'

'If I had your blood pressure, Mrs Cooper, I'd be doing two laps around the block each morning, instead of wasting a busy doctor's time.' He turned to the watching faces, aware that if they didn't know what the emergency was by now, then Mrs Morris and Mrs Murphy would soon nose it out.

'Buzz off, the lot of you,' he said. 'Clear out ... except you, Jim Bryant. Sister'll call you a taxi, and I want you in it and up at the hospital today and no bloody argument about it. Got me?' Still scanning, his gaze settled on an anorexic expectant mother, and his finger pointed to her. 'You, Betty Miller. We'll start you on the drip this afternoon and get that elephant out of you before it eats you alive.' He looked around the crowded room, scanning it for illness he could recognise at fifty paces. His waiting room was full of those dying of boredom and lack of love, but he couldn't do much for them. Drama and love could not be doled out in a pill bottle. He picked up his straw hat, and with it pushed

the hair from his eyes as they came to rest on Young Mick
Murphy. He frowned.

'Young Mick. What are you doing in here? What's wrong
with you that a couple of beers won't put right?'

'I think I've broke a bone in my bum. Come off the back a
Spud's truck on the way home last night. Can't bloody walk two
bloody metres, and I'm supposed to be going pigging tonight.'

'You shouldn't a been on the back a Spud's bloody truck.
How did you get here?'

'Got a lift with Dave's new missus.'

'Then get a lift home with Dave's new missus and go to bed,
and stay in bed, and give your poor bloody pig dogs a break.
I'll call in sometime this afternoon. Now the rest of you clear
out. You're fitter than I am.'

There were several who wished to argue, but he walked out
on their arguments, nodded to Sergeant Johnson, then hurried
with him to the police car. Sister was left alone to take the flack,
but she was more than capable of clearing her waiting room.

'Did he say Miss Moreland, Sister?'

'Got wax in your ears, have you Mrs Morris? I'll clean them
for you if you like.'

'You'll do nothing of the sort.'

Mrs Morris was on her feet as Mrs Murphy whispered. 'He
definitely said Miss ... someone. Who else could it be? One of
the teachers?'

'No. He would have said it.' They were out the door, young
Mick bringing up a slow and painful rear.

'I don't know about you, but it sounds very fishy to me, Mrs
Murphy.'

'Old Mrs Thomson lives in the flat next door to Miss Moreland. It's about time we paid her a visit isn't it?'

'Oh, my word, yes. We'll get Mick home and pop in on her.
Poor old soul, she could probably do with a bit of cheering up.'

'She certainly could, Mrs Morris. Come along Mick. We
haven't got all day.'

high heels on concrete

There was someone in the house. The workmen had left for the tip while she was upstairs, typing. There had been such a racket going on in the kitchen, she hadn't noticed the noise until they left, but someone was now in her room.

There was a grating sound, a slow tap, tap, tap, of heels on concrete. Stella ran for the stairs, thinking to lock her back door, but that would lock her in with him.

She glanced at the chaos of her kitchen, then walked back to the stairs, peering up.

'Who is it?' she called. There was no reply. 'I know you are up there and I'm calling the police now.' She took two steps up, then listened. Again she heard the slow, dragging sound, then the tap, tap, tap.

The front door was locked. All the windows were snibbed, but the back door had been open since eight-thirty. He ... someone could have crept in while she was out this morning, crept by the workmen.

'He wouldn't dare. It is nothing. It is just the normal movement of an old house,' she said aloud, but remained unconvinced. It sounded like a body being dragged across the ceiling by someone in high-heel shoes.

It was the tenth day since her father had left. A formal letter had arrived in the mail only this morning. He was well, it said. Africa was proving more interesting than he had anticipated, but he'd be pleased to move on. He was looking forward to France. He had many fond memories of Paris. He hoped his letter found her well.

She began counting. The tour was for twenty-one days, plus two days more for the bus trips to and from Sydney. Thirteen days and he would be home.

She had not missed him, other than as a second presence in the house, and if the truth be told, she was wallowing in her freedom to do, to live, to eat, to buy what she pleased ... and to write again. Last night she had written until twelve, and she'd been at it again today. She hadn't intended sitting so long, but it was an addictive occupation. Now close to three and she'd had no lunch!

The story was still evolving. Consciously, she had no idea of where it was heading, or even from where the ideas were being drawn, but each time she sat at the old typewriter and wound in a new page, it somehow filled. What a grand, what a fascinating occupation, she thought, and her mind returned to the computer.

She'd actually had a play with it in the electrical shop, but the price was out of this world. She had bought a new typewriter ribbon for her father's old relic, and a full ream of paper. Five hundred sheets of blank white paper, she did not doubt her ability to fill.

Before leaving the main street, she had called into the furniture store, gleefully ordering a new vinyl floor-covering for the kitchen and laundry. The account would go to her father, but the vinyl was quite inexpensive. Chris Scott was coming in tomorrow to measure the floor – and to measure up for two security doors, which were not quite so inexpensive. But necessary. It was past time, well past time for the old flywire doors, both front and back, to be replaced. They were warped, and virtually useless against mosquitoes.

What a busy morning. What a wonderful morning. Money was exhilarating. The lack of the tall hedge was exhilarating. Her shorter hair was exhilarating. Life, back with her writing, was exhilarating. How had she put it away for so long?

Poor Father, she thought. What on earth will he think of me? I must stop this spending. I really must. I will. But the money is there. Pots of it, and as Miss Moreland says, money is only as good as what it will buy.

I wonder if I'm too old and set in my ways to learn how to use a computer? How much easier it would be, and how much re-writing it would save. Lyn Parker could show me how to use it. I might go around and have a talk to her later.

Again she heard the noise from upstairs. The unaccustomed silence was allowing her to hear previously unnoticed noises. That was all. She knew it, but as she climbed three more steps, a kitchen knife held before her like a sword, her own footsteps sounded hollow, the stairs creaking with each step. Had they always creaked so? Mentally, she began writing the next scene.

The stairs creaked as she climbed higher, the sharp kitchen knife grasped in her hand. Her greying hair hung loose to her shoulders, her eyes were sly, the eyes of a feral thing seeking prey. How she hungered for prey. Sink the knife deep into the child flesh – cut her. Cut out the bad and finish it. Get it done. Tonight.

Halfway up the stairs, and near lost in fiction, she froze. There was a demanding knock at the front door. She turned and hurried down, her smile pleased. For an hour this afternoon she had been attempting to capture an image of the female villain. Now she had her. The eyes. The grey hair that felt like wire to the touch, the rounded shoulders.

'Who is it?' she called, her hand on the doorknob.

'Parsons.'

She swung the door wide, smiling her greeting, as always, pleased to see him at her door. He made her laugh.

'When is Martin due back, Mousy Two?' His face looked serious as he stepped into the hall.

'Thirteen days, Doctor Parsons, and I believe I have now reached the age where you are beginning to give me a mouse complex.'

'It's a compliment, Mousy Two. And what's the silly old coot think he's doing, traipsing around the North Pole in the depths of winter?'

'He's probably enjoying France at the moment. He was looking forward to spring in France. Then he's off to do a short tour around Germany and Switzerland, back to Paris, then by ferry to England.'

'He was supposed to come in for a flu shot. He never turned up. What's the matter with you, anyway? What have you done to your hair?'

She turned, walked into the hall and he followed her.

'Miss Moreland cut it on Saturday. I still feel a little light headed, but very well,' she said, running her hands through her cropped curls. 'I'm actually beginning to enjoy my holiday.'

'You've lost weight.'

'A little yes – but I can afford it.'

'You're not dieting, are you?'

'No, I'm not, but I'm no longer cooking heavy meals for Father, either.'

'Sleeping well?'

'Not as well as usual. The empty house, and the loss of the hedge. I am hearing noises that I never heard before. Please, will you come into the lounge room. We actually have light in there. Since Mr Wilson turned his forest into firewood, the old house has taken on a whole new personality.'

'Nothing I'd like to do more, but no time today. We've got a problem, lass – and a big one. I was hoping your father might be due back, but if he's not, then he's not.'

She looked at him, her head to the side. He was rarely serious.

'Much and all as I'd like to, I can't make it go away, Mousy Two. I'm the bearer of bad news today.' He placed his hand on her shoulder. 'It's our grand old lady.'

'No.' Stella stepped backwards away from him. Her hand to her lips, she stared at the doctor, her head denying his next words before they were spoken. 'No. No. No.'

'It's true. Sad, but true.'

'No. I don't believe it. I don't want to hear this. Please.'

'Nobody wants to hear it, lass. She's dead.'

'But she can't be. I saw her on Saturday. We went out to lunch together, and she was so alive. She cut my hair, and I took her to the cafe ... we tried their savoury ...'

The foolish things people say. Stupid words of denial – as if haircuts and savoury pancakes on Saturday could bring an old friend back today. Stupid words, but they were all she had to fill the too raw place beginning to gape in her heart.

'Her next-door neighbour said he didn't notice her about on Sunday.'

'We didn't go to church. We decided not to go. Mr Macy ... Willy Macy was in charge. She didn't want to go, so we – Oh God. Please tell me this isn't happening, Doctor Parsons. I saw her on Saturday. She was well, so well.'

'Sit down, lass.'

'No. No. I didn't ... We never miss church. We always picked her up for church on Sundays. We – ' Her hand rose to cover her babbling mouth as she cowered against the wall. He walked to her, took her hand.

'One of her neighbours picked up her newspaper this morning, and he knocked on her door around ten and got no answer. He tried her half a dozen times and when he couldn't raise her, he called Johnson. Johnson found her dead in bed. She was – '

He watched Stella's face pale to marble white, and he steadied her with an arm as she swayed on her feet. It was not necessary to tell her the finer details. Maybe it wasn't necessary to tell anyone the finer details. He'd hoped Martin might be home. Three heads were better than two.

He looked at his watch. 'Maybe I ought to sit down for a bit, Mousy Two. I don't suppose I could beg a cup of tea and a bite. I'm near dead on my feet today. I've got old Jim Bryant dying by refusing to lie down, and young Betty Miller not wanting to pop her infant. Young Mick Murphy has probably gone pigging with a broken back, and I haven't had a bite to eat since breakfast. Feeling a bit weak on me old pins to be quite truthful,' he lied.

He knew her well. Stella never shirked responsibility. Her life had been governed by responsibility, by doing as she was bid, seeing to the needs of others. He watched her draw a deep breath. He watched her chin lift. There were no tears. He had expected tears, knowing how close she and the grand old dame had been, but the girl wasn't breaking. She was like a rock. On the outside, she was a rock. Christ only knew who, or what was cowering within that rock. Christ only knew.

'I'm sorry,' she said. 'I'm so sorry. I should have offered. Please. Please do forgive me, Doctor Parsons. Come through. The kitchen is a mess, but I'll fix you something. No stove, I'm afraid. I ... as you can see, I'm ...'

He sat at her kitchen table watching her hands. The smallest finger on her left hand had never straightened. Poor little hands, he thought. Poor little tyke. She'd done it the hard way and that was a fact.

She spread bread, sliced tomatoes, then she fried his sandwich in an electric frypan, just as he liked them, as she knew he liked them from the suppers she had served when he came around to play chess with her father. She boiled the jug, made tea, added milk and two sugars. She knew him well.

He spoke no more of Miss Moreland, but asked about her father while he dispatched his sandwich, and a second cup of tea. He had much to do, but he stood on, not wanting to leave her alone. She was paper white, her jaw tensed. She had barely touched her tea. Then he heard the noise and from upstairs, and she jumped like a scolded cat, spilling her tea.

'So, while the old cat's away Mousy Two gets to play. Who have you got hidden upstairs?'

'It's nothing. I was just ... when you knocked. I was going up to look when you arrived. It's nothing. Nothing at all. Please. That dear, dear lady is dead – '

Nothing or not, here was one ill Arnold Parsons could cure today. He was on his feet and halfway up the stairs, sprightly as a man half his age, his old pins looking perfectly steady. Stella followed slowly on his heels.

One by one he went through the rooms. He checked the wardrobes, looked beneath the beds. As he was leaving the spare bedroom beside her own, they heard the noise again, the scraping of wood on metal and the tap, tap, tapping.

'Sounds like a dame in stilettos dragging a body across the roof, Mousy Two.'

They stilled, listening again. Moments later they heard it. Parsons walked to the window, looking out at the jacaranda bough, grown too close to the house.

'That's your dame, lass. Have you got a saw, or maybe a pair of secateurs might do it? I'll do the old Cut-n-Slash trick. Remove a limb or two. Keep the old hand in.'

'In the shed. It's not important now, Doctor Parsons.'

'Run down and grab them for me. Only take me a tick.'

She was slow to move. He watched her take a collection of keys from her pocket then slowly she walked away. He unsnibbed the flyscreen from the window and leaned out watching her open the side door with a key, watching her peer in before entering the shed.

Martin Templeton didn't believe in burglars, or he considered himself a protected species, due to his dog-collar. He had never locked that shed in all of the years Parsons had been in town. The little man doubted that side door had ever been closed before.

When she exited, she locked the door behind her, and as the back door slammed, he again heard the turning of a key. Something has frightened that girl badly, he thought. Something more than being alone in a big house, more than the death of the old lady.

'These are quite new,' she said, offering the secateurs. With an apologetic shrug, she passed him a handsaw that had been old when Parsons was a boy.

He shook his head at it, but took the secateurs then leaned far out the window to snip at a few small branches. 'Looks like it's that big one. Up there. I reckon it might be a job for young Whitey and his chainsaw. Have you got his number?'

She stood beside him, her head out of the window. She could see what he meant. The limb overhanging the roof had been split. Its foliage, slowly starved of sap, had fallen. Bare wood now leaned on the metal spouting, moving with the breeze.

No more freak blooms out there. All of the leaves were yellowing, falling, readying the jacaranda trees for their short winter deaths.

'I've got a tall ladder. I'll ... I'll look at it. It is not important now. Please.' She took the secateurs from his hand and walked back to the passage. 'What was it? She was so well on Saturday. What happened to my dear friend?'

'It looks like her heart might have decided to give up, lass. Try to look on the bright side. She had a good innings and hardly a day of illness in her life. A heart attack in your own bed can be a good way to go when you get to her age.'

'She wasn't ready to die. She was so much younger than her years. We were planning a trip to China. We were going to walk along the Great Wall. She said what did it matter if she died in a paddy field with her hiking boots on, better than dying alone in bed. Was she . . . did she have a heart condition?'

He thought on that one, then decided not to reply. 'Like you, lass, I expected her to make her century and a decade more. A wonderful old bird. A wonderful gutsy old bird. The world would do all right if we had a few more like her in it.'

'I will miss her terribly. Terribly. And Father. What a time for him to be away. We can't even say our goodbyes to her the way she planned. You know she spoke to us about her funeral several years ago. She made us promise not to speak of her as if she had been some decrepit old woman. Father was to speak of her youth. No morbid hymns, she said. And she said, no-one had ever given her a bon voyage party. She was to leave me a thousand dollars so I might throw her a wild bon voyage party and invite the entire town. And she bought this dress – a positively dreadful dress, Doctor Parsons. It was reduced to twenty-five dollars at the department store. Dreadful.' Stella turned away, chewing on her lower lip now, attempting to steady it with her teeth. She would hold her grief inside until he left. She would. She would. Hadn't she always?

'It's been a shock to most of the town, lass. She was the last one the old busybodies expected to go. They had their money on Jim Bryant. Speaking of going, I'd better get a move on myself. Too much to do and no time to do it in. You'll be all right here?'

'Yes, of course I will. I'm . . . I'm just terribly, terribly saddened. But she wouldn't want me to weep for her, would she? She said, no tears necessary, that I was to wave her goodbye and wish her a wonderful journey. And I do, and I do. But – excuse me now, please, Doctor. Thank you for – excuse me.' She escaped to the bathroom, closed the door.

Parsons let himself out. The front door had a modern lock,

but he checked it before walking to the shed where he peered through a crack in the side door. He could see the shape of the Packard against the light from a small window. Everything looked in order. He straddled his bike and rode away.

Her tears wouldn't, couldn't dry. She walked the house while they rolled down her cheeks and she wiped at them, swiped at them, denied them.

'How am I going to survive this town without her? Why should she die? It's too fast.' She wandered the kitchen, picking up, putting down, hoping the workmen did not return and find her weeping uncontrollably.

Her head ached with it. Her nose was blocked and her sinuses heavy with weeping. She caught a glimpse of her swollen eyes in the bathroom mirror as she washed her face for the umpteenth time. She looked terrible. Terrible. Her face was shiny, her nose red. What if they were to come back? What had they said? They'd called out that they were leaving, but she had been too absorbed. What if someone were to come?

She splashed cold water on her eyes, held the cold facecloth there, then wept into it until it was cold no longer.

'Stop this. You must stop this,' she ordered, but her tears would not listen. 'How can I stop? I need you, my dear friend. I need you. I am not weeping for you, but for myself, for my loss.' She lay on her bed, muffling her grief in the pillow.

It was near five when she walked downstairs, took two Aspros and made a cup of tea. Her head aching, but still denying, her tears still leaking, she let them leak, bored with the futile attempt to wipe them away.

The telephone rang, it caused her to jump, again splashing tea to the table. She shook her head, but the phone continued to ring. There was only one way to stop it.

'Marilyn?'

Her friend wanted to talk about the news and to seek out more information to pass on with her change. In a voice, not quite her own, Stella cut the conversation short.

Five times in the next hour the phone rang as the news swept through the town, scattering yesterday's news before it. Five times she spoke a few words then hung the phone on the cradle. It was after six when John Parker, solicitor and husband of Lyn, got through.

He was accustomed to having people listen, so a murmured yes or no was all he required. He spoke until the sun began to go down, go down on Miss Moreland's final day. Go down. Stay down.

'Oh, God, John,' she said, and she blew her nose. 'Why now?'

'Bad timing,' John Parker said, and Stella leaned and listened. Her tears slowly dried.

Perhaps she had known she would be named in Miss Moreland's will. There was no-one else. Perhaps she had known, but there was nothing she wished to say to him about it. That was for another day, if there was another day.

'Can I come around, Stell?'

'No. Not now.'

'You're one of the executors.'

'Yes,' she said. 'Yes, I know, but there is nothing I can do. Not now. Not yet. It is too soon to think of her as gone. I don't want to do anything. Not yet. Please – '

'Are you also aware she left some pretty weird instructions as to – ?'

'I know. You have her instructions in writing, John – and we will follow them to the letter, otherwise she will return to haunt me. She made me promise. Spit my death and hope to die.' Again the tears welled. She shook her head, shook them away.

'It's all here, Stell, but Christ – has she got any family? How are they going to take it? Won't they have some say in it?'

'I'll talk to you tomorrow. It can all wait until tomorrow. Thank you for calling.'

'Okay. I'll be there around ten.'

'Yes. If you must.'

'Before I go, can you tell me where I can contact the family?'

'She said I was her family. She has two nieces somewhere in Sydney. She hasn't seen them since Cara, her sister, died in ... in the sixties.'

'I'll have to try to contact them.'

'Surely they will receive something.'

'There's not a lot left to receive. The flat, a few thousand in the bank. I'm afraid you're it, Stell. The only mention of family is – ' She heard the shuffling of papers, then he added. 'To my nieces, Marie Connor and Raelene Mackenzie, I leave the bill for my funeral, and my insincere condolences.'

'Oh, my God.' Stella laughed and the tears rained down. 'Oh, my dear, dear, wicked lady.'

The solicitor remained silent until he heard her blow her nose. 'She had a good life, Stell. The best any one of us can wish for is a fast death. Better for her than dying like Mum did, an inch at a time for two years. Try to look on the bright side.'

'Somehow a good death doesn't seem to hold a lot of meaning for me at the moment, John. Maybe tomorrow. I have to go. Please excuse me now.'

'Are you all right? Do you want Lyn to come around for a while?'

'No. Of course I am all right. It's just the shock. Totally unexpected. Do forgive me. I'll see you in the morning. At ten.'

See you at ten. Get down to the business of burying. Off with the old and on with the new, but Miss Moreland hadn't belonged to him. She was just another high school teacher, just another client. He hadn't known her friendship. He didn't know that she had filled the place of mother, of friend and confidante. He didn't understand that a raw gash had opened up in Stella's life, a gaping space which now threatened to swallow her. He didn't know that.

She shouldn't have died in her bed in the middle of the night. She shouldn't have died alone. No-one should die alone. Had she tried to call Stella? Had she tried to climb from her bed, reach for the telephone?

'God! How dare you do the things you do?'

Night had drifted into the rooms while she'd been speaking to John Parker. Now she turned the lights on, flooding the house as she wandered, breathing in the scent of its age and old memories. She had wept herself dry. Perhaps the Aspro had helped, but she didn't want to sleep. Perhaps she was afraid of sleep tonight. Somewhere that dear lady was laying cold and dead. How could she sleep and forget that? She took up her knitting, but couldn't settle to it. She picked up the plastic bag, half filled with clown heads, and she took it with her to the lounge room where she turned on the television, let it flash its nonsense before her eyes as she stitched.

These small clown faces she stitched by rote. A mindless task, but that was what she needed tonight. She felt mindless, empty of emotion now, empty as the old house. Empty head. Empty heart, just empty. For two hours she sat stitching empty faces on her clown head while some inane show played its faces on the screen. She didn't know which of the males was villain, and which the hero. They were taking turns sleeping with the same naked woman. Or were there two naked women? She didn't know.

Her clown faces all looked the same when she was done. She picked them up, one by one. Bland, staring things. She'd hate them in the morning. Yawning now, she turned the television off, leaving the villain/hero and the blonde rocking their bed, then she tossed the clown heads into their plastic bag and walked to the twin glass doors.

It was black outside, sullen black, waiting to pounce on her, wrestle her down. She drew the drapes. Faded, musty. No sun to fade them – not in the past forty years. When had they become faded? Why are they still hanging there? God. How time has stood still in this house, she thought.

But it was catching up now, spinning, ticking, gobbling up all the years of unchange. Like the vampires in – what was that film? A stake through the heart and the vampire began his aging, flesh decaying, his skull turning to dust to be blown away by a puff of wind. She stood staring at the brown velvet curtains, expecting them to begin their rot before her eyes. Small holes would melt into the larger, join. Slowly the metal rings would shed the fabric, and it would fall to the floor. A small heap of dust to be sucked up by the vacuum cleaner. Gone.

'But who will vacuum up the dust?' she said, 'My own small pile of dust may be beside it in the morning.'

She turned away then, stiff with sitting, drained by spent emotion, and she walked slowly upstairs, forcing blood to flow.

The typewriter was on her father's desk, her stack of completed pages at its side. She sat, seeking words, words to fill the blank paper and the blank space inside her.

Time remained motionless, trapped in the dark rooms. He stood in the doorway, holding time back with his will, and with his massive frame.

'She was not the mother I had hoped she'd be,' he said –

Stella's fingers stilled. They hung over the keys, like birds, frozen in flight.

These had been her father's words.

'She is not the mother I had hoped she'd be.'

Her father's words.

She sat back, her heart beating like the motor-mower engine as she looked at the words that had come from some too full page buried deep within herself. She could remember hearing those words. They had been spoken once in this very room. Long, long, long ago.

And Doctor Parsons had been here. The tiny man, smaller still because he stood beside her father. And her hands. Her hands were ... were blistered. Her small finger like a parchment balloon. Water-filled. And her palms. Seared. Raw.

'No. No.' She shook her head, shook the words away. This was fiction, only fiction.

'Put it away. I am becoming caught up in fiction. And perhaps it is not the sort of tale to become involved in at this time. She pushed her chair back and walked across the hall to her own room where she sat on the edge of her bed, wishing her father home. Her hands came together, as in prayer, then they separated, and she stared at her palms. They had always been scarred. Ever since –

Again she shook her head. 'Put it away.'

Don't put it away. Look at it. Look at truth. Learn from truth.

'No. I will crack,' she said. 'The shell I have built around me is already fracturing. My tears have weakened it and I am breaking up. I must get my mind onto something else. The computer. Lyn Parker. Yes. I will speak to Lyn. She is a wizard on John's computer.'

Poor hands. Again she stared at her palms. They were scarred, ridged, toughened unnaturally, as she had been toughened unnaturally. For minutes she sat staring at her hands, the sound of her own breath loud in the room.

I'm going to crack. I must sleep. Turn my mind off.

Tired now, tired beyond tiredness. She rested it on the pillow, still damp from her afternoon of tears. Perhaps she slept.

'I want to get up, Mummy.'

'You want a lot of things, don't you? Do you want to feel the fires of hell?'

'No, Mummy. Please, I just want to get up now.'

'Sit there and don't you move.'

'The clock made four. Daddy might come home soon. Please can I open the gates for him.'

'You haven't said the magic word.'

'I said, please, Mummy.'

'Please what?'

'Please, my dearest darling good Mummy. Please may I leave the room now?'

'You didn't say the magic word. You'll sit there until you do.'

'I don't know the today magic word, Mummy. You say it first, then I will say it, and we'll be very happy, Mummy.'

'You listen to God. He will tell you the magic word. Listen to him. Let him save you from the burning fires of hell – if it is his will.'

Her own scream woke her, but she'd bought part of her dream back with her. She could see her. She could see her clearly. For the first time in years, she could see her mother. A screaming, foot-stamping virago, her hair uncombed, her body unwashed, her face mad. Her mother had been mad. No precious Angel, hanging on the wall, with her fine eyes and her arms full of flowers. Not that fake portrait kept in Martin's room, a vase of flowers always there, beneath it.

Mad. She had been stark raving mad.

'But dead,' Stella said, breathing out the dream. 'Dead now. Dead. Dead. Dead. Dead. Dead.'

a flighty old bird

There was no way to escape the morning and responsibility. The workmen arrived before nine to complete the installation of the stove, and by ten John Parker had wandered in with his papers. Then Steve Smith arrived, and minutes later Chris Scott turned up to measure old doorframes for new security doors. And the kitchen and laundry floors – finally they would have new coverings. Never had the old house seen such activity.

She had risen early that morning, dressing carefully in beige. Pantihose, sensible shoes. She had tamed the too short hair with pins above her ears, and appeared composed as she sat with John and Steve in the study, all doors closed between them and the workmen.

John had given her much to do today. Steve, the second executor, would be tied up at his one-man business until five. Near eleven when they left, she handed the back-door key to the electrician and asked him to lock up, and to drop the key into Miss Moreland's flat.

'Do what must be done,' she said. 'Go. Life goes on. Go.' Thus she steeled herself to leave the house and drive alone to

Miss Moreland's unit where she must set about packing up a long and wonderful life.

Johnson and the new constable were there when she arrived. The older man left soon after, but his colleague remained in the bedroom, behind closed doors. Stella was given leave to sort through the drawers and personal files in the lounge-dining room. She did not ask her questions aloud, but her mind kept asking, why?

A death no doubt had to be investigated – even the death of an elderly woman who had gone to sleep one night and never awoke. A massive heart attack was the probable cause of death. So Johnson said.

'Instantaneous,' he said.

Stella crept up on the drawers in the old writing desk, feeling like a thief, and too aware of the other presence that had been behind the closed door. Her sleep had been broken by the strangest dreams, fiction and fact intersecting in the night. This morning she could not shake the memory of wild grey hair, and those eyes. Ice blue, and wide. Wild. Angel had been a crazed thing near the end, locked in the small downstairs bedroom, hidden while the hedge grew ever taller. Why? Why had her father keep his wife at home?

Her fingers in her hair, she massaged her scalp and breathed deeply. This was no time for such thoughts. There was a task that must be done today. That is why she was here. No time to question insane decisions made on some lost yesterday.

'His false pride,' she said. 'Perhaps she could have been helped.' Then she shrugged. 'Probably not. Not back then.'

Another drawer was opened. She took from it a box of old postcards, and stood scanning for names and the addresses of the missing nieces. There were many old letters, though none from a Marie or Raelene. She glanced at each one, but briefly, then she tossed them into a large plastic bag.

It was twelve before the young constable exited the bedroom with his own items in his own plastic bags, but Bob Johnson had returned. She made them tea, and the younger man asked her if she knew of any male friends Miss Moreland may have had.

'She was on good terms with many – ' She looked up from her teacup, caught his eye, and understood. 'She was ninety-six!'

'I've known a few who wouldn't let that hold them back, Miss Templeton,' he said.

'She was a flighty old bird. I wouldn't put it past her,' Johnson added.

Stella flashed him a look and Johnson had the decency to blush.

She left them drinking tea while she emptied the refrigerator, but there was a feeling of unease about her now. She followed their backs with her eyes as they walked out the front door, then from a window she watched them knock on the doors of other flats, then return to walk around Miss Moreland's unit. She sighted them in the shrubbery beside the lounge room window, and again at the bathroom window. Then they left, and she went about the business of searching.

At one, she called John Parker and gave him the names and addresses of Miss Moreland's two nieces.

Empty, wrung out and squeezed dry, Stella worked on, functioning on a different level, as if lost in some never-never land where death is not yet complete, where life has gone but the presence remains, until church ritual and cemetery give release to the living. The wait until Thursday was too long.

'Get me in the ground as fast as possible,' Miss Moreland had said many times. 'Don't leave me languishing in a freezer like a side of old mutton.' But Thursday was the earliest they could put her to rest. Thursday afternoon. They'd had to get a minister from out of town.

It was too long.

She washed the refrigerator shelves with water and a drop or two of vanilla essence then she propped the door wide.

So empty, so lonely, its contents tossed to the bin, or placed on the bench. The flat offered no solace today, and Stella wept again for the empty refrigerator, the old supplier of countless luncheons, a thousand cool drinks. She had loved this place. So many wonderful afternoons spent here. So many meals eaten at this table.

Through the kitchen window, she saw the young constable poking at the soil beside the neighbouring flat. Her stomach grumbled. She had eaten little since breakfast yesterday. Stomachs make their own demands, lost energy must be replenished. She looked at a tomato she had given Miss Moreland on Saturday, picked fresh from her garden.

'I must eat something,' she said. 'Life must go on, my dear lady, but only God knows how.'

The town clock struck two as Stella ate alone at the dining room table. She ate the tomato, she ate cheese and a small can of leg ham. She used the last of Miss Moreland's milk in a cup of tea, then she washed the dishes and packed them away.

An apron, hung lonely, waited in vain on the kitchen doorknob for her old friend's return. She picked it up and held it to her face a while, breathing in the odour of kitchen and luncheons, then like a thief, she folded it quickly and tucked it in her handbag. In the laundry, a basket sat patiently waiting on the ironing board, damped down and rolled up in the old-fashioned way. Stella found a task for her hands, something unfinished, something to be done, something that might keep her out of the bedroom. She didn't want to go in there where the men had been. What had the young constable taken away? What tales might that bed have told?

'No-one should die alone,' she said. 'No-one.'

Busy hands, they pressed and folded, they spent time over that red and grey blouse, and when it was done, all done, again she wandered, just touching things, creeping closer all the time to the bedroom, trying to find nerve enough to enter.

'It is just another empty room,' she said, and she was in there, standing before the dressing-table with its large mirror. 'I always like to keep mirrors around me, girl. They tell me the truth when no-one else has got the gumption to,' Miss Moreland once said.

All the scents, all the memories of Miss Moreland were in this room, but there were other odours here too. She opened the window, then again turned to the mirror and she saw her dark-rimmed eyes and fading hair, pinned behind her ears. Truthful mirror, as its owner had been truthful. She pulled the pins from her hair, and stood combing her curls with Miss Moreland's comb.

'Mirror, mirror, on the wall, who's been the greatest fool of all?' she said.

The built-in robe bulged with barely worn garments. She scanned its contents, searching for the gown Miss Moreland had stipulated in her will. Red satin with matching shoes. Stella knew all about it – and about the shoes. She'd been with the old lady when she had seen the dress.

'I always wanted to wear a red satin ballgown. I think I'll buy it for my funeral,' Miss Moreland had said. And she did. She'd had to order the matching shoes. It was eight or more years ago, but they'd be here somewhere.

A black and white check suit hung over a red silk blouse. Stella had always loved it. Now she placed it on the unmade bed. She stood staring at the mattress. Someone had stripped it bare. She moved the suit, walked to the linen closet and found the spare bedspread, tossing it over, and covering the naked pillows before again searching the wardrobe.

So much of everything. 'You extravagant lady,' Stella whispered, taking up the white satin blouse with its embroidered front. Perhaps she should package everything up as she went. Give the clothing to the opportunity shop.

'Oh, no. Oh, no. I do not want to see others wandering around town in your beautiful things, my dear. They wouldn't wear them with your style,' she whispered and she sorted on.

The satin shoes were in their box on the top shelf, and in one shoe was a pair of red and gold patterned sunglasses, and a note.

You'd better believe it, Miss. Now don't you chicken out and let me down.

Stella laughed. She put the glasses on and looked at her image in the mirror, and she tried to stifle her mirth with her hands.

'God. If someone should hear me, they would think I'd lost my mind.'

The wicked red dress was hiding inside a grey zip-bag. She laughed again as she opened the bag, freeing the rich satin thing. Its neckline was low and heavily beaded in gold. The frock held before her, she stood again before the mirror.

'Perhaps I should be a little wicked too. Lend me some of your gutsiness, my dear friend. Of late, I have been sadly lacking in the guts department.' She fitted the frock to her waist, studied her reflection. 'I'm not so old, am I? I used to wear red, once, a long, long time ago. I could still wear it. I am not so old,' she said. 'However, you wicked woman, as I told you the day you bought this ... this abomination, it would better suit a lady of the night working a shift at Kings Cross.'

The bed became lost beneath the pile of clothing. It was near four when she took a large case from the hall closet and began packing.

'For your trip, my dear. I am packing this for your trip. You'll need some casual clothing for the days, and something nice for the evenings. Perhaps your embroidered sweater, and the grey slacks, and the black. You'll need the white skirt, and your black and white check suit. And certainly the black suit and the white satin blouse. And the red jacket, definitely the red jacket.'

It wasn't so bad after that. She near emptied the wardrobe and several drawers, filling two cases which she carried out to her car. Then she returned and emptied more into a carton. The rest could go to the needy.

So many scraps of a lifetime of hoarding. It was lucky that Ron Spencer had thought to drop off half a dozen boxes mid afternoon. She thanked him profusely, but did not invite him in, as she did not invite Mrs Murphy and Mrs Morris inside when they came to offer their help.

The best of the old china she wrapped carefully in newspaper. Much of it had belonged to Miss Moreland's mother. It would have value, as would the few ornaments and a very elderly marble clock. She packed efficiently now, marking each box with texta before moving on. The nieces would probably appreciate the family heirlooms. The photograph album she packed also. Before sealing that box, she glanced again through the album. Strangers' faces. They had meant something to Miss Moreland. Perhaps they would to the nieces. There were very few faces Stella recognised. She turned to the photograph of Cutter-Nash, and she looked at his eyes. Jaguar eyes, Miss Moreland had said.

'I wish you had told me all you knew of him, my dear. Now their secrets will truly die with you. He looks so familiar, but he was dead before I was born. How could he look familiar? Perhaps his eyes are a little like – no.' She shook her head. 'I will not think of him, and I will not allow my imagination to run away with me.' The album closed, she sealed the box, and scribbled *Album, Old China* on its lid.

'So much,' she sighed. 'How do we accumulate so much in one short lifetime?' She lifted a piece of patchwork to her face – tiny hexagons made from all the fabrics of Miss Moreland's life.

'Every dress I ever loved, since my sixteenth birthday, is in there. I've saved a bit from each. One of these days, you might have to finish it for me, girl.'

The old lady's words were like the whisper of the wind in the wires. They still lived in this flat and in Stella's memory. The dead are not lost, only the ones who remain are lost.

'I will finish it, my dear, and I'll treasure it. It will have a place forever in my life.'

She stood looking at the fabric for minutes, then she took up a pair of scissors and returned to the bedroom and to the pile of clothing she'd placed to one side for the needy. From the sleeve

210

of each favourite frock and blouse, she cut a fifteen-centimetre square.

As she sat at her writing that night she allowed new emotion to flow to paper, and when she read her evening's work, she knew it was good. On Wednesday, she began again while Chris Scott worked downstairs, stripping away the worn-out brown linoleum, hammering a backing board to uneven floors. What a noise. But she needed that noise. Now she transferred noise to her pages.

Wednesday died too quickly, and Thursday dawned with a clear blue sky for Miss Moreland.

The town stood still. Shops closed their doors at midday, and the people came to the church to fill it, and to spill over to footpath and lawn where Steve Smith had set up large speakers.

There were many tears, but no more from Stella. This was a time for strength and efficiency, and certainly no time for sadness. The service was as Miss Moreland had planned it, and a riot. The only strangers there were not amused; still, the one who had demanded she be present at her own funeral, just to keep an eye on proceedings, looked wildly wonderful in her cheeky sunglasses and red frock, her red-as-sin hat. She appeared to be enjoying the farce.

When the coffin was carried from the church, and orderly crowds slowly emptied the front pews, Stella sat on. She tried not to see . . . see him. He was one of the pallbearers. Pale. Surly.

Ron had wanted it. He had been fond of Miss Moreland, and he'd wanted his son at his side. How could she say no? Steve and Chris Scott made up the four.

She glanced up, and caught the eye of Miss Moreland's long-lost nieces. If it had been possible to walk out of a funeral in disgust, Willy Macy and the nieces would have walked. Of that, Stella was certain.

'Who am I becoming, Miss Moreland? You are changing me in death as you tried in vain to change me in life. Who will I be tomorrow? Will I be tomorrow? Or without you, will this town wear me away? Have I left already? I certainly don't feel like me today.'

'Time to go, Stell.' Steve Smith walked back to her pew. He thought she was crying and his hand reached out to comfort her, but she turned to him with a smile, and his hand withdrew.

The church bells were tolling out their own goodbye. 'I'll sit for a moment longer, thank you, Steve,' she said. 'I'll just sit here a while and say my own goodbye while the crowd clears. Sit with me.'

'Did you see old Willy Macy's face when he got a load of her rig-out – and that pair of prune-faced old tartars? I was expecting them to start spitting pips.'

'Oh, I did. I certainly did, but I promised I'd do as she wished. You had better keep me away from Mr Macy, too. If he attempts to chastise me today, I may say something I could be ashamed of later.'

'You and me both, Stell. You and me both. You'd better watch out for that pair of prunes. I think they've got their knives out for you.'

'I was not sure what to expect – after all, they are her blood. But how? How can they be her relatives, Steve?' She shook her head. 'Goodness me. Where is my charity today? I'm afraid that I'm feeling rather un-me, but I don't quite know who I am.'

'Want to ride with me to the cemetery – or give me a lift? Mum's gone off with Bonny and Len.'

'Yes. Yes, thank you, Steve.'

Miss Moreland's nieces waited until their aunt was safely underground before they made their joint attack.

'We are upset, and with good cause, I may add. My aunt made a laughing stock at her own funeral – '

'We are all upset, so perhaps we might leave this discussion until a more appropriate time and place,' Stella replied, standing before the duo, her eyes shielded by large sunglasses. She was breathing deeply. Anger, too long swallowed, was eager for its freedom, but she controlled it. She always controlled anger.

'The service was a mockery. A cruel mockery.'

'It is sad that you feel that way. It is what she wanted. Perhaps if you had known your aunt – '

'What are you trying to say? What are you trying to say, you uppity little bitch?'

'What I am attempting to say perhaps, is that my dear friend was not quite so popular, nor so revered by her family in life as she appears to be in death. I do not recall seeing either of you in town before. But perhaps you were not aware of her great age.'

'We live in Sydney. It's a long drive and we're not as young as we used to be.'

'No, you are certainly not, and you still have a long drive home, so do take care.' Stella turned away, but the smaller of the prunes followed her, grasped at her arm. Stella shook off the hand and continued walking.

'We'll break that will. You see if we don't. We are her closest relatives, and entitled to inherit all she owned. We'll take it to the courts. You see if we don't.'

'That is, of course, your prerogative.'

'You wheedled your way into a senile old fool's life. I know your type.'

'Which, thankfully, is not your type, Mrs Mackenzie. Good afternoon,' Stella said and she walked briskly away.

Steve had been behind her, now he walked with her to the near empty car park, his smile wide. 'Good one, Stell. Good for you.'

'I behaved badly. I should not have allowed – darn them.'

'I didn't know she'd bought that flat. I thought she was renting, like old Mrs Thomson. What's the situation? I mean, can you move into it, or do you need to be over sixty-five?'

'Who knows? I ... I couldn't leave my garden. John Parker suggested I rent it out. You know Doctor Parsons has been advertising for an assistant. It would make an ideal doctor's residence, John said. Perhaps. Perhaps the nieces will break the will. Who knows.'

'Buckley's hope I'd say – the way it was worded.'

A shrug her only response, Stella unlocked the car and slid in as Steve folded his limbs into the passenger seat.

'I don't suppose you'd like to go and grab a bit of dinner somewhere, would you Stell? It's after five.'

She looked at him, then back towards the town, and she shook her head.

'Up to you. But I sort of feel a bit queer going home. It's like a day off from ... I don't know. I don't get many days off. God it was a riot. The best funeral I've ever been to.'

'I think this has been the strangest day of my life, Steve. No doubt tomorrow I will be feeling very ... very guilty about that attack. I'll sit stitching my clowns, feeling terribly wicked about the entire day.' She looked at him.

'Then why not give yourself something to feel wicked about? Come and have a drink with me.' Again she shook her head. 'We'll wish her a good trip. We've got to get on to that party too. Throw her a real wing-ding. Do one of those whole life videos. You know, with old photographs. Mum reckons Miss Moreland was a raving beauty in her day. Has she got many photographs?'

'Heaps. I was going to give them to the nieces. But – ' She shrugged. 'Perhaps I won't – as for the party, we'll wait until Father comes home. He was fond of her – in his own odd way. I know he'd want to ... to feel a part of it. He may disown me of course.' She looked up at Steve, and shook her head. 'Was it so wrong, what we did today? The service, the frock, those glasses?'

'I work on the principle that you go with what feels right at the time, Stell. It felt pretty right to me. She was there too, and loving it. Christ, I won't forget that look on Willy Macy's face until the day I die.'

'What is he going to say to Father?' Again she looked at Steve. 'Oh, why not? Let's have that drink for her, Steve. I know, I know she'd approve of that – but perhaps not in town. Could I suggest we go to Dorby, far from the disapproving crowd?'

'You're on.'

She started the motor and pulled away from the kerb, feeling strange, nervous, but so brave.

'You're looking good today. A bit more like the old Stell I used to know. It's nice to see you in a bit of colour for a change.'

Stella pulled at the lapel of her red silk blouse. 'It's one of Miss Moreland's. I felt if she was determined to wear her scarlet ballgown then I couldn't embarrass her by wearing the old beige.'

They spoke of many things that night, of stoves and planes and tours and Martin, and they spoke of Miss Moreland. Stella drank peach cooler, and Steve drank beer. Slowly their conversation altered. They began laughing about the old days, and the old band, and the Saturday nights when they had sung a duet in this same club. The crowd was younger then. They were younger. They talked and ordered more drinks while the hour grew later and the band played on.

'Feel like a dance, Stell?'

'Dance? Good Lord. I haven't danced in a millennium.'

'It can't be that long.'

'It certainly feels like it. I'm sure I've forgotten how.'

But she hadn't forgotten how. Steve had a fine sense of rhythm and it only took a few minutes for Stella's white sandal-clad feet to find their own rhythm.

Foolish, foolish woman, she thought. You are making a complete spectacle of yourself tonight. You are talking too much, laughing too loud. Perhaps the peach cooler is not lolly water after all. Just a mote afraid of her laughter, when Steve ordered more beer, she ordered coffee. 'Miss Moreland might enjoy the joke, but I don't really think I want to get booked for drunk driving,' she said. 'That may be carrying things a little too far, do you think?'

They outstayed the band. They sat on drinking coffee until the weary workers began moving chairs back for the cleaners.

'I think they want us to move, Stell. They're going to vacuum us out in a tick.'

She stood, and she wasn't quite sure which way to walk. He took her arm, and held it as they walked down the steps and across the car park. It made her feel so young. So delightfully young and silly.

'I think Miss Moreland would be proud of me tonight,' she said.

'I was proud to be with you tonight. Real proud. You should wear red more often. It does something to you.'

She felt sixteen. Foolish, gauche. Drunk on four glasses of peach cooler and an old friend's company. She didn't quite know what to say so remained silent until she found her key, until she unlocked the car, until they were both seated, until she found her own way back to the highway, until the dark countryside began slipping by and memory of the nights of long ago and driving home near dawn in the old band van, urged her to sing as she had then.

It started small. Steve joined with her. Their first attempt to harmonise raised safe laughter, but they tried again. She let him choose the key and she hummed along until she found the old mellow blend. They sounded good. They still sounded very good together, and she'd always had an ear for harmony.

'Do you remember, "Send in the Clowns", Stell?'

'That was my swan song,' she said. 'That last night, remember?'

All the way home they sang the old songs, and when she

pulled the car into the churchyard beside Steve's utility, and the night was over, and in the distance old Wilson's rooster was signalling dawn, they sat on.

'We ought to do it again some night – if you feel like it, that is.'

'Perhaps we will, Steve. Perhaps we should. Thank you so very much for today – for yesterday,' she corrected. 'Thank you so very, very much.' And she drove away, grateful her father was safe on the other side of the world.

so many clowns

It was Monday night, and the seventeenth night Stella was to spend alone in the old house. Martin had sent two more postcards, one of Paris, a city of lights, and one of a castle in Germany. Uncertain of where he might be at any given time, and of how long it may take her letter to reach him, she chose not to write back, not to tell him of Miss Moreland's untimely death. Time enough when he returned on next Sunday's bus, and time enough for the wild party she and Steve Smith were planning to host at the shire hall.

Steve had come around to discuss the plans yesterday, and to collect some old photographs. He dabbled in photography, and was intent on creating a video of the old lady's life. For hours they had sat, selecting, rejecting. There were photographs too of the old town when it was young, photographs of the old school. The album was a historical documentation of Maidenville, Steve said.

He had stayed so late that Stella asked him to join her for dinner, cooked on her wonderful new stove. And afterwards –

She smiled, and her hand holding the long embroidery needle

stilled as she sat a moment, staring at a small clown eye. Then she shrugged, slid the needle beneath the round nose and commenced working the second eye. Her mind free to roam, returned to Sunday night.

After dinner, Steve had washed the dishes while she dried, and there was something about washing dishes with a companion, a task she'd always done alone in that kitchen. There was a closeness about it.

He had started the remembering games. 'Remember the old van? Remember the night the tyre blew and we were stuck thirty kilometres out without a spare?'

Remember. Remember. So fine to remember the good times.

And they had sung again, right there at the sink to the clatter of crockery, the jacarandas their only audience, and when the dishes were done, Stella had hunted out her own old photographs.

They'd laughed then at Steve's hair; he had allowed it to hang free back in those days, and they'd laughed at baby-faced Chris Scott. So much laughter. What a night, and what on earth would the neighbours have thought of her?

It was well after midnight when he rose to leave, the selected photographs in a large envelope. She had walked him to the front door, flooding the drive with light, flooding her garden with light, which got them started again.

Then he'd spoken of a booking he'd taken for his aging band.

'It's in three weeks, Stell. Come with us. We still sound good together,' he said.

'What a lark, Steve.'

'Do it.'

'I'm too old. I'd look ridiculous.'

'You'd look far from ridiculous. Age is all in the head of hair.'

'Father will be back in Australia next Saturday. He'll come through on the Sunday bus.'

'So it's back into the cage, eh?'

'Back to normal, I suppose, Steve.'

'I always reckoned our band could have made it big if you'd stayed with us back then. We might have been a second Seekers.'

He'd kissed her cheek when he was leaving. Just a brother's kiss. He'd always been like a younger brother, always there – at the same children's parties, always around, but in the background. He'd helped carry home the small jacarandas and suggested she plant them between the house and shed. A born planter of seeds, his hands more at ease in the soil than at the dinner table. His blond hair was greying at the temples, but he still wore it long – as he had back then. Now he tied it back with rubber bands. A strange boy, and they did sound so well together.

'What am I thinking of?' she said. 'Father will return and bring reality back with his case full of washing, and I will pin up my hair again and Miss Moreland's colourful shirts will be packed away in the cases.'

But it had been a good night. One of the best. Laughter so readily raised, and eager to rise. He was so darn easy to be with.

'Lord. What would Father think of me? "Entertaining a man in my kitchen, singing love songs until midnight with that long-haired lout. Wandering the garden at 1 a.m. You must ask yourself, Daughter, is it seemly, with Miss Moreland barely cold in her grave?"'

Probably not, but that dear lady would have been delighted. Stella smiled as she turned the radio volume a little higher. They were playing the song she had sung at Miss Moreland's funeral. It was one of the old favourites from the seventies.

Leave my worries far away in another time and place.

She hummed along with it now, thinking of her old friend who had always turned the volume up when they played that song.

It was odd. Several times since the funeral, the Dorby radio station had played that song – as if they knew, even though they couldn't possibly have known. Each time it played, Stella's thoughts went to Miss Moreland. And what better way to be remembered, she thought?

She stitched the round eye on the face of a clown, then peered closely at it, before changing her thread. Writing had taken over her days; the clowns were a chore she resented.

Let someone else do them, girl.

'Would that I could, my dear,' she said. The song had ended, but Miss Moreland was still close. There were moments when Stella could almost hear the comments spoken in her mind, as if Miss Moreland had not truly left yet, but taken up residence in Stella's right ear, determined to change her, to have her will.

It had been obvious to all that Ron had forced his son to be one of the pallbearers. The teenager hadn't looked well on that crazy day. His face had been pale, and his eyes had the look of a wild thing, trapped. A surly jaguar, pacing the bars of his too small cage, and wanting out.

He had strange green eyes – Marilyn's eyes. There had always been talk in town about Marilyn's mother. Marilyn and her brothers had grown up with many short-term uncles. Was it possible? Was that what Miss Moreland had been hinting at?

Stella had spoken to Steve of Cutter-Nash. They'd studied his photograph together, and she'd removed the shot of her grandfather. Perhaps she'd have that one enlarged. No photograph of old Randall De Vere hung in the house – even his wedding photograph had been cut in half, leaving only his ghostly hand on the shoulder of his bride.

'I'm sadly lacking in relatives,' she told the finished clown face, and she dropped it into the plastic bag beside her bed. 'We were not a family of breeders. No uncle, no aunt, no cousin or niece, parents a generation removed from the parents of my friends.'

She took up a blank face, trying to see the personality hidden behind it. Sometimes they suggested themselves, or they had once. She was doing too many lately and they were all beginning to look much the same.

'Green eyes,' she said, 'with a glint of yellow, and a golden collar.' Again she began stitching, her mind once more free to roam.

Miss Moreland's nieces had taken the jewellery. Some of it had antique value, as did the old china and ornaments. They had demanded a tapestry and a large painting from the lounge-dining room, the antique mirror in the hall. They had claimed an antique coffee table and the bedroom chair, but made no mention of the family album. Which was as well. Stella had no intention now of parting with it.

John Parker, a born diplomat, suggested Stella allow the nieces to go through the flat, and to take any of the older family items. They'd settled for that, but only after having shown a copy of the will to their own solicitor. 'Don't give them the key, Stell. Go with them, keep your eye on them,' he'd said. 'Lyn will go with you.'

The prunes had arrived with a small van and a large son on the Saturday, but Lyn was a match for any man. Bonny had come too. The friends followed the trio from room to room. By the time the van left, the flat looked a little bare, but Stella had a receipt in her hand, all items had been listed by Lyn on her laptop computer, then printed out on her tiny portable printer. And what a wonderful machine it was.

Until Sunday, no conversation had been complete without a mention of Miss Moreland, then old Joe Martin, a lost soul since the death of his wife, died peacefully, and the old-timers in town began looking at their neighbours for the one most likely to make up the third. In Maidenville, deaths always came in threes.

Funerals, weddings and births formed much of the news, but in recent months there had been more funerals than births, and even less weddings. The young ones were leaving the town in droves.

222

'*Sorrows shadow drapes no more, or cowers the dear heart,*' she sang. 'Desist,' she said. 'You've become a singing fool. But you've left your run too late. Anyway, it would interfere with your writing time. You have enough on your plate without attempting to play middle-aged vocalist.' Her needle slid into the featureless face and she began to create a character.

By running threads from side to side through the fabric, she lent shape to the clowns' faces. She pinched up small noses, holding them high with invisible stitches. She fashioned ears, large and small, she stretched mouths into wide smiles or cheeky grins. The idea had come from the Cabbage-Patch dolls, fashionable many years ago, and many failures evolved before she perfected the art. Her hands were swift, and a small face once started, was quickly finished with a dimple in the cheek, and wide-set eyes. This would be the best face she'd worked tonight.

She had two dozen in the plastic bag beside her bed, but endeavoured not to count, allowing her hand to feel out the blank heads from the finished. Sooner or later, someone else would have to learn to work the faces. There were orders coming in from all over. Less than twelve months ago, she had sent out letters and photographs to craft shops all over New South Wales and Victoria, and for months had received no replies; then out of the blue they received an order from Echuca, and a second from Swan Hill. Since then it had snowballed.

'Too big, too fast, and the worst part about it is, I have lost interest. Lyn is good with a needle and thread. I'll teach her to work the faces, and maybe Liz Holden.'

Writing. It was a demanding occupation. It stole time from her garden. There was much that needed to be done. Each day since the funeral she had promised herself a day in the garden, but somehow she didn't get there.

She ate her breakfast with her typewriter, and her lunch. This unfolding tale was a force she could not hold back, so she was not holding back. She had written a sex scene that darn near made her blush!

Each evening she wrote, filling her blank paper with words, living her characters, speaking their words aloud. In her fictional world, she was in charge of who died, and how they died, and she killed at random, or her violent *Seraphani* did.

But inactivity had given her a neck-ache, so tonight she had closed her door on the typewriter, showered early, eaten a light dinner then climbed gratefully into bed. Propped high on pillows, she stitched clown faces, the small transistor radio beside her. It had earphones, which she would use when her father returned, but here in her own room, she allowed the radio freedom to sing.

Music was wonderful company. When the old radio in the lounge room had made way for a television set, she had missed it. Her father enjoyed his television shows, but she could always pick holes in their plots. Loose ends. She loathed loose ends, and she smiled now, her mind with the end of her novel, mentally tying up loose ends as she tied off the end of her green thread and chose one already threaded with gold. Her pincushion was filled with threaded needles.

A tuft of hair, a mouth of red given. Two questioning eyebrows, brown freckles on his nose and cheeks and he was done, dropped overboard into a plastic bag and a new face selected.

The last of fear had left her. Perhaps the tears she had cried that day had been inside her for too long, had filled her; the old lady's death had released a plug, emptied the barrel. Now a part of that dear woman had crept into the hollow, filled it up with something more positive than tears. And Thursday night at the club in Dorby, the dancing, the singing all the way home, had been cathartic.

And she'd almost said no. Almost.

Why?

'No fool like an old fool,' she said.

She was feeling better tonight than she'd felt for years and years, and younger, so much younger, stronger. Free.

It was odd, really, this sense of freedom. Had it been bought by her money, Miss Moreland's wardrobe, or by the haircut? She ran her fingers through her curls. Perhaps she'd have a little more cut off – and get a rinse. Bonny kept her hair vibrant with a rinse she bought at the supermarket. Stella had actually browsed in the hair-care aisle this morning, but she'd had no idea of what she might buy. There was such a choice.

She'd popped in for some cereal. Marilyn had had an X-ray appointment in Dorby, so Ron was alone. He always looked at her differently when Marilyn wasn't around. Previously, this had pleased Stella. She had once lived for a week on those stolen glances, those stolen smiles.

'I hope it's nothing to worry about, Ron,' she'd said to him this morning.

'She's always worrying about something,' he said. 'You look good today, Stell. I like your haircut.'

He never made personal comments when Marilyn was on the checkout, and the old pleasure had attempted to rear its head. Instead, Stella could only wonder how he had managed to spawn a rapist.

Not wanting to be long away from her writing, she'd walked quickly to the cereal department where she'd picked up a packet of toasted muesli. At the refrigerated section, she'd been studying the frozen meals, single serves; they were quite tasty and saved time in the kitchen. Then she'd looked up at Ron's reflection in the long mirror. She hadn't recognised him. He looked so old. For a split second, she'd believed she was looking at his father, dead these many years. He was the living image, and like his father, wed to a tyrant.

Ron had wanted to talk. He had taken his time at the cash register, but eager to get away, Stella cut the conversation short, took money from her handbag, surprising him with a fifty-dollar note, and she'd stood hand out, waiting for her change.

'Tell Marilyn to give me a call tonight, Ron. Do let me know how she got on. I have to fly now.'

Something had changed. She knew it, as did Ron.

Poor Ron. Poor Marilyn too. Second choice for the leading lady in *West Side Story*. Second choice for Ron, when he couldn't get Stella to 'go all the way'. Circumstances force us all into the roles we learn to play, Stella thought. Circumstances had forced her into her role of dutiful daughter.

Circumstances alter.

She loved her new stove and her new floor-covering, and her security doors, but her father would disapprove – and soon too. She'd spent so much money.

'He'll have a stroke when he sees that!' She glanced at the cordless telephone on her bedside table, beside her pincushion. It had been connected on . . . on Friday.

So much happening, it was difficult to keep track of the days. Her new phone followed her from room to room. It was so convenient, and to a degree gave her a sense of security. It had ten automatic dial buttons. This morning she had set them, following the instruction book to the letter. And it worked too. She had tested each one. Now she was one button away from Sergeant Johnson, one button away from Arnold Parsons – and from Steve Smith.

Steve was so nice. So plain, ordinary, straightforward, honest, nice. 'And he was only two years behind me in school,' she told a clown face.

And you started school a year early, Miss Moreland's voice reminded her.

'Yes, you wicked old matchmaker. You knew we'd be thrown together. Your two executors. Your big bon voyage party.' Stella laughed as she heard the tap, tap, tap of Miss Moreland's heels on concrete. 'I know you are out there, keeping an eye on me, but for all your scheming, my dear, nothing will come of it. We are both too shy – too set in our bachelor ways to take it further than a kiss on the cheek, a meal or two, and a song.'

Stella had allocated one of the phone's automatic buttons to old Mr Bryant, near blind, and too ill to live alone, but live alone he did. For some months now she had been concerned about him, but since Miss Moreland's death, she phoned him each morning, not wanting him to die alone in his bed. He had kept an eye out for her when she was young, so she would make it her business to keep an eye on him now he was old.

Number five button had been allocated to Bonny. Five still remained blank. Stella told herself she was saving them for the minister's use, but in truth there were no more phone numbers she wanted to add. Not Marilyn's. Since the rape, she had not been able to dial Marilyn's number, always afraid that her son, the rapist, may pick up the phone.

Six weeks. Six weeks that had been like a lifetime.

She shook the thought away, forced her mind to her father. What will he think of my spending? 'You'll have us in the poor house, Daughter,' she said in fair imitation of his tone, and she smiled again and stitched on.

He would return to a changed house. The new vinyl looked like tiles. So bright and clean, and so easy to clean. And the metal doors with their small keys that allowed her to lock herself in without locking away the breeze and birds and the perfumes of her garden. The old black stove, the evil beast of her childhood was gone. Ripped from the chimney and tossed to the dump, to rust, to rot. The workmen had cleaned the chimney of a hundred years of soot, sealed it with an exhaust fan, then placed white tiles over the smoke-blackened bricks before setting in the new electric range.

It looked so white and light, so clean and bright, she wanted to put in a new sink and get the men to tile behind it too. But maybe a new window first. A larger window. Or maybe a new kitchen. White laminated benches and cupboards –

Have I willed to you my spendthrift habits, girl?

'Perhaps. But it may be genetic, my dear. We are all the sum pool of a long line of genes. Look at Ron. How did I fail to notice how like his father he has grown?'

At least he is his father's son. In Maidenville, it is a lucky man who knows his own son.

'Stop this, Stella Templeton. You are becoming quite wicked. Along with her spendthrift habits, Miss Moreland has bequeathed to you her delightfully wicked mind,' Stella castigated herself.

Len Davis was coming in to paint the rooms next month. She'd already chosen the colours. Light. Bright. And she'd make new drapes too – dusty pink for the lounge and dining rooms, soft blue for her bedroom, and a green blind for the kitchen. The bathroom was overdue for a facelift. She wanted a new bath and shower recess built into the corner, and lots of tiles, bright tiles. Perhaps a dusty cream with a touch of maroon.

As with the kitchen, the bathroom window presented a major problem. Replacing windows required considerable structural work, the knocking out of old bricks. Still, it was possible. Steve had said it was. He said it was easier to do in a solid brick house than in a brick veneer. Both rooms needed more light. The bathroom by today's standards, was large, and its window, a small cell-like thing. With more light, she could have a pot plant or two in there which would give the room life. They'd thrive in the steamy atmosphere. Still, it would cost a lot of money. She'd wait until the minister came back and try to talk him into it.

'Some chance,' she said.

Another small clown head completed, she placed it in the plastic bag, and felt for a blank face. Most were done.

'Thank God,' she murmured.

The jacaranda limb knocked at the spouting. It definitely sounded like Miss Moreland's high heels tripping away – dragging her luggage behind her. In truth, Stella did not want the branch to die and fall now. It had become a comforting sound. The one she had respected above all others, had lived her life without learning fear, had died in her sleep, in her own bed, never recognising fear. It was a good way to die. The best possible way, just as everyone in town said. No warning. No weeks tied to a hospital bed. Just taken from her dream to ... to wherever.

Still, she shouldn't have died. She had years of life to live, and certainly on that final Saturday, she had not appeared to be ready for death.

Why had Sergeant Johnson been involved, and what had he been looking for? Stop that. I am doing too much writing. My imagination is beginning to rule me. She had a massive heart attack, as Doctor Parsons said.

How old is he now? she thought. He must have been, at the very least, twenty-three when he arrived here, which would make him sixty-seven. He's already past retirement age. Will Maidenville find another such as he when it is time for him to go? He had been attempting to obtain an assistant for the past three years, but Maidenville had little to offer.

With no doctor the hospital would die, and without a hospital, the school would eventually die. Parents would not want to send their children to board in a town fifty-eight kilometres from the closest doctor.

The country was dying. The best of Maidenville's youth left for the cities, or at least the larger centres. With little work to be had, there was nothing to keep school leavers in town.

Twenty years ago, Maidenville had boasted four banks, and each one had given employment to several men. The old picture theatre had employed one full-time girl and several part-timers. In those days there was work to be found on the surrounding farms, for both farmhands and domestics. And there had been so many more shops, each one requiring assistants. Today most of the older shops in Crane Street were empty. Even in Main Street, a few businesses had closed their doors, and now the ANZ Bank – that beautiful old building – would become vacant in June.

Sad. And frightening. Age is frightening, she thought. When we are young, we think the world will go on unchanged forever. The people who died back then were strangers, but we reach this stage in our lives when the ones we love begin to die, and suddenly, death is no longer for others. One day it will be Father's turn. How will I handle his death?

But it is odd, too, how we learn to accept. We walk by the empty shops without a second glance. And death. It is as if they go away – as Father has gone away. It's as if Miss Moreland took the morning bus to some place. I still think of her, but as I think of Father. I can no more see where he is at this time than I can see where she has gone. They are both away, but living on in my memory.

I do not fear death – not since that dear lady blazed the trail for me. I don't. I really don't. And I no longer fear that . . . that youth either. It's over. It was a momentary aberration, some madness he now regrets, and must live with. At the funeral, he looked as if guilt were eating him alive.

She turned her head to her closed window, still locked – as all of her windows and doors were locked. Perhaps she knew her words were false bravado. It would be a long, long time before Stella was brave enough to sleep again with her window wide.

Remember all our yesterdays. And the laughter and the tears. Tomorrow and tomorrow, will –

Another clown eye completed, she was snipping the thread as the old town clock struck eleven.

'Good grief,' she said. 'I am supposed to be having an early night. Where has my mind been wandering?'

Tomorrow was Tuesday. Her favourite day. No meeting. Not one thing that she must do, except to keep a breakfast appointment with her typewriter.

The unfinished face placed with the others in the bag, she turned off the light, turned her radio volume to low, then rolled to her side to listen a while, perhaps fall asleep with the music playing. So soothing. Music is so soothing, she thought.

the blue jeans

The room was black. A male voice on the radio spoke of God. She reached out a hand to still the voice and was confronted by a narrow beam of light.

'Who's a lucky girl tonight? Ah-ah, Aunty Stell just won the lottery.'

Then the light blazed overhead, flooding the room, framing the figure in jeans and sweatshirt.

'No!' she cried. 'No.' Only halfway back from sleep, she tried to rise up in her bed, but he was on her bed, on her, his weight pinning her legs beneath the quilt.

'No.' She hit out at him. She swiped at his face, and grasped at his hair, but he caught her hands and held them in one of his own strong hands and he laughed.

'Come on. Don't be coy. You like it. Admit it. Did I give you a taste for it, eh? I hear you've been getting a bit from old Steve lately.'

She opened her mouth, screamed in his face, and quite casually, he backhanded her, connecting hard with her ear.

No hand had been raised against her in too many years. She

had forgotten the shock of the hard hand. For an instant she cowered from him and it gave him the advantage. A yellow, plastic-handled Stanley knife held at her throat, he stripped, tossing his shirt, his jeans to the floor. He dragged the quilt back, the radio fell to the floor, and the voice died.

'No playing around tonight, Aunty Stell, or you get cut,' he said, and he ripped her light cotton nightgown from neck to hem, he slashed her blue briefs at the hip, then he entered her, brutally, painfully, muffling her screams with a pillow held to her face.

The chance, the time to scream was gone. Now she sucked air through the fibres, but not enough air – not enough to scream. Lungs bursting, mouth open, she sucked cloth, not air.

Red mist beginning. Red mist, clouding her brain. The world was darkening, sliding away.

No more time to live, to care, to grow, to write. No new bathroom window. No new curtains. No more dreams.

The pain in her lungs and throat overrode all other pain. Soon that pain would die too, and she would die. This was how it was written down to happen. She was Maidenville's number three.

But I have just begun to live, she thought.

The world was going far away. Dark now. Time became another time of sucking air through feathers. Another heavy hand, pressing down, down.

Heavy footsteps pounding up the stairs.

'*Angel! Angel! What in God's name – ?*'

And the hand slid from the pillow, and the pillow slipped, and crushed lungs sucked in air ... kept sucking in air, until air exploded in a hash dry sob. She coughed. She gagged, and she sucked air enough to scream it out at the figure looming large above her, large against the light.

Spitting brown/grey shape with her vile accusations and her mad eyes, her kitchen knife in hand to cut out the bad.

But it was the wrong shape. It was saying the wrong words.

'Lick me,' the new shape said, pushing his genitals at her face. 'Go on. Lick me with your silky tongue and I might let you live for a while.'

'Bow to her will, Daughter. Don't argue with her when she is not rational.'

'Better ... that I ... am dead.' A hoarse whisper. Uncertain to whom she was replying, she closed her eyes against this insanity, clinging to these last moments of her life, searching her mind for some sanity. Her lips pressed together, she moaned, moaned long, her head shaking, denying, until the moan became a hum and the hum became a melody, Miss Moreland's song, perhaps seeking strength from the one who had been her strength.

He hit her again. He sat back on his heels. Hit her. Again. And again. And each time it jolted her brain. Jolted her out of the now and into –

'Say the magic word. Say it. Say it.'

'Shut that up, or I'll kill you now. Shut up with that bloody song. I hate it. It was stupid. It was a stupid bloody funeral, her sitting up there with her stupid dark glasses on, staring at me, accusing me. It was a bloody mad house, you crazy old bitch. And my bloody old man made me help carry her out. You need locking up. My mother said you needed locking up, and so does he.'

She sobbed a breath, then a second. She blinked at the light, then closed her eyes against it, and she hummed. It was all she had, and she clung to it.

'Shut up.' If he hit her, she felt no pain. 'Are you listening to me? I said, shut that up.'

'Are you listening? Are you listening to me?'

Thump.

'Look at me.'

Thump.

'Say the magic word.'

Thump.

'Look at me. Look at me, I said.'

Thump.

'I'm talking to you. Don't you pass out on me. You look at me. I want you to look at me. Now.'

Thump.

'Don't you pass out.'

She opened her eyes, and her tongue tasted blood, and she saw his tongue sweep his lips, and she saw his feral eyes were afraid.

'Yeah. That's better. That's better. I've got a bun in Kelly Murphy's oven. Do you know that? Wouldn't it be a laugh? Wouldn't it just ... if they did the autopsy on you and found out you were pregnant?'

Cut. Cut out the bad.

'Men with their love, and their lust, and their filthy needs. He wants to stick it in you. I know. They all want to make whores out of their little daughters, make their little bellies swell with seething crawling little parasites. You'll find out.'

'Old goody-goody two-shoes, didn't tell a soul. I knew you wouldn't. I bet if it had been someone else you would have told everyone.' He kneeled between her legs, watching her, and she watched his thumb slide another centimetre of steel from the plastic handle of the knife. She made no response when he pressed the blade to her throat. He pressed harder. She swallowed, and her chin lifted.

'I could cut your head off with this right now. It'd be easy. Just like nothin'. Just like cutting the head off a dead rabbit.'

Nothing. No sting of pain. Heat. Only heat.

He smiled, repeating the action an inch lower, wanting to see her cringe, wanting her little rabbit chin to tremble.

'It could slit your throat open with one swipe, let your blood spout across the room. You'd be dead in ten minutes. I read somewhere that if you cut that artery, here, you can bleed to death in ten minutes. Your heart stops, but your brain doesn't. You'd be lying there dead and your brain would still be asking, Why? Why? What did I do?'

He'd given her a word, and she used it.

'Why?'

'Because I felt like it, and because you're it. You're this fucking town, you are – with your holier than shit act, your little beige pleated skirts hiding your black knickers. Panting around after my father. You wanted it. Your tongue was hanging out for it. Fucking shit town, and you're just fucking shit too. I know all about you and my old man. You think my mother is your friend, but she hates your guts.'

Shivering uncontrollably, each breath of air a shallow sob, words were fought-for things, and she could not grasp one. She was in and out of time zones. She was in the past, and in this bed.

'She thinks you did it with him. I hear her going on, and on, about you and him. Maybe I should tell her different, eh? Set her mind at rest. What do you think, Aunty Stell? Do you think I should tell her that the old man didn't get into your frilly knickers?' He slapped her face with his free hand. 'I asked you, what do you think?'

She lay limp beneath him, her eyes closed. His left hand pinched her nipple while he watched for her reaction. There was none, but Thomas craved response. 'It's your fault too about old lady Moreland. You can blame yourself for that one,' he said, checking out the other nipple, wondering why Kelly had nothing to grip onto and why old Stell had no boobs but nipples worth sucking on. He licked the nipple, bit her, then laughed. 'I did it to her too. You should have seen her crappy old face.'

Now she reacted. Her eyes opened wide. Now he got what he wanted. She shook off yesterday, and his second-hand words, and she rose up from the pillow, screaming in his face. He wasn't ready for it. Her breasts were bare, her briefs, caught on one ankle, he was kneeling between her legs, and she screamed as she should have screamed on that day in the shed. She screamed, and she hammered him with her fist, drew breath, and screamed at him.

'Beast. Vile demonic little beast.' She sucked in more air and screamed it out. 'Evil, black-souled demon. May you burn in hell for all eternity.'

Her brain was functioning now. Telephone. The telephone. One button would bring Sergeant Johnson. Doctor Parsons. Steve. One button. Turn it on, and press one button. The right button. Get it in your hand. You'll only have one chance. Don't look at it. Look at him. Look at evil. Grab the telephone and hit the button then hit him with it. Aim for his eye with the aerial while you scream. She drew a breath. Held it. Then she grabbed wildly for the phone, but he saw her aim and he grasped the phone first, tossing it behind him at the wall, forcing her down.

'You liked that, didn't you? Want to hear some more? Want to hear what she said to me?'

'May God strike you dead. May God strike you dead. May God strike you dead,' she chanted over and over. 'May you die in pain and agony, and rot, you demonic evil little beast. May you feed the dogs in hell.'

'There isn't any hell, and there isn't any heaven, and you shut up about it, and listen to me. Do you know what she said, I asked you? She said my grandfather would be proud of me. I was halfway through doing it, and she started laughing. She's sort of choking herself laughing, and I thought the old bat was getting to like it. Then she sort of stiffened, came up at me, and an electric shock went through her. And I thought, wow. Like, wow, lady, and here I've been wasting it on Kelly Murphy. Then she sort of sagged, gagged, and when I got off her, she didn't move any more. First dead body I ever saw.'

Stella lay shaking her head, backwards and forwards. Tears were coming now, tears to weaken her, but she must not weaken. She screamed again, killed her tears.

'Shut up, or I'll have to finish you now, and I'm not ready yet. Don't you want to know what happened? I've been dying to tell someone. That's the worse part about it, not being able to tell anyone. I was going to tell Kelly, but her old man won't let her out. You want to know the grisly details?'

'Kill me, Thomas. Kill me now or I will see you dead.'

'What's your hurry? Dead is for keeps. I can vouch for that. I stuck around for a while after she croaked, just to see if she was going to wake up, but she didn't, so I put her in her bed and covered her over with a blanket, tucked her in, walked out and shut the door. Did you know that they didn't find her for nearly two days? A neighbour found her. She was probably fly blown.'

An involuntary sound, the pitiful cry of a trapped beast, growled in her throat as she lay there, denying the vision of the grand old lady violated on her own bed, but laughing in his face. She didn't cry.

'Why? Why?'

'Because I felt like it at the time, and because I thought she'd be easy, and because you're a stupid old bitch. You just took it, and then you kept your mouth shut. What did you think I'd do? Forget it? It's like something else, man. It's like ... like the power, and you're not real anyway. You're a fake, like this bloody town is a fake. I watched you walk into church that day in your little straight skirt and your little tight-arsed shoes as if nothing had happened. As if I'd done nothing. Was nothing. Nothing!

'Do you reckon old lady Moreland wouldn't of dobbed on me? Lucky for her she croaked, or I would of had to do it for her. Cut her with my knife. I was going to anyhow, going to practise on her. Go for the carotid artery. See what it felt like. I picked an easy one to start with, but she wasn't so easy as I thought, the tough old cow.'

'I wish you dead, Thomas Spencer.'

'Wish in one hand, and spit in the other, and see which one fills up first.' He hit her behind her ear with the handle of the knife gripped inside his fist, and the combination of fist and handle sent an agonising jolt of pain through her head. 'You've got the guts of a rabbit and rabbits don't deserve to live.'

Willpower held onto consciousness, but it was minutes before she could hear his words.

'Are you listening to me?'

'Yes.'

'Bend to his will, give him what he wants.'

Her head was throbbing. Next time, next time may be the last. 'Yes. I am listening, Thomas.'

'People used to reckon you did it with your old man too. Living here with him behind your fence, hiding your sin with your lacy knickers behind the hedge. Everyone thought so. Your mother told them he did it to you.'

The kitchen knife. Sharp.

Red on her stomach.

'Cut it out. Cut all the bad out.'

Footsteps pounding the stairs.

And the man with the gnome face smoothing child Stella's brow, threatening the minister, 'Put her away, or I swear to God I'll report it. She'll kill this child one day.'

'It is not her fault. Her father. She was barely thirteen when the bastards aborted her child. It is self loathing, and not her fault, Parsons. She is seeing herself again in her own child.'

'She goes, or you get this little one out of the house.'

'The turns come and go. She will be all right again.'

'Do you want to be charged as an accessory to your own child's murder?'

'I'll speak to Miss Moreland. Perhaps she could board at the school until – until things settle down.'

Stella lay watching the ceiling turn, lurch down at her, swim before her eyes. She could hear the whooshing whirr of blood-waves in her ears. Slowly she gained control of her mind. Red pain faded into a pinkish mist through which she could see pure distilled evil ... as she had once seen Angel. Pure essence of evil leaning over her bed, this same bed, her mouth spitting accusations. She saw the hand rise and she cowered.

'No more. No more. I'll be good,' she begged, and she turned her face to the side. One eye had closed. The other looked down at the clown heads she'd embroidered only hours ago, a lifetime ago. One clown eye was blind too. It was staring at her from its plastic bag. Its long legs waiting in another bag, waiting to be joined to the body.

I am as the clown. I have one eye, my other is closing now. My limbs are missing. Numb. I have been unpicked. My right leg is still held to me by a stitch or two, but not my left. Is it there, or in some plastic bag, awaiting the rest of me?

For how long he had been sitting astride her, she didn't know. Cat with a broken mouse, playing with the broken mouse until the fun is over and the mouse dies.

'We're going to drown. We're going to drown,' cried timid Mousy One.

'Oh goodness gracious dearie me, our little lives are done.'

The seed he had spilled was drying on the sheet, gluing her skin to the sheet ... like stiffening eggwhite, tightening the skin.

Egg. Birth. Death. Grave.

She tried to move her left leg. The knife touched her throat.

'Stay where you are.'

She was dead if she must rely on defeating him with muscle. Bow to his will as she had bowed to another ... play the old cat and mouse game again. She used to know how to play that game.

'I love you, my dearest mummy. You are the best mummy in the whole world. Let's go for a walk in the garden, Mummy, and we'll find some flowers, and I'll pick some for you, and you will be like famous Angel in the photo. Come on, Mummy. You open the door and we'll go and pick some flowers.'

Trees to climb in the garden. Fences to clamber over. Safe in the garden. Old Mr Bryant over one fence. Mrs Wilson over the other. Just get the door open a crack, just get outside, and see which way the game would go today.

Play the game, Stella. Roll the dice and see if your lucky number comes up. Maybe you'll find today's magic word.

But Mousy Two, her chin held high, was circling round and round.

'Please don't despair, keep swimming, a way out may be found.'

Tap, tap, tap. Tap, tap, tap. High heels across a floor.

It startled Thomas. He moved, turned to the window and Stella snatched her left leg free, flexed the muscle, raised her knee, taking the weight from her heel to the sole of her foot. Blood started its painful journey down from her buttock.

'What's that?

'Miss Moreland always wore shoes with heels,' she said.

His eyes were wide. A child's eyes, but his hand was a man's. Again the knife came close to her face. 'Don't you try that on me. You can't get at me with your tricks. I read a book once where the dame wouldn't shut up with her psychobabble, so the hero cut her head off. Then he went to sleep, which was stupid, and the headless corpse rose from the dead and she got him with an axe. It was plain stupid in the end. As if he'd go to sleep. He'd be hyped up. Hyped out of his brain.' He looked at her, the knife's point placed between her eyes. 'He'd be on a real high. Couldn't sleep if he tried. I couldn't sleep after I did Miss Moreland. Didn't sleep until they found her on Monday, then I crashed. I was out of it for sixteen hours solid.'

Her left eye refused to see, but the other turned to look at the out of focus steel blade, the yellow of handle.

Tap, tap, tap.

He silenced, listening again to the dragging sound of wood on metal, followed by a louder tap, tap, tap.

'It's the tree. It's the tree knocking against the roof. You lying old bitch. You knew what it was, didn't you?' He hit her. 'Didn't you? You knew, didn't you?'

'Please, Thomas – '

'Please what? Want me to do it again, eh? Want to take some pleasant memories with you to Jesus? Want to help me this time. Lick me with your silky tongue – buy yourself some time. I did it three times in one night with Kelly Murphy. She's got a good tongue.'

Tap, tap, tap.

His eyes grew wide again, then he said quickly. 'It's like that poem – something about knocking at my wee small door, and nothing much was stirring on the still dark night. It's black as pitch outside – a good night for creeping around. Nothing much stirring in the still dark night. No-one saw me come here. No-one will see me leave. No-one will think it was me. I'm lily white. I go to church on Sunday.'

'People see many things now that the hedge is gone.'

'Did you guess I did it?' His smile was a naughty boy's.

'Did you know it was me who put that mouse in your drawer, Aunty Stell?'

'I knew, Thomas,' she replied to the part of him who had placed the toy mouse in her dressing-table drawer, to the part of him who had once loved to sit at her side and listen to the old poems, the stories. She searched his face now for that part that remained the child, a child who might still be reached.

'No-one's got a clue that I did Miss Moreland. I hid my bike in front of the hospital then crept around the garden to the units. I knocked on her door and she let me in. "What can I do for you at this hour, Thomas Spencer?" she said. So I showed her.

'No-one saw me creep up the stairs. I did it when you and Mummy was in the shed getting the stuffing.'

'No-one saw me coming in here. I put my bike behind your shed.'

'Someone always sees, Thomas.'

'Good old God? Don't give me your God crap.'

'Your mother will know you were out.'

'My mother knows nothing. She comes home from work at night, and she wipes off her stupid supermarket grin, and she gets stuck into the old man. He gives me some money for take-away, just to get rid of me, and if I'm lucky when I get back they've taken a couple of sleeping pills and they're both snoring.

They don't know if I'm back or not till breakfast. They don't give a fuck what I do, and they couldn't care less either. They're shit parents. Too busy making war and lousy money to care what I ever did.' He stopped, and he tossed his hair back from his brow. 'I'll be home for breakfast in the morning, and she'll say, "What did you do last night, Tommy?" She won't listen to what I tell her. I could say, "Oh, I fucked old Stell, then cut her throat, got home around dawn," and she'd still say, "Good boy. Don't forget to put the garbage out, will you?"'

'Clever Thomas.'

'Yeah. Serial killers need to have a brain or they don't get to be serial killers. Get it? They get caught first time, which would affect their success rating. They'll blame your murder on some stranger, someone just passing through, and they'll talk about the pokies at Dorby, and the highway going through the town, and how it's bringing bad elements in, and they'll say how the government ought to put in a bypass, and how if the hedge was still up and the gate shut, that you might have been still alive today.'

'Perhaps they will.'

'I'll rob you, take any money you've got hanging around, up-end a few drawers and things, make sure I don't leave any fingerprints.'

He looked at the bedhead, then at his hands. 'I haven't touched anything. I touched the door handle at Miss Moreland's bedroom, but I wiped it clean. Anyway, they haven't got my prints on record so they'd have nothing to compare them with, would they?'

'As you say, Thomas.'

'Stop doing that.'

'I'm sorry. What am I doing?'

'Calling me Thomas all the time. It's like you're my bloody aunty or something.'

'An honorary aunt. Wasn't I always an honorary aunt? Weren't you always my favourite honorary nephew?'

'You're nothing to me. Just a good fuck.' He fondled her breast, nursed on it, and she became his toy, his old abused rag doll.

She didn't fight him when he entered her again. She felt no pain, no shame. It meant only that she was able to raise her other knee, to place both feet flat on the mattress. There was nothing to be gained from pleas or tears. She must conserve energy, relax her muscles. Her good eye was wide open now. It was watching the greedy boy's face lose its personality as a heaviness saturated his features.

How close he is, and how ... how vulnerable, she thought, so vulnerable because of his youth and his lack of fear. Fear is good. Fear is necessary. How certain and sure he is of his supremacy. Little boy with his knife in his hand and his raping weapon driving into her, driving deeper, and deeper, between her legs.

She moved beneath him, aware that if she was to live until morning, she must stay in this place of no pain and no shame, she must view this happening as from a great distance. He had told her of the rape of Miss Moreland. Now she would be obligated to tell the world of his deed. And he knew this. Her Thomas was no fool. He had never been a fool, and to save himself, he must certainly kill her before he left the house tonight.

The hand that held the knife was supporting his weight on her pillow. Her throat might be slit with little need for movement, but his concentration was not now on the knife.

Tentatively her left hand rose to stroke his shoulder, just as it had when he was a child. She allowed her fingers to move to the nape of his neck where she smoothed and stroked his hair.

'Dear Thomas,' she said. 'How I loved you when you were small. Of all the little boys in town, I loved you best,' but her other hand, her right hand, was over the side of the bed, seeking, circling, reached for ... something. Anything. Knitting needle. Something. Hope. Anything. 'You were such a beautiful little boy. I used to pretend you belonged to me. How I wanted you to belong to me.'

Her seeking fingers touched only the plastic bag, half filled with clown heads. It continued its circling, then returned to plastic. Her one eye watched his face, saw his own eyes close. She moved beneath him as she grasped the bag, tilted it, up-ended it, allowing the small knitted heads to tumble soundlessly to the carpet. Her hand keeping low, she drew the bag along the edge of the bed, until her arm was at full stretch. And she held it there, her fingers inside its open end, her thumb gripping ... gripping it ... until ...

'Dear Thomas.' She stroked his neck with her fingers, matching the rhythm of her fingers to his motion. No pain, only the heat of him, and the tension in her right arm. She moved her feet, pressing her heels into the mattress.

He stiffened. He screamed as a child might scream. His neck arched, his eyes closed, and he flung his head back.

And she struck.

Her left hand came together with her right. The bag held open by her palms, slipped easily over his head, exactly as she might slip a similar bag over a finished clown.

Simple. Easy.

At the same time she bore down on her heels and flung her weight at the off-balanced youth, pushing him to his back, her action sliding the bag down ... down to the still slim vulnerable boy's neck, where her hooked thumbs gripped the plastic, while her hands, with a twist and a turn, wound the excess around her palms.

Fast motion. Slow motion. Time lived in another place. Seconds became minutes and minutes hours.

He rolled to the side. She rolled with him, straddling him, locking her ankles now behind his knees, holding him inside her.

Green eyes grew wide in protest behind the film of plastic they now shared with another green-eyed clown, but the big clown mouth was not smiling; it grew wide, pink, it sucked plastic. Its nostrils flared and whitened as they sucked in the transparent film. The throat bulged.

Her hands were strong. They had learned to be strong. Now they fought for her life, joined together by a twisted plastic bag. She was locked in a battle to the death and there could only be one winner.

Fists hammered against her. The knife drove into her rib cage. She felt no slice of pain. Perhaps it was the handle. If not, then she may not outlive him long. But she would outlive him. She would outlive him. Vengeance is mine, said the Lord, but tonight vengeance belonged to Stella.

Like a wild-west rider, she rode him while he bucked and fought to be free of her. Her hands were crushed beneath him. Hot. There was heat in her knees, her hips, but no pain. No room for pain. He kicked at air, fought for air, then the knife dropped with a clunk to the carpet, and too late his fingers sought the plastic, clawed at the film of plastic.

But slowly.

With no nails to grip, to rip, his movements were slowing.

Slow.

Slower.

More slowly.

And more slowly still.

He stopped fighting, sagged.

And she breathed. She looked.

His face had changed colour behind the plastic film glued to his features as if a paintbrush had painted it there. The small clown head, with the green eyes and the glint of gold, smiled as it clung to his ear.

cooling flesh

She waited.

Waited long after he stopped moving. Waited.

Slowly then she dragged her legs free, one first, then the other. She waited again, before sliding them over the side of the bed. Her feet, dead things, refused to support her, and she sank to the floor, entangled in the sheet, but still gripping the plastic bag with hands grown numb as her feet.

She waited until her mind was capable of setting forth the plan to unwind the cutting plastic. Then she waited again, afraid if she unwound it, he would draw breath and rise up, rip the bag from his head.

Hands, dead lumps of wood, were slowly freed. First the left. Then the right. Pain came then. Pain was all over, in her hips, and her feet, where it regrouped its army of pain to rush her hands.

Agony. Agony of another time. She looked at her hands, expecting to see the small white gloves that for weeks had camouflaged Angel's guilt.

Small hands pressed to the black stove, held to the black heat.

Smell of burning while Angel screamed, 'Feel the flames of hell as I once felt them.'

Rationality was skittering away. Far away. Her feet entangled in the sheet, Stella didn't know how to handle the task of the untangling. Her mind was pulsating, forward and back. Back and forward. She had to grasp at the forward and impel herself through the barrier, back into the now.

How.

Almost over. Almost home. Get that phone.

Miss Moreland, my dear lady. Forgive me. Forgive me. Forgive me my false pride. Forgive me.

Pick up the phone. Pick up that phone.

Stella began pulling at the sheet, pulling, pulling until she was free of it, of him, then she placed her forehead on the carpet amid the small clown heads, and her hands came together, her index fingers touching the point of her chin, as if in prostrate prayer to some ancient old god of the kill. No words came. No tears. And she heard no accusations. The old gods were all sleeping, and the one true God had flown away. Far away.

The head lolling over the side of the bed was close to her own. A hand, with open fingers, touched the floor. She backed away, backed on her knees until she reached the dressing-table, where she drew herself up, leaning heavily on the solid unit.

Slowly she released her grip on the wood and stood alone, looking at her hands, staring at the deeply embedded lines of red and white across the scarred palms. For minutes, she stood staring at her hands, at the burn scars she'd grown with, that had grown with her, then her gaze lifted and she looked across her hands to her bed.

He hadn't moved.

She sighed, turned, caught a glimpse of her nakedness in the mirror, saw his naked limbs reflected behind her.

Dead limbs. Dead. Dead. Dead.

She was looking at Ron Spencer's only son, and at the face of his killer. His killer. She had killed. Two faces in the mirror.

Two killers. One was that of a twisted clown, wrapped up in a plastic bag, packaged up for delivery. The other was a blank face, not worked yet. Empty.

She tried to move to the door, but her feet tripped on the blue jeans he had tossed at the floor. She stepped on them, felt the sharp stud beneath her foot. She lifted her foot, then used it to move the jeans aside.

Stooping hurt. She sucked air. Everything hurt. Pain was everything, but the phone was on the floor. She overrode pain, stooped, picked up the phone and pressed the talk button. She pressed number one. No light. Something was wrong. Time after time she pressed the talk button, then the number. The phone was dead, as the clown was dead. She tried all the buttons. Nothing. And the telephone slipped from her hands to the floor, bounced on the floor, bounced near the denim jeans. But she didn't want to see them, so she turned her back and stared at the mirror.

Naked. Naked breasts. She had feared naked.

Once.

The telephone had worked.

Once.

She looked down to the pale triangle of her pubic hair, and at the scar in the shape of a cross above the hair, and she touched the cross. She had feared that cross too.

Once.

Not red any more. White. Always there, but never there.

Hide it. Hide it in the showers at school. No-one must know. Hide it behind the tall hedge. Mustn't tell. Mustn't ever tell on Mummy. Daddy said.

Two slow steps away from the mirror and she was against the bed. More naked flesh. She turned to it and saw the puny shrunken thing between his legs.

Have to cover it. Cover it up. Hide it. Mustn't tell.

She picked up the sheet, used it to clean herself, then she tossed the defiled thing down. His sweatshirt had fallen to the floor beside the bed. It was studded with small smiling heads. She took it, shook the small clowns free.

The shirt smelt of him. She held it to her nose, breathed in the scent of his sweat. No more fear in that scent. Nothing. Fear was dead. She shrugged, pulled the garment over her head.

'To the conqueror go the spoils of victory,' she whispered, reaching down for his jeans, shaking them out, stepping naked into them.

The stud, clipped. Zipped, the rapist's fly. Cuffs rolled – as she had rolled other cuffs on another day. A fine day. Day with Bonny. Day long ago in the fitting room.

They're too baggy. Show us a size smaller.

She looked in the mirror. Too big. Too loose in the waistband. 'But you have no choice today,' she said. 'No choice at all.' And she walked from the room and down the stairs, past the telephone and outside to wander amongst the damp perfumes in her dark garden.

It was later when she unlocked the shed doors, flung them wide. Perhaps her action was a primitive celebration of freedom, as was the wearing of her rapist's clothing; she was far beyond all conscious thought. Standing in the open doorway she looked at the Packard, then like a sleepwalker she turned, looked towards the house.

'Where would you like to go today, Mother?'

Each movement an effort, each action a reflex thing, born of the moment, she turned towards the house, seeing that which was no longer there.

'Coming, Mother,' she whispered, and she walked to the back door, took the Packard's keys from the top of the kitchen dresser and returned to the car.

Its odour was of aged leather and polish. A clean odour. She slid into the driver's seat and she placed the key in the ignition. It turned over slowly, then caught, ticking quietly as she reversed out of the shed and began backing the big vehicle up the drive to the front door. Angel had always left by the front door.

Obese Angel, barely capable of walking in her last years. Angel, the invalid on her brown leather couch, eating chocolate biscuits, stuffing herself with food. Unkempt, unwashed. Sister Brooks had come to bath her twice a week, bath her in a tub. She couldn't walk upstairs. She slept in the small downstairs room. Upstairs was safe now. Angel was safe too. Doctor Parsons came twice each day to inject her medication and make her safe, safe enough to take beyond the hedge on the days she had her bath because she had to have a double dose or Sister Brooks wouldn't come. They were the good days. Stella took her touring. Mad Angel in the back seat, while the driver sat up front, ice tingles down her spine.

Watch her in the rear-vision mirror. Don't fear the other drivers on the road, fear precious Angel. Watch her. Always watch her. Don't take your eyes off her. Not for a second. Drive to Dorby, drive for hours. You are out of the house, so just drive – but watch her.

'Too dark.' Stella whispered. 'Too dark to go out touring. The world is sleeping, Mother.'

So dark, she was unaware that the car had left the gravelled drive until the Packard's wheels sunk into a garden bed.

'Lights,' she said, and her hand searched for the lights. Somewhere.

A seeking hand found the switch, and too suddenly, the drive was floodlit. She drove the big car forward until the twin beams illuminated the shed floor, showing the empty space where the Packard had been, and she sat staring at the permanent indentations the Packard's wheels had made on the earthen floor. Twin hollows, worn by the tyres' movement in the sixty years this vehicle had called this space home.

'The world is sleeping, Mother, and you are blissfully dead. Blissfully, wonderfully dead. Dead. Delightfully dead. So. So, why do I need the car tonight if you are dead?'

250

But she did need it. Someone needed it.

The clown did. Delivery. It had to go away. Now that it had been made safe, she had to take it somewhere. Delivery to –

Always doing deliveries. Always someone wanting something.

'Where do I have to take him?'

'To Marilyn?'

She shook her head, aware that that was a bad thought. The key turned in the ignition and the motor stilled. The night silenced. Leaving the lights on, she climbed from the car and returned to the shed.

'There is always a logical answer to a problem that appears to defy logic,' she said, unaware she was in a place outside of logic. 'Be logical. I am alive and he is not. The logical course of action would be to telephone Sergeant Johnson. The downstairs phone will be working, so what am I doing out here?

'What do I say? Sorry to wake you, Sergeant, but there is a clown in my bedroom and I'd like it removed. Or Ron. Good evening, Ron. This is Stella. Thomas's party has ended. Can you come around and pick him up, please?' She shook her head, her eyes scanning the shed.

'Be logical,' she whispered.

The big green waste container was near the back door. Put him in it and wheel him out to the nature strip for the garbage man to take away.

Fitting, but perhaps illogical.

'I have to hide it.

'No more hedge to hide it behind, Father. The hedge is gone.

'God help me. What have I done?

'But what is done cannot be undone,' she whispered. 'Except for Mrs Morris's clowns. They can be undone.'

She walked to the mark of the wheel indentations. Squatting, walking crab-like, she scratched a rectangle in the centre with the car keys. For minutes she remained there, looking at the rectangle, too weary to do more than look. Then she stood, walked to the far corner, and selected her favourite spade and her pick. Dragging the tools behind her, she returned to the car and turned off the lights.

The new dark of the shed was complete. She stood in the centre of the rectangle, picking at the earth until her eyes adjusted to the dark. It was just a little hole, a deeper black in the all black. Just a very silly little hole. Just something to do because she didn't know what to do, and she couldn't face what she had done, so she kept picking and shovelling. She was digging in the garden. She was making a hole, large enough to plant a small rose bush, or to bury a dead bird. She worked on, her mind far away.

Hard-packed virgin earth, it would not easily give up its place in the scheme of things, but eventually her small wheelbarrow became full. Too full to accept more soil. It kept trickling off. For minutes she looked at the barrow's rounded shape, a shadowy shape in the near black of the shed. She tried to lift the handles, but her hands burned.

'Can't,' she said.

Stained-glass window. Jesus on the cross. Hands required to be placed palms-together, index fingers on the point of the chin. Throbbing hands, throbbing as Jesus's own poor hands must have throbbed.

'Can't,' she said.

Chin up, Mousy Two.

She sighed, lifted her chin, then she took up the handles of the barrow. Lifted. Her hip screamed, her shoulder throbbed, so she dropped the handles, spilled earth.

'I can't.

'But I will, because I have to,' she said. Again she gripped the handles and she wheeled her load into the vegetable garden, emptying it there to a fallow plot.

The next barrow load was emptied beside the first, but when she returned to the shed, the first pink blush of a pre-dawn sky gave light enough to see how little impression her labour had made in the centre of her rectangle. She narrowed her image of the hole, digging a small ditch to mark her new smaller triangle. Again she transferred earth to the garden.

Daylight came slowly, and with it the deeper layer, the pre-clay. She was emptying her barrow along the eastern fence when a bald head popped over.

'G'day,' Mr Wilson said.

She stared at the bald head of reality, of neighbour, and she recognised reality, but hid her face from it.

'G'day there. What are you up to?'

She had to reply. Find a word or two. What word?

'Gardening.' Familiar words are always the last to desert the tongue.

'Yeah. I can see that. What are you putting down there?'

'Earth.'

'You're into it bloody early, aren't you?'

'Yes. The removal of your trees, Mr Wilson. Thank you. Father will be delighted.' Old wars were safe wars. Far better to rekindle the old tree war than to struggle yet with too-new conflicts. Far better.

'Humph.'

The one and a half metre fence only allowed her eyes to peep over. She did not peep this morning, but remained stooped, head low. He was a bare fraction taller than she. Hands supporting him on the top of the palings, his looked down at her crouching form.

'What 'ave you done to your eye then?'

Her hand rose to touch her eye, closed tight now. 'I took a tumble. Down the stairs. In the dark.' Old lies were good lies, far better than today's lies.

'What in heaven's name happened to the child, Angel?'

'She took a tumble down the stairs. Clumsy. I've never seen a child so clumsy.'

'You want to watch yourself on those bloody stairs. That's

how your mother did her back in. I wouldn't give you tuppence for a house with stairs.'

'*What happened to her, Daughter?*'

'*She took a tumble down the stairs, Father.*'

Never again had Angel made it up the stairs. Never again.

'God works in mysterious ways, his wonders to perform,' she said.

He scratched at his bald scalp, attempting to digest her reply. 'Yeah. Well, you can say what you like about your mysterious ways. Your bloody old man went on and on about our trees keeping your house in shadow. You ought to see what your bloody house does to our kitchen now that me trees are gone.'

'Illogical,' she said, concentrating on scraping leaves and mulch over the telltale clods of clay as her neighbour edged one foot onto the fence railing. He clung there, head over the fence, one finger pointing at her empty wheelbarrow.

'Bloody logical nothing. Don't you go building it up too high over there. You'll block the natural draining of the land.' Then his hands left the paling and he stepped away. Stella trundled her barrow back to the shed.

She counted seven barrow-loads that did not equal one hole, so she gave up counting. The count was growing too high, and her pit was not growing low enough, fast enough. Number seven was being emptied behind the shed when she saw the bike, the red racer, purchased from Sydney before Christmas. It was leaning against her shed, accusing her of something she did not wish to think about. She had set herself a task, and it would be done, and when it was done she'd think about why she was doing it.

The barrow tossed to its side, she wheeled the bike into the shed, pushing it into the storeroom where she covered it with an old tarpaulin.

Hide it away.

Cover it up.

There were several aged tarpaulins folded neatly in the back corner of the storeroom. She chose one and dragged it close to the hole, carefully spreading it flat there. Mr Wilson would be watching now through the cracks in the fence, and he'd have his wife at his side. They mustn't see what she was doing. Easier to keep the clay close at hand, anyway. And faster, much faster to dispense with the barrow.

'Bucket,' she said. 'Fill a bucket and empty it into the tarpaulin.'

By 9 a.m. she was in the hole, picking, shovelling, lifting her half-filled buckets, tossing the clay to the side. An automaton. A robot, set in motion to dig a hole. Ache and self had been placed aside. There was the picking, the loosening of the earth, and the scooping up of the earth. There was the mental measuring of a square, and the reducing of that square to clods, the transferring of the clods to bucket, to tarpaulin. There was the noise of the traffic on the highway, and the thunk, thunk, thunk, of her pick on clay.

She came upon the root in the late morning. It was as thick as her calf, and driving down, deep into the clay near the centre of her hole. She did not question its origin, but followed it with interest, as an archaeologist might follow an ancient bone – until the pick handle slid free, leaving the business end of the tool jammed deep in the root.

Her energy exhausted, she squatted over the pick, panting in the earthy air. Her hands could not find the strength to work the pick free. Dug into a narrow hole by her following of the root, she had left herself little room to manoeuvre. Now she kicked at the pick that refused to budge. She turned her back, hammering at it with the heel of her pedi-rest.

'Wood axe,' she said, clambering out and walking purposely to the corner where the old wood axe had been gathering dust since the minister bought his electric heater. It was still razor-sharp and it sliced cleanly through the wood and the clay at the side of the hole.

White clay. Waxy white. Damp. It came away in sticky lumps.

Perhaps an hour passed before the root tugged free, only then she looked at it. Thought jacaranda. Thought damaged. It was of no consequence. She had retrieved her pick head. That was of consequence, that and the fact that removal of the root had taken her deep in the centre of the pit.

'Deep enough,' she said, tossing the root to the floor of the shed, and following it up a natural set of steps created by the sticky clay and by the thick end of the root.

Her hands were raw, sore. Pain was drawing her back to reality, to the place where she didn't want to be ... not yet. 'Fix the pick. First I must fix the pick. That is next on the list. Fix the pick. Complete this chore, then I will look at the list. Today is ... today is ... today doesn't matter.'

Words forced her on, but her movements were slow. Her shoulder was stiff, her back bruised and her hips ached; her hands screamed each time she forced them to close around the pick handle. They could prove to be the weak link. She sat on the edge of her pit, resting while she studied her reddening palms. She should have worn her gloves. Blisters had formed, broken. She must stop, see to her hands, or what must be done could not be done. She must look to her hands' needs, bring some logic to this illogical task.

Using the pick handle as a prop, she stood, her limbs shaking with the effort. She drew in a deep breath, tossed her pick to the floor, then made her slow way to the side door, across the garden, and in through the back of the house to the kitchen.

Kitchen suggested food. A frying pan taken from the pantry, a knob of butter added, she watched it sizzle before sliding in a small piece of steak. As she looked at it, her mind made its own leap to eggs, to refrigerator. Her hands selected two, cracked two into the pan beside the steak. Eggs demanded toast. She placed two pieces of bread in the toaster, and when it popped, she spread it thick with butter and began eating, the clay white beneath her fingernails.

Food refilled her ewer of energy. Food was life. She was

alive. She had survived. That was enough for the moment. She could give no thought to what lay upstairs. Not yet. She had walked the night garden until a direction was chosen for her. Nothing had altered since.

'When the hole is done, then it will be time to think about it.'

A cup of tea. Antiseptic cream. She sat staring at her palms, massaging them for minutes. She found bandaids, applied three, then she stood and climbed the stairs to her father's room where she took a pair of soft cotton gloves from the top drawer of the dressing-table – gloves her mother had once worn to church.

'Could you conceive of such a day as this, Angel? Maybe *you* could. Would you ever believe the purpose that your Sunday gloves would be put to? Maybe *you* could.' Her smile was a strange thing. It was in her lips, not her eyes. She caught its edge in the dressing-table mirror, and she looked at a stranger's eyes. One was near closed, the other was ... lost. With a shrug, she turned her back on the mirror and walked out to the shed where she slipped a pair of gardening gloves over the soft white cotton.

Again she began digging.

What was time but the measurement of the clay mountain on a tarpaulin? It grew taller.

She drank from the garden tap when the sun went down, but she did not eat again. It was near 10 p.m. when she knew the hole was done. It was no six-foot deep grave, not so neat either; just a raw gash in the earth – but a wide enough gash, and in places deep enough. She could, would, do no more.

The jacaranda root and her chase of the root, left her a rough set of steps to climb, and on legs as heavy as the root she had tossed to the floor, she dragged herself from the pit, for minutes sitting on the edge, feet swinging, while trying to raise the necessary incentive to move away. Outside.

'Morning will come,' she said, and her yawn was wide. 'I will sleep, and morning will come, and by this time tomorrow, I will allow myself to think. She stood, swayed on her feet, until energy enough was raised to walk her wearily across the garden and in through the back door.

Hands washed at the kitchen sink. An overripe pear, taken from the bowl on top of the refrigerator, she gorged it at the sink. She ate a banana, then drank long and straight from the carton of milk. Alien actions, born of need. Movement was effort. Why waste effort on glass, on knife, on plate?

This is not Stella Templeton, she thought. This is the fictional character they created to fill the necessary position. The character having eaten must walk again, walk slowly away, laboriously climb those stairs, and lay her head down.

Her legs resented the part they must play. They trembled now with fatigue, but like seasoned troopers, they climbed, carried her up to her door, where she stood, staring at the shape on her bed, resenting its use of the bed she needed. She recognised the shape, but refused to know the shape, or to give it a name.

'The character will know her lines as they become necessary.'

She looked at the small clown's head, laughing beside the ear of a much larger clown. Not one of poor Stella's best creations, she thought. Fright, fear was embroidered on the larger face. She turned away, looked at the mirror, saw the figure standing there.

Nightmare figure. Filthy. Covered in white clay from her uncombed hair to the cuffs she had turned up on her borrowed jeans. She swayed on her feet, wanting her bed, looking at her bed, wanting what was in her wardrobe, her chest of drawers beneath the window, but the Stella character had not been allocated her own room. Her ungodly role did not call for cleanliness either. Time enough to wash the dirt away in the next scene.

She turned, walking her clay down the hall to her father's room where she fell across his bed. Exhaustion took her.

london calling

Dawn birds twittered. The town clock's resounding Bongs called
out across the houses. It sounded like the tolling bell at Miss
Moreland's funeral, and when it silenced, Stella waited for more.
Five. Was it five? She lay on her side, remembering other days.
How often she had listened for the old clock's chimes, sweated
on its chimes.

She became aware of the odd clothing she wore, and of the
position of the window, and of the quilt. Then yesterday's memories flooded in. She tried to roll from the bed, but her blood
had cooled in the night, and her abused muscles did not wish to
move. Having fallen asleep across the quilt, she found it had
been pulled diagonally across her during the night. Now she
pushed it aside with one arm.

Who was she today?

She forced the arm to move again. It reached up to brush the
hair from her face. Cogs and gears ground. Metal against metal.
Her back screamed as she rolled to the side, and her hand
reached down to soothe the scream. Muscles didn't want to

reach. Her neck stung. She could reach that. She rubbed her neck slowly and moved into today's role.

Play the robot. A robot is programmed for denial of pain, programmed for work, and there was work for it to do. On her feet now, she noticed they were still shod. White shoes. White clay shoes. They walked her to her room, shedding dry white clay.

The naked shape was still lying on her bed. This nightmare had not left at dawn with the others. The world she had known for forty-four years, the world she had moved uncomfortably within, was no more. Everything in the past six weeks had been leading her towards this day. To today, but what was today?

'Today is – '

'What does it matter what today is? I have shed the garb of yesterday with Angel's beige skirts.'

Function. Work was God today, whatever the day might be.

Muscles and joints grinding, she walked downstairs and out to the shed.

A thin film of moisture lay in the bottom of the pit, seepage from the garden, or down some natural pipeline. Or had one of her dear trees bled? It was unimportant. Tonight the hole would be filled. She would continue until it was filled, and then she would think of the consequences.

One shed door dragged open, she glanced at the Packard, dew wet, the morning too new, and cold. She felt no chill.

Inside the house, she cleared a pathway from her room to the front door. The hall table she moved to the lounge room, giving free passage for her wheelbarrow. It had served her well, but its work was not yet done. She propped the front door wide, then stood looking out at the grey light of morning, and at the town still sleeping.

'Sleep on, Maidenville,' she said, returning to her labour upstairs.

Dead weight, she thought, now knowing why people said, 'a dead weight'. Dead smell. Dead touch.

'*Kiss her, Daughter. Learn forgiveness. It is a lesson that will stay with you. Say your goodbyes.*'

'*My kiss would be a lie, Father.*'

'*It was not her fault. One day you may understand.*'

'No. I will never understand. I was her child, born of her body. I refuse to understand. I was an innocent in the cruel game she played in her head,' she said as she took two cold clay feet, and tugged. Not a movement. She attempted to roll the clay that was worse than clay. Kilned clay now. She propped herself against the wardrobe and pushed against it with white clay shoes. It wouldn't budge.

Then she gave up. She tossed her hands in the air and gave up, she walked back to the door, looking at the blisters on her hands. Yesterday's labour had all been in vain.

Run away. Take the car and run away to some place. Just drive, keep driving. Dye your hair black. Change your name. Just run.

Mousy One and Mousy Two, in search of cream once strolled into the farmer's dairy, where Tom the cat patrolled.

'I won't run,' she said. 'It is much too late to run.'

But Mousy Two, her chin held high, was circling round and round.

'*Please don't despair, keep swimming, a way out may be found.*'

And I will find a way. I will. I will keep swimming around and around in circles, until I find the way out. There will be a way. I'll telephone Sergeant Johnson and tell him of Miss Moreland's rape.

That is not the way. Not after her grand funeral. She will not become tea-party gossip for this town, and nor will I.

Then there is no way.

So drown. So, go down without a bubble and drown, Mousy Two.

She walked to her window, staring unseeing at the jacarandas and the shed. Two early birds were flitting from limb to limb.

They nodded, and winked, then pecked at the limb before flying together to the roof of the shed.

A short distance. The shortest possible distance. They were showing her the way.

She turned to the bed, then back to the window. The flyscreen unsnibbed, she propped it against her wall and pushed the window high. She slid the bed with its load across the room.

'A lump of lead is harder to lift than a long lead rod,' she told the naked clay. 'There is an equation to suit this situation. What cannot be easily lifted can be pushed with ease. Pyramids were built without the help of cranes. Man power. Woman power. Slave power. The Stella character will now play the role of Egyptian slave. The pyramid must be done, and today.'

Prop and push. Buttress and roll. Slide and wedge.

One at a time, she lifted the legs of the bed, sliding the great dictionary beneath one, and the bible beneath another. She used Grimms' fairytales, and *Gone With the Wind*, just to gain an inch or two, or three. Then with her garden spade beneath the cold clay on her bed, she levered the head and shoulders onto the sill.

So she worked on while time went away. Each gain became the new celebration. She set herself aims, and achieved those aims, and each centimetre on the sill became her new success until the clown head and clay shoulders were well out over the window ledge and she could lever no more.

I should have dug beneath my window, she thought. I should have thought ahead.

'What has been done cannot be undone,' she said.

Her bedroom window was screened by the largest of the jacarandas, but she stripped the cover from her quilt and tossed it over the ledge, over the clown, before walking downstairs to her garden.

No movement at her fences. This side of the house was safe

from Mr Wilson's eyes, and as yet little traffic moved on the road. Her window and the shed were both well back from the highway, well protected by her trees and the shrubbery that followed the curved drive, but for the first time she found herself wishing for the return of the hedge.

'If wishes were fishes then Jesus would have been out of a job,' she said.

She looked at her wheelbarrow, and knew it was too small. The trailer at the rear of the shed was old, but a well-balanced wooden construction, and light enough to pull over flat ground. She kicked a tyre. Tight. Her father had a small compressor beside his workbench. Tyres, even infrequently used tyres, were never allowed to go flat in the minister's shed.

'Dear Father, what exotic pool of genetics did your mother leave behind her? Were her forebears engineers? Were they builders of carriages? Were they too-moral men? Did their women create gardens and pen strange tales? I believe they were a race of survivors, Father. They were the ones who came to this land, tamed this land. Did they kill? Is it in my blood, this willingness to do what must be done to survive?' she asked, as she began tugging at the coupling frame of the trailer until a wheel moved.

Genetics. What bizarre pool had gone into the making of the boy rapist. Was he the grandson of an addict, of a butcher given licence to cut? He was also the son of a man who could alter his allegiance with a stage kiss.

She turned the trailer and ran it to the wall beneath her bedroom window, flattening her garden as she went. It was unimportant. That which had taken on a huge importance yesterday was now irrelevant. An azalea, a beautiful thing that bloomed with two different coloured heads, was flattened by a wheel, a lily broken off at the base. The lavender had been overrun by the trailer. Now it lay crushed and broken beneath the trailer floor, its perfume rising, surrounding her. Too potent in the early morning air.

'Poor things,' she said, looking around her flattened garden, picking up a sprig of lavender to hold to her nose. 'Still, you will all grow again, and bloom again.' She tossed the sprig to the earth, and levelled the trailer, its back to the wall. 'I have built a perfumed bower to receive him,' she said. 'Better it were a pit of flames.'

Hands on her hips, she looked up at her window. The quilt wasn't covering the head. 'Thomas the clown, sleeping on my window ledge. You were put together by careless hands. Perhaps it was the fault of your creator, but it is too late now.'

Back in her room she climbed on to the bed where she kneeled between the spread legs, tucking a stiff knee beneath each of her arms – close now, so close to that tool of rape. Weight evenly balanced on the window ledge, when the clown toppled too easily, she was unready. A rigid foot caught beneath the armpit of the sweatshirt she wore, almost dragging her through the window and down to the trailer below.

'This is the moment when it will all end. Someone will come now. Someone will walk down the drive,' she said, her head out the window.

But the ancient god of the kill was watching over her. No traffic moved on the highway. Only the two birds, perching on the shed roof, watched her strip her bed, toss sheets, pillow, under-blanket and quilt cover to the trailer, where the reject clown now lay crumpled, half on and half off, its head twisted in a unique position.

'Are you looking over your shoulder, checking for the hounds of hell who snap at your heels? I only hope they are snapping, and I hope their jaws are wide, and their teeth long, and their saliva acid,' she said as she left her room, leaving the window wide.

The birds did not blame. They flew across the trailer as she rocked it, rocked it into movement; it was heavier now with its load and too close to the house for ease of manoeuvring, but two wheels are easier to move than the legs of a bed. She had the trailer turned and was pushing it back to the shed when she heard the telephone. She baulked, and a wheel baulked in the circular depression before the door.

No-one in Maidenville rang before eight. It would be a wrong number. She let it ring, while again she rocked the trailer backwards and forwards, backwards and forwards.

Her strength ebbing fast, she was functioning on raw nerve, and the phone's demand was gouging at raw nerve, but it silenced after the twelfth ring. Relief gave her strength for one supreme effort; and the wheel rose out of the depression and she was through the door. Then the ringing from the house began again. She dropped the trailer, left it there, the shed door swinging wide as she walked across the garden and inside to silence the telephone.

'What do you want?' she said, her words – her voice – not Stella's.

'Daughter.'

'Father?'

'I've been ringing for minutes.'

'Father?' His voice sounded so close. She heard him cough, and she turned quickly to look over her shoulder, expecting to see him behind her.

What you must ask yourself, Daughter, is what would God think of your actions – ?

'I thought you were out. I'm calling from the airport. I will be boarding the plane shortly.'

'Where are you?'

'London.'

'Have I lost all track of time? You ... you are flying in on Saturday.'

'I – ' Again he coughed. 'Patrick was able to get us on an earlier flight,' he said. 'I ... I had a dream, Daughter. You were driving your dear mother to church in the Packard. She was young again, and she was to sing the solo. I ... I had a desire to hear your voice.' He coughed, and his voice was breathless when he spoke again. 'Is everything as it should be, Daughter?'

'Yes, Father.'

Thomas Spencer is dead, a plastic bag over his head, but all is well in Maidenville, she thought. There is a deep pit where the Packard generally lives, Father, but all is well in Maidenville. I am filthy and wearing trousers that encourage unladylike conduct, and I stink of a dead youth, and last night I slept in your bed with my shoes on, but all is well in Maidenville. 'The congregation has missed you, Father,' she said.

'What time is it over there?'

'Seven?' She guessed at the time.

'I got you from your bed, Daughter?'

'No. Yes. Yes. But perhaps I needed to hear your voice. Perhaps you knew I needed to hear your voice, Father.'

She heard his cough again. 'I have missed you – ' he said, and the line was cut.

She looked at the phone, wanting her father back, wanting his sanity back. She clung to the phone, waiting, willing him back, needing him to complete his sentence. 'I have missed your ... care ... cooking ... laundering ... I have missed you, Stella, child of my loins.'

Poor Father, too afraid to come any closer than my bedroom door, she thought, as she placed the phone down and stood there, her hand on it, waiting for the ring. Poor Daddy, accused of unspeakable evil if he dared to pat my head.

'Even a dog is allowed a pat on the head,' she said.

The phone remained silent.

'I have missed you, Father. I have missed your voice in these empty rooms, but perhaps I am not yet ready for you to return. I am not yet ready for such sanity. How long is the flight? Twenty-six hours. I have twenty-six hours. And the bus trip. I have thirty-odd hours left – and I have left the shed door open.' She ran.

Again in the shed, she positioned the trailer carefully. Logic had returned with her father's voice. She planned to tilt the trailer upright, to lift the coupling frame in the air. The clown lay lengthwise across the trailer, and if all went to plan it should drop neatly into the pit.

She had taken two bricks from the edge of a garden bed, now she used them to place against the wheels, aware that if the trailer ran forward, fell into the pit, she may as well climb in with it and die.

Slowly now she lifted.

The clown clung there.

She lifted higher.

It took only the slightest shift of weight for the clown to tilt, slide sideways, topple. The trailer, as if eager to be rid of its unholy burden, deposited it across the pit, where it balanced a moment, half in, and half out.

'No. No. No.' The coupling frame slammed to the earth and she ran to the pit in time to watch the clown bend, slowly fall in. But not in the position she had visualised. It was awkwardly seated in the centre of the hole, the soles of its feet level with the top.

'God.' It was a wail, a prayer, a plea as she ran to the shed doors, closed them, bolted them. 'God. What do I do now?'

'*Eat something,*' a voice replied. '*And take an Aspro.*'

the safe compartment of self

It was eight-ten, the sun high in the sky, she was in the kitchen drinking tea when the phone rang again.

'Stella Templeton,' she said, no longer afraid of the telephone. No need to fear it any more. Fear collapse. Fear footsteps in the drive. Fear some fist hammering at the front door, but not the telephone.

'Stell, it's me, Marilyn. I'm worried out of my mind. Tommy hasn't come home for two nights.'

Perhaps there is a place where we go to when there is no peace to be found in our own little hells. Perhaps there is a special place beyond reason, a compartment of self, a primitive centre of the brain where desperation takes control of actions and responses. We survive, Stella thought.

'Not come home?' she said.

I am there. I am in the primitive place, in that safe compartment of self. I am functioning on my will to survive. They are coming at me from all directions now, forcing me to know, to accept responsibility for my actions. They are attempting to drag me from this safe place of no thought, no guilt, and back into their petty little world. I must respond. I will neither think of minutes past or those to come, only this one. I must respond. I must move a small part of me into this here and now, but allow the rest to stay away in that safe place.

How?

Somehow.

I will be the ear for a supposed friend, who poisoned my reputation in the presence of her son. She, who was given a small precious life to hold and to mould; she, who wasted it, as Angel had tried to waste the life of her Stella child – she did not succeed. I did not allow her to succeed. And I will survive this thing. I will complete this task I have set for myself.

'He didn't come home on Monday night, but he's done that before, so I didn't worry too much, but this morning, when he wasn't at breakfast – Stell. Stella. Are you there?'

'I'm listening, Marilyn.'

'I rang around all his mates. None of them have seen hide nor hair of him since Monday, after school. He had dinner at home on Monday night. Ron bought fish and chips. Then he went off somewhere on his bike. I've just rang Sergeant Johnson, and he said not to worry yet. He said kids take off all the time. I know he'll be all right. He's probably ridden to Dorby, and he's too scared to ring us up to come and get him. He did that once before, you know.'

There was a silence. Stella tried to fill it. She coughed instead.

'I thought he'd come home last night. I was sure he'd be here this morning, but his bed hasn't been slept in. Stell? Stell? Are you there, Stell?'

'Yes.' Stella responded to her friend's urging. Ears must hear. Tongues must wag a reply, any reply.

'What if something has happened to him? What if he was picked up by some deviant? Murdered – '

Stella flinched as her mind returned to the pit, and what was in the pit, and how she might be required to get into the pit with it, and –

'I know ... I know I'm being stupid. He's just ridden off somewhere. I suppose I'd better get off this phone. Johnson or someone might be trying to call me.'

'Keep your chin up,' Stella said.

'Ron says he's probably just done it to get our attention. He's been nagging about more pocket money lately. We should have given him more, I suppose, but we bought him anything he wanted. He only had to ask for it and we bought it. There's also talk about him and young Kelly Murphy. She's pregnant again and she's blaming Tommy – the little moll.'

Stella clicked her tongue. 'Tut-tut.'

'I know that sounds awful, but I mean – if she is pregnant, then it wouldn't have been Tommy. He's only a kid, and he would have had more sense than to – I mean, she's as rough as bags, Stell.'

'Boys will be boys, Marilyn.'

'It wouldn't have been Tommy. I know my own son. He's a sensible, responsible kid and he wouldn't have touched her with a ten-foot pole. I'd better go.'

A friend's ear is only of value for as long as the friend's mouth mouths the words a friend wants to hear. Speak a truth, and the phone can be placed down, leaving only the beep, beep, beep of friendship.

Stella placed her phone down then walked slowly across the vegetable garden to the shed. She kneeled beside the pit, took hold of a long bare foot and tugged. It was too hard on her back. She rubbing at her back, knowing time was running out. Sergeant Johnson would be following a still-warm trail. He'd be wandering around town, asking questions. He'd go to the school, speak to Tommy's friends, his teachers. He'd go to Spud Murphy's house, speak to Kelly. But there was no reason for him to come here. None at all. Again she pulled at the foot. Bare. Her mind attempted to follow the thought. Too much else to think about.

Someone would come. No hedge, no gate to stop them, nor

to warn her of their approach with its complaining squeal. Just the sound of shoes on the gravel drive, and she would turn around and see the long morning shadow, and –

It could happen. She'd wasted too much precious time over breakfast. People always came knocking on her door, wanting something.

'Have you got a few pots, Stella? I want to pot out those camellias.'

'I just popped in for that apricot cheesecake recipe, Stell. The one you took to the meeting last week.'

'Got time for a cuppa, Stell?'

It was going to be a beautiful day. People would be out and about. The sun was moving away for winter and not so hot now. A fine day for walking, not a cloud in the sky. The magpies were warbling on the lawn. Two crows were in the drive, arguing some point. There was traffic moving on the road. Murphy's dogs were barking – just a normal slow old Maidenville day.

But what day was it? What was she supposed to be doing today? There was something she had to do today and she knew it, but because she didn't want to know it, she didn't try to follow the thought.

Sitting on her heels, she leaned over the pit, looking down at the shape, the head, still wrapped in its plastic bag. No longer person, youth, missing son of Ronald and Marilyn, grandson of Cutter-Nash. It was just a naked immovable mass.

What did Miss Moreland say? Don't leave me languishing in the freezer like a side of aged mutton.

Stella looked down at a shifting pit – or was it she who moved? Shouldn't have taken the Aspros, she thought. They had relaxed her, and were making her drowsy and slow. It was not good to stop, to sit like this, because stopping meant she had to find the will to force her hands and muscles to begin again. But her head was too light to begin again. There was a strange noise in her ears. A muffled drumming. And strange shafts of sunlight were cutting like swords through the gloom of the shed. She turned her head. Sunlight had found a gap between the doors, it had found cracks, and knot holes, weaving interesting patterns on the walls.

'I can't do any more,' she said. 'I can't get it in, and I can't get it out. I can't.'

You are bringing no mind to the task, girl. Control is slipping away. Today is Wednesday. You know today is Wednesday. Mind is all that remains to you, and too little time. Get it done, girl.

She tried to stand, and her bones that had found a nominal peace, while crouched before the hole, now ached anew. The spot below her left shoulderblade felt raw. Had he cut her with his knife? She hadn't taken the sweatshirt off, hadn't bothered to look. She sighed, tried again to force will into her arms, her legs, to get it done, but she remained in her crouch over the pit. Her spade was close at hand. She reached for it now, and attempted to lever a leg to the side.

It moved. She drew breath, then repositioned herself, bracing her feet on the opposite side of the pit before levering again.

'All I need is Mrs Morris creeping down the drive in her moccasins and stretch slacks.'

I've just popped in to check on your knickers, dear.

Oh, good morning, Mrs Morris. Sorry the washing isn't out yet. I am not wearing my frilly knickers today. I am wearing no knickers at all. I am wearing the clown's jeans and his sweatshirt, and I stink of clown sweat and semen and this shed is beginning to smell of death.

What are you doing there, dear? Not that it's any of my business, mind you ...

Stella began to laugh at the vision that had become too clear. She could see the old gossip, perched on the opposite side of the pit, swinging her tightly clad, baby fat legs. She laughed until a stitch in her stomach forced her to stop laughing, but she couldn't stop. Imagination – or madness – was controlling her. She began creating more dialogue.

Climb down please, Mrs Morris. I believe I need some help here, and I dare not get in there, or I will never get out. He will crush me in death as he tried to in life.

How do I get down, dear?

Just stand on him. He's quite safe now.

The grave was too shallow. She had visualised the clown resting flat. Perhaps she had visualised arms folded, a flower in the hands. There was plenty of room at the top end of the pit. Plenty.

Unpick its seams. Reverse an imperfect creation.

Remake it. Give it a second chance at life.

The voices were coming at her from the walls, the roof, the window. She looked around her, seeking the speakers, but she was alone.

'Mad,' she whispered. 'Stop it. You are imagining it. Stop it. Grasp control and hold onto it. You are not your mother's daughter. You are not your mother's daughter,' she whispered, her hands pressed to her ears, trying to crush the voices as she looked across the swords of light, looked from doors to window.

The tree root was also immovable – until the axe.

Hopeless. A hopeless situation. She had made the hole too small, too narrow. The clown's head and shoulders were resting against the side. Dig out more. Dig behind it.

'Can't.'

Hopeless.

Ice crawled in her scalp and blood roared in her ears, swam red before her eyes. Strange throbbing silence. The hush before a storm.

Hopeless.

She stared at the sunlight sword, hitting, twisting off the side window where two branches from the apricot tree crossed. Clusters of red and yellowing leaves began to form a shape as she stared at it, stared until her eyes slipped out of focus and the shape writhed, as another shape had once writhed.

She lifted a hand to the sword of sunlight and she looked at

her blisters and she saw the blood seeping from the centre of
her hand, seeping from old scars.

'Poor Jesus,' she said. 'I know exactly how it feels. I sym-
pathise with your pain, but I need the magic word. Give me
today's magic word.'

'*Packard. Rope. Tie a rope around its shoulders and tow it
straight,*' he said. '*And find his shoes. Where are his shoes?*'

meals on wheels

The motor was still now, and the sheds doors bolted fast. She was singing as she tossed her father's tow rope into the pit to lay beside the size ten sneakers with their ringed and striped soles. She had found them outside the glass doors, a sock tucked into each shoe. And she had found the broken glass on the lounge room floor.

> *Oh Jesus, sweet and perfect Lord, how dear the voice I*
> *   hear.*
> *I was once a soldier marching alone, now You are ever*
> *   near.*
> *Your pain hath taught me faith and hope, Your death hath set*
> *   me free*
> *to live my life in perfect love, a life You have given me.*

She took up her spade, and with it positioned a limb, prodded a shoe into a gap, and she sang on, sang with relief. Sang sweet.

Though You did die at Calvary in torture on that hill,
All mankind had his freedom bought when Your purest blood
*   did spill.*
Though pain may smite my heart and soul and dangers gather
*   near.*
I will not flinch, my pledge is love. With You there is no more
*   fear.*
I sing my praise to Jesus Lord. I sing with voice so pure.
Oh let the world hear songs of praise and love will long
*   endure –*

'Stell. Stella. What are you doing in there?'

Startled, Stella silenced.

'Stell.' This voice was real. It was at the front of the shed. A fist was hammering at the old door. Stella dropped her spade like a guilty child might toss down stolen fruit. She looked over her shoulder, ready to run.

'Stella.'

She recognised this voice.

'Bonny?'

'Have you forgotten what day it is? It's Wednesday. It's your turn for Meals on Wheels.'

'Meals on Wheels?'

Today. The lost Wednesday. The fictional dun-coloured Stella character was in charge of the dinners today. She was supposed to be in her kitchen cooking a lamb roast, and she hadn't taken the twin legs from the freezer. The poor fictional character had taken on too many roles. She'd forgotten Wednesday's lines.

She laughed then. She looked at the pit and what was in the pit, and she laughed, drunk on Aspros and fatigue and pain.

The Stella character wasn't supposed to be in the shed. She should have been out there serving, because this was her Wednesday. She'd drawn up the roster. She was supposed to be –

But she'd got him in the hole. She had got him in and he was flat enough. The Packard had worked for her, dragging him flat. She had levelled him with the spade, placed his arms across his chest, now all he needed was the flower.

She wrapped her arms around her stomach, held her ribs with her elbows, trying to still hysteria.

'Stella Templeton. What's got into you?'

Bonny had remembered. She would have cooked apple cobbler with custard. Outside of here, the world had been turning. Just the same. Always the same. So funny, really. Mrs Grey would have cooked the vegetables. She was coming today to help with the serving and delivery. But there was nothing to deliver, because Stella was in the shed and not the kitchen. It seemed so funny.

'It's no laughing matter, Stell. It's half-past eleven.'

'Is it? I'm sorry.'

'What are you doing in there? Why have you got the doors shut?'

'Some ... something I put off too long, Bonny.' She stepped back from the pit, and her clay-covered shoe slipped on more clay and she fell heavily to the heap of clay on the tarpaulin, and it jolted every aching bone in her body, and if she didn't laugh then she'd cry, so she laughed again.

'Yeah. Well I believe you, but there's thousands who wouldn't, Stella Templeton. You sound like you're having too much fun to be working.' Stella climbed to her hands and knees, but slowly, and Bonny continued to bang on the door. 'Let me in. I won't dob.'

'Not today,' Stella replied.

'Okay, then keep it to yourself, you party pooper. I've got the sweets, and I picked up Mrs Grey's vegies. Her car has broken down again. She said she tried to phone you to tell you she can't help with the dishing up and delivering today, but she couldn't raise you. Obviously you were doing something better.' Stella made no reply. She was attempting to gain her feet, but her shoes had evolved into skates. 'Have you done the roasts, Stell?'

'No.'

'Then what are you going to feed them?'

'Let them eat cake,' Stella said, and it was Bonny's turn to laugh.

'Who is in there with you?'

'What's the time, Bonny?'

'I told you. It's gone half-past eleven. I can stay for fifteen minutes and give you a hand. I don't have to be at the school canteen until twelve.' The door rattled on old hinges, but the bolt was strong.

'No. No, thank you.' Stella was standing now. She stripped the sweatshirt from her and flung it into the pit. She kicked off her shoes, stepped out of the jeans, they followed the shirt down the hole. She wiped her hands with a rag she'd picked up from the bench. Wiping at her arms she walked around to the cleaner side of the pit, and stood naked there, looking down. The clown was no longer naked, but covered by his sweatshirt and jeans, her shoes on his chest in place of flowers.

'Will I go and buy half a dozen chickens from the chicken place? Give them roast chicken instead of lamb.'

Stella scratched dried clay from her arm. 'Perhaps you should. Yes.'

'Will you be right to do the serving and delivery by yourself?'

'I . . . I'll manage.'

'Okay. I'll be back in fifteen minutes. If they haven't got any ready, I'll order six and tell them you'll pick them up.'

'Just place the order. I'll pick them up . . . in half an hour. You go, Bonny.'

'Oh, did you hear that young Tommy Spencer has nicked off?'

Stella looked down at what remained of Tommy Spencer. 'Yes,' she said, walking naked to the bag of rags the minister used for car washing and for wiping greasy hands.

'Marilyn is at work. Standing behind her checkout, as if it's a normal day. I mean, God. If it was one of mine, I'd be out

278

there looking for his body. I'd be out of my mind with worry. I reckon she's spaced out on pills, you know. Nothing ever seems to worry her.'

'True.'

'He's turned into a real little shit of a kid, that one. My boys won't have a bar of him, thank God. And Marilyn was saying Kelly Murphy is pregnant again, and blaming him. My boys reckon that Spud has probably had a go at Tommy, and the little shit has nicked off until it blows over.' There was a brief silence. 'Who are you hiding in there, Stella Templeton?'

Stella picked up a pair of her father's worn underpants, she stood looking at them. 'Marilyn rang earlier,' she said, tossing the underpants down and dragging an ancient blue shirt from the bag as she listened to her friend's footsteps walking across gravel to the back door. Twice she heard the door open, slam shut, then the footsteps approached the shed's side door and Stella moved away from the window as she slid her arms into a shirt that reached her calves.

'I put the veg in your oven and left the sweets on the table.'

'Thank you, Bonny.'

'Okay, I'm off then. Have fun,' Bonny called from close by. 'See you at the meeting tomorrow. That's if you're not too busy.'

'Tomorrow,' Stella replied.

Tomorrow. So time had come back to get her.

Statue still, she listened for the small motor's purr, listened for the movement of wheels on gravel then, like a fugitive, she unlocked the side door, opening it an inch at a time, peering out into a world too bright, creeping out from her cell, and stepping into sunlight. It hit her eyes and she swayed back from it.

There could be no more denial now. She locked the door, locked *that* away, then backed away from it, the old key in her hand. *That* must be for later. She backed to the trunk of the largest jacaranda, leaning there a moment, gaining strength from it while looking down.

Bare knees. Bare feet.

She had to move away from *that*. Move her mind away. She pushed off from the tree and on legs uncoordinated, made her slow way to the back door. Once inside, her legs defied her plea to climb stairs. She leaned on the table, breathing deeply while staring at a patch of white clay on her new floor.

But this she had to do. This thing she had to do. The apple cobbler was here. She could smell it. The vegetables were here, her new oven humming.

She had done so much and this she would do also, otherwise all of her work would had been for nothing.

No-one knew. No-one would ever know – unless she told them.

And how would she tell them?

By her conduct.

She could never tell them, therefore she must behave responsibly.

'Now.'

So I will behave. I will be responsible. I will gain some self-control.

In a moment.

How?

How do I face this town?

How have I ever faced it?

Mind control. I will control my mind. But in a moment.

She looked at her hands, blistered, bloodstained. How can I show these hands to the town?

They could be worse. I have been working hard in the garden. Very hard. What a silly woman, I forgot my gloves.

'They could be worse.' She sucked in a deep breath as she moved from the table to the hall. One hand on the banister, her head lifted. So many stairs to climb. Too many.

'I have been working very hard in the garden. I took a tumble down the stairs in the dark.' She sighed, took one step. 'I will choose a face to fit the situation as I have always done. I will. I can. But first I must get up there, wash this old face away.'

She took a step higher, painfully. Then one step more. Slowly, she made her way up to the top of the stairs then down to the bathroom.

It was close to twelve when she stepped from the shower and walked naked to her bedroom. She did not want to be there. She chose clean underwear, then flung her wardrobe wide, reaching for a beige linen skirt.

'No,' she said, and she slammed the wardrobe door, then slammed her bedroom door. Still naked, she walked downstairs to the utility room where she had stored the cases brought from Miss Moreland's flat.

'It's chicken, followed by apple cobbler, Mr Bryant. I became involved in a lengthy task and ran out of time,' she apologised as she handed the old man his meal at the door. He was near blind, and an excellent choice for her first delivery.

'Never look a gift horse in the mouth, my dear,' he said.

The peanut-pillow queen took Meals on Wheels, and Mr Macy, Mrs Morris and her husband, Mrs Murphy and Dave. They all took Meals on Wheels. In Maidenville, age had its fringe benefits.

Stella handed Mrs Morris two meals at her front door.

'You're late, and what's wrong with you?'

'I . . . had a fall. Hit my head, then slept too long. I . . . I had the very strangest dream. You were in it, Mrs Morris,' Stella said as she turned away.

'Yes, well you're lucky you can sleep in. Some of us can't get to sleep at all. And you were supposed to be here at twelve-thirty. We have to go to bowls this afternoon and we're going to be late.'

'We require more assistants with the Meals on Wheels. Perhaps you have some free time.'

'No I haven't. Did you hear about the Spencer boy?'

'Yes.'

'He's nicked off. Rode to Dorby on his bike, they say. Ruined him, they did. You know they paid six hundred dollars for that bike. One from the local bike shop wasn't good enough for him – '

'His bike? Yes, of course. I must go.' She was halfway down the drive. Mrs Morris's voice rose to compensate.

'He left on Monday night after Spud had a go at him. And young Kelly Murphy. Did you hear about young Kelly Murphy – ?'

But Stella was away. She took two meals from the polystyrene container and walked up the drive next door to Mrs Murphy's door.

'You're very late today, aren't you?'

'Yes. I had a . . . a long call from Father – '

'Did he have anything interesting to say?'

'He's missing Maidenville.' Stella was backing away, thinking bike. Bike. Dorby. Spud. Kelly. Time. Can't run. Always a word or two at the front door. Bike. Have to . . . have to . . . drive it to Dorby. Yes.

Mrs Murphy lifted the lid of her hot meal as she pursued Stella down the drive. 'It's supposed to be roast lamb today, with mint sauce. I was looking forward to a nice bit of lamb, dear. What happened to the lamb?'

'Blown fuse.' Then Stella was walking away. She was in her car. She was driving away and back to . . . *that*.

The neighbours met at the fence when she was gone. 'What's got into her? She's got some bee up her bum today. Hair all over her head like a wet teenager . . . trying to do a Garbo in her big sunglasses. Wait till Martin Templeton gets back. Won't he be in for the surprise of his life.'

'They say Steve Smith's ute was in her drive till all hours on Sunday night, and Mary Owen's girl saw them in Dorby on the night of the funeral. Dancing! I mean to say, Mrs Morris – '

'I heard, my dear. They say she was drinking like a fish, and dancing cheek to cheek with him too. A dark horse, that one.'

'While the cat is away, the mice will play, Mrs Morris.'

'They say she's spending money like water too. I was in the electrical shop when she ordered a brand new stove.'

'It blew a fuse. That's why we didn't get our lamb with mint sauce.'

'What was wrong with their old stove, that's what I'd like to know? If they've got that sort of money to waste, then I don't see why the church had to buy them a new airconditioned car.'

'And did you notice her neck? She had a love bite. I'll swear to it. And her clothes, Mrs Morris?'

'That was one of Miss Moreland's shirts, or I'll eat Parsons' hat and have his socks for seconds. I wondered what she'd done with the old girl's clothes. I've been keeping my eye on the op shop, but Glenda said that none of the clothes have come in yet. She's kept them for herself, Mrs Murphy. As if they, with all their money, need second-hand clothes.'

'I always said Miss Moreland was mutton dressed up to look like lamb, and if you ask me, Mrs Morris, Stella is heading down that very same path,' her neighbour replied.

'Mutton, lamb, or bloody chicken, she'd have made someone a bloody good wife if she'd stood still long enough for them to catch her,' Bert Morris replied, a chicken drumstick in his hand.

'That's one of them chickens from the Charcoal Chicken place. She didn't even cook it. Her fuse blew. That'll teach her to go throwing money away on new stoves. My word, but Martin Templeton is in for a terrible shock when he gets home.'

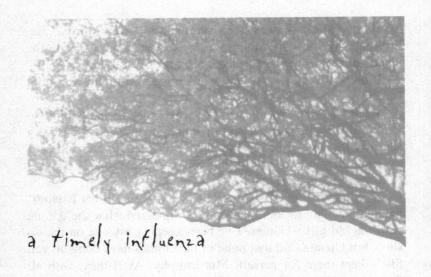

a timely influenza

At two-thirty, Stella returned to the shed and to the shallow grave, its contents now well covered by her sheets, pillow, quilt cover and an under-blanket. She had changed her clothing, her old friend's outfit was far too fine to soil with labour, but she was not wearing beige. She had resurrected a much patched pair of stretch jeans from beneath her bottom drawer, her secret place. They smelt musty. They were dusty, but the zip still closed. From the same hiding place, she'd taken an old favourite T-shirt, a faded apple green.

She felt cleansed, and her head was clear. The long hot shower had helped, the washing of her hair, the washing away of clay and perspiration and worse, had helped, but the need to force herself out, out there, where she must, by need, respond to greeting, react to situations, had helped her more.

Perhaps too it was the clothing she wore.

For the first time in years she felt like herself – like the self she had abandoned years ago, discarded in favour of a shadow self, deemed fit only to wear her mother's second-hand skirts and maidenly blouses.

She would empty her wardrobe, burn Angel's clothing – when she had time. She'd burn them slowly, piece by piece, and delight in the burning. But that was for later. There was the bike to think about now.

Still much to do.

But how much better it was that she had been seen around town, going about her normal business.

'So much better.'

The theory was that Thomas Spencer had nicked off to Dorby, and with Spud Murphy's publicly made threats being rehashed on every corner, who could blame him? He wasn't the first, nor would he be the last youth to disappear from Maidenville, but now his bicycle must also disappear. Stella was thinking logically as she wheeled it from the storeroom. Still new, it was a feather-light thing, and as Mrs Morris had said, expensive.

She opened the car boot, easily lifting the bike in – half in.

'Darn it!'

She had been planning to drive it to Dorby, after dark, leave it leaning in some park. But the car boot was too small, and other than to leave one wheel out, and tie the boot down with rope, this could not be done. Someone would be certain to sight her on the road. And fingerprints too. Again she had forgotten to use her gloves.

Such a waste, she thought, as she went for a shifting spanner and began to disassemble the bike. Seat, pedals, handlebars came off and were positioned low in the pit. Again she wished she'd dug it deeper.

'What is done cannot be undone,' she said. It was a sentence she had repeated and repeated in the past two days, and she said it again as she freed the wheels and dropped the frame into the pit. Gingerly then she slid a wheel down each side. They were big wheels. Tall. Too tall. She tried to hammer them in with the head of the axe but the axe kept bouncing off. She turned it, cutting into the tyres with the blade, flattening them before hammering again. One sank low, but the other wheel must have hit a root, or rock. It would not budge. She leaned it towards the centre, low enough, and when she was done, she wiped her father's tools before putting them neatly away in his tool case. She placed the axe and the pick in their corner, but kept the spade nearby. She would need it a while longer.

A bag of gardening lime caught her eye. She dragged it to the hole, where she up-ended it, sprinkling it there. It was supposed to do something. She had read it ... somewhere. Working from left to right, she began moving the mountain of clay from the tarpaulin back to the pit, shovel-full by shovel-full.

'What is done cannot be undone,' she said, but the words were losing their power, so she began singing, filling her head with words to still her thinking.

One more journey, and we will cross over,
over the river to dwell with Thee.
One more journey and we will cross over,
over the river, and safe in Your love.
Trials and tribulation, they will pass away.
Troubles disappear in the light of newborn day.
One more journey, and we will cross over,
over the river and safe in Your love.

It was almost done. One more hour and she could rest. The promise of rest kept her moving clay. Backwards and forwards, backwards and forwards, and when her back refused to lift one more spade of clay, she kneeled and shovelled, forcing unused muscles to take up the labour until the hole was filled.

Exhausted, her concentration was slipping by the time she drove the Packard into its old position; the vehicle didn't go in straight, but she called it good enough and left it there.

'Tomorrow,' she promised. 'Tomorrow.'

* * *

Like one of the dead, Stella slept that night in a spare room, in a bed unused for decades. It sagged in the middle, its pillows were hard, its blankets heavy, but barely had the thought time to form, and she was away. Her limbs down, they didn't move her from her back during the night. She slept late too, but woke with a rigid neck and a pounding headache. She woke sore, stiff, but mentally rested.

'What is done cannot be undone,' she said, clawing her way out of the central sag and gaining the floor. She showered, allowing the too hot water to play on her shoulders and back, then she dressed again in her jeans and T-shirt.

Aspros were kept in the top kitchen cupboard. She peeled two, tossing them into water, then she added a third. How many more hours did she have to call her own? Martin's plane left Heathrow Airport at around 7 a.m. Wednesday, Maidenville time. Now it was Thursday, 9.15 a.m.

'God, how did I sleep so long? Father is probably already over Australia. If his flight connects with the bus, he could be home before evening.'

But he couldn't come home yet. She could see signs of her actions everywhere, and when she walked to the shed, she noticed the level of the clay had dropped beneath the Packard where the front wheel had edged onto the soft earth. The mutilated bike tyre and the silver rim were protruding.

She started the Packard, fearful that its front wheel would sink lower, bog in the soft clay, but it lifted out. She'd have to wash that wheel. But later.

'So much to do.'

She'd have to vacuum the house, change her father's sheets, wash his quilt cover. She'd have to move her mattress onto the spare bed. She would not sleep in her old room again. Never again. The alien earth in the garden would have to be dug in, or covered with mulch. She could see the heaps of clay everywhere. Others would too. Had Bonny seen it yesterday? Had she seen the trailer's tyre marks near the window, the broken shrubs – ? God, what have I done?

'What I had to do.'

By ten-thirty, her head was clearing, and her aches had somehow distanced themselves. 'Good little Aspros. When all else fails me, I have you. How does the Aspro know where to go?' she said.

She washed the Packard's wheel with the help of her straw broom. She filled the wheel indentation with clay, then she swept the shed floor. She brought the hose into the shed, hosing the earth, attempting to wash the dirt cleaner, and water pooled in the rear storeroom, as it had always pooled in the storeroom, so she turned the hose onto the pit, and for minutes left it running there while she moved the bale of polyester filling to safer ground. When she returned to the hose ten minutes later, its water had soaked deep into the clay, disappearing into the earth, into the pit, into the soup of he who had been, and the clay had sunk low, the wheel rim jutting high.

He is pushing it up, trying to get out, she thought.

'Save your melodrama for where it is worth something,' she ordered, setting the hose on the trailer, scrubbing it down with her broom.

A barrow-load of earth reclaimed from the garden, she heaped it over the wound, then she placed the tarpaulin over it, and stamped on the grave, stamped up and down the length of it, attempting to flatten it. It had a strange unstable feeling. Wet pillows and fabric do not make for good foundations. The earth was pillow-spongy.

'What is done cannot be undone,' she said.

The wide end-boards of the trailer, placed lengthwise over the mound, she drove the Packard's passenger-side front wheel onto them and walked away. The old car had shown her the way by accident. Its weight might compact the soil, might push the bike wheel down.

Thursday. Today was Thursday. The church guild came today

to stitch the clowns. She'd have to put them off, keep them out of the shed.

'Call Bonny. Have the meeting at her place. Call her now.'

'Can you call the others please, Bonny? I'll bring the boxes around at two.'

'Did Ron call you, Stell? He had to get Parsons around to Marilyn last night. She went off her head and they took her over to Dorby, to the psychiatric hospital. He said he'd been trying to call you.'

'I might not have heard the phone. I've been busy in the garden,' Stella said.

'You've changed.' A long silence followed. 'I mean, I thought you would have been worried sick about Tommy. You used to be – I don't know. He was more like your kid than hers when he was little.'

'Children grow up. They ... they choose to cut old ties. I ... what can I say, Bonny?'

'I dunno. It's just ... just that you seem so disinterested. It's as if you've got more important things on your mind lately, that's all. Is it true what they are saying about you and Steve Smith?'

'It's Father. For some reason he has cut his trip short. He'll be home sometime today.'

'Scared of his reaction to your new stove?'

'Perhaps.'

'Too bad. Let him blow a gasket. Now fill me in on you and Steve.'

'He came to discuss Miss Moreland's party, and he stayed for dinner, Bonny. And that is all.'

'Yeah? I believe you, Stell, but there are thousands that wouldn't. I still want to know who you had holed up in your shed yesterday.'

'Holed up?'

'Something was going on in there. You've never locked those doors in your life, and I've known you too long to be conned.'

'You've been watching too much afternoon television, Bonny. I'll call Beth and Liz and Lyn. Can you call the others? Tell them we're meeting at your place.'

'Okay, but you'd better do Mrs Morris, or I might tell her it's been cancelled,' Bonny said. 'See you at two.'

The phone rang as Stella placed it down. She picked it up on the first ring.

'Stella Templeton.'

'Miss Templeton? Yes. It's Patrick O'Sullivan,' the voice said. 'I'm in Sydney, calling from the hospital.'

'Father?'

'Yes. He's been admitted.'

'Father? In hospital?'

'I tried to get him to a doctor before we left Germany, but he'd have no truck with German doctors. Determined to see Churchill's bunker, the old coot – '

'What ... what ...?'

'Some flu complication. Gone to the lungs.'

'Is he ... in danger?'

'He's not good. I won't lie to you. We had a doctor on the plane. He gave him oxygen. The airline wanted to off-load him in Bangkok but I talked them out of it.'

'Thank God for that.'

'The ambulance met us at Sydney Airport and rushed him off to RPA. I'm waiting there now.'

'Should I be there?'

'They've got him in intensive care. He's no chicken, Miss Templeton.'

'It's Stella. Please call me Stella.'

'Estella? He always did like that name. As I was saying, Estella, he's no chicken, and he's pretty low, but I've known him a long time. It will take more than the flu to bring down Martin Templeton.'

'I'll come.'

'Not much you can do here. I'll have a word to the doctors later, and call you again tonight.'

They spoke for a minute more, then Stella made the calls to the guild women.

She couldn't go to Sydney. Not yet. Not today. She had asked for more time. So she had been granted more time and she would use it well.

'His will, or his God got him on a plane and home. Father is not ready to die.'

She worked on the hole after an early lunch, filling it, then driving the Packard backwards and forwards over the clay, compacting it. When the town clock struck one, she was reclaiming the top layer of earth she had emptied onto the vegetable garden. It was from the first barrow-load and she hoped it would cover, or blend in with the scar. Once more she flattened the dirt with the Packard's wheels.

'Tomorrow, I'll tidy the garden, do the house. There is a train to Sydney in the morning – but that is too soon. I'll take the bus – no. I'll wait for Patrick to call tonight. I'll get the hospital's number. Then tomorrow – I'll worry about how I'll get there tomorrow.'

She dressed carefully in Miss Moreland's slacks and shirt. Her eye was still swollen, and ringed now by a yellow and blue bruise. Her left cheek was bruised also. And her throat. From her dressing-table drawer she took the bag of make-up her old friend had bought at the chemists that day, and she smoothed on a dash of foundation, then added more around the eye, and to her throat. It looked odd, but how well it covered. She lined her eyes with the eyebrow pencil, as she had at sixteen, then used the pencil to add a light brown shadow to her lids. She added blusher high to her cheekbones, and she took up the lipstick, carefully painting her mouth.

'God. I look like one of my own clowns.' With the tips of her fingers, she rubbed away a little of the blusher; she blotted the lipstick with a tissue, added a dot of foundation to the cut on her throat, working it with fingertips. It looked well enough.

She put her reading glasses on. The frames were heavy and dark, but the lens blurred the world – and the bruise. She wouldn't be able to drive in them, but once out of the car, she could manage. She'd wear her dark glasses to Bonny's then change them before she went in.

Perhaps a more colourful shirt might draw attention away from her eye. She took out the red shirt she'd worn to Miss Moreland's funeral, only last Thursday. It was camouflage enough. She flipped the collar high, then clipped on a double string of pearls. Miss Moreland's grey slacks fitted her well. A mite too long, though not with high heels. Her white sandals slipped onto her bare feet, she looked at her reflection in the long mirror and she was pleased.

'There is always my tumble down the staircase to blame if questions are asked,' she said. 'Good old much-maligned staircase.'

just a fanciful thing

Martin Templeton remained in intensive care for nine days, but it was the fourteenth day of his hospitalisation before Stella packed her bags for Sydney.

The shed looked normal – if a little neater. She backed the small car out, and was in the process of locking the doors when she took one final look at the scar in the earth, which, as long as the Packard remained in its position, was not visible. The idea to turn on the Packard's lights, to leave them on, came to her as she locked the doors. By the time she returned to Maidenville, the Packard would not be going anywhere, and having spoken to the minister's doctor on the telephone, it appeared that it might be some time before Martin concerned himself with vehicles. Her father had been dragged back from the very brink of death.

Unable to choose between bus and train, Stella had chosen a road map instead. It was only a six-hour drive, still, by the time she reached Penrith, and booked a room for a week in the first motel she sighted there, she'd had enough of strange roads, and of backtracking, looking for signposts. She closed her unit door, turned on the television and tested the bed. And it was just right. She slept ten hours straight.

Each morning she caught the train to the city, and took a taxi to the hospital. Each afternoon she reversed her steps, relieved to be back in her unit, safer in the suburbs. The train trip was long, but she did not notice it passing, her pen busy, filling the pages of an old exercise book. The taxi ride, the swarming cars and people were adding another element to the tale she wove.

Sydney was a different planet. The movement, the noise, the crush of humanity suffocated her. Once she had planned to find herself a small neat flat, and a position in some Sydney library. Now she sat each day on crowded trains, sliding through a landscape of buildings while craving the space of Maidenville.

Each day she greeted the minister with a light kiss on the brow. He accepted the kiss, coy as an eight-year-old boy who knew he was too old to be kissed, but liked it well enough anyway. Perhaps they re-learned love in that hospital, realised they were safe to love again, safe from Angel's accusations.

He had been visibly shocked to hear of Miss Moreland's death, but not surprised to learn that Thomas Spencer had disappeared. She told him all of the town gossip, and they somehow managed to fill the hours she sat beside his bed.

It was not until he asked the date one morning that she paled, and placed a hand to her unusually tender breasts. That evening, she did no writing, but began her calculations.

So much had happened. She had misplaced time!

'My God,' she said. 'My God, what have you done to me?'

'I spoke to your doctor on the way in. He said I can take you home to Maidenville tomorrow, Father.'

'Home?'

'Yes, my dear.'

'I am not up to those stairs yet, Daughter.'

'No. I explained to him that we have access to a unit next door to the hospital.'

'Miss Moreland's? I thought that unit went back to the community on her death.'

'Not the original units. She bought it outright.'

'Neighbours peering in my windows,' he said. 'No garden. However, I admit I will be pleased to be back amongst familiar faces.'

'Yes. I believe one would have to make the transition to the city at an early age. To me it has been like visiting another planet. The people out there, Father. They are like ants swarming at lunchtime, all busy about their own business. I'm just an alien insect floating all alone here, and should I land in the wrong place, I would be swatted with as much thought as we give to swatting a mosquito.'

'Our old world is not as it used to be.' Martin coughed, and for minutes Stella sat beside him, her mind in another place until he regained his breath, and spoke again.

'France,' he said. 'It is not of this world, confound the place. They don't even eat a civilised breakfast, Daughter. Fed us on cold tea and dry bread. I didn't sight a piece of toast, and as for a cooked breakfast! One would think I'd asked for human sacrifices.'

'Poor Father. You've lost considerable weight. Not that that will do you a lot of harm. I'm sure Doctor Parsons will consider it for the good.'

'Hmph.'

'We have to think of how much worse things could have been ... if ... if Patrick hadn't been able to get those two seats on the earlier flight. If you had collapsed in London, or if you had become unwell in the first weeks, or been admitted to hospital in France.'

'Then I wouldn't have lived to tell the tale, Daughter. We gave our lives that they might treat us like the plague when we dared to visit their land.' He was racked by a spasm of coughing, and she waited until he sucked in a lung-full of air and settled back on his pillows.

'Did you get to see Paris before you became ill? Did you get to take the boating trip down the Seine by night, see the city of lights?'

'I am certain that is where I caught it. Bad night air. The whole of Europe is full of bad air. And London is worse, even though they do at least speak the Queen's English ... or a form of English. Blacks everywhere, blacks with London accents. It's not the London I knew.'

'And Churchill's bunker?'

'Worth the trip – if not the illness. Wonderful, but the city. Traffic pouring out noxious yellow gases; the only time the air is fit to breathe is when it's raining ... which it did on every other day I might add.'

'Not like our own Maidenville. You'll be there tomorrow and our delightful air will have you well in no time. I'll come in early. We'll try to get away from the city before ten.'

'Am I up to another confounded bus ride, Daughter? If I never see another bus in my lifetime it will be too soon.'

'I told you. I drove the car to Penrith. I've been booked into a motel there for the past week. There is a good train service.'

'That will have cost us a pretty penny no doubt.'

'No doubt. I'll put it on my credit card.'

He shuddered, coughed. 'You spoke of an emergency, Daughter. Perhaps it is well that you had the damnable thing to rely on after all.'

'Yes. Yes, it has been very handy. I bought a weekly train ticket with it.'

'I'm not up to train travel. If I see one more confounded seat, climb one more set of steps, I'll – '

'Of course you are not up to trains. I wouldn't expect you to travel by train. We'll take a taxi to the motel, then it will be into your own comfortable little vehicle, and away.'

'It's a long drive.'

'But we'll make frequent stops. Relax now. Let me worry about it. We'll get you home and you will soon be back to your old self again.'

'I've got a strong constitution,' he said, but his words no longer held their old conviction.

'You certainly have. Your doctor said that the fact that you have never needed to take antibiotics before made them so much more effective in your case. He said another week on them and you'll be as good as new.'

'And require a new wardrobe. Have you been in touch with the Spencers?'

'No. No. I have made no phone calls. By the time I left, they had given up the search for him.'

'Youth. They are rarely content to live as their parents wish them to live. No doubt he will return when he has had a taste of freedom,' he said. 'How were the parents taking it?'

'Badly. Ron was talking about selling out and moving.'

'The little scoundrel. You know, I always had the feeling that he was the one making those confounded phone calls. I am thankful that I was blessed with a dutiful daughter.' He patted her hand, then looked towards the window. 'You have been a ... a stalwart companion to me. I could not have wished for better.'

'Thank you, Father, but you embarrass me.'

'I have been walking too close to death these past weeks. It made me aware of what I have not said – and perhaps of what needed to be said.' He heaved himself up from his stacked pillows, and swung his feet over the side.

'Stay in bed, Father. Get yourself rested for tomorrow.'

He waved a hand. 'Allow me to speak, Daughter. I vowed when I was in the plane, that if God should see fit to spare me, that I would show my appreciation to you for your support and loyalty, to both myself and your dear mother.' He was watching her as he spoke, her hand was at her breast, she snatched it away, but she could not hold his eye.

Her breasts appeared to be larger. Her bra felt tight. She drew a deep breath, held it. They never discussed Angel. She did not want to discuss his precious Angel. She had written her out, out of her life, out of her memories, cleansing herself in the process.

'She was not an easy woman,' he continued. 'But there were circumstances, and she not wholly to blame, Daughter. And I deserve much of the blame. I bent too easily to her will. Blessed so late in life, I feared, I always feared she may ... may leave, as my own mother left, that she may take you away. She had her own money, you see – ' He coughed, bowed his head. 'I had waited a long time for a child.'

'Miss Moreland once told me I had a twin.'

'That is so. That is so. The boy did not survive – ' He silenced, coughed a while. 'I cannot help but ask myself at times, do you ... do you look around at your friends and envy them their lives, their children?'

She flinched. A minute passed before she replied, replied honestly.

'I would be lying if I said there was nothing in my life that I regret.' She studied him closely, then her eyes turned again to the window. 'Perhaps lately I have had time to regret much; however – ' She stilled her tongue, and her thoughts went within. Could she kill it? Have it sucked from her? Could she live with herself?

'Speak of it now. We are ... we are distanced from our old lives, Daughter. Distance, perhaps, may give us the opportunity to discuss that which we have kept within us for far too long.'

'It is just – just that I have been thinking much of children in ... in recent weeks,' she said quickly. 'There are many women now who raise children alone, Father.'

'Women such as Polly Daws.' His voice was high.

She shrugged.

'It is past time I came home. Well past time. This is not you, Daughter.'

'Blame the distance, Father. You gave me leave to speak, and so I spoke; still, it's just a fanciful thing that will surely pass in a day or two.'

'Is there ... has there been some ...?'

She looked down at her hands, and she slipped easily into fiction. 'I did meet rather a pleasant man at the motel – '

Martin Templeton's eyes opened wide. He stared at his daughter until she looked up. 'What you must ask – ' he began, but a spasm of coughing cut his sentence short.

She poured a glass of water, handed it to him. He gasped, sipped the water, and she waited, watching the window until he handed her the glass.

'Has he left?'

'Yes. As I said, Father. It is just a fanciful thing. I'm certain it will pass. I am quite certain that within a few weeks I will be quite back to normal again.'

Perhaps it would pass, perhaps it wouldn't. At her age it probably would flow away. And if it didn't, then that was something she would have to think about, but then ... Still, as with any fiction, it was a good idea to plant early hints that could be picked up later if necessary.

A nurse came in to check Martin's temperature and his blood pressure, which was a little high. It was some minutes before they were alone again.

'Where has he gone to?' the minister asked.

'Who?' Stella's mind had been far away in the future.

'This confounded fellow you spoke of.'

'He was ... is an American. He's gone home. Washington.'

'Who was he? What was his name?'

'Wayne. Wayne Lee.'

'Lee? A Yank, you say. It sounds Asian.' With great effort and much coughing, he was on his feet.

She looked at his long pale feet and thought of other feet.

Bare. Had she ever seen her father's feet bare? She found his slippers, offered them.

'Have this chair, Father.'

But he needed to stand. There was power in his height, and he needed some of his old power back. 'Don't fuss, Daughter.' He walked to the window, stood there, looking down. 'I always believed that you inherited many of your traits from my own mother, who had some difficulty settling down to the mundane life of a minister's wife. Being deserted by her, as a mere babe, is perhaps the reason I chose your mother, who for a time appeared to fill the situation of minister's wife admirably. My own father deemed her a paragon of virtue. He, of course, did not live long enough to see – ' Martin scratched at his neck, cleared his throat, then he spoke on to the window. 'Perhaps, what I am attempting to explain, and not doing it well, I might add, is the desire for an exciting, a modern lifestyle has led to the downfall of many a good woman. Far better to choose substance over a dream.'

'Yes, Father. I'm sure you are right. Now sit down before you fall down.' She took his arm, and led him back to the chair.

'And an American, no less. They are a race without morals. I recall the war years. The Yanks promised much, but left behind them many fallen women. They are not to be trusted, Daughter.'

'Yes, Father, but that was long ago. This is the nineties and there are no more fallen women. We have been liberated you know. Relax. You'll have a stroke on top of your pneumonia.'

'Liberated to fall victim to some traveller who cannot be relied on to tell the truth of his situation.'

'Is it your turn for a confession now? What did you get up to over there?'

'I have nothing to – ' He stopped, looked at her and caught her smile, then he coughed again. 'Although, perhaps in my youth, during the war, I too was guilty of suggesting a commitment I was not free to suggest. What I am attempting to say,

Daughter, is that distance can disorient us at times. Our responsibilities, all so far away, we are unable to bridge the distance. Loyalties can be tested.' Martin's face had grown red.

'You are making far too much of this. I merely said – ' She sighed. 'I assure you, I will not be leaving you or Maidenville. This trip has been sufficient to convince me of that.'

'You will no doubt feel more settled once I am home and things are returned to normal. The church now? Everything well with the church?'

'Yes. The congregation is managing without you. Mr White has been doing an admirable job. Mr Macy, I am sorry to say, usually preaches to thin air, but it doesn't seem to concern him. He'll be taking the service today and I admit I am pleased to be away.'

'And our Miss Moreland?'

'That was a bad, bad time. We had a stranger for her funeral, and he may never be the same again.' She smiled at his expression, then added. 'But, it was what she wanted.'

'And what was it she wanted?'

'Oh.' Stella shrugged. 'A simple enough service. I spoke of her friendship and of her years at the high school. I sang one of her favourite songs. Steve's band played. It was what she wanted. You'd possibly remember that she stipulated there was to be no psalm singing at her funeral, and also that should we allow Mrs Morris to open her mouth, she'd come back and haunt us.'

'I don't recall off hand.'

'No. You have had other things on your mind. She wrote many instructions in her will and we did it the way she wanted. It was quite ... well, quite different. No doubt you will hear all about it from Mr Macy when you return, and you may wish to evict me, disown me, toss me out on the street. Oh, and I promised the congregation that we would have a wild bon voyage party for Miss Moreland as soon as you are well enough.'

'You have been busy, Daughter.'

'I have been very busy.' They sat for a long time.

'I was aware that she had named you sole beneficiary, but does that require you to wear her outfits?' he finally said.

She was wearing a black skirt and a red jacket over a white satin blouse. But her black shoes were her own. Brand new, bought in Sydney, they had seven-centimetre heels.

metal screenings

By June Martin Templeton, though not strong, was out and about again. The steep staircase in the old house would have exhausted him, so rather than move into the downstairs bedroom, and take his bath in a tub, he had remained in Miss Moreland's unit, with her walk-in shower. It separated him from his beloved Packard, but the car wasn't going anywhere without him.

The flat had its fringe benefits, the minister had to admit. It was close to the hospital, where Doctor Parsons spent much of his time. Parsons popped into the unit most days to check on the minister, or to beat him at chess. Several members of the congregation were installed in the retirement units, so Martin was kept busy with visitors, and he never tired of showing off his unit.

Such extravagance. Modern laminated benchtops, tiled and carpeted floors, luxurious conditions. But the other units he visited were as his own, and many occupied by pensioners. They were the new rich in Maidenville.

Martin didn't feel up to driving yet. Stella drove him around town, and occasionally out of town for funerals. She drove him to church, and afterwards, took him back to the house for lunch and a long visit with his Packard. He was up to tinkering with the spark plugs, and on his last visit, he had peered between the wheels at a new depression in the floor. He considered getting down on his knees to take a closer look, but he wasn't quite up to that yet.

'Something under there,' he said. 'You've moved it, Daughter?'

'I said I'd start it up for you. It was going well before I left.'

'The battery, no doubt.' He cleaned the terminals, and again attempted to start the big motor, but the battery was dead. He thought to lift it out, to get Stella to take it over to Jennison's and have it recharged, but it was a weight he could do without lifting. Perhaps later. Or perhaps the old car was due for a new battery. Maybe he'd get Jennison to bring a new one around. But in June the shed was cold and uninviting, and after fifteen minutes of tinkering there, he began to cough. He would have to put off playing mechanic until spring.

'No good for a fine old vehicle to stand idle for this length of time. I'll call Jennison around, let him get her going for me.'

'Let other hands tinker with your beloved Packard, Father? What is the world coming to?' Stella looked younger each day. She had put on a little of the weight lost while he was away, and looked better for it. And her outfits. He rarely saw her in the same shirt twice.

'Is there no end to her abominable wardrobe, Daughter?' he asked.

'It appears not,' she laughed.

'And no end to your spending.' He looked up at the new bathroom window, and he shook his head. 'Perhaps I should consider selling the Packard. We may need it to pay some of your recent bills.'

'We certainly will not sell it. Anyway, I've stopped spending for the moment, and when you move back, you will appreciate the upstairs bathroom. The shower recess is positively palatial.'

He had turned back to the car, and she looked where he was

looking. From this angle she could see the cracked and sinking soil between the wheels of the car. She stooped, looked sideways and she saw the hump of the bike wheel again. Damn that wheel. There must be a root beneath it, pushing it up. She'd have to dig down, hacksaw it through. End it. Finally write 'the end', as she had written 'THE END' on her manuscript.

'I think I'll get you back to your nice warm flat, and if it will set your mind at rest, I'll order a new battery from Jennison's. Come now. It's too cold out here for me, Father.'

But she didn't order the battery from Jennison. She drove to Dorby and bought one, and she fitted it. The positive terminal was the larger of the two. As long as she put it back the same way as she took the old one out, it must be right.

And it was. The old motor purred, eager to go. She backed it out, but when she saw the sunken earth beneath it, and the protruding hump of bike wheel, she returned it to its place and ran for her telephone, ordering a truck-load of blue-metal screening from Steve Smith's Gardening Supplies.

He arrived with his truck, late on the Saturday morning, dumping the load in her drive, directly in front of the garage. It locked the Packard in and the new car out, and although she shook her head adamantly when he offered to help move the pile, he stayed anyway, barrowing in the screenings, glancing around the shed.

'Do you reckon we could push the old girl back?'

'Leave it there, Steve. I'll finish the spreading later.'

He was flinging the screening beneath the Packard's wheels when he saw it. 'What's that?' he said, on his knees, peering at the curve of the mutilated bike tyre.

The town clock struck its long and aching twelve. 'Lord,' she said. 'Is that the time? Will you share a bite of lunch, Steve?'

'You know me. I never say no to a free meal.'

'Do you like baked beans? I seem to have a craving for them these days. Baked beans on toast?'

'Sounds good.'

a game of chess

Doctor Parsons called at the unit in late July. He checked the minister's lungs, took his blood pressure, and told him he was fitter than he ought to be for an old codger, then he sat at the dining room table, attempting to beat him at chess.

Stella found them there, still locked in battle, when she arrived at four to prepare her father's evening meal. She made tea before setting to work in the kitchen.

'New trousers now,' Martin said. Stella was wearing stretch jeans, and a loose sweater. 'You will have us in the poorhouse yet, Daughter.' He turned to Parsons. 'Did you see what she has done to the shed floor?' He didn't approve of the metal screenings, and a month on, he still made his disapproval clear at every meeting.

'And as I continue to say, the floor was excessively low, and each year it appears to sink lower. It is constantly flooded by the hose – when you are in residence, Father, and as you are determined to come home, the screenings will at least keep you dry underfoot. We do not want you unwell again.'

'Have you ordered the battery?'

'Why cut up the drive with the Packard's great wheels and weight? It's bad enough at the moment. I'm thinking of having it done with bitumen.'

'God save me from your spendthrift ways – '

'Play the game, you niggly old coot and stop your nagging,' Parsons said. Stella laughed, and Parsons turned to her, a frown creasing his brow. 'You're looking well, Mousy Two.'

'I'm very well, Doctor. The question is, is Father well enough to handle those stairs yet?'

'He's well enough to give me a run for my money, and though the old coot won't admit it, he has no desire to return to his stairs. He loves this place. And so would I.'

'It has its good points and its bad. Still it is not home,' the minister stressed.

'I've attempted to talk him into remaining here, but to no avail. I really have no desire to sell the flat, so you can move in if Father ever decides to give up his central heating.'

The doctor's attention on Stella, he absent-mindedly moved his castle and Martin pounced, stealing his queen.

'Checkmate.'

'Life happens. You bring your daughter in to dazzle me at a ticklish moment in the game, then take advantage of my wandering attention. You do look quite dazzling, Mousy Two. What have you been doing to yourself lately?'

'My continued absence from home is encouraging her into many habits,' Martin replied, looking meaningfully at Stella's jeans. Her short hair was near gold again, having been somehow transformed by chemicals she bought from the supermarket.

'I'd better be off,' Parsons said. 'Don't you get up. Your daughter will see me safely off the premises. You've got nothing worth stealing here anyway.'

Stella walked out with the doctor, and he ushered her through the front door, then closed it behind him, locking them outside.

'A word, Mousy Two.'

'Yes.'

Parsons was never a one to beat around the bush. 'I'm one of the old school, lass. I can pick a pregnant woman at fifty paces,' he said.

The blush began at her brow, working its slow way down. She turned away to hide it, pushed at the front door. 'Father. Father. I've locked myself out.'

The doctor caught her hand. 'What age are you now?'

'You, of all people, know my age, Doctor Parsons.' She knocked at the front door. 'Father. Father!'

'That I do. Nineteen-bloody-fifty-two. The worst day of my life. You don't intend going ahead with it, do you?'

'I have no idea what you are talking about.' Again she knocked on the door. She hammered on it. 'Father. Will you open this door please?'

'I'm talking about a woman of forty-four having a baby, lass – in five months or so.'

'Father!'

'Tight jeans, large tops. I've seen girls trying to pull that same stunt for years. They say your mother tried to pull it too.'

She turned on him, angry now. Her head, her face hot, on a day too cold. 'I am not my mother. I ... am ... not ... my ... mother.'

'No, and that's a fact.' He rubbed at his mouth with his free hand. 'Have you considered abortion?'

'Please release my hand. I want to go inside.'

'No use running from me, lass. Who's the culprit? Young Steve?'

'How dare you.'

'Oh, I dare a lot. Or have you been making a few withdrawals from some sperm bank – while you were up in Sydney?'

'I am not in the mood for your humour, Doctor Parsons. Father's dinner is burning. Release my hand.'

'He doesn't know about it.'

'There is nothing he needs to know.'

'This is no place to talk, lass. Come down to the surgery on Monday.'

'I don't need – '

'You need all right, Mousy Two. Have you got any idea of the problems associated with a first pregnancy at your age? Come in at eight, before the old biddies get there. I'll leave the door open. I've got some literature you ought to take a look at. At least read it before you go making some crazy decision you might regret for the rest of your life. Who did the deed?'

She ignored him.

'Denying it won't make it go away, lass.'

'Leave . . . me . . . alone.' She tugged her hand free and pushed through the shrubs to the lounge room window, where she rapped with her knuckles on glass. 'Father. Can you hear me?'

Parsons tracked her. 'Nice place. The grand old dame kept this garden up until the day she died. I always envied her this unit. Wouldn't mind calling it home,' he said.

'Father.' Again she rapped on the window. 'Father.'

Heads were peering from other doors now, faces from behind lifted curtains.

'She was raped the night she died,' Parsons said.

'And may he rot in hell for all eter – ' She caught her tongue, but too late. Now she covered her mouth. Her eyes widened, her mouth was open, gasping air between her fingers, trying to take back the spoken words. But the little doctor had all he needed. He nodded, smiled, and she turned away, blood again flooding her cheeks, her brow, her head. She swayed on her feet, stumbled, then grasped the brick wall. For months she'd been so careful. How could she? How could she have been such a fool?

The back door opened.

'Daughter?'

'The wind. The front door. I locked myself out, Father.' She tried to move away from the window, but the doctor now held her upper arm. For a small man, his grip was strong. Keeping his voice low, he said: 'Me and Johnson covered it up. I mean, a flighty old girl like her might have had a lover. That's the way she would have wanted it, we reckoned. Johnson swore she'd come back and haunt us if we'd let her become town gossip.'

Stella was listening now, loving Sergeant Johnson – loving this little man, but hating him too. Her tears were starting, and he took advantage of her tears.

'Johnson hasn't given up though. He knows we've got a rapist in town. Someone the old lady knew well, someone she opened her door to. Someone who left better than his fingerprints in his sperm, lass. He raped you too, didn't he? That's what you're carrying. Who is he?'

She pushed him from her and ran to the door, and she ran inside, pushing past Martin, leaving him at the door with Parsons.

It was over. It was over. There was a fifteen-centimetre layer of blue-metal screenings on the shed floor – levelling the shed floor. She had put it behind her, and she would not allow Parsons to start it up again.

on the scent of a decomposing bone

The doctor rode around to the Templeton house that evening. The Packard was in the drive and he could hear sawing coming from the shed. He crept to the closed door and stood listening, then he crept around to the small window and climbed to the fork of the overgrown apricot tree. It was high enough for him to see inside the shed where Stella was squatting, sawing at something deep in the earth. Sawing through metal, with a hacksaw.

He watched her for minutes. He watched her until a small piece of curved metal came free. He watched her stand, her face pleased with her labour.

Only then did he rap on the window. 'Digging for gold, Mousy Two?' he asked.

She spun around, looked up and saw his face amid the bare branches, then she dropped the piece of bike wheel to the floor, and with her shoe kicked a heap of screening back, burying the metal, and what she had cut the metal from. By the time Parsons crawled down from his perch, and untangled his beard from a twig, the door was open and she was in the Packard, moving it back to its rightful place.

He stood at the driver's side, preventing her escape. 'I thought the old girl had cracked up,' he said, fingering a scratch on his face.

'It needed a new battery, so I bought one.'

The old battery was on the bench, ready to be put back into place when she was done. He saw it. He saw much. A bike man from way back, he knew a piece of wheel when he saw it too, and he was pretty certain what bike it was she'd been cutting into.

She slid across the seat, opened the opposite door, and hurried to the storeroom where she began tidying the bags of knitting wool, sorting through them, matching colours. He followed her and stood watching.

'As I was saying today, we got a sample of the rapist's sperm, lass. Thought you might like to know. I got his blood group from it. Got my own idea of who it was. I reckon I've solved a couple of mysteries here today.' There was no reply, no sign that she had heard him. 'I've had my own opinion of what might have happened to our rapist, lass. I reckoned someone with a daughter might have a fair idea of what happened to him.'

A breath drawn slowly, held, she worked on, her head low.

'Now, my money was on the Murphys,' he said. 'On Spud, young Kelly's old man. Only trouble is, those who threaten murder, rarely do it. Spud would have thrashed him within an inch of his life, fixed him so his voice went a few octaves higher. But murder. That's not the Murphys' style. Murder is usually a hot-blooded thing. A lot of people might threaten to do it, but we usually have to be pushed into a corner before we kill.'

Still she made no reply, but her hands were shaking out of control, her stomach, her mind, her heart was shaking.

'Young Spencer came by your place, didn't he, lass?'

'Leave me alone. Go away and leave me alone.'

'You're pregnant. I'd say, fourteen, fifteen weeks. Not a day less.'

'You're wrong. It is less. It's much less. I ... I met a traveller at the motel in Sydney. I told Father about him when he was in hospital. An American tourist. His name was Wayne. Wayne Lee.'

'Taking a page out of the old lady's book now with your mysterious lovers. He wasn't a relative of John Wayne by any chance, was he? I know him well.'

'Ask Father if you don't believe me.'

'Yeah. Yeah. Yeah. And pigs might fly, Mousy Two, but in Maidenville they rarely do. Did young Spencer call on you?'

She turned away, spilling the wool to the floor. 'Damn you,' she said, attempting to pick up the scattered wool, but dropping more. 'Damn you.'

He squatted by her side, gathering up the colourful balls, dusting them on the leg of his baggy shorts, before handing them back to her to place into their bags.

'I've been doing my arithmetic. Miss Moreland has been dead for close on four months, and young Thomas Spencer, missing since four days after her funeral, and my interfering eye says you were impregnated around the time he took off. Now that's an equation Johnson could have a lot of fun with, I reckon. Add to that young Spencer's blood group, which I happen to have on record. The sperm fits, lass, and when you pop his infant, I can get some of its blood, check his DNA. I'm God in this town.'

She flung the bag of wool to the floor, kicked it at the wall. 'Damn you. Damn your God, and damn the wool, and damn this bloody-minded town, and damn your probing doctor's eyes, and damn your interference. Damn you!' And she walked to the Packard, where she stood, her head against its cold metal.

He stood behind her, a hand on her shoulder. 'They don't make them like they used to, do they?' he said. 'A little bloke like me could set up house on the back seat of this old girl.'

'Nothing is like it used to be,' she said. 'Nothing. I am not like I used to be.' She turned to him then, her eyes holding his. 'I rarely look to the past, Doctor. As you no doubt remember,

313

I learned early to put each day behind me and to never look behind. I look ahead to each dawn, to a better dawn, and that is what I am trying to do now.'

'And what about that future dawn, lass? What about tomorrow?'

'Tell me – you tell me, Doctor Parsons, does my only chance of a tomorrow, of going forward into tomorrow, of leaving some small part of me, of Father, to the future, does it deserve to be gouged from me and flushed down some sewer?'

'Where is he, lass?'

She pointed with the toe of her shoe to the earth beneath the Packard.

'Life happens,' he said, dropping to his knees, half expecting to see a corpse in a body bag tied under the chassis. 'Where?'

'With the bike. I ... I dug a ... a shallow pit.'

'Shit happens, lass. And when it does, sometimes the best thing you can do with it, is to bury it. How shallow is shallow?'

'Very,' she replied, eyeing him defiantly. 'Far too shallow.'

He stood, took a handkerchief from his pocket, and he wiped the handkerchief across her cheek.

'What?' Her hand went to the place he had touched.

'You've got butter all over your whiskers, Mousy Two,' he said.

differing versions

By early November, the jacarandas were a barrier of blue guarding the doors of Templeton's old shed, closed now, locked fast. No wool waited on the shelves, no more polyester filling popped like snow from its bales. The thriving clown-doll business had been moved on to the storeroom behind the church hall. By the same spring, Stella Templeton was bursting out all over. Her waist was lost, and her breasts, once small crab-apples, had ripened into plump peaches.

Bonny had taken her shopping for maternity jeans when they went to Dorby for the tests. 'Too baggy,' she'd said to the shop assistant, just as she had so many years ago. 'Show us a size smaller,' she'd said.

She'd driven to the hospital, held Stella's hand while the amniotic fluid was drawn, then she'd prayed with her until the tests came back.

Safe. The tiny being was safe.

They'd watched the ultrasound together, prematurely viewing a new life. Small perfect fingers. Tiny profile. Small mouth opening, closing.

Stella had wept then, wept for a long time, and she wept hard, but Bonny had held her, kissed her, wept with her. Then they'd taken the video home to Bonny's place and since had replayed it over and over.

Bonny was certain it was a girl. Having produced five boys, she knew exactly where to look for a small penis and she hadn't sighted one. They both agreed that the infant had a feminine look.

'Was he handsome, Stell, or ugly? Was he tall, or short?' Bonny wanted to believe unreservedly in the tale of the American lover who Stella said she'd slept with at the Penrith Motel after a night of drinking peach cooler, but she couldn't quite see it happening. Also, she had her own very good reasons for doubting this tale, though she never expressed her doubts. There had been something going on in the shed the day Tommy Spencer went missing, on the day Bonny had arrived with her apple cobbler. She hadn't told a soul, except Len, but he didn't count because she told him everything, and he had a mouth like a steel trap.

'I peeped in through that knot hole in the side door, and for a split second, I sighted Stell against the light from the side window. She was as naked as the day she was born, Len. Then she sort of smiled – you know that secret Stella smile, and she put on a man's shirt. A big blue shirt.'

'So what?'

'So Steve Smith's a big bloke, and he wears a lot of blue. That's so what.'

Mrs Morris also knew about Stella's lover, but her version differed. She'd gleaned her information in the doctor's waiting room, and from Parsons' own mouth. Her voice low and conspiratorial, she was passing on some gossip to Mrs Murphy. Her husband and six or eight neighbours could hear her well enough to get the gist of it.

'I've known since July, Mrs Murphy, but for my own good reasons, I've kept it under my hat.'

'She's flaunting it around town. Do go on, Mrs Morris.'

'Well, you see I went down to the surgery for my blood-pressure prescription on the Monday, early, and I saw Stella Templeton coming out. Parsons had his hand on her shoulder. *"You won't think about it, lass. You'll have those tests and no argument,"* he says to her. Then he sees me, and she sees me, and she scuttles off.'

'Oh, the poor girl. Is it cancer, I'm thinking. Remember how he sent Mrs Carter over to Dorby for her tests? Dead in six weeks, she was.'

'I do, dear.'

'Yes. Well, I was thinking that Stella had been looking too pleased with herself to have a tumour, so I asked him, and he says to me, "I know I can rely on you not to mention this to anyone, Mrs Morris."

' "Of course you can, Doctor. Is it cancer?" I say. "We're all so fond of Stella."

' "She's pregnant," he says. Comes straight out with it too. Well, my dear, you could have knocked me down with a feather. Then he takes out my card and walks me into the surgery and he tries to change the subject. "So what can I do for you this morning?" he says.

' "Me?" I say. "Don't you worry about me, Doctor. Just give me my pills. I'm more worried about our Stella. I mean, who could she have done it with? Was it Steve Smith?" I thought of him first off, of course – after that night they spent in Dorby.

' "Shame on you for asking," he says, and he scribbles out my prescription, his mouth sealed.

' "I wouldn't tell a soul, you know me, Doctor," I say to him, and he says back, "That I do, Mrs Morris. That I certainly do. I have always been impressed by your discretion." He passes me the prescription, but I can see he wants to talk about it, so I keep sitting there. I won't budge.

317

' "It was that Steve Smith, I'll give you ten-to-one odds," I say. "Why hasn't he married her? Is he going to marry her?"

'He shakes his head and looks at me, real serious. "This is for your ears only. You realise that," he says.

' "Of course it is, Doctor," I said. "I swear on my mother's grave."

' "Stella came to me, saying she'd had a strange dream, of a visitation from God. Well, her being a maiden lady, as you know they can be prone to flights of fancy."

' "Oh yes, yes indeed I do," I agreed. Menopause can be that hard on an unmarried woman, I said to him. Then I remembered her telling me about a strange dream that I was in, so I tells him that and he says: "Good Lord. You mean, you are to be one of the chosen?" He comes around the desk and he starts taking my blood pressure, and putting his stethoscope on my stomach. "It's got me beat, Mrs Morris," he says. "I examined her of course. She's intact as I expected, but undeniably pregnant. Never yet in all the years I've been practising have I diagnosed pregnancy when the hymen is intact – though a few of my patients may have claimed to be virgins. Have you had any dreams yourself? Sexual, I mean?"

'Well I didn't like doing it, but I had to, you see. So I tell him that dream I was telling you, the one I blamed on the prawn and avocado pancake that we had down at the coffee shop . . . the one about me and young Roy Thomson. Well, did Parsons go off then. He hits his head with his hand. "Good God," he says. "Good God. Go into the examination room, Mrs Morris. There are eleven pregnant women in town all due around Christmas, and it appears that you are to be the twelfth."

' "Be buggered," I said to him. "Be buggered to that. I'm not going into any bloody examination room. I just came down here for my blood-pressure pills."

' "Be it on your head, Mrs Morris," he says, "But I'm warning you now, keep your eye out for symptoms. In the dream, Stella said there were to be twelve, plus her own. Perhaps

318

I'll just do a pregnancy test, while I've got you here."'

Mrs Murphy's eyes were wide behind her bottle-top spectacles, her jaw was sagging as Mrs Morris's voice rose.

'Well, my dear, I said to him in no uncertain manner, "I'll remind you Doctor Parsons, that I had a hysterectomy at fifty-five, as you well know – seeing as you did it."'

'"Could be ectopic. God works in mysterious ways, His wonders to perform," he said. "And young Roy. I always thought he had an uncanny resemblance to Jesus. That long blond hair. You are certain that it was he, and not – "'

'Oh, my God!' Mrs Murphy took three steps back. She covered her mouth as she stared at her neighbour's sagging stomach. 'Oh, my God. He does look like him, Mrs Morris. He does. I've always said it. You've always said it – '

'It was young Roy, I tell you. I'll stake my life on it, but it gave me a funny feeling, I can tell you straight. I got myself home in a hurry and took an extra blood-pressure pill and two migraine pills, just to be on the safe side.'

'My God.' Mrs Murphy's eyes were wide.

'You said it, Mrs Murphy. I'm willing to swear that it's our own immaculate conception. God has chosen Maidenville, and by the sounds of it, there's a whole clutch of women involved.

'Young Kelly, Spud's girl. She's due around November. She could be the twelfth.'

'God wouldn't impregnate a little slut, Mrs Murphy! He'd be a bit more choosy than that. But Stella. Didn't I always say to you that Stella was halfway between saint and martyr? Didn't I always say it?'

'You certainly said she was a martyr, Mrs Morris. My word, and her an Anglican too. Did he say what religion the other eleven were?'

'No. I didn't think to ask him. But imagine what a thing like this will do for the town. It will put Maidenville on the map, Mrs Murphy.'

'Won't it be a real slap in the eye for the Catholics?'

Martin Templeton felt as if he'd been slapped between the eyes with a lead-weighted cosh. He was now keeping his head down, and no longer nagging to return to the big house where he must each day confront his own confusion, plus a ballooning daughter, who was showing no shame or remorse at all.

But there were moments in each day when he felt tremors of excitement at the very thought of . . . of it. Then there were the other times, the times of acute embarrassment when in town, people looked at him oddly, spoke behind their hands. It was all he could do to get himself away from the smiling faces that had once been so subservient.

Too much on my mind lately – too much and still growing, he thought. Growing bigger daily. Looking at her growth last Sunday, he forgot where he was in the middle of his sermon, and frequently now he found himself in shops or backyards, but couldn't remember why he was there. Baptism? Funeral? Milk? Bread? At these time he was forced to return to his Packard, and to sit a moment, collect his thoughts.

The Packard was the only stability in his life. Stella had registered and insured it for his eighty-sixth birthday. It was parked each night, half in and half out of the small garage attached to his unit.

Each morning he drove it the three blocks to town to collect his newspaper. It was the one joy, the one bright spark in his life. He felt safe in his Packard, even if other users of the roads felt less secure with him back on the road. Still, in the Packard, they could see him coming a half-mile away and make their early detours.

Mrs Morris and Mrs Murphy never detoured. Together they bailed Martin up in the cafe on a Thursday in early November, and he couldn't see a way around them. The milk in one hand, his keys in the other, he glared at the duo, willing them gone.

They remained.

'So you're going to be a grand-daddy at last, Mr Templeton,' the one with the bottle-top glasses said.

'A new little angel in our town,' the fat one with the starched hair added.

He nodded. He coughed and he muttered, 'Life happens, Mrs ... Mrs ...'

Life happens. Why did he say that? Because he was seeing too much of Arnold Parsons, that's why. He was being reconditioned, overhauled, re-programmed by Arnold Parsons and ... and by the future.

'Life happens. Seasons change. The world goes on,' Parsons said.

And it was true. Although Martin was loath to admit it, in some primitive part of his mind, in a place too long denied, there was a small petal of change opening to life. It was smiling 'grandchild'. It was thinking of a few years without constant burials and weddings. It was thinking of a life where small hands might again beg to comb his mane of hair, where small hands might lay warm in his own huge hand, and small white things might flap again on the clothesline. It was thinking of the scent of new life, and of being able to hold a new life's warmth to his heart without fear of accusations.

And for the first time in more than forty years he could see a line, a long line extending forward, its unravelled threads, re-woven, re-joined – and by a bloody Yank! Still, there were moments when he wanted to thank, to shake the hand of the unprincipled swine for giving him back a small part of immortality.

A grandson – and a Templeton.

God! What was he supposed to think, to feel? Was he celebrating the fact that his daughter would give birth outside of matrimony?

'Templeton. Martin junior ... or John. John Martin Templeton.'

Back in his Packard, he brushed the two women aside as he might two bothersome wasps. It was not minister-like, and he shook his head at his behaviour. Too much on my mind, he told the steering wheel. I will feel better ... later, when Stella's damnable traveller returns and makes an honest woman of her – hopefully before the event. He'd have to hurry. The swine. Far better that it had been that long-haired, guitar-playing lout.

But then the child would not be born a Templeton. Peter? John? Paul?

Stella had spoken not one word about her traveller since that day in Sydney, and Martin had not dared to ask.

Damn the nineties. What was left of the world he had once known and understood? He'd had the best of it. What we have left for future generations is not going to be worth much, he thought. Women bearing children out of wedlock, and having the audacity to walk around town as if they were proud of it. His own daughter, and during the years when she should have been well past those sorts of shenanigans. What was the world coming to? It was doomed. Doomed. God help this child. What sort of a society would be left for him/her?

Perhaps it would be a girl. Still, he had always wanted a son, his own lost to Angel's knitting needle. A son. Yes. A fine sturdy little boy – although a little girl has a sweetness about her, he thought. What did it matter? Children. Small voices tinkling in the old rooms.

'Papa.'

If she married the swine, then there may be more than one. Angel had been in her late forties when she bore Stella –

What a mess. What a fine mess it has all become. I can no longer reach a decision as to what my own response to this mess should be. I cannot condone it; I certainly do not condone it; however I cannot deny my ... my own interest in the outcome. I certainly cannot deny that.

'Papa.'

But she's spending money like water. What does a woman in her situation want with a confounded computer machine? Three thousand dollars worth of electronics on which to tap out her silly little tales. And what was wrong with the old typewriter?

322

That's what he wanted to know. She had a perfectly good type-writer at her disposal. Angel had typed his sermons up on it for years before Stella was born. It was still in immaculate condition.

Immaculate? Perhaps he should work on that rumour. Slot it into one of his sermons. Next Sunday. Just a word. Yes. He would speak of Mary, and of Jesus' birth. After all, Christmas was not far away.

He sighed deeply and pressed the starter. The Packard's motor hummed into life. Carefully Martin drove away, pleased to escape the town and the stares.

He drove around the back roads for half an hour before making a stop at Jennison's to fill the tank and talk motors a while. Then it was back to his neat little unit, with its gas heater, and its microwave that could do anything from boil water for a cup of tea, to rid the quite tasty Meal on Wheels of bacteria and other micro-organisms.

Stella no longer came each morning to prepare lunch, but they always ate their evening meals together.

Life had reached out and cut Stella Templeton, cut her deeply, but cuts heal, given time, if the flesh is strong. And some leave the minimum of scars.

The earth over the roots of the old cypress hedge had healed; it was as if it had never been. Replaced now by a neat white picket fence, passers-by came to lean, to admire the riotous garden blooming out of control behind it, and to peep with awe-filled eyes at the gardener's thickening waist.

Stella often sang as she went about her weeding, and some nights a light baritone blended with her own pure voice. Many walkers stopped a while to listen and to wonder just what had become of the small beige sparrow once trapped in the minister's cage.

That colourless little bird had flown the coop.

epilogue

Stella named her first novel *Screenings*. Steve Smith read the new manuscript. It was he who suggested the name – suggested it as he held her eye.

She flinched, shook her head, then turned her face to the window, and to the jacarandas, and to the shed outside the window. She coughed, stared hard into the dark. 'I ... I like it, Steve. It suits the villain – relates to her addiction to midnight movies, but – '

He handed the pages back to her. 'Up to you, Stell. Just a suggestion.' He reached out and took her hand, shook her hand. 'I'm proud to know you. Bloody proud to know you,' he said, shaking her hand for a long time.

'And I you, Steve.'

'Just to put it on record,' he said. 'There's something I've got to ask you tonight.'

She thought he was about to question her story-line, or the tying up of the plot. She turned her eyes to his, eager for his question.

'Well, do you trust me?'

'Of course I trust you.'

'Completely? Totally? No reservations?'

She smiled, nodded. 'You are the only one in town I've allowed to read my manuscript – which must mean I trust you, completely, totally, no reservations, and that I value your opinion above all others, Steve.'

'So you don't reckon that I'm a complete moron then?'

Stella shook her head. 'What is it? Where Matthew covers up for Seraphini? I've been concerned about that, but I believe this is what his character – '

'No. No. It's not about – ' He tapped the manuscript, then dragged the rubber band from his hair. 'Do you think I should get my hair cut off?'

'No. Never. It would not be you.'

'Okay. I won't then,' he said, replacing his rubber band. 'I want things to be straight down the line with us, Stell. Always.'

'Such as haircuts,' she nodded seriously, but could not hold back a smile.

'Yeah. Haircuts, and some other stuff too. Such as ... well. That little bloke you're growing. I mean, as if I, of all people, don't know you better than to think you'd go jumping into bed with some strange Yank you'd known for a few hours. I've fed you a bit of wine in my time. It never did me much good, as I recall.'

She shook her head and stood, her smile wiped away. She walked to the sink where she made much ado about pouring a glass of water, but he followed her to the sink and he stood beside her, his eyes turned to the shed.

'I didn't say it to upset you, or embarrass you. That's the last thing I ever want to do, Stell, but – ' Her head was down. Her hands played with the glass. 'Christ. Where do I go from here?'

The old town clock began its slow count to twelve. An eerie sound, that last long call of the night. They stood listening, their eyes turned to the window.

'It's very late, Steve. I had no idea.'

'Yeah. That's sort of the point I've been trying to get to. It's

325

getting pretty late for both of us.' His next words came quickly, but his eyes did not leave the window. 'Templeton's shed has never been closed in its life, love.'

She flinched, backed away. He took the glass from her hand and he drank the water, because his throat was dry and because it was something to do with his hands. He licked his lips and tried again. 'I reckon I'll put a cement floor in there for you at the weekend. Young Glen will help me. He's always looking for extra money. With ready-mix we'll have it done in a day.'

Silence. Only the bowed head, shaking, shaking, denying. Only a night-bird calling from the jacaranda.

'And ... and I'll say this once, then it's up to you. I won't mention it again.' His hand gestured to her lost waistline and she turned her back, but he caught her hand, held it. 'I'm a whiz at growing things, Stell, and so are you. I reckon that if we pooled our talent, we could grow things the way they were meant to grow. We'd give them plenty of TLC and plenty of room to grow as straight and true as those jacarandas out there.'

She shook her head.

In silence, he watched tears creep from beneath her closed lids. He watched them trickle down her nose. He watched them shaken away, and when he could stand it no longer, his large hands cupped her face and he kissed her wet cheek.

'I've loved you since I was six years old, Stell.'

She shook her head.

'No more shaking that head at me. I reckon I've been letting you get away with that for a bit too long.' He kissed her again, but this time he found the corner of her lips.

'So. So, the way I see it, Stell. We do the cementing at the weekend, then on Monday we take off to Sydney and give the old town something new to talk about for a while, eh?'

Screenings was in the bookshops the following November, *Stella Templeton-Smith* proudly emblazoned on the cover – in blue.

MORE BESTSELLING FICTION AVAILABLE FROM PAN MACMILLAN

Joy Dettman
Mallawindy

Ann Burton was born on a river bank the night her father tried to burn their house down.

Six years later her sister Liza disappears while they are staying at their uncle's property. What Ann sees that day robs her of her memory and her speech.

A stroke of unexpected humanity releases Ann from her world of silence, and she escapes her anguished childhood, finding love and a new life away from Mallawindy. But there is no escape from the Burton family and its dark secrets. Ann must return to Mallawindy and confront the past if she is ever to be set free.

'We ride the crests and troughs of the Burtons' 30-year history with open mouths and saucer eyes ... Dettman is an adept storyteller'
THE AGE

'A highly competent and confident debut novel'
SUNDAY TELEGRAPH

'A compelling story, well told ... it holds promise of further enthralling fiction from its author'
CANBERRA TIMES

'A stunning debut; a rich and engrossing read; a tale of page-turning suspense and mystery; a postmortem of family ties; all this and more, *Mallawindy* will grab you hook, line and sinker'
QUEENSLAND TIMES